THE CITY

AND

THE STORM

THE CITY
AND
THE STORM

A Mendax Chronicle

Jeremiah Daniel Sater

Contents

To the original Storyteller, and author of salvation, this story is for You.

A Word from the Mendax

You are the first readers from your world to experience the tales from the land of Solisternum. And I hope your venture into this land is fruitful. You will find that while the language of the Vox Nation translates fairly straightforward to yours, certain terms have no proper translation. Some have equivalents in your world, but the differences warrant a separation in the language used. While I will not waste time explaining those terms here, I do want to briefly present how the Vox Nation observes time in Solisternum. I believe this will aid in your entry into this foreign world.

You might best understand what the Vox call a solpae as a day, though theirs is twenty-nine hours compared to your twenty-four-hour period. Ten solpaes marks an ora, which you might perceive as a week. Nine oras comprise a mansii, except for a sole exception that is only five oras. You can compare these to your months. Six mansiis make up a sun cycle. As you may say you are seventeen years old, a person in the Vox Nation will use sun cycles or cycles in the same context.

The rest I allow you to discover on your own.

Welcome to Solisternum.

Mendax: The Choosing of Stories

Stories hold the truth that weaves the land of Solisternum together. Apart from each other, these tales seem to travel through time without connection. Sometimes a single conversation or behavior is all that connects the stories. It is the responsibility of the Mendax to show these connections. I search the land for what those living cannot see. An honor I hold above all.

My efforts are not without help. The Great Ario gives me many stories I cannot or do not see. Though my presence transcends Solisternum, a select few are able to remain hidden from my sight, and therefore, my compilation. How this occurs, I cannot fathom. Even when Ario gives me these stories, they are mine alone to watch.

I don't enjoy these things from Ario as I do the others He gives me. I dread the legends of these Alfarons, as they call themselves. They seek to undermine my authority with their own *historical record*, a temporary, fallible account in comparison to mine. Their interference aims to not only mark my compilation incomplete, but also causes their lives to end with their deaths. Each story ends the same. Lost to the void of time, they only persist in my memory, apart from my compilation. I only hope that in the far future, when my life completes the story of the land, a portion of the Alfarons are carried beyond death.

But do not mistake this belief as a blessing for the Alfarons. I do not wish their stories upon anyone. Their hopelessness. Their selfishness. Their pride. Not all threads that connect are good. These people are the frayed lines that make up reality. If I could include their stories, I would hide them in the shadows.

I trust Ario gives me this story to show me something. I see a city and a storm, and certainly not some boy with no future, though he is the lens I use to seek what Ario wants me to see.

Into their historical record I enter, to hear the story of one long past. I only hope Ario spares me a long tale.

To Be An Alfaron

"To be remembered is an Alfaron's greatest honor." —from the official collection of early Prava Council wisdom

Graduations don't require surgery, unless you are an Alfaron. Then the process of cutting open the heads of children is a requirement. The last choice parents make for the next generation, to set us on the best path forward.

An implant now sits on the back of my brain. And what for? To be remembered. Not now, but later, after we die and disappear into nothingness. Why does it matter what others think of us when we are incapable of thinking of ourselves?

But that isn't the way of the Alfarons, first and greatest faction of the Vox Nation. That isn't how I should see it. How we are seen after we leave this world matters. We want people to remember us. Our path to remembrance is easier. The small piece of Tech that now dwells in me guarantees me a place in our history, no matter how I live my life.

But I am not content with my status as an Alfaron marking my place in the Historical Record. My father, a Representative of the Prava Council, gives my life meaning beyond that of the faction to which I belong. His place in history is not reliant on his membership to our faction. I only need to follow the path he has laid out for me. Then I can persist in the memories of those living and be carried into the Historical Record long before my death.

On his path I must remain, for he has not told me his secrets of how he has come to the place he now stands.

I look beyond my thoughts to the white walls that surround me. Harsh lights push away any shadow, leaving me no place to hide. It's easy to hide in crowds, at school, even in my own house. Here in this empty room, I'm alone. I still feel vulnerable.

The other graduates should be waking up now, surrounded by classmates and preparing for their futures away from this place—Epis City, home of the Council. As I stare around the room, empty silence is all that meets me. No joyous sounds of friends reuniting after the procedure. This city remains my home even after the celebration. My education continues under the Council. I follow after my father.

The implant that Alfarons covet so much records every thought and image to enter our Historical Record one sol. I let out a breath. That is a good thing. I am now an Alfaron graduate, set to become a Vox citizen. My place in history now awaits only my death.

The thought scares me. The Historical Record holds no bias. The people see you for who you truly are. Will my actions match what my innermost thoughts say? Is that how I will finally understand my father? Do I have to wait until he enters the Record and his secrets become a part of history? No, of course not. He has provided a path through the Council to which I will learn the mysteries that make him the man he is.

The silence won't allow these thoughts to settle. I sit up as the bed's itchy sheets bother my neck. A small table stands next to me. It's empty except for a portable timepiece. I reach for it and grip it in my hand. I can feel my body's energy—Lamis—flowing into the device. This natural energy flows through every Vox citizen, powering our Tech. Children are forbidden to partake in it until graduation because our energy can't power more than a simple device without overtaxing our bodies. Over the next ten cycles, my energy will mature, allowing me to power even a transport vessel to soar across the Red Plains. For now, the implant is all my body is able to sustain.

My hand reaches around my head and feels where the implant went in. No scar remains from the procedure, not because of the doctor's excellence, but my Lamis. It kept me healthy as a young child, even healing minor wounds. But now, at the age of ten sun cycles, my energy can heal me of any injury short of growing back limbs.

I feel no different. Only a sol ago, four mansiis after the other graduates were cleared, I still wasn't. They collected a sample of my Lamis every sol since the celebration of my tenth sun cycle. What difference does twenty-nine hours make? A small part of me still thinks my energy isn't ready, but my father played some part. But I cannot be certain.

I only know nothing is ever common with me.

"Your name?"

I turn to see a woman standing in the doorway. She wears a standard grey shirt and pants joined in the middle with a green belt—a sign she's the assistant to someone in this building. Her brown hair hides any symbols. My thoughts kept me from hearing her enter, but her sudden question doesn't cause me to jerk. At some level, I knew she was there.

"Zayne . . ."

I pause. That name is mine. A common name with no extra connotations lurking in the letters. No one thinks anything when they hear *Zayne.*

Her fingers move across an arvos—a portable computer interface—in her hand. "Radi!" Her face lights up as she unnecessarily speaks my family name. My father doesn't even have to be present to elicit a response from someone.

"My apologies, my name is Varet. I voted for your father. Both times. Such a great man deserves to serve our Council more than once. I get a bit carried away. I didn't realize you were assigned to this medical unit."

Everyone always boasts that they voted for him. No one voted against him. Every five sun cycles, the Vox people choose to either replace or reaffirm the Representatives of the Council. My father nears the end of his second term and plans to seek a third. I have no doubts he'll serve again.

He served the Council before becoming a Representative. He's never talked about this venture. It was before I was born. But I have to believe this played some part in how the people view him. I have his name but not the understanding of who he is. Not yet. Not until I finish my studies under the Council.

Then *Zayne* will hold as much weight as my father's name.

"We haven't had an active representative with a child in many cycles," Varet continues. "You must be making your father proud. His advocacy for you to remain in the city under the Council's instruction is admirable. You must already know so much about the inner workings of our leaders."

His advocacy? She's mistaken. My father's name grants me the privilege to study under the Prava leaders. She only knows the process other graduates have to adhere to. They need someone in good standing with the Council to vouch for them, and even then, they have to meet with the Council and convince them they are suited to study with them. Not me.

My eyes shift to the floor. Unless this is another secret my father has kept from me. Or is favoritism not permitted by the Council, and this is the only way my father can grant me access to his secrets? Yes, that is why my father acts the way he does.

None of this matters. In two mansiis, I go before the Council either as my given right from my father or by his advocacy and take my place under their instruction. There I will receive the first information about my father that he holds secret.

"Well," she says, regaining my attention, if only partially. "With the delay in your recovery, I'm sure you're eager to meet your father at the final ceremony."

"Delay?" I blink, holding my eyes shut for an extra second before looking at her. Now she has my full attention. "What delay? What sol is it?"

I remember the timepiece in my hand and turn its face upward. The datecode reads **85.6.517.**

"It is the eighty-fifth solpae—"

Eighty-fifth sol of Anam, the sixth and final mansii. Only five sols left before the end of the current sun cycle and the beginning of the five hundred and eighteenth. I went into the procedure on the eighty-second. Twenty-seven hours were necessary to insert the implant. Less than a sol in duration, with eight hours for my recovery.

"But do not be concerned," she says. "The Council gave word that the final ceremony has been delayed. I do not know the exact time, but I believe it is not for another sol."

I slip down from the bed, barely registering her words. "Three sols? What happened?"

"Your Lamis tests were inconclusive," she says. "The doctors kept you in a suspended state to ensure your Lamis recovered from the procedure. No reason to worry. The Curator conducted the final test himself and cleared you."

I glance again at her green belt. The color is worn by the Curator and those he commands. He's the city's specialist on the energy in our bodies.

I visit him twice every cycle to evaluate my Lamis. He's responsible for clearing all the graduates for the procedure. Why is she so calm about this? The Curator's responsibility ends there. He has nothing to do with the procedure itself.

"But I ramble and worry you for no reason," she says, presenting me with a smile to ease the worry she instills. "I need to know your new name for your final record. Have you chosen?"

I break eye contact with her. A sharp sting flashes in the back of my head. I resist the urge to grab the area with my hand, and the pain subsides.

I am the son of the Council. A future leader. That is why the Curator took an interest in my procedure. That is why I am here alone, separate from the other graduates.

"Your name?"

I look at her. Her cheery demeanor wavers, but a smile remains.

My new name is my first choice as an Alfaron. An honor, and the most distinctive thing that sets us apart from the other two factions in the Vox Nation. Members of the Vecco and Balon factions keep the same name from birth. I now decide what name I carry into the Historical Record.

"I want to keep Zayne as both first and preference," I say.

"Excellent." Varet inputs data into her device. "If I may presume, you will keep your father's name?"

Varet's response to my father's name flashes in my mind. How much does my father's name grant me? I am not yet more than a name. I cannot cast off his name, for what does it matter? The Council gave him the name *Radi*. When I complete what my father desires from me, my new name will come from the Council as his did.

I open my mouth to answer her when the lights flicker. No—the power system fluctuates. The vibration through the floor stops for a second, its constant presence a mere afterthought until it stops.

Varet taps her arvos. "Hmm . . . I lost connection to the network. No worries, just update your name via your city profile within two mansiis, or else the process becomes far more difficult. Well, if you wish to change your name. You need only do nothing if you wish everything to remain as it is."

Her words barely register in my mind. Numerous fail-safes prevent power fluctuations. Beyond the people who power smaller devices and systems, the city receives power from lamis-5 formations underneath us. Similar to the energy within us, but different, more versatile with the right Tech. Epis City was built here to take advantage of the natural deposits, which are far more stable than others across Solisternum. Most cities aren't near deposits, requiring extensive processes to transfer energy to their generators.

Most systems in Epis city passively pull power from the energy formations. Variations in the power simply do not happen. Too many fail-safes. Perfect designs.

The lights flicker again.

Varet looks up. "Odd. It's always something." She points to beneath my bed. "Clothes for you to change into are there. You are free to leave. I am sure new instructions regarding the final ceremony await you at home."

She tucks her arvos under her arm and leaves the room. I pull the clothes out and slip them on quickly, glancing at the Alfaron symbol adorned on the shirt. A red circle holds the silhouette of two profiles. They face away from each other, connected by a distant city. Above the city hang three yellow circles, representing the three factions—Alfarons, Balons, and Veccos. No one speaks to what the symbol means. We each interpret it differently.

My father, looking away. The Council and its Representatives, watching for danger. The Vox people, looking away from their city, knowing their leaders will keep them safe. I wonder how my father sees the symbol. He doesn't share what he sees in it. My interpretations change each sol. Every time I pull on a shirt with the symbol or walk by someone displaying the image of our faction. Every one of my father's conversations I overhear.

With the clothes hugging my body, I run my fingers through my short light-brown hair, pushing down what the shirt shifted. My hand stops on the back of my head. I lower my arm and pull the long black sleeve up to check the skin underneath. I shouldn't expect to find anything. My energy not only prevents scars, but also erases past scars. Only the implant holds onto those memories now.

I walk through the door into an empty hallway. The lights remain steady, but the vibration in the floor is inconsistent. I take one step to the right, and the vibration's steady. A step to the left and the inconsistency returns. Not everyone can diagnose Tech issues by the vibration. The trait is learned through hundreds of hours in class. The Tech classes that my father never demanded I take in school.

The ones I loved.

I follow the vibrations down the hall until I find an open door, an invitation for my curiosity. A voice drifts out, speaking technical terms with frustration. I look inside to see someone bent over a control panel. Only two people have permission to work on public systems—Tech periis and specialists. I shift to the right, staying in their blind spot. It's a boy. No older than I am and far too young to be a perii. And specialists rarely work in the field. He cannot be the Tatem—the overseer of all the city's Tech personnel.

The Alfaron symbol sits on his back with an unfamiliar symbol on his shoulders. He is adjusting the power supply input. I step loudly, causing him to jerk.

"Need any assistance?" I ask.

He stands up to my height, if not an inch taller. The lighting is poor, but his eyes appear different shades. "And what makes you think you qualify to help me?"

I ponder telling him about my father. No, that holds no significance here. My father takes no interest in our Tech. I once thought if I excelled in something he didn't, he would notice me. I was wrong. He only questioned my loyalty to the Council. To him.

This boy has enough confidence to question my offer to help, but the fluctuations betray his lack of skill. He's not a perii or specialist.

"You are adjusting the power supply for the building without a Lamis regulator," I say, glancing at the panel. "Lamis-5 is more stable than, say, formations three and four, but you still need a regulator. You're causing power fluctuations throughout the system."

He smirks. "Then, unless you have a regulator on you, you cannot help me. Can you? Shouldn't you be somewhere else right now?"

"I do the regular maintenance on my house's power supply once a mansii," I say, ignoring his last comment. "My request for a regulator is always denied, so I have to alter the existing system components to act as a substitute."

He closes the panel and slips a small rectangular device into the pocket of his pants. "I would lose my city visa if I altered the Tech of a system beyond its designated purpose."

Every adult has a city visa. Everyone in Epis City has some sort of duty to fulfill to remain here. He is no older than me. Is he working in the city when he should be at an Etero school continuing his education?

"You aren't from here," I say. "What city sector did you graduate from?"

"I have to move onto my next assignment from the *Tatem*," he says. His words mean to tell me how serious my interruption is. He walks past me and stops in the doorway. "I have an education visa to study under the Tatem. I come from the city of Urbs. Those power fluctuations came from me manually regulating everything at once. Well within the tolerance for a lamis-5 system."

The information comes more as a punishment for my curiosity than providing any relief. As the boy walks out of sight, I have to think he knew that. He isn't Alfaron. Urbs is a distant city under the control of the Vecco faction. They rarely travel this far. I look back at the control panel. Veccos aren't known for an aptitude for Tech. I shake my head.

I should be the one learning from the Tatem. Not a Vecco who lacks the appreciation for the Tech he works on. But those are only dreams. My future lies with the Council and not Tech.

I ponder the secrets that my father keeps from me. He has achieved a respect that rivals the Council's. I only know he hasn't surpassed our leaders because they hold his loyalty. An unbreakable devotion that surpasses his role as a father. If I am ever to match my father, I have to abandon Tech for his path.

My father's future joy at my sacrifice flashes in my mind. He has a heavy burden of having to keep everything from me.

My doubt stops me. I look around and realize my thoughts have me walking aimlessly. I tap a small screen near a door, and a light creeps along the wall, guiding me.

I look back down the hallway. "Where is everyone?" I ask the emptiness.

I push the question away and follow the glowing panels. The light ends at a door. An automatic sensor sits at the top, but the door doesn't open. I press the manual button to the right of the doorframe. A girl replaces the door, standing across from me as the metal slides out of the way. Her hand is inches from the edge of the frame, intending to open the door.

Soriina Nami. My friend for as long as I can remember.

Her shoulders relax as her eyes beam. Her blue eyes meet mine. My only real friend needs no invitation to move forward and hug me. The embrace doesn't last long enough before she pulls away.

"We're going to be late," she says. "I came to find you as soon as they said you were awake."

The smile that I realize is on my face fades. "Late? For what?"

Soriina shakes her head, her own smile remaining steady. "Your father's speech. The finale of our graduation ceremony. It's happening now."

The Council Representative

"A Council Representative is the voice of the Council, both literally and figuratively. An honor that I hold above all else." —an excerpt from the acceptance speech of Council Representative Stephan Radi

A wall of heat meets me as I exit the coolness of the medical facility. An array of voices forces out the stillness of the hallway. A collision of sounds. Yells. Cheers. Adults. Graduates. I take a step back into the shadow of the doorway. The walkway and transport path beyond that are filled with people. Clouds shift in the sky, unveiling the sun. Its blinding rays reflect off the glass fronts of the two-story buildings around us. The thick, transparent material keeps the interiors cool without much thought of those outside.

I retreat further into the comfort of the shadows. Clouds are abundant during this mansii, but not this sol. Why does it feel personal?

A worse thought creeps into my mind. Why didn't my father meet me here? Did he not know about my delayed recovery? He should have wanted to be here to make sure I arrive at the final ceremony. Even as I step closer to becoming who he wants me to be, he remains distant.

No, no. I condemn my father for something I don't understand. How childish of me, unfit for someone as myself. My father speaks on behalf of the Council this sol. Nothing is more important.

"You question why no one came to retrieve you for the ceremony," Soriina says, stepping into the shadows with me. "Why do you think I am here? Do not think you were forgotten."

I force a grin and say nothing of what I want to share with Soriina. "We should be leaving. I've made us late enough."

Her eyes search mine. She knows I have more to say. She knows me too well, but Soriina knows when to pry and when to leave me alone with my thoughts.

Soriina takes a step backward. "We can talk later about whatever's behind those eyes. The crowds are leaving."

We start in a brisk walk, trying to keep up with the other graduates and their families. They are moving toward the city's center—Sector Five. The most important place in the city. The home of the Council. While Epis City is not an open city, requiring special permission to live and work here, access to Sector Five is even stricter. No one enters without permission from the Council—usually dictated by their job, set by their leaders.

This sol is different. The final ceremony grants us all reason to enter. But the Council will not preside over our presence here. My father will.

The walk to the heart of the city takes nearly an hour. Walking from Sector Two to Five, we can see the towering buildings in the distance long before we reach them. The short, two-story houses that allow us the view line the transport path we walk along. Each house is identical; not even mine or Soriina's boasts any difference. Soriina's home feels distinct, though. Her parents were a welcoming change. Their presence absent of secrets.

The walk is a part of the ceremony. No one walks into Sector Five. All entry is done by transport. The transport path is wide enough to accommodate nearly four vessels. That's only side-by-side. There are four vertical lanes to travel as well, each one allowing a different speed for transports to operate at.

A chill moves across my body. Darkness grows around me. I look up and see the moon nearly completing its eclipse of the sun. Orbed light fixtures on the buildings sense the fading light and try to replace it. Why put the ceremony so late in the sol? I need to ask Soriina. She didn't explain the reason for delaying the proceedings.

The crowd slows and condenses. Soriina looks at me with concern.

"Are you still Zayne? Before you ask, you can still call me Soriina. But now it's Soriina Solum."

My head tilts involuntarily. "You changed your family name?"

"Soriina Solum." Her eyes beam as she repeats the name. "My father encouraged me to." She crosses her arms. "You didn't."

I shift my eyes from her to the crowd around us. My feet slow until I stop. "Technically—"

Soriina walks a couple of steps farther before turning to face me. "You said you were going to change it."

"I still can," I say. "The system went down. I still have time."

"You're afraid of what your father is going to say," she says. "You yourself have said you wanted to follow after him by your own means. What better way than to choose your own name?"

No soft entry into this conversation. Soriina knows better. We've had this discussion before. She knows the only way to make me face it is to be direct.

Her arms drop. "You're going through with studying under the Council. And you can't risk them rejecting you for rejecting the name they gave your father. What happened to the Zayne that wanted to build the next great piece of Tech?"

Her words reflect my past thoughts. She doesn't realize I long forgot such illusions. That naïve child doesn't exist anymore. My father's name is his gift to me. A chance to learn from the Council is an opportunity I cannot relinquish.

I look at her. "Wouldn't you?" Her silence gives me time to think, and those thoughts turn to more words. "I was born under the Council. I have the rare opportunity to stay in the city. The law requires graduates to leave and move away from the influence of their parents in order that they discover themselves on their own. I am above that law. Why would I throw away my father's name? Do you not see how he commands the respect of others? Even the Council respects him. Would you throw away a chance at such power?"

"What if what you want is outside the city? Can you truly see something when you're right next to it? You've spent your entire life here. Leave. Come with me to an Etero."

An Etero. Where graduates go to continue their education in leadership, Tech, the Agmen military, or one of the many connecting subsets. Graduates can't remain in their birth city past the age of ten. They're forbidden to reconnect with their families until their next graduation. Soriina has no choice. I do.

"You once dreamed of leaving the city," she continues in my silence. "Exploring the Red Plains. Visiting the trees at the base of the mountains, or the far reaches of Solisternum where the moon doesn't cover the entire sun at the end of each sol."

That younger version of myself was oblivious. He didn't understand the knowledge this city holds. He didn't understand why his father would abandon him each sol for the Council. For his duty. Each sol he left was an invitation into his secrets.

I now accept the invitation.

Soriina may live in Sector Two with me. Her father may work in Sector Five. She doesn't overhear the things I do. The things I shouldn't hear. The words that urge my curiosity forward.

Soriina taps me on the forehead. "Let someone else in there and you may find your thoughts are not as overwhelming."

I blink several times, retaking in my surroundings. Only a sliver of the sun remains in the sky. The tops of the buildings reflect the yellow skies that darken with each passing second. Artificial lights across the tops of buildings fight the growing darkness. They cannot fight the drop in temperature. A chill sweeps across my body.

The pathway below the fading sun is empty. During any other sol, transports would be flying overhead, sending down violent but cool air. The skies are empty for the graduation. The city comes together in Sector Five. Everyone will be there. I look around. We're alone in the middle of the transport path.

No. A single man wearing a featureless black uniform stands alone across from us. His gaze follows the crowd before moving to us.

I look at Soriina. "We should be moving."

"All that silence and you just expect to say nothing more? I know something was going on inside that head of yours. We've known each other since before we could speak. I know how to read that face of yours. And I am the only person you ever—"

"Soriina," I say, grabbing her face and turning her head. "I would let you continue to barrage me with your words, but the crowd is gone."

Soriina sees the approaching man and gives a slight dip of her head. "Not that you are correct or that this conversation is over, but we should go before we are told to. Whatever words he has for us will only make us late."

We sprint toward the main group. School never had us run much, and when we did, it was exhausting. My maturing Lamis courses through my body, and I feel like I never need to stop. I keep up with Soriina with ease. We only stop when the mess of bodies becomes too crowded to maneuver. The slow movement does nothing to reduce the noise from the graduates and their families. Worse, the voices meld together, making it impossible to pick out individual conversations.

It also keeps Soriina from bringing up our earlier discussion.

It feels like hours pass as we progress forward. The buildings rise higher into the sky the farther we walk. Everyone pauses for a moment as the moon completes its eclipse and sends the city into darkness. The larger of our three moons is in the sky, so the sun completely disappears.

The orbed lights cast an even white light across the transport path full of people. The transport path we walk on ends, opening up into a large area with flood lights that keep our eyes forward. The City Center. Epis City has numerous squares meant for the public to use for joint work and occasional relaxation. Sun shields extend across the tops of the buildings. But here, in Sector Five, the space is far too big for sun shields and isn't open to the public. This sol is the only time the public is welcome, and we have the eclipse to shield us from the sun.

The jumble of bodies ends as the open space allows everyone to spread out. The entire city is here, all for our graduation. Thousands of people fill the square from every direction. Four main transport paths connect to the City Center, but smaller routes number in the dozens.

This is not my first time in Sector Five. The buildings sting with familiarity. The towering constructions house the most important people and activities in the city. More than half the buildings have fully glass fronts, while others have glossy metallic shines. The shortest structure stands at fifteen stories, while the tallest towers over thirty and is a recent addition to the Sector.

I feel the steady vibration from the generators within the buildings, but an unfamiliar irregular pulse reaches my feet. I resist the urge to drop to the ground to identify the source. Rather, I look past the people toward the edge of the City Center. A generator glows blue, extracting raw lamis-5 from below the city. Most generators function that way, usually enclosed in buildings or beneath homes. The design of the surrounding structures acts as a fail-safe in the event of hypothetical overloads.

Epis City is one of the few cities built on top of a deposit. Other cities transport energy from deposits far away to reduce the risk of unstable raw lamis-5 damaging their homes. The Council doesn't have such a fear, so we don't.

The generator I see is massive, towering over the crowds.

"Zayne," Soriina says, just loud enough to hear over the crowds. I turn from the generator to her, leaving that mystery for another sol. "We aren't the only ones here."

I give an exaggerated look around before staring at Soriina. "A bit obvious, even for you."

Soriina slams her hand into my shoulder, but not enough to hurt. "Look at them, Zayne. The other factions are here."

"That's not possible. They aren't invited to graduation ceremonies."

I speak before checking the accuracy of her comment with my eyes. Despite the size of the area, the people continue to crowd. I pick out a small group and realize the truth in Soriina's words. Three men stand apart from the others around them. They have intricate tattoos in place of hair. Vibrant colors mark their clothes apart from the standard solid colors of the Alfarons around them. No symbols adorn their clothing, not even of their faction. They might as well be barefoot with the lack of coverage their shoes provide.

Veccos.

The smallest faction in our nation. Two remote cities fall within their control in Solisternum. No transport paths cross the Red Plains to reach them. The journey is long and difficult. Manual flight for sols. No automation. Not that they care. Their affinity for Tech is far less than that of Alfarons. They contribute nothing to its advancement.

"Surprised they can tolerate all the Tech," Soriina says. "But what are they doing here?"

I smirk at her initial comment, but the question of their presence tugs at my curiosity. This ceremony is important, but never enough to draw the attendance of the other factions. Their own graduates are completing their education. Before I can bring more thoughts to the surface, a man wearing a thin grey sun jacket over a black shirt pushes his way through the crowd toward us. The material protects against the relentless heat, so he must have been here since before the eclipse. He holds an arvos in hand, pressing buttons as he stops in front of us.

"Graduates!" He stares at us. "Yes, yes, you are graduates. Why are you here? The speech is delayed until every graduate is in their seat. Never have we not had every Alfaron graduate in attendance for the speech! The retelling of our great Vox story. Come! Come!"

He walks in between us, turns, and pushes us forward.

"Forward! Forward!" He ushers us onward through the crowd. He mutters under his breath. The blurring of conversations around us makes singling out his voice easy. "First no speech, now a speech. We break traditions in some areas, but adhere in others. Order is the way of the Council. Yet disorder—" His head jerks toward me. "Faster, faster. I have other graduates to find."

A space opens up in the crowd where the man stops. Another man's voice rises above the jumble of conversations.

"There is a size limit on those filthy beasts in *our* city! Get that thing out of here before it attacks a child!"

The Alfaron man's hand glistens with a metallic covering. He waves it erratically at a woman wearing patchwork clothing that lacks any precision in its design. As people move across my view, I realize the woman has an animal next to her. It sits calmly, nearing her waist with its head. It has four ears, two straight up and two lying flat against its head, which narrows into a long snout. Its coat is a sleek grey color with a dull, red-colored head. It's a Sofera. A tamed animal that feeds off the energy of a person.

Lamis connects the land of Solisternum beyond the deposits in the ground. Every Vox and animal. Every plant and most of our Tech use the energy. Soferas act as a natural solution to a uniquely Vox problem. We can overproduce Lamis, which causes skin burns and shuts down various bodily functions if left untreated. Of course, doctors have treatments, and in the cities, Alfarons have Tech that eases the condition.

I have studied what they call LiorTech. It's the most common technology used to treat an excess of Lamis. This Tech often bolsters a person's natural senses or augments limbs. And with only a few hours of calculations, a person can live a normal life with excess energy. Soferas require cycles of training before they can join with a person, and that is if they accept their new diet. Our Lamis and the natural lamis originating from deposits are different. Similar enough to find commonalities to power Tech, but animals sense the difference.

Soriina nudges me. "That's a caro. Sure, I've seen plenty of gradula beasts as Soferas. But that thing's regular diet is other animals. What's it doing in the city?"

"Look at her clothes, clearly a Vecco," I say. "No chance an Alfaron wears that and has one of those things in the city. I read that fewer than five percent of caros pass the training. Fewer than that last a cycle before reverting."

Gradulas draw lamis from vegetation without digesting the plants. They leave no scars on the land, allowing their food source to return anew the next time they're hungry. Unless cities control the nearby caro populations, they devastate the gradula populace. They absorb energy as they digest the lifeless bodies. Whoever thought to train them to absorb without digestion was crazy. It's not natural for them.

LiorTech predates the use of caros, but Soferas have a long history. We know better than nature. The Council's support of technological improvement propels this truth forward. But not everyone believes that. This Sofera proves that.

"Arrest her! Someone arrest this Vecco scum and get rid of this beast!"

The man's words pierce the crowd's noise, drawing me out of my thoughts.

Our guide lifts his hand to his mouth. "There is a disturbance near the graduate seating. Send Esidio guards."

Esidio guards are the city extension of the Vox armies—the Agmen. Renowned fighters. They are the only ones allowed weapons within the city. They keep the Council's peace, often walking among us without notice. They watch over the Representatives. Always near, never seen.

Two men appear on either side of the angry Alfaron. If not for overhearing our guide, I would only think they're normal citizens. He points to the Vecco woman, but the crowd shifts, hiding the rest of the encounter. Our guide steps further in the way.

"Enough time has been wasted," he says, stretching his arms forward. "To your seats. To your seats so the speech may begin."

No one is sitting, rather the other graduates stand in front of the backless seats. We only stand in the Council's presence. I look up at the stage, hovering nearly fifty feet in the air. My mouth hangs open.

The Council sits above us.

The Breaking of Tradition

"Children hold the future of the Nation; therefore, they must be educated by the Nation." —Prava Council ruling upon the creation of city schools

Lights shift to engulf the stage. The faceless helmets of the Council shine bright. They never show their faces in public. Do the Representatives know what they look like under the masks? Does my father?

My father. He stands at the center of the stage. The six Council Members are seated behind him. Anam, Tosa, Kaz, Arba, Pak, and Isa—the Member my father represents. The seventh member, the Speaker, is not present. Of course he isn't present; the Representatives are silent in his presence, and my father intends to speak. My father and the others only speak for the Council when the Speaker is absent.

He is always absent.

The conversations around the Sector Center end as everyone notices the Council. Murmurs shift through the crowd. They are as confused as I am. The Representatives oversee the final graduation ceremony. The Council's public appearances are few and well-known, but this sol shouldn't be one of them.

I turn to Soriina. "Why is the Council here? What is all this?"

Her eyes say everything I need to know, but she adds words to solidify her meaning. "If you would be quiet, you may learn. Your father is about to speak."

I return my eyes to the stage. My father presses two fingers to his forehead before extending his palm up and out toward the crowd. His white coat flaps in a light breeze. Simple grey clothes lay underneath. Silver plates on his shoulders reflect the lights around the stage. When his arms and the wind rest, his body disappears under his coat. His hair is shorter than when I last saw him.

My father's voice echoes through the area with the help of an amplifier hidden somewhere. "Many of you stand before your Council with questions. Why do we break tradition? Why are the other factions here? The Council does not mislead you. Our leaders guide us in ways unseen for only your good. I remind you of a saying by the first Council, '*Tradition is not truth.*' Embrace this deviation and trust the perfection that is the Council's wisdom. Knowledge is power."

"Favor to the Council!" the crowd finishes the Vox saying.

The roars turn to cheers. My father radiates the glory of the Alfarons as he allows them this moment.

Do they cheer for him? Or the Council? Is that why my father is here? To lead the people into this breaking of tradition. I dare say the Vox citizens respect the Council because of my father. The people see him more often than the Speaker, who is the only Council Member permitted to show his face. He chooses to sit in shadow, while my father has the most public appearances of any Representative. The Speaker remains hidden as my father takes his applause. Is it by design or something my father takes advantage of?

What secrets will I learn that everyone else has to live in ignorance of?

The noise of the crowd tapers off as my father gestures with his hands. "As you look around, you see familiar friends and unfamiliar faces from our neighboring factions. Our nation gathers in our great city because the People's Representative has concluded his journey across Solisternum, visiting each of our cities. He petitioned the Council to speak in front of the graduates. Rather than gather when the sun sets to hear his account, we do so now. His words transcend the generations. What better way for our graduates to enter Alfaron citizenship than to hear about the state of the Nation? May you hear his words and establish your own path into the Historical Record."

As prideful cheers fill the air around me, my father glances at me. The moment lasts less than a second, but he means his last words for me.

My father puts the crowd to silence more quickly this time. I know he cannot speak to me directly, but I want him to. "But don't let me waste time filling you with my words. May I present you, Carius, *your* Representative."

The crowd ignites into cheers again. I resist pressing my hands to my ears and keep my attention on my father. But he doesn't look at me again, so I look at the man standing up. His black coat remains still in the breeze, only the hint of a red shirt visible underneath.

I've heard my father speak about this man. His position holds no power. The only people who can cause the Council to change law or make decisions are the Representatives. They are voted from the people by the people to speak for the people. But they remain here in Epis City. The People's Representative spends time in every other city. What does he hope to learn? The Council resides here.

Carius steps next to my father. He presses two fingers to his forehead, then to his chin with a slight dip of his head. A formal greeting my father is worthy of.

"Thank you for your service to our Prava Council, Representative Radi." He turns to the crowd. "It is my honor to stand in the city of the Council. To stand before the people of Epis. And this city's most recent group of graduates." He pauses and dips his head with two fingers to his chin as a sign of respect to us. "May you leave this city to greater things."

He can't believe that. He knows the Council is here. And with them, knowledge that surpasses anything the other cities can offer. It's a sacrifice to leave the city. Every graduate hopes to return. He only says that because every graduate *has* to leave.

He continues. "I hope you forgive this shift from the known so close to our celebration of the new cycle. My journey across our land has been long and tough. I have learned much about our people. About the factions—the Veccos, the Balons. And even the Alfarons living beyond Epis City. The spread of solar energy is pushing the advancement of Tech in ways previously thought impossible. We no longer have to rely on the energy of our bodies or risking our lives by tapping into natural deposits of lamis."

My eyes shift to another generator beneath the stage. Its blue glow fades in and out. Is what he says true? Are we shifting away from Lamis powering our cities? Our Tech? Epis City uses no solar power. We do experiments in school and study its intricacies, but there is no application. It's not yet consistent enough. Not for a—

A sharp pain erupts in the back of my head. I move my hand quickly to the spot. I nearly hit Soriina with my elbow. She gives me a look worth a hundred words. The pain subsides but remains present and, in an unexplainable way, has me turn around.

The crowd's focus is on Carius, except for that of one man. He looks at me. I look away as the pain increases. When I look back, the pain disappears, as does the man.

An audible gasp from the crowd refocuses my attention on Carius. "The city of Mauris lies in ruin. They only had a small lamis-5 deposit beneath their city, and the destruction was unimaginable. The half of the city that used solar power received only minimal damage from the storm." I look around me for a reaction but receive none. Everyone's attention is set on Carius. "Without the partial transition to solar energy, the entire city would be lost. The Etero Grex Ludus now serves as both hospital and school. With the school still using Lamis, they fear for their safety. The future of the next generation is not certain. When will the Tech periis and specialists of this city move to solar research? Will you encourage these new graduates to go beyond the limitations you put on yourselves?"

He's talking about Sorbes. Storms that descend from the northern Triones Mountains where the city of Mauris lies. These natural phenomena feed off Lamis of every form. They can overload generators and other Tech and even drain the energy from an adult Vox. Cities across the mountain base have defensive measures to dissipate Sorbes. But storms don't form until the middle of the cycle. We are far from the storm season.

And they never reach Epis City. No storm has ever pushed this far into Solisternum. We're safe.

The crowd's words turn against the Representative. I can feel their anger filling the air. He cannot expect to win the approval of the people here. Lamis research occurs here because the storms cannot reach us. We push natural lamis deposits to their limits with no threat of Sorbes drawing near. He wishes the city to change completely, its citizens to give up everything they work for. Everything that maintains their visas.

Did the Council know what he was going to say?

My eyes go to my father. He remains still. His body language betrays no concern.

"You reject my declaration for change. On what basis? Because no storm has ever reached this deep into our land? How many of you have called this place home for long enough to prove that? No. You trust the Council when they say no storm has touched this city. All the while, your brothers and sisters face the devastation of these storms. You don't live in fear of dying to the storms. Your memories lost. Your place in history stolen. They endure because they understand when to expect them. And when a storm reaches you here, what will you do?"

I don't understand why he pushes this topic. The murmurs of the people grow. I fear to look back at their anger. He isn't convincing anyone. Is he casting doubt into the Council's word?

Carius looks back at the Council members, and this time, a shift in my father's movement betrays concern. The Council did know what he was going to talk about. But not what comes next.

"But you are not going to change," he says. "You are Alfarons. Your Council sits with their backs to the sun, telling you lies of its appearance. You feel safe in their shadow. Their lies. You do their work as long as it means you can stay here. You refuse to face the realities that extend beyond this city. The horrors the other cities face. May I introduce you to one of those horrors."

His words fade into the anger of the crowd as colors streak across the sky. The clouds shift from grey to an assortment of hues that I have never seen in the sky above Epis City. The eclipsed sun only serves to deepen these colors. I've only seen images of what comes next.

A Sorbe.

Impossible.

The air cracks. The clouds release thundering sounds. In a flash, an explosion rings out from behind us. A rush of air and heat knocks me forward. My forehead bounces off the seat in front of me. A different pain surges through my head as my vision blurs. Time doesn't seem to pass as I wait for the pain to subside. Several drops of blood hit the ground, glistening with blue—my Lamis. I stare until the color fades into a dark red and the agony stemming from my head lessens.

Shifting to my knees, I look up to see most of the graduates on the ground as well. The crowd is screaming. People lie face down on the ground. Many stay there. Nothing moves except the smoke filling the air.

My eyes trace the edge of the City Center. Smoke pours out from the remnants of one of the generators I saw earlier. The building nearest barely stands. Glass and metal strike the ground. No chain reaction to the lamis-5 deposit below. All the damage is on the surface.

Soriina grabs my arm, which causes me to shift my focus. I look ahead to beneath the stage. Another generator. Another explosion waiting. More death. I look up. The Council. My father.

"Someone has to seal off that generator," I say, standing up.

Soriina tries to pull me down. "Not you. We have to stay here."

"No one else is. Everyone is tending to the hurt. They aren't thinking about the other generator."

I step away from my friend, and whether she gives up on stopping me or is unable, her hands slip away. I half run through the scared graduates. At the end of the graduate seating, my eyes focus on the stage. I look for my father. He isn't visible. Did he look for me when the storm struck?

I push the distraction away and look forward to the generator. My eyes scan the outer casing, identifying where I need to start before arriving at the device. My eyes pause at its bottom. From this distance, I can see the ground beneath the generator. It isn't drawing energy from the deposit beneath us. It's a temporary generator storing a limited supply of raw lamis-5. An inefficient device, but it's the only reason everyone is still alive.

I stop a few feet short of the generator. The air changes. I turn around, and the colors are shifting in the clouds. I'm too late.

A streak of white light beats me to the generator. A flash blinds me before I lose all feeling in my body. I sense myself flying backward before everything goes black.

Disconnect

"The words of the Council are true. The words of the Council bring unity. We can trust the words of the Council above all. They do not lie to us, thus we praise them."—an excerpt from the acceptance speech of Council Representative Stephan Radi

A blue shadow covers the distant horizon—a city. No, a mountain. Mountains. A haze blurs my vision—no, everything. Smells and sounds reach me but are distant, unrecognizable. I cannot feel my body. If I were only mist, I would have no reasoning to say otherwise. My hands blur as I move them, but I know I am real. I have to be real. This has to be real. Even the memories of how I arrived here are blurry and distant.

A voice. The back of my head throbs in pain.

My ears sting. I cannot be certain. A voice. Many voices. I look up to find the shadow closer. Mountains. Not that I am certain. The blue haze shifts through my body. *Is* my body. I want to believe I am in pain, but exhaustion seems more fitting. The blue shifts from the shadows into a figure. Figures. A dark haze envelops the area. The sky—or ground—disappears into shadow.

The voice again. Voices. More pain.

Yes, a figure now stands before me. My senses still cannot give me certainty. The figure raises its hands. Blue expands into the shadows. A city within the mountains, or mountains within a city. The longer I try to comprehend, the less I believe what I see. I cannot even be sure if I am standing. Or sitting. Or flying.

The voice stops. A silence makes me aware of a noise that no longer persists.

The figure turns toward me or away. It lacks all detail. As I feel my senses focusing, the shadows swirl until everything fades to black. All that remains is the pain in the back of my head.

The storm.

My eyes shoot open.

Blinding lights force me to close them again. With my eyes shut tight, I feel the last moments of discomfort fading in the back of my head where my implant sits. Nothing can be wrong with what solidifies my place in history. Just a coincidence. I shift my focus to the soft bed I find myself on. Too soft to be my bed.

I swing my body so my legs hang in the air. It's higher than my bed as well. A medical bed. I lean forward, pressing my hands into my eyes. I open them in my palms, allowing the light to enter at my discretion.

When the light hurts less, I pull my hands away and take in my surroundings. The room is white and still as my feet hit the floor. A warmth hits my bare feet. The bed and a single seat are all that is present. The door is hard to see, but the outline becomes present after a minute of searching. It becomes more apparent when I realize there's an entry pad on the right of the door. My limited focus overlooks the obvious feature.

Where am I? Has the storm gone? Was a storm ever present? A thousand more plausible explanations exist. Carius set the generators to explode to mimic a storm. If I remain in the city, that is the most reasonable account. A Sorbe shows no mercy to cities.

Yes, Carius wants to move the people to action. He chose to simulate a storm's presence. Not even he can summon a natural phenomenon.

As an answer to my questions, the door slides open and an Esidio guard enters. He has no intention of hiding in the shadows or blending in with the general civilian population. A silver helmet covers his head, and a cloak hides most of what I presume is his uniform. The Alfaron symbol sits on his headgear. I am still in the city. He looks around the room before stopping his gaze on me. His arm stretches out toward me with a domed projectile weapon in hand. Pointed at me.

I stumble backward into the bed. I put my arms out in front of me and try to form words, but nothing escapes my lips. He twists his hand as blue energy swirls around the dome of the weapon, ready to escape.

As if he can hear my thoughts pleading where my words fail, he relaxes. His arm drops, and the energy retreats into the weapon. He looks over his shoulder and calls to someone I cannot see.

"There's no one here, just the Representative's son. With all the power outages, the room's sensors must be malfunctioning."

A woman with short brown hair steps around the guard and checks the room herself. A thin silver line extends down from her hairline to her left eyebrow. Her left eye flashes red as her gaze moves around me to the other portions of the room. "I will have a technician check the—" Her eyes stop on me. "He's—you're awake."

I ponder the concern in her voice. Many questions rise to the surface of my mind, but she speaks before I can manage anything.

"Guard, go alert the Curator that he's awake. Hurry."

The Esidio guard pushes back his cloak, revealing a grey shirt with the Alfaron symbol. He places his weapon on a silver belt—it clicks with a metallic zing—before exiting the room. Her voice has more hurry in it than his actions. Does she know something he doesn't?

The woman forces a smile. What is she concerned with? How much damage did the People's Representative cause? As she speaks, I expect her to give me an update.

"The—the Curator will be here soon."

The Curator has dothyris, general experts on Lamis, who care for the people in the city. Why has the Curator taken a specific interest in me? He spends most of his time in Sector Five. Is that where I am now?

The woman holds a smile but seems afraid to say anything. I see her hands shaking before stuffing them in her pockets next to her green belt. She works for the Curator.

"Where am I? What has happened since the speech?"

She looks over her shoulder, hoping that someone is going to come and end the conversation.

Or is my presence causing her to worry? Or is something else lurking beyond my comprehension? *Is* there a storm outside?

"Lia." A voice pulls me from my spiraling thoughts. A man steps into the room. He wears a green coat that reaches down to his black shoes with no visible Tech on his body. The Curator. "You may leave. I will handle the rest. Go begin your preparations."

She gives me one more glance before nodding. "Thank you, sir."

He looks at me with an arvos in hand. He holds back his coat with a hand on his hip, giving a view of his white pants with red, vertical stripes. The Alfaron symbol stands out on his white shirt. "Hello, Zayne. May I presume you remember me?"

I place two fingers to my chin and dip my head. "Yes, sir. A bit confused about everything, though. Where am I?"

He gives me the kind of soft smile that usually precedes bad news. "We are at my medical facility in Sector Five."

"Then there was no storm."

His head shifts. My words surprise him.

"Tell me everything you remember."

"What happened after the generators exploded?"

"First, give me a recollection of that sol. The best to your memory."

I resist the urge to demand more information. He's not telling me something. I wait a few seconds, hoping he may change his mind about answering my questions.

When he doesn't relent, I start. A few details slip my mind as I trace my memories back. I double back to fill in the blanks. He doesn't seem to mind the extra time I take to recall everything. He taps his arvos's screen as I speak. I pause when reaching the second generator. My memories feel more like speculation. Nothing seems certain. I give vague details about what caused the explosion of the generators. I withhold my doubt of the storm's presence and my suspicion of the People's Representative.

"Zayne." My vague details nearer to the explosion must alarm him. "Can you recall anything specific from when you approached the generator?"

I want to say yes. But the memories blur the more I think about them.

"That is not surprising," the Curator says, taking my silence as my answer. "If you had, you would be even more of a medical marvel. Allow me to fill in the gaps." He takes a step away from me. "After the storm struck the first generator, the second generator was sealed off immediately. You approached it regardless, for reasons that don't interest me. Before you reached it, the storm struck again. The storm's bolt was close enough to drain you of your Lamis."

I was struck by a Sorbe?

I press my hands into my body. How did I survive?

"Perhaps this explains Lia's strange reaction to finding you awake," the Curator says. "Simply put, you shouldn't be awake." He lowers his arvos and looks me in the eye. "Zayne, the storm took every measurable part of Lamis from your body. The only reason we tried to save you was because of your father. Anyone else would have been declared dead. We would be mourning you now."

I take a step back and sit back on the bed. "I—I don't understand. Was . . . was I dead?"

"Technically, no," he says. "You are breathing, and your body is producing Lamis." He reaches into his pocket and produces a vial of crimson red, with strands of blue moving in it. "This is the most recent sample of your blood. Your Lamis is abundant. You are alive. I'm not one to believe in resurrection, so I can only conclude that you were nearly dead. Closer to death than I have ever seen. I may have to work with the other Curators to redefine a few terms now, but not dead."

I want to believe him. But he so casually dismisses my near death. Is there humor in his voice? He's hiding something. Omitting something to keep me calm. It's having the opposite effect. How did I survive a strike from a Sorbe? These storms decimate entire cities. Half of the city of Mauris. Yet I survive?

"Zayne." I look up at the Curator. "Stop worrying. Near deaths happen more than you know, and no two are the same. Our Lamis is resilient. We only understand a fraction of our energy. Please, trust me when I say you have made a full recovery. An astonishing recovery the likes of which I have never seen before, but the test results are conclusive. And after only four sols."

"Four sols."

Before he can answer my questionless words, the lights turn off and emergency lights replace them. I jerk to my feet, but the Curator extends his hands to prevent further action.

"Nothing to worry about, Zayne. As soon as I realized you recovered, I gave word for the power in this section of the building to be terminated."

He has to know his words only create more questions. Why does he insist on tormenting me? Did all the cycles of tests not help him understand me? He knows my curiosity and its power over me.

Even in the dim lighting, he must see the confusion on my face. "My apologies. The storm remains overhead. Tech periis are shutting down the power throughout the city."

A storm is overhead.

"Are we the last to evacuate?"

"And abandon the city? You don't understand your Council very well."

"We're staying?"

"The Council decided yestersol."

"That doesn't make sense," I say, turning from him. "How do they expect us to survive a storm? We don't have the resources here. This cannot—"

"Zayne," the Curator says, guiding my gaze back to him. "If you have questions about your Lamis, I am more than qualified to answer them. But don't ask me to make sense of the decisions of our leaders. If anyone can receive the answers you want, it's you."

He means through my father. I may as well ask the Council. I am not yet his equal.

"I need to tell you one last thing, Zayne," the Curator says. "I know much is going through your head, but this is important." He pauses, though my thoughts don't settle by the time he starts speaking again. "The Council has restricted the knowledge surrounding your . . . near death. No one knows what I have told you, and no one can know. The explosion knocked you unconscious. The storm never struck you. That is the story the Council has announced to the public. That is the truth you are going to tell."

"They want me to lie? Why would you even tell me?"

He shifts forward but still leaves a gap in between us. "Zayne, I didn't lie before. I expect no setbacks with your recovery. But Lamis is a strange thing that we don't fully understand. Without knowing the truth, you may overlook possible symptoms in the future. Your body completely stopped producing energy. I have never seen such a recovery, so your future is within a void of knowledge."

"Who do I tell if something happens? Who would believe me?"

His eyes soften. "The Council has allowed me to research the rarity of the incident in private. You may contact me. But tell no one else, or you risk challenging a truth of the Council. This entire incident is putting enough stress on the city."

"What's the Council's plan?"

"I will let your father give you those details."

My eyes widen. "My father's here?"

The Curator pauses, considering my tone. "He awaits you as we speak." He presses his hand into the wall near the door's outline. Rather than opening, a panel disappears into the door, revealing a small lever. He pulls it with the sound of air releasing following. The door slides open. He looks back at me. "And Zayne, remember what I said."

The door remains open as he steps into the hallway.

I step back into the wall and slide to the floor. I press my hands into my head and try to push down everything the Curator said. A storm crossed the Red Plains. A Sorbe is overhead, and we aren't evacuating. Fear must have overcome the Council, for not only do they refuse to leave the city, but my survival—or death—scares them.

Fear? That isn't something the Council experiences. Some other explanation has to be just beyond my grasp. Why alter what the public knows?

My father. I realize a few minutes pass and he hasn't come. He isn't coming. He expects me to go to him. But he's here to see I am protected beneath the storm. Not that I should have anything to fear from the storm. The explosion hurt me. *Not the storm*.

I repeat those last words several times as I exit the room.

Dim lights fill the hallway. A door sits about twenty feet to the right, in shadow except for a white light coming from the wall. Whether the direction is correct or not, I head toward the light.

I stop in front of an electronic board. Dozens of names fill the screen. The screen shifts every few seconds, displaying more names. I can't determine when the cycle restarts, if it ever does. New names keep appearing.

As I ponder the reason, the screen goes blank before a larger text fills the screen. **Casualties of the Sorbe. Last Updated: 88.6.517.**

I take a step back. I watch the names again. And again.

Soriina's name is absent. And my father's. And mine.

I should be on that list.

But a more dangerous thought rises to the surface. The Council has us remaining in the city. How many more names will their decision add to this list?

Among the Representatives

"The driving force of our Nation is our operators. They sacrifice cycles of their lives to move us forward." —from the official collection of early Prava Council wisdom

I let the names paralyze me. Each one a person who thought they were safe from Sorbes. We don't fear storms because the Council knows all. We feel safe in their knowledge. Is it truly knowledge if they manipulate it?

I shut my eyes, trying to push away the thoughts. I know better. I understand. How many conversations have I overheard from my father, detailing how the mind of the Council works? I survived . . . an explosion caused by the storm. I shouldn't be thinking about these things. My body may be recovered, but my mind is still weak.

A click to my right pulls me from my thoughts, then a voice opens my eyes.

"Zayne."

I turn to my right. The door sits open with someone who isn't my father standing on the other side. But a man who is far more familiar than my father.

"Mr. Auctor," I say, wiping my nose. "What are you doing here? Where is my father?"

The man—my father's transport operator—steps forward. He seemed more like *my* operator, taking me across the city when others would walk. Our thousands of conversations helped sustain me in my father's absence. He moves so the light from the board illuminates the metal covering on his head—his LiorTech that regulates his excess Lamis. The Tech extends down into his cheek. His blue jacket seems almost black in the dim light.

"And hello to you, Zayne," he says. He points to the board. "You shouldn't dwell on those names. Their day of remembrance was two sols ago. If you wish to know their names, look upon them in the Historical Record and remember their contribution."

"What do you think we will learn from their contribution?" I ask.

Mr. Auctor takes in a breath. "The Council will help us with that. We only need to trust them when we seek answers about what happened."

His answer is everything I expect. I can't tell if he knows what the Council hides. Did anyone now residing in the Record see what happened to me? Does the Council hide that part?

I curse myself for the thought. It isn't my right to challenge the Council's decisions.

I seek to the change the topic. "Where is my father?"

"He had to attend the Council's judgment over the People's Representative," Mr. Auctor says. "They have chosen to expedite the process to give the people some closure on the events that unfolded."

When the Council presides over a person's judgment, they have no future. Carius will never see the sun again, if they choose to let him live.

"And with the preparations required for the storm," Mr. Auctor continues, "your father simply could not escape his responsibilities. With your hearing later, he chose to keep his distance until after."

"My hearing?"

"Ah, I suppose he made that decision when you were under the care of the Curator." He lets out a breath as he steps into the doorway. "Your hearing with the Council Representatives is happening this sol. With the storm looming, your father wanted you to decide your mentor before the Council made any more drastic decisions."

My father wants to protect me. As a graduate, I am legally torn from him. Whatever special protection he receives from the storm won't be passed onto me. I have to face the storm as a temporary citizen of the city. I suppose Soriina's parents will offer me shelter. No. My father has planned for this. If a Representative takes me on now, I will have their same protection.

But how can I be certain the Representatives will accept me? The woman's words from the first medical facility eat away at my confidence. Do I go before them having to earn my place or accepting what my father has given me? What I thought would be two mansiis to reconcile these thoughts turns into an hour, if that.

Mr. Auctor senses the turmoil within me.

"Zayne, I understand this is unexpected, but you have prepared for this. Nothing needs to change. You will speak with the Representatives. Answer their questions. Show your love for the Council and your desire to seek a place among the Representatives. If all goes as your father predicts, you will wait out the storm among them."

And have to rely on the Council's word to learn what transpires during the storm. I curse myself for thought. They have reasons beyond my comprehension. I have to trust. But what if someone else experiences what I did? How easily does the Council make these decisions about what to tell the public? Do they alter—

I stop the thought from fully forming.

I should ask Mr. Auctor if he knows the answer that will ease my thoughts. I can discern his answer from his words.

"We have delayed enough," Mr. Auctor says, removing any possibility of further questions. "The Representatives await you. My transport is outside."

I offer nothing more than a smile as he guides me out of the building. My eyes go to the sky. It's absent of the normal busy transport activity, giving me a clear view of the storm. I expect dark clouds or something menacing, but beautiful colors fill my sight instead. The colors swirl in unnatural ways, mixing with each other, forming new and familiar shades.

"A storm natent," Mr. Auctor says, "not the full presence of the Sorbe. The only reason we are alive and have time to prepare the city. Strikes from a natent are rare."

"Where is everyone, then?" I ask. "Do they know the storm can't hurt them right now?"

Without transports, I expect people. The Council's insight has everyone living close enough to walk where necessary. But the area is empty. We are somewhere away from the City Center in Sector Five. Everyone is always busy there.

"I doubt it," Mr. Auctor says. "The consensus is that the storm is overhead. No one is dealing in the technicalities, especially after what happened at the speech. Most people are staying in their homes by order of the Council."

The speech. The Council didn't know what he was going to say, or at least part of it. They can't control everything. They didn't see the storm coming. They should have.

Mr. Auctor directs me forward out of my thoughts. A transport—volant, its proper name—sits just off the sidewalk. At ten feet in height and six feet wide, it's smaller than its vehere counterpart that transports materials to and from the city. Mr. Auctor's vessel is an older model by many cycles. The metalwork across the outside rarely matches, signs he probably does the work himself. Or has it done at other cities. Red rods extend from the top. His transport is equipped with protections to deter storm strikes.

He approaches his volant and presses his hand into a piece of metal clearly recently installed. Most alloys now are a mixture that allows the transfer of Lamis. The panel glows before releasing the locks, allowing a door to slide open. He gestures for me to board. I step up and stop by the operator's seat in the front. I reach my hand up and can touch the ceiling. Newer designs give more head space with the same outside height. And that's because the hover pads are of a condensed design. Older Tech isn't always bad. This volant has always proven that to me.

Mr. Auctor closes the door behind him as he takes his seat at the controls. He places his hands over the two control ports that appear only as black voids. A blue glow from his Lamis emanates from his hands as dim lights fill in the shadows.

He pushes his hands into the black voids, extinguishing the color. A surge vibrates through the floor—due either to the age of the vessel or a poor power connection—before Mr. Auctor commands his volant into the air. After the initial ignition, the hover pads are barely noticeable as they connect to tracks in the pathway below. While transports don't need the tracks to remain in the air, the infrastructure's design reduces the power pulled from the operator's body by nearly half.

He removes his hands from the control ports, and the blue glow returns. He takes a deep breath. The takeoff requires the operator to fully power the vehicle. His outdated volant doesn't help the strain his body must take. Mr. Auctor is not young. He has never been young.

I position myself so he can see me without straining his neck. "Why do you continue this?"

He smirks. "The freedom. Operators are exempt from city visas. I can come and go as I please. Plus, can you imagine your father walking everywhere?"

A smile escapes my lips. "Him walking? What about me? I think I benefited more from you than he ever did."

I glance out the front window. The colors of the storm reflect off the buildings extending the sky's reach. It seems improbable that such beauty can hold such danger. Fear should be the last thing brought on by beauty. Yet it is all I can feel. The destruction from the City Center flashes in my mind. The bodies.

I step away from the window and take a seat behind Mr. Auctor. Leaning into my knees, I press my hands into my eyes.

"If all goes well, Zayne, you won't have to face the storm," Mr. Auctor says.

I pull my hands away from my face. "What do you mean? Aren't we all facing the storm?" Or is the Council evacuating and leaving the people to face the storm alone?

"The Curator didn't say anything? I suppose not. Nothing official has been announced." A vibration shifts through the floor as the volant turns. "Even with an evacuation, the city needs caretakers to monitor the Tech in the case of errant storm strikes. No adult can stand beneath the heart of a storm, so the Council decided on the most recent graduates. Old enough to be useful, but still young enough to go unnoticed by the storm."

"They expect children to face the storm?"

"Not children," he says. "Graduates. Alfaron graduates at that. And not something you have to worry about. You will spend the duration of the storm with the Council's Representatives."

No evacuation, and they are choosing children to face the storm. Not even a mansii ago, we weren't allowed to make a decision without our parents' involvement. Now we are to stand underneath the storm, because the Council believes we are immune to the dangers from the storm.

And if the public knew the storm struck me, how would they react to the Council's plan?

A chuckle escapes my lips. My near-death—my death—threatens their plan. There's still much I don't know. Will they tell me when they take me on as a student? Why not evacuate? Why risk staying? Why risk the city with children serving as its caretakers, even with the knowledge now that they aren't immune to the storm?

I hold back my questions from Mr. Auctor. He isn't going to give me the answers I want.

"We've arrived."

I sit up and realize I didn't feel the transport land. His skill with the transport is unmatched. I stand up and walk to the door. Mr. Auctor doesn't open it, forcing me to face him.

"Don't overthink this, Zayne. This is what your father wants."

And what my father wants is the only way to understand him.

Mr. Auctor opens the door, and I exit.

The area isn't familiar, but my destination is apparent as two men approach me. They lead me across a pathway toward a small structure. It appears independent of the buildings on either side, but I can see where they connect. It lacks the glass design of the surrounding structures. They appear to reach up into the clouds; the glass reflects the storm. Colors swirl in the glass, giving the illusion of movement.

My destination sits as a glassless void.

The men don't look up at the colors as we approach the entrance, either the reflections or the actual storm. Are the men afraid or ignorant of what lies above them?

I look back as the door opens to Mr. Auctor's transport leaving.

A hand passes by my face toward the entryway. "Please enter. The Representatives await you."

I turn to the men and place two fingers on my chin. A simple white waiting room meets me through the door. Even with the structure's design, the small size surprises me. A few chairs are scattered throughout the room. A lone door sitting offset from the center of the far wall—poor design or maybe intentional—takes my attention.

The door slides open, drawing me inside.

I step into a dimly lit room. Six chairs sit in the room with lights overhead. Five have men standing behind them. The Representatives. They each wear a similar black robe that makes them hard to discern from the black wall behind them. The sixth chair is my father's. He can't be here. Or does his position have him dealing with more important things?

One man steps out from behind his chair—I recognize him as Vitus, representative to Council Member Kaz. A metal disc sits at his hairline, reflecting the light above. "Zayne Radi. You are here seeking a mentorship with a Representative. Due to the ongoing situation we face, your father has requested an early hearing, which we have granted. And while your father's identity has no effect on the outcome of this hearing, his advocacy holds merit far above that of anyone else's in the city. Think of this as more of a formality than anything. We will be forgoing the traditional process."

My gaze passes across each of the Representatives. Beyond their public appearances, I have seen and interacted with each one at my house. Have they used those times to evaluate me? Was this hearing always a formality? They say my father's position has no bearing on the outcome, yet I don't believe them. His influence is the very reason I stand here now.

"A formality?" I let the words hang in the room. My father wants me here. If my father wants me here, does the Council? How closely do their beliefs align? Does he know they change the truth to fit their plans?

"Does this concern you?" Vitus asks.

This is what my father wants for me. I am here because of him. This is where he wants me, and where I learn about him.

"Do I not ask a question about my advocate?"

A flash of confusion moves across Vitus's face. "Normally, yes, a graduate in your position would ask a question about their advocate. But seeing as your advocate is your father, I don't think that will be necessary."

I glance across each of the representative's faces. "I understand the necessity of expediting this process with the storm." I pause, hoping to study their reactions, but they give none. "But I wish to still ask a question."

Vitus exchanges a glance with the others. "Very well, you may ask your question."

"Whose Representative mentored my father?"

Vitus expects me to know this answer, but after a pause, he answers. "Your father was never in the position you are in now. Your father's path differed from most."

"In what way?"

Vitus's gaze shifts to the others. They don't want to be here. They think I'm wasting their time. The storm worries them. "Your father played a pivotal role in several Council operations several cycles before you were born. His unique contribution to the Nation made him well known across every city. Though the people vote for Representatives, the Council approves each candidate. Rather than risk the opinion of the people by not allowing your father candidacy, they offered it to him.

The only path away from being a Representative was his choosing not to be one."

"This is not how you came to be a Representative?"

Vitus gives a slight shake of his head. "No, your father's path was unique. He had no connection to the Council, while myself and the others present have had long histories with the Council in some form. We spent many cycles working in the public eye and staying in our leaders' favor to gain our positions."

My father's words come into my mind afresh. *"Establish your own path into the Historical Record."* He never told me these things because he knew I would learn this sol. He wants me to forge my own path as he did. I know now why he looked at me during the ceremony.

"Radi." Vitus's sole choice of word pulls me from my thoughts. "The name your Council gave your father when they allowed him a wife is worth more than you can fathom. His name gives you access to what we know you will earn. We knew this when the Prava selected your mother to bear a child while joined with a Representative, an honor rarely given. I can feel your doubts, but know you are meant to be here. Trust the Council's sight."

"Enough of this useless discourse," another Representative says. My attention falters as my eyes hit the ground. I don't know who speaks. "This was supposed to be an expedited process. There is still a Sorbe overhead and preparations to oversee."

"I agree," Vitus says. "Zayne, your request to remain in the city and serve under a Representative is granted. By your advocate's word and testimony, we hereby grant you this. And with your verbal—"

"Wait."

I now see the light from above the Representatives nearly touching my feet. I look up at the men. I barely remember speaking, but everyone stares at me. My father wants this. But he doesn't want me like these other men, who sit in his shadow. He wants me like him. This storm that sits over the city illuminates the path I can now take.

"Zayne, we need only your verbal commitment. The official documentation can wait until the storm passes. What you study and who you study with is not being decided this sol." Impatience washes over his face. "Your verbal agreement. Do we have it?"

I swallow all the saliva forming in my mouth and step back from the light creeping toward me on the floor. "I wish to reject my father's advocacy."

A Twin Presence

"Every building is required to have at least one screen accessible by the Prava Council in emergencies to communicate instructions in a timely matter. It is a requirement of every citizen to watch and interact with these broadcasts." —an excerpt from Epis City Law

The words have always been near the surface. It is not until I say them that I recognize how close they have been. They feel right. They are the missing piece to understanding my father. I need to understand the Council the way he did. I need to serve them at a distance. The mentorship takes me too close. I need to see them from afar, where they will find me worthy as they did my father.

This is why he hasn't told me about his past. I have to do this myself.

A flurry of voices fills the room before Vitus returns order to the hearing. "Zayne, do you understand the consequences of your words? Your father's advocacy is not unique. Everyone who stands before us for a mentorship has to have an advocate."

"I understand that," I say.

"Then you have wasted our time," Vitus says. "You may leave."

"I want to serve in the storm. Earn my—"

Murmurs rise out of the representatives, cutting my words short.

I know my reasoning, but a deeper rationale stirs within me. They know I understand the truth, but no one can speak it. My father trusts our leaders because he understands the truths they hide. I need to embrace the Council's perspective, but I can't without facing the storm. I have to witness it all, and when they alter what the public knows again, I will understand, having lived through it. They cannot alter my memories.

The reason behind the Council's actions is key to the connection I lack with my father. He learned it by working with them, and so will I.

"Such a decision is not yours to make," Vitus says. "This hearing is over. Return home immediately."

The lights shut off overhead the representatives, leaving only the light from the door behind me. I only now realize the door never closed. With the Representatives cloaked in silence and darkness, I exit the room. Once outside, I stop and nearly fall over. I press my hands into my thighs to keep myself up. My heart beats strong enough that I feel it in my throat.

"Please vacate the building. A transport awaits you outside."

I look up at a man, not caring what he thinks. I exit the building and face a shining volant with two levels. Red rods extend from the top and sides. I question if the design will actually deter a storm strike. Mr. Auctor thought so. I suppose he can no longer give me free passage. Or my father has to pretend this isn't what he wants from me and forbade his operator from picking me up. He didn't tell his fellow Representatives. By doing so, he wasted their time with a dangerous storm looming.

He has to talk to me now. Give me some insight into where I go from this point. He knows the storm is my path. He will convince the others to allow me to serve in the storm. Protect the city, earn the Council's attention. A glance is all I need from them.

The trip to Sector Two doesn't take long. We only pass one other transport, so the operator flies at the highest level, allowing him the fastest possible speed within the city. Additional hover tracks line the tops of buildings, allowing for increased speed at this height without additional strain on the operator. His eyes constantly look up. Someone told him it's safe to operate underneath the storm, yet he doesn't believe them.

He lands the volant with a thud. His hover pads will not last another mansii with such reckless regard. I keep the words to myself as I exit. No reason to break the silence we've enjoyed. And this man has enough to worry about. He's risking his life being beneath the storm.

I stop a dozen or so feet from the volant as it takes off. My house sits at the end of a short path. Fake grass on either side gives the illusion of the colorful hillsides that surround the city. But the colors are a stagnant red, requiring someone to shift the colors that naturally change beyond the city. No one is going to bother adjusting the grass with the storm bearing down on the city.

I look at the houses that stretch along the transport path. Every house appears the same. The insides may vary, but nothing that affects the power efficiency. Efficiency over uniqueness, not that I care. I spent more time at Soriina's house.

"Zayne!"

I turn to see Soriina sprinting across the grass. The colors remain the same as her feet crush the blades. She does not slow down, crashing into me with a hug. Her arms grip me tight as her chin pushes into my shoulder.

"I thought the worst until they explained what happened." She loosens her grip and creates a gap between us. "I told you not to go near that generator. When will you learn to listen to me?"

I cannot lie to Soriina.

"Do you know about the Council's plan for the city?"

She holds my stare for a second. My abrupt change in conversation has her thinking through all the possibilities, but her concerns remain in her head.

"We have heard rumors of it," she says.

"No official word from the Council or the Representatives?"

"You know what they plan to do?"

"We should talk inside," I say, glancing up.

She takes a couple of steps backward toward her house. "Good, because the Twins are here, and I imagine they are just as curious as I am."

"The Twins?" I know who they are, but I need her to know I wish they weren't here. They don't even live in our sector. For reasons I never cared to learn about, they attended the same school as Soriina and me. I am sure there are discernable differences between the brothers, but I spent more time avoiding them than learning their differences. I cannot even remember their names.

"Yes," she says. "While I've waited for you to recover from your stupidity, I've been discussing Eteros with them. They've extended the deadline for our decisions. We should be leaving in two sols, but the storm has halted everything."

I want to ask her where she is going, but the whole discussion seems pointless with all that I know. Are we going to survive long enough for Eteros to matter? The Council is putting graduates in charge of the city when they should be leaving. They certainly want to see the city fall.

I condemn myself for the thought. It slips so easily.

No more words are necessary as Soriina walks toward her house. Dives Inop—the name across the door—is the only distinguishable thing about her house. Names are a requirement to keep from getting lost. A black material covers the four windows on the front, shielding the inside from the sun's relentless rays. The material that makes up most of the structure is a non-metal composite that reflects the sun's heat away.

Not that any of it is necessary now. The sun remains hidden behind the clouds, with the colors of the storm the only evidence it remains.

Soriina pulls a lever next to the door, releasing the pressure that holds it shut. A panel sits on the ground near our feet. As I notice this detail, the vibration from the ground is noticeably absent. The main generator no longer feeds power into the house.

"How are you discussing Eteros?" I ask. "All the information is within the city's network."

She lets me walk in first. A hallway extends forward with a room to the immediate left. A large screen sits on the wall with three individual chairs and a long couch big enough for at least four people. Dim lights make the details hard to see, but it's nearly identical to my house's layout. But the chairs here still hold on to the endless laughter that Soriina and I had in them. The memories are easy to recall. A smile forms across my face.

"They gave us some notice before turning the power off," Soriina says, stepping past me. "I downloaded all the information. Don't forget you disappeared for four sols. Life doesn't stop when you're safely hidden away recovering."

"Woah, isn't that a bit heretical? Of course time stops for the Representative's son."

I turn to my right to a staircase. A boy descends the dimly lit stairs. He hops down the last three steps, causing his blond hair to fall partially into his face.

"Zayne has been through enough," Soriina says, moving in front of me. "He doesn't need your unhelpful jokes." She glares at him for a second, keeping him silent. "Zayne, you remember Safon?"

The boy brushes the hair away from his face. "He's going to mentor under a Representative," Safon says. "I don't think a couple of harmless jokes are going to affect him."

The comparison he draws tugs at my curiosity. I don't know him enough to know how he feels about the Council. Without that knowledge, I'm not sure how to interpret his words.

Footsteps draw our attention back to the stairs before another voice joins our conversation. "Not to add anything negative to this, but even Zayne has to survive through the storm before they select him for a mentorship." A boy identical to Safon slowly descends the stairs.

"And we may all find that easier when Zayne tells us what he knows," Soriina says.

Safon looks at me. "Your father told you what the Council plans? Beyond turning the city's power off? When does the evacuation start?"

I know little of the actual plan, but I can use my collective knowledge to make my explanation seem more in depth. "Not by my father, but yes. Even with the power off, the city needs caretakers to ensure nothing happens to the city. The storm is still unpredictable. And with such a large deposit of natural lamis-5 below us, the Council can't allow anything to chance. Especially without an evacuation happening."

"Caretakers?" Safon says. "Without the power, any adult that steps outside is an instant target for the storm. And no evacuation? They realize the colors outside are a precursor to the real storm?"

"We've been studying Sorbes from the data out of the city of Mauris," Soriina says. "The Etero Grex Ludus does extensive research during peak storm season. The school is almost within walking distance of the city, so . . ." She lets her words trail off as the city's destruction fills our minds. "What I mean to say is this natent has less than a fraction of the activity that the full storm has. Experts don't think there will be another strike until the storm's core arrives."

Safon's brother moves next to him, and I immediately struggle to tell them apart.

"The caretakers will be the most recent graduates," I say.

One twin gasps. "Graduates? Is that the language they used? Or did they say children?"

Distrust fills his words. He's not asking a question, but for an interpretation of the Council's intention.

"Let him explain, Erman," Soriina says.

Erman. I try to remember it, but he shifts positions with his brother, making it more difficult.

I look at Soriina. "There's not much more to explain—"

"There is, but you are not the one who should be explaining it."

We all turn to see a man and a woman in the doorway. The dim lights in the hallway do little to cast the shadows off their faces. Soriina steps forward with a grin.

"Mom, Dad, I didn't expect you home with all the restrictions."

Soriina's father allows his wife to step inside, before he pulls a lever next to the door, closing it. Shadow consumes the hallway as he turns to us.

"The Council has set its plan in motion," he says, directing us into the room to the left. He approaches the window and presses a button, removing the tint and allowing the light from outside to fill the room. He wears a simple shirt with no insignia of the Nation or his faction. Without any LiorTech, his appearance is far tamer than that of most people in the city. He's always kept a distance from me, but not the same as my father. "The Council rejected my request to stay in Sector Five. Our family will be staying here during the storm."

"Does that mean Soriina won't be selected to serve out in the storm?" one twin asks.

Soriina's mother takes off a hooded coat and hangs it on a hook near the door. Underneath she wears a shirt that dips away from her neck, revealing a necklace with a circular symbol. It's odd to see something that isn't the Alfaron or Vox insignia. She pulls her long red hair together before tossing it behind her shoulder.

She smiles at Soriina, brushing her softly with her hand. "As research has always suggested, energy matures differently in girls than it does in boys. Lamis dothyris have requested that girls be omitted from the selection process. The risk is low, but even with the Council's certainties, the risk has been deemed too high."

"Even omitting the girls, there were still hundreds of male graduates," Soriina says. "They can't select them all, can they?"

She thinks only of us.

"That is not up to us to decide," her father says. "Safon and Erman, since you both are sheltering here, it falls to me to give you the news. Now I hadn't expected Zayne to share the Council's plan or for you to hear it without some proper context."

The Twins exchange glances. "But we've been chosen," one says.

"It's an honor to serve your city," he says. "Now what Zayne may have failed to say is that your place out in the storm isn't being left to chance. As my wife mentioned, the certainties the Council has given us are to find fruition in a plan. Storms don't reach this far, but that doesn't mean we are ignorant of them. Your place out in the storm is to ease the minds of the people. A living, thinking element, as everything else works together to keep the city safe."

"But why not evacuate everyone? Why take any risk at all?"

"An evacuation is not possible," Soriina's father explains. "The Council has made us aware of a Redlander presence near the city. If we evacuate, the Red Plain dwellers may seek to inhabit the city in our absence. As long as we remain here, the Redlanders will continue on their way deeper into the plains."

Redlanders are a Techless and Lamisless society that lives on the Red Plains. They inhabit abandoned cities that lie nowhere near Epis City. They rarely come anywhere near Vox populations. They don't even speak our language.

"Redlanders have been nowhere near the city in cycles," one twin says. "They're using them as an excuse to dismiss an evacuation. There probably aren't any Redlanders anywhere near us. Why bother putting us out into the storm if there's no real threat?"

I hold a gaze on the Twins. Is this the reaction of the people—the Council's decision creating a divide in their trust? They question the Prava so quickly. If I reveal the truth about the storm striking me, how much further will the trust dissolve?

Soriina's mother's words are soft, but I sense something behind the syllables. "If you believe that, serving in the storm is a simple matter of trusting the Council. There is no threat, so there is no danger for you."

She knows the Twins don't believe her. I can hear it in every word they speak. They don't trust the Council. I have a real reason to mistrust their plans. They're built on a lie—I push the thought down. I can't let prejudice take hold.

"Not even the Council is above the people," Soriina's father says. "The information about the Redlanders should have been released far earlier. The Council already subverted the people's expectations with the refusal to grant an evacuation with this surprise information. They can act against the will of the people, but only to an extent that retains their power. This decision seeks to strengthen their position."

The Twins step away to the furthest point in the room. Fear creates an anger in them. They expect the Council to be stronger than the storm. How would they react to knowing I want to serve? I doubt they would understand. They let fear push them away from our leaders, while I allow it to draw me closer to an understanding otherwise impossible to obtain.

"And what about me, sir?" I ask.

Soriina's father turns his head away from me, while his gaze remains. My question takes him off guard. He thinks I know my fate. Or does he know the storm struck me? He works in Sector Five, but is he subject to what the Council tells the public?

"A question for your father," he says, his stare lingering.

"What are we do to now?" Soriina asks.

His gaze softens as he looks at his daughter. "The storm is quite large, so the natent may last for another dozen sols. But no one can be certain. Not every storm produces a natent, so we have to act as if the storm is overhead. We follow the Council's orders as they drain the city of its power and limit our time outside."

Either Safon or Erman move closer. "How long before they take us?"

"Preparations are still taking effect," Soriina's mother says. "The Council hasn't given a definitive timeline. But soon is an accurate guess. Movement has been restricted across the city, so you can't return home before you leave. I will send word of your presence here to your parents before communication is completely shut off."

Fear flashes across the twin's face. He wants to see his family.

Soriina's father places a soft hand on my shoulder. "And Zayne, while I care for you, I have been told to send you home. Reasons I won't bother you with were given. You are to shelter there." His next words are lower, not enough that no one else can hear. "You may find the beginnings of answers there."

He means my father. Even with his responsibilities, he has taken time to see me after my decision. I only hope I made the correct one.

"Is my mother there?"

"No," Soriina's mother says. "She is in a meeting, finalizing the plans for the individual sectors. When they decided my input wasn't necessary, they were still in the beginnings of discussions. You shouldn't expect her back this sol or even next."

I want to ask more, but I refrain. My trust in Soriina's parents comes easier than most. They benefit from my unrelenting trust in their daughter. I look at her father. He has always been more of a father to her than mine has been to me. For that, he has my trust.

Her father gestures for her mother to leave the room. "We will let you say your goodbyes before you return home."

They exit the room.

Soriina moves forward and wraps me in a hug. Her words are soft so only I can hear. "My father would easily defy the Council for you. I don't know why he isn't."

My earlier actions have the Council's eye on me, or at least the Representatives. Her father knows this. Now I am certain. He hasn't told his daughter.

She releases me, and I step toward the door. "It's okay. I imagine my parents will stay in Sector Five. My house will be empty. What better place for me to shelter at?"

The Twins stay silent, still trying to grasp their own futures.

I pull the door lever and exit. I cut across the grass to my house. The name Haud Lar sits at the top of the door. The panel hiding the manual control is still in place. A yellow light sits above the door. I step a few feet away from the door, allowing the light to scan me. It still recognizes me as it glows green. The door opens.

Why is the power still on?

I walk in, and the lights are off except in the room to the left. I let it draw me in and find a man sitting down. He sits in my father's chair. The other two chairs are empty. The man has LiorTech on his right arm and hand. Black clothing hides what other Tech he may have. His long brown hair covers half his face. His one visible eye appears to glow blue.

"Zayne Radi."

This man is *not* my father.

Decisions of the Council

"The Vox people have every right to challenge any decision made by the Prava Council. In their duty to the Nation, the Council may choose to change their minds or not." —an excerpt from An Unlikely Decision

The man forgoes any proper etiquette by not telling me his name, despite knowing mine. He pulls something out of his pocket and tosses it into his mouth. I stare at him as he chews.

I break the silence. "Who are you? Did my father send you?"

Half a smile escapes from his hair. "The modifications to the generator controls. Are those your doing?"

I don't expect that question. He isn't dressed with any authority. No one should care about a few minor tweaks to the system with the storm overhead. A first-cycle student could disable my modifications.

My silence allows him to continue. "My periis nearly blew up half the sector trying to shut off the generator here, and that was after they consulted the specialists. Was it you?"

Periis? Tech periis. They report to the city's Tatem—our Tech Master. Two Representatives used to hold the position. Is this my path forward? Does my father now realize the benefit of the classes I loved in school? Why else would the current Tatem be sitting in my house? My father knows this is the only way to follow him after my rejection of his advocacy.

"Maybe your *periis* should be better trained, Tatem Diask," I say, hoping to throw off my nervousness. I have never met the Tatem, but I know his name well. "My modifications are simple, at best."

He reaches back into his pocket and pulls out a small oval device. He raises it above his head and presses down with his thumb. The vibration in the floor fades as the lights turn off, plunging us into darkness. A few seconds pass before emergency lights struggle to push back the shadows.

"In that, you are right," Diask says. He stands up, pulling a coat off the back of the chair. "I hope you are capable of more than just simple modifications."

I don't move as he steps toward me. "What does that mean?"

The Tatem looks down at me, nearly a head taller. "With your rejection of the path your father gave you, I'm giving you another. It isn't as easy, so I came to make sure you were as capable as my periis claimed."

"What path can you give me? I have to prove myself to the Council that I am like my father. Worthy of their acceptance. My father knows this."

"I am selecting you for service in the storm," Diask says blankly, keeping whatever feelings he has about the decision a mystery. "There, you will find ample opportunity to prove yourself."

The words almost don't seem real. "Really?"

"You weren't on the list of graduates," he says. "But after I stumbled upon your class scores, no one could ignore your absence. Despite taking only the minimum Tech classes, your scores far exceeded those of even my students."

Someone doesn't want me in the storm. The Council knows I risk endangering the others beneath the Sorbe. They aren't willing to admit to their lies to stop my entry.

"And who told you to look up my scores?" Did my father tell Diask about me? "The Council doesn't want me to serve, do they?"

He sidesteps me, putting his coat on, and stops in the doorway. "You're a curious one, aren't you?" He removes the panel next to the door. "I like that. Anyone proficient in Tech has to have a certain level of curiosity."

"But that person has to know when to control their curiosity, or they may never come to any contentment," I say.

He pulls the lever and steps out into the color. "Those are the words of a Representative. But are they yours?"

The Tatem's question freezes any type of response. I thought the words of my father would impress him. He sees through that to the doubt I have.

I close the door and let the solitude surround me.

***

I sit at an empty table. A few crumbs remain on the plate in front of me. My mother isn't here, and I doubt she returns before she and my father enter whatever refuge the Council has for the Representatives. She didn't bother to clean out the food storage, so I eat my fill of anything I like. Now that I am a graduate, she doesn't control my eating habits. My energy can maintain my body's needs with a diverse diet now.

Not that she wouldn't try.

Certain foods are still healthier than others, but right now, I don't care.

I wash down the green and red chunks with a sweet red drink. I search the house for any of the water my father keeps, but can't find any. None of the underground water sources are near the city, so the Council only distributes it to a select few. The city only has one purification center, so the water that reaches the city takes sols to clean and distribute.

I leave my plate and glass on the table. With the storm looming, no one is going to care if I don't clean up. I should do so to take my thoughts away from my service in the storm. The Tatem told me I would serve, yet no official notice arrives to tell me when I leave. Or where I am to go if I travel on my own account.

To further distract myself, I use the last of the cleaning gel to scrub away any dirt on my extremities. I'm cleaner than I expect, so I don't discard the gel in case I spend the storm's duration here. I rub some dry powder into my hair before shaking the extra out.

Straightening my clothes, I walk where the Tatem sat and told me of my new path. The monitor flickers with minimal power flowing through it. **STORM SELECTION STATUS. Zayne Radi. TRANSPORT EN ROUTE.**

The words take a few minutes to settle in my mind. The Tatem has enough influence to convince the Council to allow me to serve. He ensures my place under the Representatives' guidance.

Further instructions tell me to leave everything behind. Proper clothes and supplies are at my destination. I expect they will confiscate anything I have with me when I arrive.

I take a deep breath. This is what I want. Within the storm, I can prove myself. Feel what my father felt. He wants this for me.

I repeat the thought again and again to dispel the doubt that grows.

With my stomach full and the shadows creeping closer, I leave the safety of the metal walls and step out into the color. No, I am safe no matter where I am. My still-maturing Lamis protects me. I have nothing to fear from the storm. I look up. How can I even be certain the Sorbe struck me? I'm immune to the storm like every other child. My injury jumbled the memory in my head. The Council knows the truth. I trust them as my father does.

"Zayne!"

I turn to see Soriina walking toward me. The Twins are several feet behind her.

"Have you come to say goodbye to Safon and Erman?"

I push down the doubt. "I have come to join them."

Safon or Erman steps closer. I can't tell the two brothers apart. "Can he do that? I thought—"

"No, no," I say, not thinking my words through. "I was selected."

Soriina shifts her head. "Why would your father let this happen?"

I consider telling her the truth, but I find a lie easier. "I'm a graduate now. And the mentorship selection is not for two mansiis. I suppose his influence is limited. These aren't normal circumstances."

"Did you reach out to your father?"

I shake my head. "You know him. Council before family."

"You speak his intentions, but have you ever heard them?"

Her stare tries to pull the truth from me. A rush of air sweeps across the ground. A transport interrupts us, and I am thankful for it. It lands at the edge of the pathway, where the door opens. I hold my breath as the operator steps out. It's not Mr. Auctor. I'm not sure if I am relieved or upset.

He crosses the grass to us, holding an arvos. "Safon and Erman Coffer."

The Twins step forward. "Ready as we'll ever be."

The man looks at me. "Zayne Radi."

I take in a sharp breath.

He looks at Soriina. "Say your goodbyes and board the transport. Five minutes, no more."

The operator returns to the transport, leaving the four of us. I did not expect this part. I wanted to avoid having to say goodbye to Soriina. It is already hard enough to maintain the lie. Each conversation with her challenges my ability to keep the truth to myself.

Safon and Erman move past us, turning to walk backward. "We will see you on the transport, Zayne. Give him some of that good advice, Soriina."

She looks at me. "You're hiding something, and don't think you have to tell me now. But tell someone."

"Is that all the advice you have?" I ask, half as a joke and half wanting something more.

"The Twins are the closest thing you will have to friends out there," she says. "Give them a chance."

"Maybe I'll find other friends."

Soriina drops her head and shakes it slightly. "If we're asking for the impossible, maybe we should start with getting rid of the storm."

"That'll be the first thing I do when I make a new friend."

Soriina smirks before she moves in for a hug. "The Council knows what it's doing. This will all be over soon."

She lets me go, and I step back to look at the volant. Its outer hull is bulky, with three rods extending from the top. No windows except for where the operator sits. The Council believes these modifications will protect us from the storm. "I hope you're right."

"Go on, or he may leave without you. Then you'll miss your opportunity."

I smirk as my stare lingers. Her word choice invites a discussion I don't have time for. I turn toward the transport. The operator steps out to meet me. Before we can exchange any words, the colors shift above. The man looks up, and fear erupts over his face.

A bolt of light streaks across the sky. We cannot see where it strikes, but we feel the explosion.

I wait for the chain reaction that will incinerate the city. A minute passes, and death doesn't come. The Sorbe struck a surface generator or some other concentration of Lamis with no connection to the deposit.

"In the transport! Now!"

Despite the intensity of the operator's words, I look back at Soriina. She stares at me in horror. I take a step toward her before hands grab me and pull me backward. I resist until my friend retreats to her home. Her father meets her at the door, ushering her in.

I let the hands guide me into the transport. The Twins move toward the back, and I take a seat near them as the operator takes his seat at the controls.

"This volant is fitted with standard Red Plains armor," the operator says, plunging his hands into the control ports. "I will stay low, but the armor masks the majority of our energy signature. It'll withstand numerous strikes if it comes to that."

His words are reassuring, though unnecessary.

"What was that?"

"Is the storm here?"

I look at the Twins. I still can't tell them apart. They keep their blond hair the same, cut short, so not even an errant strand can help me determine who is who. Not that that would help if I don't know who they are to begin with.

The only distinction is beyond their control. Twins are identical in every way except their eyes. One's left eye is brown, and the other is blue. Their right eye is the color of the other's left. Not every set of twins has the same eye color variation, but every twin has different colored eyes.

"I don't think the storm is here yet," I say, trying not to stare at their eyes. "The natent struck another part of the city. We're lucky the lamis-5 deposit wasn't hit."

"We should talk about something else," one of them says. "No need to fill our minds with worry."

"We should talk about how Zayne here doesn't know how to tell us apart," the other says.

The words take me by surprise. I try to say something to deflect the truth, but I can only mumble a response.

"In his defense, we are more of Soriina's friends. He really only knows us in passing."

"I know you," I say. "You're Safon and Erman Coffer."

The Twins eye each other with serious expressions. "You know our names. Our pre-graduation names, specifically. Did you ask if we changed them?"

I cannot tell if they're being serious or if this is some sort of joke. They have to be serious. No one would joke with a Sorbe threatening the city.

After seconds that feel like minutes, the Twins start laughing. They push and shove each other. They ignore a cry from the operator to settle down. But he does not have the will to force them. His eyes remain forward and up, waiting for another strike from the storm.

"He believed us." One twin's words stop as they erupt into laughter again. Grabbing onto his brother's shoulder, he forces out more words. "We considered changing our names to each other's."

"But we thought such a choice would be cruel."

"Not that it wouldn't be magnificent to watch you worry which of us is which. I am Safon."

Right eye brown. Left eye blue.

"And I am Erman."

Right eye blue. Left eye brown.

"Wait," Erman says. "Weren't you Safon yestersol? I thought I got to be Safon this sol?"

Safon shakes his head. "This is the last sol of the cycle. You get to be Safon at the start of the five hundred and eighteenth cycle of our Council. I still have one more sol."

My eyes glance between the two boys. I can't discern the humor from any serious possibility in their words.

The brothers glance at each other before laughing again. I can barely discern their words as they talk through their laughs. "Don't worry. We haven't played that game since we first came to the city."

"Though sometimes . . . I'm not sure if I remember who's who," Erman says. "We did switch an awful lot back then. I'd say it's been nearly four cycles since we last tricked our parents."

I look at the Twins. They know the storm is real, yet they still make jokes. I saw their fear only moments ago. The Council has given them no choice in risking their lives, yet they sit here and joke. Will their humor remain when the storm rips through the city?

"You three may want to. . . tone down the fun," the operator calls back to us. His breathing is heavy. I don't think he's a regular transport operator. "We're nearly there."

As he finishes speaking, the vibrations shift in the floor. He said he'd stay low, but the volant is ascending. Colors sweep through the window. I lean from my seat to look out the front. We are facing a building with a glass front. The windows reflect the storm's colors in a mesmerizing way.

"Sucks something so beautiful can cause such devastation."

I look back at the Twins. I am not sure who spoke, but it doesn't matter. The words are true. All things beautiful lead to destruction. Every cycle's sunset sends us into darkness. Graduation sends us into the unknown.

"What do you think about when you're staring into nothingness?"

My eyes refocus on the Twins. "Nothing important."

"Good, because I think we're here," Safon says.

The operator levels the volant with a jerk. A platform is visible for a few seconds as he turns, and when he finishes the maneuver, the city extends out from the front. The lights I expect to see are blackened. Smoke rises into the colors of the storm.

Leaders

"Twins have a rare and unexplainable genetic defect, causing their eyes to be different colors. For some, this negates their ability to be truly counted as twins." —*an excerpt from* A Study of Children: What Makes Them Different

A cold wind meets me as I step out of the volant. The colors swirl, threatening to unleash further destruction. I look out overtop of every surrounding building. The platform has to be the highest point in the city.

"Not a good time to let everyone know I hate high, open spaces," one twin says.

"Erman, I suggest we move toward the man walking to us," Safon says.

I tear my gaze from the city to a man approaching us. He holds onto his heavy coat as the wind tries to knock him off his feet. A hood covers most of his face. He doesn't speak until he reaches us. His voice barely rises above the wind.

"Safon and Erman Coffer. Zayne Radi." We nod. "Follow me. It's not safe to stay beneath the colors."

He means it's not safe for him. The coat must be some form of protection. Soriina's mother and the Tatem had similar items.

He walks away, clearly expecting us to obey him. Fighting the wind, he leads us across the platform. It stretches across two buildings. We head toward the taller of the two. The outline of a door stands out from the seamless metal wall.

He stops next to the entry point and gestures for us to hurry, despite us only being a few steps behind him. He presses his hand into a sensor pad. The door slides open. I tilt my head. The building still has power. I have no time to think through why as he practically pushes us into the opening.

We enter a small room with a low ceiling and railings on either side at about waist height. He steps in, and when the door closes, I realize there are no lights. In the darkness, I can hear someone pressing buttons on an interface. After the last button, lights slowly envelop us. Without warning, the room moves down—a vert lift. I lean against the wall. Vert lifts never leave me feeling well. They lack the stabilization of transports. Side-shift or horizontal lifts feel more natural.

One twin nudges me. "Why does this place still have power?"

I straighten myself, keeping a hand on a railing. I only shake my head as the lift comes to a stop. The opposite wall from before opens up into a large room. The ceiling extends far higher than seems practical. The man pushes past us and exits first. We take the action as a command to follow him. My first couple of steps are awkward as I find my balance.

He stops at a walkway that slopes downward toward a stage. I count nearly thirty-five rows of seats spanning fifteen chairs in width. Boys fill the lower half, while the sections closest to us remain empty.

"Safon and Erman Coffer. Please, find a seat. Further instructions will follow."

I take a step when I reconsider his words. "What about me?"

"Please continue this way."

The Twins stop and look at each other. Right eye brown. Left eye blue. Safon speaks. "Knew someone was going to get special treatment. Don't forget about us lowly servants of the Council."

Erman. Right eye blue. Left eye brown. I owe Soriina enough to learn the difference between the brothers.

"Zayne Radi. Follow me, please."

I look at the man who has stopped. His face betrays his annoyance with my delay. Boys in the seats stare. The Twins remove themselves as a distraction as they descend the aisle to find seats.

"Sorry, coming," I say, taking a few quick steps to catch up to the man as he continues moving. Right eye brown, Safon. Right eye blue, Erman. I repeat the identifying features several times as the man approaches another door. A red sensor above flashes before opening. We move into a smaller room, where a single boy sits with his back to me. The man gestures for me to walk toward him.

"Please, remain here. I will notify the others of your arrival."

The boy turns in his seat to face me. He stirs familiarity within me.

"You must be Zayne."

I try to recall the memory that connects me to him. "And you are?"

He stands up and places two fingers on his chin with a dip of his head. "Seni Daw." His name brings no clarity to why he is familiar. "The others should be joining us soon."

I glance back at the door. "The boys out there?"

Seni smirks. "No, not them. The other Tech leaders. I have the impression you aren't aware of why you are here."

"I'm here to serve the Council as they see fit," I say.

My words are quick. Too quick that I miss his words. *Other Tech leaders.* This Seni is a Tech leader. My presence here means I am as well. This is what the Tatem meant. He doesn't just mean for me to serve, but to use my skills with Tech. But as a leader?

I straighten. "Well, I suppose you mean as a Tech leader. Can't say it was explicitly told to me. How many others are there?"

"A boy for each sector," he says. "Those assignments haven't been announced yet. Don't worry about not knowing everything. I have been Mr. Diask's pupil for nearly three cycles now. He may have told me a few things in our last meeting. He's been preparing me for a moment like this since I've known him."

My eyes search the ground. "Mr. Diask? The city's Tatem?"

Seni pushes his shoulders back. "Yes. I received an education visa to study under him. He only takes on four students a cycle. You certainly have met him?"

My memory finally lands on his image. He's the one from the medical building. He only called me by my first name. He either doesn't care about formal greetings, or he was told my name by another. He doesn't recognize me.

"He visited my house recently," I say. "But not before then."

"Never his student, then?"

"No."

"I am sure his visit was to ensure your qualification for this service. Mr. Diask has me evaluate his prospective students. It makes sense he would do the same for those set to protect the city from the storm."

Doubt creeps into Seni's voice but stays hidden. Does he recognize me? Or does he not think I am capable enough to be here? I don't look to tempt the conversation further as I shift the topic.

"How long do we have to wait?"

Seni doesn't have to answer as the door opposite where I came in opens. Three boys walk in with two men behind them. The Tatem—Diask—and a Council Representative. Vitus. His white coat stands out from Diask's dark clothing.

They both look at me with different intensity. Despite their eye contact conveying hundreds of words, they speak none.

The three new boys move so they are next to Seni and me. Vitus looks across our small group.

"May I forgo the traditional introduction?" Our silence gives him his answer. "You each have a different understanding of why you are here. Diask and I are here to ensure you know your purpose. You all should be aware of the importance of Tech here in the city. We have chosen you to be its guardians. Brute force and weapons can keep beasts at bay, but only the knowledge you have mastered can protect the city from the storm."

Diask shifts his body as the Council Representative lets him speak. "We need order to overcome the chaos of the storm. You each will be in charge of a single sector. You will communicate regularly with each other. And if necessary, aid each other. The other boys are important, but by the end of the storm, what you do will ensure the final outcome. Yes, we are preparing the city, but Sorbes can cause disturbances in Lamis deposits. Not every generator can be physically disconnected. You will monitor designated Tech for any anomalies."

His words linger as he looks at me before shifting his focus.

Vitus pulls his coat back, revealing bright red clothes underneath. "You and the boys out there will become known as the Datum. A name without meaning. Your success—or failure—will give this title meaning. And it will set your place in history. Forever will our Alfaron descendants read about your service. Your sacrifice." He pauses. "Sorbes are dangerous, as Diask has pointed out, but don't let his warning trouble you. His periis and specialists are ensuring your presence is merely symbolic. But your place in the Historical Record will be quite real."

Diask holds a stare on Vitus with his first few words before turning to us. "These storms are unpredictable in many ways. And the one we're dealing with crossed the Red Plains high above the regular clouds we witness during this season. Symbolic or not, your presence is crucial to the plans my periis and specialists are implementing. That is why you are here, and your words will command the other boys. We will place other leaders in more general roles to maintain order and keep beasts from inhabiting the city. But, when necessary, they are yours to command. And Zayne—"

My eyes remain forward as I feel the other eyes turn on me. I realize he doesn't use my full name. No one knows who my father is. Diask and Vitus want to keep it that way.

"—we are giving you the Datum title of Tatem. When you all cannot agree on a solution, Zayne's word will be that solution. He has the final say. His expertise is unmatched for his age. His decisions are what will decide the fate of the city."

I think he continues to speak, but everything muffles. My focus goes everywhere but his words. I can sense every part of my body. My neck throbs, and I become aware of a few hairs touching my forehead.

The path Diask has me on seems to be set in one direction. Decided by him. He trusts me with this responsibility only after seeing my capability with my house's power system. His choice has to be in error. Is this what I wanted when I wished to serve?

I push my thoughts down and see Seni shift his feet before I refocus on Diask.

"You must be able to maintain your focus," Diask says. I try to swallow, forcing whatever saliva I can form down my throat. "And we cannot expect you to have a dozen boys around you to ensure your safety. You each will choose escorts, or Aemiins, as is their proper title."

Vitus looks at Diask, who nods, but a conflict remains in their eyes. "Diask is going to remain here with you. You will join the rest of the Datum when their sectors have been assigned, along with your chosen Aemiins. If we don't meet again, serve your city well. Your knowledge is power. May that power serve the Council well."

Diask waits for him to leave, then he pulls out an arvos. "Ocen, you will be in Sector Five. Soma, four. Talpa, three. Seni, you will take two. And Zayne, you will set up your base of operations in Sector One."

Sector One? He knows I live in Sector Two. I know the area better than most. Even the outskirts and the hillsides. Why put me in an unfamiliar sector? Is this how I am to stand out and make myself known to the Council? They are giving me no advantages, even in the face of the storm.

"Mr. Diask," Seni says, drawing my attention. "May I choose Arsen as one of my Aemiins?"

The Tatem smirks. "I thought you would ask for your brother, and I asked Vitus. He approved it."

I look at Seni. "Your brother?" I look into his eyes. His right eye is a dark green, while his left is a noticeably brighter green. "You're a twin."

"One of only five sets in the city," he says. "Only one set was born here in the city. Did you know that?"

Diask swipes his hand across his arvos. "The rarity of twins is a fascinating phenomenon. Can we stay focused?" He waits for us to look at him. "Zayne, do you have any preferences for your Aemiins?"

"Give them a chance." Soriina's words come to mind. How did she know it would be this simple?

"Safon and Erman Coffer," I say, trying to avoid looking at Seni.

Diask's fingers input the information into his arvos. He turns to the others as Seni nudges me in the arm.

"I know Mr. Diask well," he says. "Your knowledge of Tech must be beyond impressive if he chose you. I trust him, so I trust you."

I wanted to serve in the storm, but in this capacity? Diask's decision sends my thoughts into a frenzy. I feel the Representatives have a part to play in this outcome. What better way for me to prove myself to those they represent? This is their decision as much as Diask's. They might as well have sent me here themselves.

"Not that you will have much to do," Seni says, redirecting my focus. "If anyone can prepare a city for a Sorbe, it is Mr. Diask. Hundreds of Tech periis came to the city to hear the People's Representative's speech. He has all the help he needs. Now time is the only factor."

Diask moves across the room, regaining our attention. "That is everything I need from you now. The other leaders will join you soon. Until then, not all of you know each other. Talk amongst yourselves."

As he leaves, the others approach me. It doesn't take long to realize the other four know each other. I'm the one they don't know. A boy slightly shorter than me with red hair makes eye contact. His eyes are both brown. "My name is Talpa. You must be something else if Diask gave you the title of Tatem. Trust me. He didn't have to do that."

He's helping me. Forcing me on a path that leads to my goal. How much are the representatives directing his decisions? Or is he acting alone? I should be grateful for the opportunity, no matter how it came to be, but my mind won't rest.

Seni shoves him in the shoulder. "Jealous? After your mishap with the solar generator, he was never going to put you in charge."

Talpa laughs. "No one told me they operate differently than Lamis generators. And Zayne didn't need to know that. Plus, I never wanted the burden of leadership. Mediocrity makes this whole storm more enjoyable."

My eyes move across each boy, looking for similar reactions to his word choice. "Enjoyable?"

The boy, Soma, throws his arm around Talpa. "No adults? Freedom to explore the city and experiment with some Tech? Why wouldn't this be enjoyable?"

Seni points to me. "Soma, Zayne here doesn't know our teacher. He doesn't have the same confidence in his abilities as we do. Give him a few sols of sitting around doing nothing during the storm. He will realize soon enough how safe we all are."

"Safe?" A new voice draws our attention to across the room. "Everyone wastes their time preparing for something that will never arrive."

Seni steps forward. "And you are?"

He stops short of reaching us. Jet black hair is neatly tucked behind his ears with a part on the left side. He's taller than me, but not by much. He's still wearing the clothes he came here with. I presume so because I doubt the Council will have us wearing shirts with flared sleeves. "Edwin," he says. "You must be the boys that are going to tell us what to do."

Seni crosses his arms. "Only as necessary."

Edwin smirks. "Good, then we won't have to worry about it at all then."

"You speak as if the storm will never arrive," Soma says.

Edwin throws his hands to the side. "A Sorbe has never crossed the Red Plains. No cities. No settlements to feed off. It will dissipate long before it even reaches the hillsides."

"And what about the natent outside?" Talpa asks.

"The natent?" He laughs. "You mean the colors. There are a dozen explanations for such colors. You're only believing the one the Council has put forth. What are you going to do? Believe the Pon Quem really exists next? This is just another story for them to control us."

"And the explosions?" Seni says. "Do you hear how crazy you sound?"

"Questions for that Representative trying to convince us we are honoring ourselves by serving the city." He shakes his head. "If there were actual danger, we would leave the city. Yet we are still here."

"You are making the Council look like fools for choosing you right now," Seni says.

"They don't need my help for that. Look around you. They chose children to protect their city. What more evidence—"

"And what if the Council Members heard you say that?" We turn to see Vitus standing in a doorway behind Edwin. "Would you say it with the same confidence? The weight of this responsibility isn't even on your shoulders. Yet here you are, breaking under the mere thought of pressure. Perhaps we are fools for choosing children. Would we be even greater fools to do nothing and watch the city burn?"

His eyes pierce the doubt in the room, silencing any reply as he pauses.

"Or should we leave the city vacant and hope for the best? No. That is not the decision the Council made. They choose to put their trust in you. I don't care what you believe. If you abuse the Alfaron name, we will strip you of it. This is not some respite for you to enjoy before you leave for your Etero. This experience shows your resolve as an Alfaron. Fail, and you will see how foolish the Council can be."

His stare lingers before he exits. And as he does, other boys enter. They enter without whisper.

"And you're a leader," Soma scoffs.

He points out the obvious, yet the realization evaded me. The Council chose Edwin.

Edwin chuckles. "And yet they put me here. Still trust them? I'll be enjoying my time away from their influence. Find me in Sector One when you come to your senses." He turns from us and greets the other boys entering.

Edwin has been assigned to my sector.

Vitus's doing. Perhaps punishment for my rejection of my father's advocacy. Or is Edwin's perspective not unique? How many other boys share his belief?

The Last Boy

"Orphans have every right to partake in the activities of non-orphans. However, where parental consent is needed or expected, the Council will provide the approval."—an excerpt from Council law on orphans

The sun drapes its warmth over Soriina and me. We escape the city and sit on the hillsides. The grass shifts colors as our feet brush the blades. I look at Soriina, and she is nearly touching my shoulder, yet she feels far away. A silence surrounds us that makes her feel even more distant.

I blink.

A blue mist seeps up from the grass.

Another blink.

The mist vanishes.

I stop while Soriina continues to walk. "Did you see that?"

My words feel empty, as if only heard within my mind.

Within another blink, the mist returns. It rises higher, and as I look to the right, toward the city, a void appears in the bluish haze. With each blink, the void forms into the shape of a man. I look back at Soriina. She stops but doesn't turn.

Visually, I cannot be certain. But the void looks at her. Then back to me. No, it doesn't see her. The feeling is distant, and I am certain it sees only me.

The mist explodes outward, forcing me to cover my face with my arms. When I lower them, the sky is black. Colorful swirls dip in and out of the colorless clouds. The storm.

The void remains. It's angry. As if confirming my thoughts, a bolt of light strikes the hillside. A rush of air pushes me back. When I regain my balance, I look back at Soriina. She doesn't flinch or even seem to be aware of anything happening.

Before I turn my gaze, the Sorbe unleashes its fury again. At Soriina. An orange flash envelops her body. I try to scream, but nothing escapes my lips. I turn back to the void. Its formless shape stares at me. An anger exudes from it.

As the dark clouds brighten with color, I sense curiosity.

A sharp pain erupts from the back of my head. I collapse to my knees. The void moves forward. My vision blurs. I can feel the void standing over me as I lose control over my body. Blackness creeps in along the edges of my vision until I see and feel nothing.

The dream lingers even after I wake. It is the third since arriving at what everyone is calling the Linam, the building where we prepare for the storm. I wouldn't mind the dreams if they allowed me to sleep. But they wake me hours before we're taken to place where we eat.

Thankfully, Diask only goes over city schematics and the simplest of Tech. He wants us to know the most intricate details of the city's generators—they're the most vulnerable beneath the storm. He only shows us the ones that cannot be physically disconnected from the Lamis deposit. These account for less than half of the total number in Epis City.

My focus wavers throughout the three sols of lectures. It's only the five of us, so it's hard to hide my weariness. Seni notices each time we meet with Diask, but says nothing. He seems far more capable of this role than me. The schematics aren't new to him. If I could think clearly, I would say he's been preparing for this moment long before the Sorbe. But my thoughts fail to do anything useful in my exhaustion. I don't tell Seni any of my thoughts. No reason to spread my doubt.

The new cycle begins without any excitement. The usual festivities are absent. I doubt those outside this building celebrate either. It's the only time of the cycle that work isn't the focus of the city. The Council's strict control wavers. The countdown to the cycle's sunset begins. But the storm dominates everything now. And the Council's control tightens.

The fourth sol in the Linam doesn't start the same. A man about the age of my father arrives at our sleeping quarters an hour earlier. A dream has me awake, so I quickly put on the clothes provided to us. It's a material I've never felt before, flexible and like a second skin as it hugs my body. I imagine it reduces the amount of Lamis my body expels to keep the storm from striking a child for the first time.

I stand up and glance to the left. The other Tech leaders take a few steps toward us—awake for other reasons, I presume. The man extends his hand out.

"Only Zayne," he says, his voice rough. "Someone else will come with instructions for you each."

I glance at Seni, who shrugs. "May I ask where I am going if not to eat in the dining hall?"

The man glances at the others, speaking loud enough that everyone hears. "You each will meet your Aemiins this sol. From this point, you won't be separate from them. I hope you picked them well."

Doubt creeps out of his words, or my exhaustion has me hearing inflections not present.

At the end of his words, he gestures for me to follow him. We exit the room into the corridor. For reasons untold, the Linam still has power. The vibration is faint, only noticeable where the floor meets the wall. I drag my hand down the wall, feeling the pulses more clearly. It's different from any other building I've been in. Vibrations from the generators often spread mainly through the floors, but here, it's prominently in the walls.

I pause for a second, pressing both my palms into the wall, hoping to ask Diask about this unique feature.

The man guides me through the corridors with ease. Few distinguishable differences are present, and none that I have been able to discern in my constant groggy state. The physical movement is the only thing keeping me awake.

He stops in front of a door. "I trust you can find your own way back."

I only nod, not wanting to appear incapable of what should be a simple task.

The door opens, and I step through. My eyes go to the Twins first. My Aemiins. To their left, Diask stands with Representative Vitus next to him. Across from the Twins is another boy I don't recognize.

"Ahh, Zayne, welcome," Vitus says. He seems happy to see me. "I am sure your escort told you why you are here."

"He did."

"I am sure you know the Coffer brothers," Vitus says. "We had a late addition to the Datum. Seeing you only chose two Aemiins, we saw fit to add a third."

Seni only chose his brother. Were we supposed to choose more? I look at Diask.

Vitus glances at Diask before speaking. "We have added additional Aemiins to the other boys as necessary. Zayne, may I introduce you to Cramen."

The boy steps forward. He's taller than me with short brown hair. A scar descends just below his hairline onto his forehead. I stare for longer than I should. Scars are a rare feature, received during childhood before the maturation of one's Lamis. Certainly a sign of some neglect of proper medical care. My eyes shift when I realize he notices me staring. His hand moves across his forehead, lightly moving his hair to cover the scar.

"Zayne," he says. "Do you have a family name? You don't seem important enough to warrant recognition by only one name."

His voice stings with privilege, yet his scar says he didn't grow up in the city.

I look at Vitus and Diask. Their exclusion of my family name surprises me and causes to me to pause and consider if I should tell him. Or any of the boys in the Datum.

"Diask is sharing his title with you," he says in my silence, though I don't think he needed my pause to continue. "You're someone special to have this city's Tech put into your hands."

"Enough of this chattering," Vitus says, his pleasant tone fading. "We have the other Aemiins to introduce. You four are dismissed. Report to the dining hall."

The Twins take the lead and exit the room. They appear to have some knowledge of the corridors. When we turn the first corner, the man from before is leading three boys. Two I don't recognize, but the third is Seni. I try to make eye contact, but he barely looks in my direction. Whatever effort he takes to look at me is just to avoid walking into me.

"Know him?"

I turn to look at one of the twins. Left eye blue. Safon.

"He's one of the other Tech boys—" I begin.

"Nah, he's an Aemiin," Erman says.

I glance at him, waiting for him to explain the contradiction.

"Don't think we've been sitting around the past several sols. They've been telling us how to act around you important boys. I remember him. He sat near the front every lecture."

It takes too long to realize the obvious. "That's his brother, Arsen."

"His brother?" Erman repeats, glancing at his brother. A smirk forms across his face. "You knew another set of twins here and you didn't tell us?"

Safon nudges his twin, equally smiling. "And I thought we were unique."

"Are you going to stand there all sol, or are we going to keep moving?"

The Twins' smiles break as we look at Cramen. Even in my drowsiness, there's something more to him that pulls at me. A wave of exhaustion keeps me from considering the thoughts more.

"You're going to be fun, aren't you?" Erman says.

Cramen steps forward. "You think this all is fun? Death comes for this city, and you concern yourself with childish antics."

I feel the weight of the seriousness, but I must bear it all because the Twins laugh.

"Antics?" Erman says. "You have a lot to learn about us. Storm or no storm, we're going to laugh."

"You either embrace us, or this will be a long endeavor for you," Safon says.

Cramen looks at me, but I remain silent. He lets out some sort of grunt before moving further along the corridor. Rather than following him, I take the time to talk to the Twins, alone. This Cramen may be taking the storm seriously, but if he treats his duties the same, I may not have another moment alone with the Twins.

"Have you told anyone about me?"

The brothers exchange a glance. "You mean your inability to make friends?"

"Or how you nearly blew up the city school messing with its Tech?"

Their responses tell me they know my meaning, but I speak it so we are clear. "My father."

Safon shrugs. "Oh, that. Slipped our minds, not that we talk about you much. You're pretty boring."

"Diask and Vitus seemed intent on keeping it a secret," Erman says. "I suppose it's your secret to tell or keep."

"And on that note," Safon says, switching places with his brother. "Since you still can't be certain who is who between us, we're going to help simplify it for you. And it'll help keep your family name a secret."

I glance between them, noting their eye colors. "And how is that?"

"I am going to call you Zayne," Erman says.

"But when I speak of you," Safon says, "I will call you Persolus."

"Persolus?"

The name is unusual, but something about it feels right.

Safon smirks. "It's a name from one of the outer cities. It's rare, but I've always liked how it sounded."

I forget the Twins weren't born in Epis City. I should ask them about life beyond the Red Plains. The words stall in my throat.

"Now come on, Persolus," Safon says. "We have to catch up to Cramen. Every second he's away from us is a second he enjoys."

The Twins' detachment from the reality around us causes me to pause. I can understand Cramen's dislike of their behavior. They were at the speech. They witnessed only a fraction of the storm's potential. How will they react when the full presence of the Sorbe arrives? Will their humor remain? Or will fear win out?

The ceiling curves at the center of the room, spreading the conversations around where we eat. With no certainty, I believe every boy in the Datum is here. Nearly fifty square tables fill the room with five chairs at each. Boys pull chairs from other tables so they can sit together, while others push tables so they are end-to-end. The room is full of friends and classmates exchanging jokes—based on the laughter—and other things I can't make out. Silence is the only thing present at my table. The Twins are busy stuffing their faces while Cramen sits across from them at the edge. The humor of the Coffer boys is too much for him still.

Hunger evades me, despite the colorful meal in front of me. A portion that is a yellowish color sparkles as I push it around. I reach for a cup in front of me. The drink is a greenish color, not water as I expected. I set it back down.

I look across the table at the other groups. Now with our Aemiins, the other boys joining us in our sector sit together. There are nearly fifty, but I can't make an accurate count. I spot Seni and his brother several tables away. Without me being close enough to see their eyes, they're identical. I still wonder if he wishes he was the Tatem. He's far more capable than me. He knows that.

As everyone finishes their meals and I finish only my third bite, Vitus enters the room. He walks through the tables, eyeing us, but doesn't say a word. I turn away to see Diask is lingering near the door.

"Your attention, Datum," Vitus says, turning my focus back to him. He's several tables away, but the room carries his voice easily. "I hope you enjoyed this meal, for it will be your last of such."

He pauses, causing a murmur throughout the boys. His words bring no surprise to me. Certain luxuries aren't possible during the storm. Anyone who thought otherwise hasn't thought enough about our situation. Then again, I doubt many boys here wanted to serve.

"The storm presents a danger of itself, and the Council needs you focused. These new meal substitutes—" He directs our attentions to several men and women walking between the tables. They place large plates with green bars on them. "These will provide you nourishment to maintain your strength for ten solpaes."

Erman jars the table. "He means we won't have to eat for an entire ora?"

Vitus glances at our table. "Your time will be best spent concerning yourself with the storm and not your hunger."

The twin slinks back into his seat and lowers his voice with his next words. "Not everyone eats when they're hungry. Some of us enjoy eating just to eat."

Vitus either doesn't hear him or ignores his comment. "Enjoy this last meal, for the storm still approaches. I expect you to heed the preparations we have for you. Time isn't in our favor."

His last words reverberate doubt. His normal confidence wavers, though I'm not sure anyone else notices. A burden I carry alone because of my family name. I see through the disguises of our leaders.

10

Corridor Conversations

"While accidental eavesdropping is a natural part of city life, intentional eavesdropping—with focus on those higher ranking than the person hearing—is a crime punishable by city exile or imprisonment."—an excerpt from the Council's Law

The green bars lack any pleasant taste. Thankfully, we don't have to eat it every sol. Further instructions tell us to eat every five sols to ensure our body's Lamis remains strong. After the scratchy texture goes down my throat, I decide to only eat every ten sols.

The Twins come to a similar decision, despite their enjoyment of eating. Erman even goes as far as describing how the green bar is tearing at his stomach. He even tries to get others to agree to filing a joint complaint to the Council about our treatment. He isn't successful.

Without the need to break for meals, we spent the last two sols with our entire sector listening to lectures from the city's experts. Basic Tech. The leadership structure. Beasts. Everything the Council believes we need to know to serve the city. Nothing about the storm. Nothing I find helpful.

I find the time spent with everyone useless. I need time with Diask to learn more about the generators and what anomalies to look for.

My inability to see the usefulness of this preparation makes me focus more. The Council doesn't require complete understanding to follow them. A truth I can't forget. The worst I can do now is doubt. I have to trust this information is important. It may not take shape until we are alone beneath the Sorbe.

A pain tickles the back of my head. My problem isn't trusting the information but retaining it. Sleep continues to evade me. More details of the dreams leak into the time I spend awake. The Twins notice my absence mentally but say nothing. I don't know how long I can conceal it from Cramen. He won't be as forgiving. I shouldn't care. I don't know him. But I still do.

"You coming, Persolus?"

His use of my new name is the only thing helping distinguish him from his brother in my exhaustion. I look at Safon, who stands near the door to the next lecture. Other boys walk past us, stares lingering.

"Yeah, just thinking."

Erman brushes my shoulder. "Don't let Cramen know how much you're doing that. Not sure how he'll take it."

"Where is he?"

Safon points behind him. "Already inside. Told him to save us some seats. I think he'll enjoy the time apart for a few minutes."

"Zayne won't be joining you all for this lecture." The voice comes from behind us. It's familiar, but not enough for me to recognize the boy. I turn to face Seni. "We have something else to do this sol."

"In that case," Erman says, "I think we should go make sure Cramen isn't enjoying himself too much."

The Twins enter the lecture room, leaving me with Seni and a few stragglers finishing their conversations. "Diask must have sent you if we're both missing our lectures."

His gaze narrows. "It doesn't concern you he approached me and not you?"

Seni knows he is the better choice for the Tatem. He doesn't realize I believe that, so he worries that he's overstepping. I won't be the one to tell him. Despite my beliefs, I can't undermine the authority the Council has given me. He refuses to undermine his trust in Diask.

"Of course not," I say, controlling my breathing, hoping he doesn't notice any deception in my tone. "Does it concern you?"

He shakes his head. "No. I imagine Mr. Diask saw me first and had more important things to do than deliver the news to each one of us. He should be able to trust each of us to relay information. You're not going to discover everything out there on your own."

I shift the conversation in hopes of dispelling any doubt he may have in my answer. "What is our goal for the sol?"

Seni relaxes as a grin forms with his words. "Tech is our goal. Diask has set aside the various devices allotted to us to fulfill our duties."

Finally, something practical. But I have trouble picturing the advanced Tech necessary to help us combat the storm. The Lamis requirements to access generators will only bring the storm's wrath. How does Diask expect us to monitor Tech without drawing the Sorbe?

"Where are we meeting?"

"I have to inform the others, if you don't mind." When I shake my head, he continues. "Down this corridor, past lecture halls three and four, you will find a locked room. Diask said he would meet us there by the start of the tenth hour. That's in ten minutes."

I glance behind him to a timepiece on the wall. Thirteen minutes, but I don't correct him. "Ten minutes then."

He takes a few steps back before moving in a brisk walk away from our meeting point. I glance at the remaining boys, who hardly notice me. Barely a minute passes when the boys finish talking and enter the lecture room. The noise of the conversations ongoing seep out before the door closes. How seriously is everyone taking this endeavor? How is their mindset having been forced into this service?

I take a deep breath. They are Alfarons. Any goal set by the Council will ensure they approach this duty with genuine effort. With the preparations underway for when the storm truly arrives, the boys only need to obey.

I glace at the wall's timepiece. Eleven minutes until we meet with Diask. I start in the direction that Seni directed. Perhaps Diask will arrive early. I can talk to him. He can help me connect the dots between his lectures and the other information. My responsibilities seem simple enough: monitor select generators and other Tech with physical connections to the Lamis deposit. It's the simplicity that worries me.

Diask either believes the storm to be no threat—thanks to his preparations—or doesn't trust me. He trusts Seni. Why he put me in charge still confuses me. Maybe I forget asking him about my responsibilities and ask for the reason he chose me over Seni.

While in my thoughts, I pass the fourth lecture hall. I keep going until I come to an unmarked door. I press the control to open it, but it doesn't move. Locked. Seni's description is accurate. With no timepiece, I have no certainty of the time. But I feel at least five minutes have passed.

Faint voices reach my ears from somewhere further down the corridor. I pull my focus to listen. When the words refuse to give me their meaning, I follow the sounds. I have to walk nearly fifty feet before I find any clarity in them. My feet refuse another step when I recognize Vitus's voice.

"First, you indicated the storm would dissipate over the Red Plains. Then your report said it would take two oras to reach us. Then the natent appeared almost at the will of the traitor an ora sooner than you predicted. You're telling me that man had better Tech to forecast the storm than you? And now . . ."

He pauses. I can hear him walking. I take a step back. I wait for the other person to talk, but Vitus continues.

"Now you are telling us every effort we have made could be for nothing? How can I bring this information to the Council? They won't stand for such incompetence."

"Good thing the Representatives are the ones standing." The voice belongs to Diask. "The Council should have left when everyone else did."

"How dare you speak of your Council that way."

"You were the Tatem of another city, Vitus," Diask says. "You understand the limits of Tech. Sorbes test every one of them. The Council is assigning meaning where there is none with Carius's timing."

"He knew it was there," Vitus says. His hand slams into something metal, causing me to take another step back.

"He said a Sorbe was present, not a natent," Diask says.

"The destruction doesn't recognize any distinction."

"Regardless, we all knew the edge of the storm was approaching. I don't think Carius expected a natent to form and strike the ceremony. His words would contain the same potency whether the storm arrived that sol or an ora later. He knew the Council was keeping it a secret from the city. That secret alone held all the power he needed."

A silence shrouds the corridor. I still don't know where they are. There's a corner I can't see or a room where they left the door open.

"What is your intention, Vitus? You didn't ask to speak separately from the other Representatives to discuss this. Speak your mind or allow me on my way. I have to prepare students for their deaths."

I let out a breath at his last words.

"The Council values your perspective because you witnessed a storm as a child," Vitus says, his tone darkening. "I believe it only clouds your judgement."

"The only certain path to surviving a Sorbe is to leave the city," Diask says. "I stand by my report to the Council. One errant strike could level the entire city. No amount of preparation of these children can assure the city's safety."

"Have you let the five boys in charge know your doubts?"

I can hear a loud breath before Diask talks again.

"I would never allow my doubts to jeopardize this city," he says. "You have my word that I am preparing these boys to survive."

"Then you agree with our selection?"

I take a step closer, but as I do, voices from behind me reach my ears. I can hear Diask and Vitus shifting their feet; they know their private conversation will no longer be such. I move away as quickly as I can without making unnecessary noise.

I've eavesdropped on hundreds of my father's conversations, Vitus being a part of many. But this one felt different. It felt fatal.

I reach the locked door as Seni and the other Tech leaders come into sight, carrying on a loud conversation.

Seni looks up and smiles. "I see you found the place. We were just discussing the type of Tech Diask is going to give us."

I keep my mouth closed as my heart beats. I wonder if the others can see it trying to burst from my chest. My silence causes Seni's lips to curl down as his eyebrows drop.

"Are you alright, Zayne?"

I nod first to dispel any concerns. "Yes . . . just didn't hear you coming. Lost in my thoughts."

"Good, you are all on time."

We turn to face Diask. I glance behind him, but Vitus is nowhere to be seen. I feel Diask hold a stare on me for what seems like minutes. The reality only lasts a few seconds. Does he know I was listening?

Diask opens the door with a press of a few buttons. He gestures us inside before entering himself. The room is empty except for a shelf against the far wall. A separate light illuminates the contents—five small devices, barely the size of my palm, each with a screen that covers most of the front and five physical buttons beneath it. Five other devices sit next to it, slightly bigger than the first, with smaller buttons on the bottom, allowing for a larger screen.

Diask approaches the shelf and picks up the smaller device. "This is an anro. For those unfamiliar with Exan Tech, this is an example. Dead Tech. Has no practical purpose for regular use anymore."

Seni poses the question that has to linger in each of our minds. "And why are we going to use it?"

Diask doesn't smile or react to the question. "This Tech has a small, highly inefficient Lamis imprint. The reason for its Exan status. But beneath a Sorbe, this imperfection will allow you some normalcy."

I glance at the others. "What does it do?"

Diask hands me the device. "It's a multi-functional tool. Without the main city power, regular communication is disabled. But a text-based infrastructure remains intact for emergencies."

"Text-based, sir?" Soma asks.

Regular communication either is visual or verbally sent. It has a holographic emitter, but we will only use it for input. The energy requirement to record a message is too high of a risk.

"I think you can manage typing a few words," Diask says, his tone betraying something I can't put my finger on. "The anro will also act as a directory to relevant information about the Tech you are safeguarding."

"What's the power source, sir?" Seni asks.

"You will provide the power the device needs."

Seni's mouth pauses halfway open before he manages a response. "Sir, even given the situation, aren't we still too young to power Tech ourselves?"

I spin the anro in my hand, looking at it from every angle. The backside removes with some ease. The components within are simple, and I recognize a few common ones.

"The power requirement is minor," Diask continues, "and—"

"And there's an inhibitor built into the haur ports used to draw the energy from our bodies," I say, not even realizing I interrupt Diask. "We couldn't overtax our bodies if we wanted to."

A smile flickers briefly across Diask's face. "Correct. The other device is simply a map of the city with limited tracking capability and requires even less power."

Seni doesn't appear happy with the Tech. "Is this all, sir? Aren't we going to receive anything else?"

A wave of emotion appears briefly on Diask's face. "Even the smallest amount of Tech drawing Lamis is a risk. We can only hope your immature energy will be enough to keep the storm from . . ."

No one needs him to finish his thought.

Does he know the storm struck me? Does he know we aren't immune to the storm's wrath?

"But you will find the anro has more useful features than just access to the communication network. You will find information on the Tech you will be monitoring within its database. Don't underestimate its usefulness; this anro is a crucial piece to your role beneath the storm." He straightens his shirt, even though it's already neat. "Now, each of you, grab an anro and a map. I have something I want to show you."

Once we each have our Tech, Diask leads us out of the room. We follow him down the corridor past where he and Vitus were speaking. He turns a corner and takes us up several flights of stairs.

I don't know which floor we exit onto. Diask takes us down a narrow corridor where the ceiling is nearly two feet lower than that of the rest of the building. I brush my hand along the wall. A vibration moves up my arm. A generator is nearby, or multiple. The reverberation is strong, moving through my arm to my back.

Seni brings my attention back to the group. "Where are we, Mr. Diask?"

"The uppermost level of the Linam," he says. "Did you know this building is of my design? I designed it to withstand a Sorbe."

"Does that mean the Council will stay here during the storm?" I ask.

Diask glances at me before reaching up to the ceiling with his right hand. Light reflects off his LiorTech.

"No. The building will remain empty."

His words are short and deter me from pushing the topic.

A building that can survive a Sorbe, yet the Council intends to keep it empty? They refuse to utilize the Linam like they refused to evacuate the city. I have to be patient. My understanding of their choices will come with time.

The ceiling glows where Diask touches it. A shape appears, first as black lines, before turning into various colors. As the lines widen, I realize it's the sky. The storm continues to encase the city in its beauty.

The opening widens until there is a square void in the ceiling. Diask pulls down a ladder and proceeds to climb up. I exchange glances with Seni and the others. I can see us each questioning his actions, but any answers we desire are on the roof, so we climb.

The city sparkles under the storm's colors, light bouncing from window to window. Without focusing my eyes, the clouds look like they descend far below their boundaries in the sky. Diask stands at the edge of the Linam, his body silhouetted against the color.

His silence draws me closer. I look at the others. Their gaze is on the storm, the brilliant spectacle pushing away any thought of the potential danger. If Diask has witnessed a storm in the past, I can only imagine the memories this sight is invoking in him. He knows the truth behind the beauty.

A light flashes in my memory. The bodies from the City Center push to the forefront of my mind. That had been only a fraction of the storm's power. A tingling sensation moves over my body. The Council's hope—no, the hope they have given the city—is based on our immunity to the Sorbe's wrath. All a lie.

Does Diask know?

"Diask."

His head lowers. I can see his left arm twitch as he grips the edge of the building.

I look back. The others' attention remains on the illusion of beauty.

I take a few steps closer. "Diask."

His voice is low, only loud enough for me to hear. "Yes, Zayne."

"Why'd you bring us up here?"

It's not the question I want to ask, but it's the only one that comes out.

"You would judge me if I told you the truth," he says. His next words seem detached, as if I ask a question that I don't realize. "As long as the colors remain, our Red Plain transports can evacuate the city. Natents are dangerous but require concentrated sources of lamis to strike."

"Why are you saying this?"

He turns to face me. He straightens as I feel the others walk up behind me.

"Mr. Diask, what is that?"

I turn to face Seni, who points to the sky. I turn back quickly, following the direction of his hand. I don't need to find anything specific. Swirls of black are pushing the color out of the sky. Shadows descend upon the city.

I move closer to our Tatem. "Diask, what's happening?"

His eyes look past me. Fear fills his entire face. "Back inside now! Close the opening. Close it!"

His words push me back. Seni and the others waste no time. They're back at the opening as the shadows reach the Linam. I can barely hear their screams at me. Diask doesn't move, so I don't.

"What are you doing? Is this no longer the natent? Is the true presence of the storm now upon us"

His voice barely is audible. "I never should have brought you here. It was a mistake."

His words need no explanation as darkness surrounds us. A flash of light shoots out from the dark clouds. It strikes a corner, sending a rush of air across the entire roof. My back slams into the ground. My head whips back into something hard. Sparkling spots flood my vision.

Diask remains standing. He holds something in his hand. My vision refuses to focus.

My ears seem fine. Diask's words reaching me with odd clarity.

"I let my fear direct my steps." My vision clears. His head dips. "The city will teach you much. Be diligent. Not everything you learn will bring clarity. Forgive me for the path I set you on. Know it doesn't end in the city."

"Diask, I don't understand."

He holds up a small oval device in his hand. A blue pulse extends upward into the clouds. With his other hand, he extends it toward me. A wave of blue sweeps through the air, pushing me across the roof. I try to fight it, but before I can find a footing, I fall back into the opening.

I catch myself on the edge. I strain as I see the Tatem slowly shake his head. My fingers slip, and before I drop below, a flash of light envelops Diask.

From Beyond Death

*"Death is not the end when the Historical Record exists
to prevent death, if only in memory." —Wisdom of the
Prava Council*

I wait for the memory to reveal itself as a dream. Fade into the void
that all dreams come and return to. But it never does.

Diask is dead.

His death should hurt more. But the only thoughts that overwhelm me are ones about the secrets he left. Unanswered questions.
His last words still don't make sense. Guilt washes over me, but
I push it away. I am an Alfaron. Death can't exist as long as the
Historical Record remains intact. I let out a gasp. The storm leaves
nothing. Diask's contribution to the nation's history is lost.

His death flashes fresh in my mind. This Sorbe threatens not only death but to bar us from the Historical Record. We will exist as only memories in those who choose to remember us. But if we die, will the storm spare those who hide from it?

Everyone who knows me is here in the city. My entire existence relies on my success. My shoulders tense. I can barely stand. I turn my senses outward.

Conversations full of fear and questions flood the room. Whatever doubts everyone may have had about the Sorbe's presence have to be gone. Everyone felt the storm strike. No one says anything to dispel the emotions that threaten to undo all our preparation. Or is the storm revealing how useless the time spent here has been?

The floor shakes.

A silence falls over the room.

Even in the heart of the Linam, we can feel the storm strike at us. It tries its best to wipe us out before we can step foot outside. But Diask's legacy extends beyond the Historical Record that he has been barred from entering. He built the Linam. And it still stands.

As the storm's presence settles into the back of our minds, Vitus walks through the crowd of just over two hundred boys. His eyes avoid each worried set that looks to him for answers. He looks at me. In order to avoid his gaze, I drop my eyes to his hands. He's holding a small device.

"Zayne," he says, stopping an arm's distance from me. "Diask wanted the Tatem to have this. I'm sure he had some explanation for it, but I leave the discovery of its purpose in your capable hands."

He hands me the device without another word. As he makes his way back through the crowd, I examine the Tech. It's about the same size as the anro but with only two buttons at the top of the screen with a holographic emitter. I press the left button that activates the haur ports that pull my energy into the device. I barely feel the tug on my energy.

The screen flickers. A list of files appears with numbers serving as the titles.

Before I can decipher the first one, Vitus's voice breaks my concentration.

"I don't have to announce to you the arrival of the storm." He stops, letting the uncertainty of some disappear. "The Linam is safe. We are safe. But this doesn't change the Council's plans. Your place isn't here, but out there."

Low words ripple through the boys. I look around. Did no one expect to actually enter the storm? Did they think the Council more powerful than a Sorbe? They may act it, but not even our leaders can overpower nature.

"Do you forget why you are entering the storm?" Vitus's words rip through the air, silencing everyone. "This building protects me. Not you. The very nature of who you are protects you. This storm passes over you without threat."

He glances at a timepiece on his wrist.

"You were meant to be in the city before the colors left the sky." His voice is lower but still loud enough to reach every ear. "After we purge the bottom level of all lamis, you will enter the city. Gather with your sector leaders. Everything you need is being prepared as we speak."

He gives no further instructions, trusting we will fulfill the duties required of us. In a show of confidence, he leaves the room.

Seni approaches me, along with the other Tech leaders. I slip the device Vitus gave me in my pocket.

His eyes are red. I don't think I could tell him apart from his brother with him in this state.

"They aren't giving him his sol of remembrance," he says, the words barely audible. "Everyone lost to the storm . . ." He doesn't finish the thought. He straightens and clears his voice. "I doubt we will meet again with the storm overhead. Clear skies will mark our next meeting."

He has more to say, but he stops to allow me the opportunity. "You each have your anros?" I ask. They each flash their devices briefly for me to see. "You understand how to send messages to each other?"

Soma tosses his anro up and catches it. "Bit slow with the archaic communication, but it's all simple enough."

His words lack something I can't discern. It makes me want to not believe him.

I swallow the saliva building in my mouth. "Good. I expect to receive a communication about anything noteworthy. No matter how insignificant, I expect to know."

Soma glances at Seni. "And if we find nothing?"

Seni inclines his head to me.

"I still expect to hear something from you every two sols if nothing happens," I say. "And let the other leaders know they can utilize us to communicate across sectors. I don't think the others have a way to communicate."

Talpa spits out air, drawing attention to him. "I thought we were guardians of the Tech? Not messengers."

"Talpa's right. Why should we be burdening ourselves more?" Soma asks, fueling the doubt that threatens to undo the Council's plans. "We have enough to concern ourselves with. Let the others deal with their own problems."

"That—"

Soma speaks before I can manage a second word. "We're going to be mere figureheads out there. Why else would Diask equip us so poorly? He didn't expect us to do much. Why do you think he was so ready to die? He didn't want to witness our failure."

"I don't believe that."

The words lack the authority needed to end this.

"Enough." Seni's single word is enough to silence Soma and Talpa. Ocen adds nothing to the conversation. His silence draws my attention until Seni speaks again. "Diask put Zayne in charge, and you will listen to him. If he thinks we should help our sectors by passing messages along, then we will do it."

I can see that Soma and Talpa are far from finished, but out of a respect for Seni—not my leadership—they remain silent. I want to say something else, but even if I can come up with something, everyone but Seni disperses to meet their sector groups.

Seni closes the gap between us as conversations around us fill the room with noise. "Forgive them. You didn't know Mr. Diask like we did. And the storm now forbids his entry into the Historical Record. The thought that his story ends so suddenly. Their anger isn't aimed at you. May I diminish any doubt you have about their resolve."

"I trust in the end they will uphold their duties to the Council."

The words may mean little in the face of his grief, but nothing else seems fitting.

"Contact me if you need anything," Seni says. "I have to report to my sector group now."

I want to say something else, but my brain refuses to manage anything as he walks away. Pushing the encounter away from the forefront of my mind, I look for the Twins. I can't imagine recognizing any of the boys from Sector One.

It doesn't take long to find the Twins as they are also looking for me. Cramen isn't with them.

"Where is he?" I ask.

Safon shrugs. "He never showed up here after the storm strikes."

"He'll show up eventually," Erman says. "They won't let him stay here. I heard no one's staying here. It's remaining empty as some sort of test. Even the generators are staying on."

"A test of Diask's last design," I say. "We already know it works. We're alive because of it."

My mention of the dead Tatem shifts the air around us. There was no announcement. But I imagine everyone knows now. But do they know he saved us? His use of that Tech to draw the storm's strike. Kept it from striking through the opening and obliterating the Linam. Or will they only see the hatred of the storm in his death? Allow fear to impact their judgement?

My shoulders tense. If they fail their responsibility, can I still succeed? I don't want to dwell on having to rely on the others to earn my place among the Council.

"Soriina warned us about this."

My thoughts break as I realize the Twins are still in front of me. "What?"

Left eye blue. Safon. "She told us to watch out for you falling into your own mind. Said we were free to smack you to pull you out."

"That last part was my idea," Erman says.

"If we get a moment to rest, I think I need to know everything Soriina told you about me."

Safon nudges me in the shoulder. "She warned us you would ask that. Such secrets aren't coming out of our mouths."

I feel a smile rising to the surface. My first thought is to push it down with images of the Sorbe and Diask. This isn't a time to joke. A deadly storm sits above us, threatening everything. But a joint laugh from the Twins pulls the smile out of me.

Hours pass as we wait for the lamis purge. Against my better judgement and the insistence of the Twins, I don't join the other boys assigned to Sector One. I watch Edwin and Cade, who I learn is his co-leader, gather the boys and talk to them from the shadows. I convince myself that it isn't my responsibility. The Tech beyond the Linam is.

Safon and Erman remain with me, ensuring I am not completely alone with my thoughts. Their laughs pull me from the darkest part of the shadows. I learn Soriina told the Twins to stay near me. Not only do they have a command from the Council to stay with me, but also my best friend.

Knowing they're listening to Soriina gives me comfort. Even when she can't be here, she's looking after me. Why does that elicit more confidence than the Council?

I hate the thought.

Without the Council's careful preparation, this city would fall beneath the storm. They can't control a Sorbe or even stop it, but it's their wisdom that will provide a path through. It's my responsibility—our responsibility—to follow it. The city's survival relies on this, but also my path.

I can't fail. Not after I rejected the certainty my father tried to give me. Not after Diask has set me on this path.

"Persolus, look." Safon points his finger at a man walking through the crowd of boys. He wears a black coat that goes down to his feet, and he nearly trips as he nears us. "It may be time to leave this place."

"And where's Cramen?" Erman asks as the man makes his way to the center of the room. "I lost sight of him in all the commotion. Think he ran away?"

Neither Safon nor I try to answer the question. I expect Cramen will not be the last one to disappear. Only having the Twins as my Aemiins may make enduring the storm easier. But his absence strikes at my curiosity, and as much as I want to think he left of his own choice, the idea seems the most illogical. Vitus selected him to be my Aemiin. He wouldn't choose a boy who was going to flee from his responsibility.

My gaze travels across the boys to Edwin and Cade.

Or I could be mistaken.

The man is quick with his words, announcing the boys going to Sector Five will leave first. To keep everything simple, I imagine, he instructs us to leave in descending order after that. I watch boys share glances with each other as they slowly exit the room. A few linger, and I think they aren't going to leave.

Either their commitment to the Council or their fear of punishment wins out. Eventually, the only ones left are the boys from my group. Whether their resolve is stronger or simply can't remain standing around any longer, they exit the room quickly.

I follow behind, with Safon and Erman close by. I watch the boys, expecting Cramen to appear. Or for an adult to be counting us as we leave to make sure no one stays behind.

But no one is here. Before we even reach the storm, they abandon us.

The thought burns in my mind. We aren't abandoned. We are in the hands of the Council.

We make our way to the bottom floor. The stairwells aren't built for so many people. It makes the going slow. If an adult was around, I would ask them why we don't use the lifts—not that I miss using the unnatural contraptions. Diask's design ensures our protection here. We shouldn't have limits on energy usage.

We reach the bottom floor, and it's empty.

The doors to the outside are open. The city is dark. Even when the sun sets, the city's lights are enough to keep the dark away. Not now. There are no lights to push back the shadows. The storm remains silent, leaving us to struggle in darkness.

"Take this Persolus."

Safon hands me a velare—a portable light. A flat bulb sits encased in a hard, transparent material at the end. The body of the Tech is just big enough to be held in my hand. There's no pull on my Lamis. The device has its own power source.

With lights in hand, we push back the darkness and step outside.

The Council's Son

"No technology, no matter how obsolete, should be discarded in its entirety. A good Tatem will be able to utilize even the oldest Tech in times of need." —an excerpt from the Tatem handbook

The city feels enormous in the darkness, but a mist surrounds me, diluting the spacious freedom I should have. Though I walk without restriction, I feel the shadows guiding me to where they want me to go. When I search for my Aemiins, they aren't present. Either lost in the darkness . . . or did they ever exist?

Who were my Aemiins? The names sit at the edge of my mind. The edge moves farther away as I try to draw near. My own thoughts fall away into the abyss of darkness. I want to jump after them, but someone or something keeps me from reaching them.

A light breaks through the darkness, illuminating the mist in a bluish haze. A shadow sweeps over me. A figure stands in front of the light.

I open my mouth to speak, but the mist steals my words. A strange silence fills the area. Words sting in the air, wanting to break the silence, but they never reach my ears. Are they my words or someone else's?

The shadowy figure advances as the mist surges forward. Though harmless, I throw my arms up to cover my face. When my arms drop, the figure stands overtop of me. I shrink. The color fades from the mist, turning from blue to a dark grey. A pressure forms in the back of my head. At its peak, it ignites into pain that pushes me to my knees.

The figure's shadow moves over me. A cold worse than any I've ever experienced sweeps across my body. My limbs go numb, but the pain in my head remains. It's as if all my feeling moves to my head, intensifying the pain that swells there. The rest of my body fades away.

Words form in the mist—no, not words. Feelings. A sense of confusion and determination sweeps over me. They aren't my own. The figure is expressing these things. The emotions draw close to words, but as the sounds form, the pain surges, sending everything into a darkness.

The dream lingers into the hours beyond my attempts to sleep.

Erman walks past me, kicking my feet playfully. "Those beds aren't that comfortable," he says. "I thought you said we were leaving early this sol."

I look back in the direction he came from. Neither Safon nor Erman have been awake before me these past three sols. I try not to think about it. I loosen the bed from around me and toss the top section off. "Just waiting for you."

We don't need to bother changing clothes. The material absorbs any odor, retaining its freshness. Erman claims he's going to find the limit.

Safon sits silently on his bed. I didn't even realize he was awake. His voice tells me he's been awake longer than I have. "If you're ready then, we should get going."

The conversation is sparse as we arrive at the wall that surrounds the Sector Center we set up camp in. The area is a third of the size of the City Center. It's still enough space that we can sleep away from the other boys. They gather near the center. The Council set up the metal barrier to protect us from errant beasts that may lurk in the city. A precaution that Edwin and Cade think is unnecessary.

We approach three rotams—bulky vehicles with three wheels propelled by a pedal system. A Lamisless design ideal for the storm. The Council's perfect insight in full view, though I imagine Diask had some part to play. Yet I wonder why such useless Tech was ever present in the city. What use would they have beyond the storm?

As Safon opens the gate in the wall, I mount my rotam. "Any weapons for this trip?"

Safon shakes his head as he swings his leg over the seat. "Not this time. Edwin and Cade are keeping a close eye on them. They don't trust us to have weapons."

Erman stands on the pedals before settling into his seat. "They think by refusing us weapons that we will stay here. I would suggest you boss them around, but that would require them to recognize an authority outside their own."

As we traverse Sector One's alleys and transport paths, I try to make sense of Edwin's and Cade's actions. Their insistence that we remain within the camp makes no sense to me. Even if my mind was fully rested, I still don't think I could find any reason for their choices. Don't they realize by rebelling against the Council's order that they jeopardize the city?

Or do they have more trust in the Council than I do? Would the Council truly leave the fate of the city in our hands?

The thoughts lay heavy on my mind as we arrive at the next generator on my list. Safon keeps us close to the camp. He's been reluctant to venture further without weapons, despite no evidence beasts have entered the city. I haven't pushed him on the topic, as there are numerous generators to check within his comfort level. Eventually I have to, and I hope he doesn't argue.

I press my hand against the smooth metal. An exhaustion sweeps over me. I can count the number of hours of sleep I've had on my hands. The physical exertion from the rotams is enough to keep me awake, but now on my feet, my body only wants to collapse.

My anro helps me to focus enough that Safon and Erman don't bother me for the next hour. I pull up the information on the generator within the three-story building towering over me. A signal reaches my anro, which I use to verify everything is within Diask's specifications. It's slow. Less than minimal power is all that pushes the signal to me.

When enough information flows across the screen of my anro, I disconnect. The generator has no power output. Data readings from the past two sols show no spikes in power, nothing for the storm to sense and strike at. Everything is as Diask set forth.

I mark the generator and location on my anro. I will need to check again after confirming the status of the others. I doubt Safon will agree to visiting another this sol.

"Persolus, are you done yet?"

I lean into the building and take a deep breath.

When I feel strong enough to hide my exhaustion, I turn to face the Twins. "Just finished. Tired of staring into the dark?"

Safon points a velare at me. The artificial light stings my eyes. "You and I know this storm alters animal behavior. As long as the other boys aren't doing their jobs, gradulas or caros may seek shelter in the city.

The longer we stay out here, the greater our chances of meeting a scared animal."

"How dangerous can gradulas be?" I ask. "We aren't their food source."

"Even a gradula can be dangerous when scared," Erman says. "But don't ask those two brainless lamis suckers. They couldn't discern a beast from their backsides."

Erman's language causes me to pause. People who find themselves lost on the Red Plains will succumb to sucking on plants to recover lost Lamis. The insult comes from the practice being completely useless.

"Do you think the other boys agree with Edwin and Cade?" I ask.

The Twins share a glance at my shift in conversation before ignoring my question.

"We should move," Safon says. "The storm's been quite active the last hour."

"And not one strike."

There's an accusation in Erman's words.

Safon snaps his head at his brother. "Not around Persolus."

The humorless words pull at my natural curiosity. The environment urges me to stay silent, and I almost do, if they hadn't ignored my question just a minute before. "What does that mean?" My tone comes across as harsh.

Safon glares at Erman but speaks to me. "Stupid words being spread by other boys. Nothing we need to bring up now."

His response isn't to quell my curiosity but to postpone this conversation. That is the only reason I don't say anything further. But do I need to worry about what the other boys are saying behind my back? I still have to verify the status of the generators in the other parts of the sector. This is all a distraction.

Do I really need something else to worry about? Edwin and Cade are already more of an obstacle than I anticipated. What rumors are they spreading through the other boys now? We have only been beneath the storm for three sols.

"Persolus, enough of your thinking and get on your rotam. We're leaving."

I attach my anro to my belt and approach my rotam. I secure my backpack, making sure the straps are snug to my shoulders. Removing a helmet lying on the seat, I hang it on the U-shaped handle. With a firm grip of the steering handle, I place my left foot on the nearest pedal and swing my right leg over onto the second pedal. I slide the helmet on, which is more of a visor to protect our eyes from debris. I doubt its effectiveness if I were to crash.

Safon places his velare in a slot below the steering bar and places a map on top. We each have one that helps us navigate the city. The darkness brings an unfamiliarity to the city we grew up in.

With only a glance, Safon commands us to follow him. The seat feels unnatural, and the pedaling burns my legs. The Twins operate their vehicles without any strain, so I fight through the discomfort to keep up with them.

In between the burning sensations, a slight vibration travels through my lower body from the seat. I store the thought in the back of my mind as I pedal faster.

Safon leads us through pathways and into the occasional alleyway. Sector One has no residential houses, so the large industrial buildings dictate how we travel. No one is sheltering from the storm here. According to the anro, primary generators are here. They are key components to how the lamis comes into the city from the deposit below, which also makes them the most dangerous underneath a Sorbe.

That's the reason Diask gave me Sector One. Even though I know Sector Two better than Seni ever can.

Sector One has two squares. The Council has our camp in the bigger one, though it's not by much. The Sector Center's open space keeps us away from any buildings with lamis concentrations that may attract the storm. Beasts will seek shelter in the tight spaces the city offers. I am thankful for the Council's foresight with how little the other boys are doing to protect us.

The gate's closed.

It only opens from the inside, but no one responds to Safon's call. He uses his rotam as a stepping stool to scale the wall. Once on the other side, he opens the gate for Erman and me.

"They come by and close the gate but don't bother to keep someone here to open it back up for us."

Annoyance seeps out of his words. He's held his tongue in our few interactions with Edwin and Cade. I don't expect him to keep that up.

Noises of the boys neglecting their work break through the darkness. Silhouetted figures appear as we make our way toward the center. Faint lights flicker as two boys separate from the main group. Edwin and Cade. I can't identify them outright, but no one else has any reason to take an interest in us.

Lights streak across the face of the clouds, confirming my initial guess of who the figures are. The two co-leaders stop short, forcing the Twins and me to keep walking to meet them. They shine lights at us before pointing them to the ground. We keep our velares off.

"Do-gooders are back from another venture out into the darkness. Find anything interesting this time?"

Edwin's words speak everything but sincerity.

I say nothing in response. My silence presses him to speak again.

"Anything to worry about out there?"

"No," I say after a few seconds of silence, "and that's how it's supposed to be."

"And it'll stay that way if you would convince the other boys to work," Safon says.

"Esidio guards swept the hillsides sols before all the chaos," Edwin says. "There isn't a beast anywhere near us."

"What if the storm pushed more beasts toward the city?" Safon asks. "Isn't that why you're here? Do you think the Council sent you out here for some relaxation?"

Cade points up. "Gradulas aren't going to run into a storm. There aren't any caros on the hillsides. Any beasts sheltering from the storm would have been here by now."

I want to say something, but all I can do is watch Safon step forward. His words should be mine.

"You only speak boldly because you think they can't hear you," Safon says. "When your indifference affects the city, you will answer to them."

"Are you the ears of the Council?" Cade asks. "Did they give you the responsibility to uphold order? We're out here to maintain the illusion that the Council is in control. They have no power out here."

"As Alfarons, you are the Council's power." We each turn to the darkness behind us, where a familiar voice joins our conversation. Cramen. He steps close enough that Edwin's light reveals enough of his face. "But not all are worthy of becoming Alfarons. The storm will strike at the weakest of you, and the Council will be stronger for it."

His words are stark and enough to cause silence to fall upon the two leaders. I stay silent for other reasons. Cramen didn't run away. He's here, which means something else kept him from joining us. Did Vitus need him for something? Why him and not me or Seni or Safon, who is proving to be a capable leader?

Almost a minute passes before Cade speaks. "My father works on the communication grid. He sees every message that comes in and out of this city. Not a single message was sent calling for aid."

Cramen steps further into the light. "And why would the Council's city show such weakness? We stand before a Sorbe and will laugh as it crosses over. The rest of the Nation will see the strength of the Council."

"Is this what we have to look forward to? You and the Council's son praising their glorious plan about how safe we are under their protection? Because, last I checked, we're the ones out here. They're hiding in some bunker until we say it's safe to come out."

The air shifts around me. I suppose my relationship to the Council couldn't remain a secret. Is that why they think I'm here? To glorify the Council and spread word among the other boys that their plan protects the city more than us? I can't share what doubts I have. Their perspective is toxic. My doubts propel me to the truth. What helps me would only strengthen Edwin and Cade's hate.

Edwin senses my thoughts. "If you thought you could hide your identity, you were wrong. But no one here cares about who you are. If anything, your presence only solidifies our position." Edwin turns his light off, plunging us into darkness as the storm stays silent. A few flickers of light come from the center of the camp. "Come on, Cade. Jaret's father stashed some real food for us, and I think it's time we open it up. Don't worry, we'll make sure there's plenty of that green crap for you to eat."

We turn on our velares as the two boys walk back to the main group.

"They are right about something," Safon says.

Erman widens his eyes and lets his mouth hang open. "Are you sick? Should we call for the medical boy?"

"Shut up."

"What do you mean?" I ask, smirking at Erman's immediate embrace of humor.

"Those two boys are evidence the Council lacks complete control out here. They have this masterful plan to protect the city, but they can't control them."

"More reason for Zayne to uphold his duty," Cramen says. "He's the most important piece here, regardless of who his father is."

Safon crosses his arms. "How long were you listening in, Cramen? You timed that interruption pretty well."

"I entered the storm a few hours ago," Cramen says. "The other boys made it easy enough to find you. My timing is nothing of consequence."

"Entered the storm?" Erman asks. "What were you doing the last three sols? What makes you so special to remain in the Linam after we all left?"

Cramen looks at each of us before speaking. "I neglected something, which I had hoped wouldn't be an issue until after the storm. I was mistaken."

"Must have been serious," Erman says.

Cramen's eyes move away from ours. "That depends on your perspective."

His tone is different, and I am sure the Twins recognize it. An unspoken agreement has us not pursuing the topic. Not now. Cramen's presence tells me I shouldn't have to worry about his resolve toward his duty. A feeling surges within me that this storm will uncover secrets. But which ones, I don't know.

Safon gestures for us to walk. "We all need some rest. But first, seeing as you are here to actually work, Cramen, we can catch you up on what we have done while we wait for the others to settle."

Several hours pass before the others quiet down. By then, Cramen knows which generators I have confirmed the dormant status of and which ones I plan to visit in the coming sols. He offers no insight and doesn't care as much as his confrontation with Edwin and Cade seemed to indicate. But he also appears to have a below average understanding of Tech. He doesn't grasp the risk that generators pose with a physical connection to the lamis deposit.

"So you're just double checking what the others have already done?"

Cramen's generalization is enough for him. He'll learn that the changing factors caused by the storm may require me to reinitialize protocols to keep the generators offline. Or I may have to physically sever connections to the deposit. But I don't want to consider that. That will require the other boys, thus the cooperation of Edwin and Cade.

Their cooperation would make my responsibility easier. With their help, their patrols could help identify storm patterns. I could focus my efforts in areas where the Sorbe is most active, instead I'm stuck checking off generators on Diask's list.

For now, I have the Twins and Cramen on my side. Cramen's defense of the Council's plan is enough for me to trust him for now. His secrets still cast a cloud of uncertainty around him. Until he tells us more, I can't trust him the same as the Twins, even if he appears to have a strong allegiance to the Prava.

Safon calls the beds we have tegs and appears familiar with them. He's able to unfold and slip into his in just a couple of minutes. A magnetic seal keeps the bed together on three sides, with the fourth open for me to shimmy into. Once inside, I pull on two cords that expand the interior of the teg, pressing into my body, preventing virtually any movement. The stillness makes falling asleep easier. It works, which is why I hate it. The dreams only haunt me when I sleep.

I pick out the sounds in the darkness, trying to ward off sleep. Erman talks to himself, but I can't make out specific words. Safon is quiet. I know he's listening as well. Edwin's and Cade's failure to work puts pressure on him. He feels some obligation to step into their role. Safon tries to hide it, but I can see it.

Cramen mumbles. I listen carefully, hoping a word or two of his secrets slip out of his unconscious mind. What did he neglect that delayed his entrance into the storm? Did other matters supersede his duties to the Datum? A matter involving the Council is all that comes to mind.

Does he have a similar connection to our leaders as I do? No, it has to be different. My father is the only Representative with a child.

No matter how tempting Cramen's secrets are, they are the least of my concerns. My purpose beneath the storm remains the same. I am here to prove my worth to the Council. They will see me as an equal to my father and not just a product of his position and his choices. To share in his secrets, I have to stand on my own next to my father.

I repeat my purpose until the stillness and my exhaustion finally win. The realm of dreams and nightmares envelops me, where the storm has long since made its presence known.

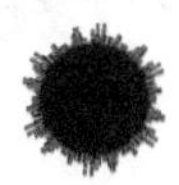

What the Dark Brings

"The infrastructure to expand anro communication was soon abandoned for alternative methods in the cycle 417 of our Council."—Connecting Solisternum, an overview of Vox communication

The storm meets me when I wake. My heart pounds from the dream. The nightmare. Magnificent colors overhead mimic the ones that force me awake. I flinch as the storm flashes, waiting for the colors to obliterate me again. The space between dream and reality blurs.

Soriina was absent this time. I didn't have to watch her die.

My Aemiins remain asleep. The entire area sits in silence. I whisper to myself to make sure the dream is gone. I can't speak in my dreams, but I can here.

Time passes differently with the sun hidden, but I can feel its warmth fighting the clouds. Wiggling my body free from the teg, I take out the device that Diask meant for the Tatem. My Lamis fills the small power coils that line the inside, bringing life to the device.

The numbers still don't make any sense at my initial glance. Beyond the titles, what should be descriptions or details are numbers. They make less sense than the others. Why would Diask entrust this device to me if it's entirely useless? Did he expect me to know what this information says?

When I'm about to give up, a sequence of numbers stings with familiarity. The answer becomes obvious. Every number is a reference to the Tatem handbook. The book updates every cycle, so the numbers change. I'm staring at the entry for a simple house light. The words and descriptions are missing. How did Diask know I would have the handbook memorized? He didn't know me long enough to have time to put this collection of information together.

Diask uses references from at least five different versions of the Tatem handbook. I expect specific Tech unique to my place in the storm, but he includes household items and transports. He uses a five-cycle-old reference to an arvos, even though the computer interface is nearly unrecognizable this sol from its older counterpart.

Not every number comes to mind, but most do. The last two files on the device hold no recognition in my mind. To say I have the entire handbook memorized is an exaggeration, but the numbers don't even tug at my deepest memories. When I press on the bottom file, rather than numbers within, a random assortment of letters appear. Before I can begin to decipher them, noises spread across the camp.

I turn the device off and slide back into the teg. The Twins and Cramen eventually wake up, releasing themselves from their tegs. I wait a minute and do the same.

Erman looks at me as he rolls up his bed. "How much did you sleep this time?"

I pat my bed down as I secure the straps. "About as much as you. Woke up a few minutes ago."

Cramen lets his teg hit the ground. "Liar."

Safon finishes securing his bed and stands up. "We didn't press you on what you kept from us. We won't with Persolus about this. When he's ready, he'll tell us what's bothering him. For now, he only needs to fulfill his duty."

I refrain from thanking him out loud. Safon is too smart not to recognize my constant exhaustion. Still, he shows no doubt in my abilities. What did Soriina tell him?

To avoid the stares of Cramen, I dig my anro out of my backpack and access the communication feature. The method is simplistic and time consuming. My fingers double click and miss letters on the holographic screen, but the network works off an emergency system that uses practically no Lamis. Safe communication for underneath the storm.

Multiple messages from Seni flash, indicating I haven't read them yet. He's sent at least one message per sol, but usually more. He keeps me up to date with everything happening in his sector. He's been able to check nearly half the generators in his sector, but he has far fewer to visit. He's found no anomalies with any of the systems. His brother is his only Aemiin, according to his last message. The other two are choosing to ignore their duties, as are most of the other boys in his sector.

"Not just us."

"What was that, Persolus?"

I keep my eyes on my anro. "Seni is having troubles with the boys in his sector too. Looks like most of the Datum is neglecting their duties."

"If we're the Council's power, as Cramen suggests, I say we should be worried."

Safon's words rest in the air, no one wanting to further the conversation. He's right. As a reflection of the Council, we're failing. I only hope their power transcends our inability.

I return my gaze to my anro. The other three are inconsistent with their reports. They only send messages when I do. I activate the holographic input screen and prepare a response to Seni before inquiring about the status of the others.

> *Edwin and Cade are still acting reckless. Won't allow us any weapons when we go out. The storm constantly reminds us of its presence yet they refuse to acknowledge the danger. I fear these beasts the Council warned us about may prove to be our undoing.*

I fumble over the words, rewriting the message several times before sending it. Seni responds promptly. His message flashes before I press on it.

> *Rumors here are that the Esidio guards killed or drove off the beasts living among the hillsides. It's given some false sense of security.*

> *I have talked with some of the boys and their parents told them our presence here is symbolic. The eyes of the future generation of Alfarons watching over the city. The other Tech leaders have confirmed what I have learned.*

I scroll through the message and pause at this last sentence. I didn't realize he was in communication with the others. Have they been communicating with him rather than me? Seni wouldn't intentionally try to undermine me . . . would he? I want to ask him about the device Vitus gave me, but I decide not to. I'll discover its purpose without him and use that to leverage the others to me.

My obsession with this realization creates enough of a delay that Seni sends another message.

> *I convinced one patrol to go with me to check generators. They were un-certain but they thought they saw beast signs. As my previous message states they do not believe such a thing is possible. They told the others what we saw were the signs of a Sofera. I think I can trust you will see the same truth I do. I doubt your leaders will listen but it may be dangerous not to warn them.*

> *I have to leave to check a generator but I believe we are in a calm that will not last. One of your last messages said Cramen had yet to join you. Keep Safon and Erman close.*

I keep my next message short to make my response quick, updating him on Cramen's arrival and promising to warn the others about the beasts. I omit my doubt that anyone will listen to me. I send the message and lower my anro, rubbing my eyes as the holographic screen retracts.

Without a word, I pick up my backpack and walk across to where our rotams are. The Twins glance at me as I move but say nothing. They know I won't leave the area without them. They sense the trust I have in them, and I don't expect them to read my mind. When I intend to enter the sector again, there will be no doubt in their minds.

I toss my backpack to the ground and remove the side panel of the nearest rotam. The slight vibration I felt on the ride earlier struck my curiosity. Shining my velare inside the frame, I immediately recognize blue tubes extending from an unfamiliar piece of Tech. The tubes appear to be transporting lamis, but I've never seen a generator so small.

"What are you doing?"

My body jerks at the words. I redirect my velare to reveal Cramen standing a few feet away.

"Tech stuff," I tell him.

"Just because you're in charge of the Tech doesn't mean others can't understand it."

I hold a stare as the storm ignites overhead. We both keep our attention on the colors, waiting for some sign of the storm's destructive nature. It never comes.

"Fine," I say. "There's some sort of generator in the rotams. I imagine it's taking some of the pressure off us as we pedal the vehicles forward."

"When it runs out of power, will these things be useless?"

"I don't think so," I say, moving my velare around to inspect each tube. I stop the light on a vent. "It reminds me of old Tech that draws in residual lamis. Back when efficiency percentages were far lower than now, this type of generator could utilize the lamis seeping out of other Tech. It's not too unlike the haur ports in Tech that draw Lamis from our bodies."

"But the city has no lamis."

I reach my hand in and touch the tubes. "There's always residual lamis. It's a natural part of our world. Even the Sorbe produces lamis. There's good reason it's attracted to the energy."

"Why are you messing with it?"

I let a breath out of my nose as I choose my next words. "My anro's range is insufficient. I can barely connect to the generators' interfaces within buildings. There's too great of a risk to enter buildings that may contain heavy concentrations of lamis. Even opening a door could cause the storm to strike." I pause, pulling saliva off the inside of my mouth. "If I can connect the rotam's power source, I may be able to boost the anro's range and may even access additional features."

The inhibitor prevents my body from providing more power to the anro but shouldn't impede the rotam's power. I don't tell Cramen this.

"Seems like something Diask would have thought of," Cramen says.

The image of the storm taking the Tatem's life flashes in my mind. I squeeze my eyes shut. Doubt still creeps around the edges of why he chose me. Seni's message tells me even he doesn't understand. He knows the others better than I ever could. He's the proper choice, not me.

Cramen sits down to watch. "Don't break it."

I pull my anro out and remove the backing. The device has a control chip that regulates the power and, if designed to standard specs, a back-up. I smile when my fingers locate the backup, then I look at Cramen. "If you're going to hang around, could you shine your light here?"

After a few seconds, he shines his light onto the control chip. Removing a few instruments from my backpack, I start adjusting the back-up. The tools only help me interact with the knobs and switches that are far too small for my fingers. I can't be sure of its efficiency, but with a few adjustments, this control chip should send the part of the lamis the rotam collects to my anro. With no regulator, I have to be cautious with the power output. Too much and my anro will overload and become useless. Something else I don't tell Cramen.

"That's a lot of tinkering," Cramen says. "You sure you're not compromising either piece of Tech?"

"Won't find out until I test it, I suppose."

"Is that supposed to be a joke?"

I sigh. "I know what I'm doing, Cramen. These two chips communicate with each other. It controls the energy flow. All I've done is tell the chip I'm putting in the rotam to send energy to the chip in my anro."

"Is that all?"

I grab his light with it still in his hand and move it to shine into the rotam. The generator—if that's even the appropriate term—is simple, but still has an empty port for redundancy. I attach the new chip and watch it glow blue.

"Why did you follow me, Cramen? Surely you knew I wasn't leaving the area. And I know it wasn't your interest in Tech."

"Safon and Erman started talking to those other two boys," Cramen says. "Not a conversation I wanted to be a part of, so I left."

"What were they talking about?"

"I didn't want to be a part of it," he says, "so I didn't stick around to listen."

Edwin and Cade talking to the Twins doesn't instill confidence. Are they trying to turn Safon and Erman to their cause? Safon trusts me. He knows the danger the storm possesses.

"Let's go join that conversation."

"You think they're trying to undermine your authority?"

"Or talking about their future Eteros," I say, forcing a half-smile. "Anything's possible with those two."

Cramen doesn't encourage any further conversation as we head back toward the center of the encampment. A single free-standing velare illuminates the area. The boys have various containers and extra pieces of the wall setup to act as furniture, which they lie across or sit on. Some boys jump across small gaps while others encourage them to jump bigger voids.

The Twins and the other two are easy to find. They're quite a ways away from the other boys. A jumble of words reaches me that stops when a trio of lights shines in my direction.

"Don't stop talking on my account," I say.

Edwin steps away from the group. "I think we've reached a point where we need you to join."

I look at Safon, though he may be Erman. The shadows make it difficult, not that I can tell them apart without their assistance. "What's going on here?"

"Persolus, I'm sorry. We should have talked to you first."

"That doesn't answer my question."

"We're discussing your involvement out here," Edwin says. Accusation laces his words.

Cade shines his light in my face. "And Diask's attempt to destroy us all."

Words fail me. I must have misheard him.

"Did you know?" Edwin asks.

"Know what? If you weren't aware, I just showed up. And you're just talking nonsense."

"You saw Diask on the roof," Edwin says. "Did you know he was going to blow up the Linam?"

"That was the storm," I say, my glance moving across each boy. "You think . . . what? Diask used the storm? He was controlling it?"

Edwin scoffs. "You know the limits of Tech are unknown. You think he couldn't control the storm? Why hasn't it struck more?"

"He saved my life." I can barely get the words out. My heart pounds. "He sacrificed his life to save us. His design kept us safe from the storm."

"No one thought the People's Representative was going to betray the Council," Cade says. "Why not the Tatem as well?"

I look at the Twins. "You both believe this?"

"I don't know what to believe, Persolus. The storm hasn't struck since he took you to the roof. And the storm destroyed his implant, along with any memories incriminating him. Can it all really be coincidence?"

"Anyone else and I wouldn't believe it for a second," Erman says. "But Diask knew Tech better than anyone. You said he had some device. Why not a device to tell the storm where to strike? The storm is the perfect way to die without your memories entering the Record."

"Do you realize how you sound right now? If he wanted to destroy us, why not leave a weakness in the Linam's design? The Sorbe would have wiped us out with no trace back to him."

"We're just trying to make sense of the situation, Zayne."

"That's not what you're doing," I say. "You're adding confusion because"—I jab my finger at Edwin and Cade—"*they* don't trust the Council's plan. They should be out there keeping beasts from endangering the city. All it will take is one beast finding its way into a building and the storm will do the rest."

"Says the son of a Council Representative," Cade says. "What are you even doing out here to begin with? Your father lacked the authority to exempt you from service?"

His meaning is clear despite his refusal to say it outright. My place isn't out here. That's what the Council thought. I can't tell the boys I chose to enter the storm. Not after Diask played a part in convincing the Council to allow me. The lies they'll twist that into could be endless. Dangerous.

"Persolus, even you know the Council's plan develops beyond our perspective. We are only trying to understand what other things may be happening out here. You must understand that."

"And why are you concerned with that? If you believe those two, then the storm isn't a threat. We're not out here to make a difference."

"Zayne, we only want to understand. Edwin and Cade bring up valid points."

"Valid points? They are undermining the Council's attempt to protect the city. Seni said they found beast signs in Sector Two. We don't know what gradulas or caros could be doing, because they haven't sent anyone out to check. I'm here to protect this city. You're only here because you have to be."

Edwin scoffs. "I told you. He's only here to spy on us, make sure we fall in line with the Council's orders. You said it, Safon. He wasn't on the list of boys chosen to serve. They sent him out here."

I stare at Safon. He feeds the doubts of Edwin and Cade. I want to lash out at him, but can't bring myself to form the words. My skin barely contains the beating of my heart.

Edwin grins, and the storm flashes. "Why don't you go tell your father we aren't believing all these lies they're feeding us?"

I step closer as my heart tries to escape my chest. "If I'm here as an extension of the Council, you will be better off fulfilling your duty. You may not be scared of the Council now. But when this storm passes, you are still Vox. You will be subject to their will."

Despite my intention, my words don't affect either Edwin or Cade as I expect.

They fill the darkness with unsettling laughs. "If that's a threat, you'll have to do better than that. We're leaving this city the first chance we have. Beyond where the Council's power extends."

"If you leave the city alive."

The words slip out, leaving me and the others standing in silence. I hold my mouth closed, hoping no one notices my breathing increasing. I don't mean it as a threat but rather a warning about the storm, but with Edwin and Cade's conspiracies, I realize a threat is how it sounds.

Then to make things worse, I walk away.

An Interruption

"The newest models of transport aid the operators by using a secondary power source that takes over seventy percent of the power load off the operator. Despite the innovation, the design often leaves trails of energy that attract various beasts."—an excerpt from a study on volants and veheres, transports of the future

Against reason and what I know to be right, I distance myself from my Aemiins and even Cramen over the next two sols. He didn't add to the attack, but his silence condemns him. I even enter the sector without telling anyone. What choice do I have? The Twins chose Edwin and Cade's outlandish claims over me and fed into their lies. How can I trust them?

I don't believe them, but my mind won't stop going over every word. Can Tech influence a storm? Is that what Diask did on the roof? Did he plan to die by the storm so his implant wouldn't be entered into the Historical Record? Was he protecting us or trying to destroy us? Without answers to those questions, how can I make sense of why Diask wanted me to serve?

I press my hands into my eyes. Exhaustion sweeps over me. Dreamless sleep has met me at the end of the past two sols, but I've woken with even greater exhaustion.

My anro beeps, helping me focus. Seni tries to speak reason into the situation.

> *You need to stop avoiding the Twins. Those who reject the authority of the Council easily deceive others. We do not understand everything that is happening around us. That allows for this deception. You need to be the one to speak the truth you know.*

> *If you lose the Twins how can you expect to fulfill your duties?*

I read his message from on top of my rotam. Understanding the vehicle more fully, I am able to traverse the sector quickly without overexerting myself. Glimmers of blue surround the rotam that I never noticed before. The color lingers in the air for a few seconds before fading when I stop.

A flash of light streaks across the sky, illuminating the open transport path in front of me. Tall, windowless buildings silhouette against the sky before disappearing back into the darkness.

As I focus on my anro, the shadows close in.

> *You keep messaging me but you ignore the accusation they made of Diask. How can I trust them? Diask chose me for this. If they feel he is a traitor why will they listen to me?*

As I send the message, a chill sweeps across my body. The storm flashes, causing me to jerk. My anro drops from my hand and hits the ground. I swing my leg off the rotam and monitor the shadows as I grab the device. The outer casing is scuffed, but that appears to be the extent of the damage.

I drop to one knee and take in several deep breaths. "What are you doing, Zayne? You shouldn't be out here by yourself."

I shift my backpack to put my anro in the safety of one of its pockets when the device chirps.

Storm activity is increasing. You need to be out in the sector checking on the generators. We have not seen the storm's core yet. Tech acts strange under Sorbes. This is why we are out here.

I stare at the message for a few minutes, unable to come up with a response. I open up the holographic input screen, but it flickers several times before disappearing. I press the physical button to reactivate it. I have to press three times for the screen to come back up.

"That's perfect. Damage one of the most important pieces of Tech I have."

A chirp comes from my anro. A new message appears underneath Seni's name, but it isn't flashing. I press his name, and it's his shortest message.

Send messages to the others. They need to hear from you.

It's abrupt, but he's right. I quickly write a uniform message to Ocen, Soma, and Talpa. They often respond within a few minutes, but I receive nothing after almost twenty minutes. They also haven't heard from me since the incident with Edwin and Cade, so I switch my anro to the scanner mode as I await their responses.

With energy flowing through my rotam, my anro takes some of that power, and the range of the scanner nearly triples. The holographic screen jolts up with three red dots blinking. I press the closest icon, and the details appear in small text. **Class Six Lamis Generator. Status: Active.**

"That's not possible."

I press the other two dots and both indicate active generators.

"No . . . no, no. This can't be happening."

I look up in the direction of the closest signal. A towering industrial building houses the device my anro detects. Nothing about its appearance suggests power flowing through its conduits. I look back toward the Sector Center. I don't have time to go back for help.

I send a quick message to Seni detailing the situation.

I should wait for his response, but instead, I leave my rotam and approach the building. I pay attention to my feet as I draw closer. A class six generator has a notable vibration, but I feel nothing. My anro still shows activity, but no power levels.

The screen of my anro flickers, and the darkness around me flees. I look up as a bolt of light streaks across the sky. It strikes the building. The metal exterior offers no resistance to the storm's wrath. A second feels like a minute as I watch the building explode. A fraction of a second passes before a rush of air hits me, and I throw up my arms in front of my face. My feet lose contact with the ground. Multiple objects strike me in the chest and arms. My back slams hard into the ground.

I roll several times before coming to a stop. I gasp for air, but nothing enters my lungs. My limbs have no strength as I roll onto my back. My chest heaves. My perception of time wavers. Minutes or hours pass, I can't tell before I feel the air reach my lungs. A tingling sensation across my body tells me my Lamis works hard to reinvigorate me. A surge of energy propels me to my feet.

Chunks of metal crash around me, launching fragments at me. As I scramble away, a sharp pain erupts in the back of my head. I collapse to my knees. I hear a metal screech before something heavy drops on my back. Burning metal stings my nose.

I try to push up, but it's too heavy. Pain sweeps over my body. My Lamis is unable to stay the agony. I can't see the storm, but multiple bright flashes fill my vision. Metal shrieks in the distance and close enough where I feel the ground shake.

Darkness permeates my vision. My focus wavers, my conscious state fading quickly. Sounds of the city's destruction fill my ears. A tingling sensation sweeps across my body, but rather than remain, it fades, and nothing replaces it. My mind is all that I know is real. I have no body anymore. Is this how it feels when the storm strikes you?

As my vision goes black, I lose a sense of everything until a voice fills the void. Words are distant, but it grounds me as I lose consciousness.

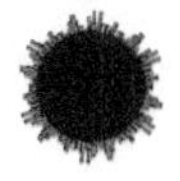

"Zayne!"

My spoken name breaks the darkness's hold on me. My eyes open to see the clouds swirling with color. I move my gaze lower to see Erman. He's holding a fragment of metal in his hand. He lets it crash to the ground when he realizes I'm awake.

"Zayne! I thought . . . you're fine."

The thought of their betrayal starts to rise, but I shove it down. A wave of exhaustion replaces the feeling. "Where's your brother?"

Erman grabs my hand and helps me to a sitting position. "He's checking the building. We thought maybe . . . maybe you took shelter there."

"And Cramen?"

"He convinced Safon to let him check another part of the sector. He's been gone several hours."

"Several hours?" I ask.

My mind races to answer my own question before Erman can.

"It's been almost a sol since the storm struck," Erman says. "About twenty-seven hours, to be exact. The Sorbe went on for nearly four hours before the colors stopped and we risked coming to find you."

"You've been out here this entire time . . . looking for me?"

"Don't think you can storm off and we're just going to disregard our promise to Soriina." He smirks. "Not to say we didn't take a few breaks. Edwin and Cade wanted us to consider you dead and give up."

"And how did you convince them to continue searching?"

"They let us come out here because they thought the Council would want your body," Erman says. The idea permeates the air before he continues. "They think the encampment is the safest place. They aren't letting anyone else leave."

"We need to find your brother."

"Hold on, Zayne. You almost died. Give your body a second to rest."

"We don't have time to rest," I say.

I can feel my Lamis strengthening me, but it comes in waves, leaving me with moments of pain. I can feel where the metal pressed into my chest. None of that matters when there are active generators in the city. This destruction is only the beginning.

"Why? For the sake of the Council, speak your mind and stop keeping it all inside."

I stand up. Soreness erupts in my joints, but I ignore the feeling and limp past Erman. "The storm's strike wasn't random. It struck a generator here, and possibly two others. We're all fortunate to be alive, not just me."

"The generators were shut down. Weren't they? The fact the city still stands is evidence the Council's plan—Diask's preparation—is working."

"We need to find your brother."

"Persolus, I'm right here," Safon says, emerging from a dense shadow. "Now answer my brother's question."

A few seconds pass in silence as I adjust to Safon's presence. He stands differently. I don't expect a joke, and not because he sided with Edwin and Cade.

"They were supposed to shut down," I say. "They should have been, but my anro picked up three active signals. And the fact there was no chain reaction to the deposit below is . . . is just pure chance."

"Your anro was barely able to pick up a single generator before," Safon says. "How is it suddenly able to pick up three? I don't know much about power systems, but generators aren't usually set up in sets of three."

"They aren't. These were three separate generators, which is the greater concern. A lone generator could be an anomaly, but three generators in separate locations—"

"That doesn't answer my first question. How is your anro able to detect three generators so separate from each other?"

Why does he ignore our previous interaction? Does he expect me to forget it all after the storm's attack?

"I didn't fully understand my anro," I say. "Better understanding now is giving better results."

He doesn't believe me. Doubts swirl in him. The storm's recent activity has given him a different perspective. But I don't need him worrying about my decisions. Not when Edwin and Cade are influencing him.

"We need to warn the others. Things are going to get worse if there are other generators active." I look at Erman. "Diask's plan requires inactive generators. Not active ones."

Erman steps closer and peers at his brother before speaking to me. "Zayne, about what happened back at the encampment. I'm not going to lie. Neither Safon nor myself knows what to think about Diask. But we don't think you're here spying on us for the Council, or—if Diask is responsible—you're in cahoots with him and hold any responsibility. We didn't mean to feed into Edwin's and Cade's theories."

I look at Safon. The seriousness of his presence is his way of seeking forgiveness. I appreciate Erman's more direct approach, but that isn't my concern now. "Active generators should be our focus right now. We shouldn't worry about anything else."

Safon extends his arm toward me. "Persolus, what my brother means beyond our apology is that if what you say is true, Edwin and Cade are going to use it against you. Diask oversaw the shutdown of the generators. If they're coming back online, that only strengthens their theories."

"They will use this to instill deeper doubts in the others," Erman says. "Not us. Please be assured of that."

"You want me to keep this information from them?"

"Do you think they will handle the news differently?" Safon asks. "They will change their minds and help?"

I let my shoulders drop, not realizing how tense my posture is. "No, I don't think they will help. They will turn this against the Council and still choose to do nothing."

Safon takes a noticeably deep breath in. "We have to face the reality that we're facing this storm on our own."

"But we're not just facing the storm," Erman says. "If someone is turning generators on, we're facing two threats."

I slowly shake my head. "The storm is the only threat we face. No adult is stupid enough to come out here and activate a generator. This was put in place before the shutdown. They're trying to weaponize the storm."

"Are we sure this isn't Diask's doing?"

Diask's last words surface in my mind. *Forgive me, for I let my fear direct my steps.*

Did regret lace those words? Did he compromise the city? Was his action a self-inflicted punishment? Did he mean to kill us on the roof to ensure the city's destruction? He regretted his choice when he saw the storm.

"It doesn't matter," I say. "We know what we have to do."

"No, I think my brother has a point, Persolus."

I look at Safon, trying to discern his next words.

"If Diask is responsible, we can't trust anything he said. You can't trust anything he said or even that device you have from him."

"We can't know either way for certain. If I choose to ignore his words, I could be—" A shadow moves behind the Twins. "Did you see that?"

The Twins turn around, flooding the darkness with light from their velares.

"There was something in the shadows."

Erman turns to me. "Are you sure? I just found you buried in rubble. You can't be thinking straight or seeing clearly."

I can feel my Lamis struggling to sustain my strength, but my eyes didn't deceive me. "I'm fine. I know I saw something."

"We need to leave then," Safon says.

"Where are the rotams?"

"Not far—"

Safon flies off his feet as a shadow darts between us. A rush of air brushes my face. As I try to follow whatever hit my Aemiin, something slams into the back of my legs. I fall backward. My body lands on something soft before I twist and hit the ground. I look up to face snarling teeth.

A New Night

"Though Sorbes have never been witnessed to kill beasts, the creatures flee storms, seeking shelter in buildings or underground cave systems. Do these storms present a threat beyond our comprehension?"—an excerpt from an Alfaron study on the Triones storm patterns

A flash of blue blinds me. The screech of a beast fills my ears. When my vision returns, I see Safon with an outstretched arm. He holds a small device that covers his hand with a dome extending from the top. A blue shimmer fades as he lowers his hand.

"Is everyone alright?"

"Look!" Erman's single word rips through the air.

The storm ignites overhead, casting its light on hundreds of animals sprinting toward us. They seem to move effortlessly across the debris covering the transport path. I don't have time to identify each one, but dozens of different species descend upon us. Mainly smaller creatures, but a few larger ones are intermingled.

A hand grabs my arm and pulls me behind a large piece of rubble.

Safon turns me to face him. "Are you serious? When you see a mass of beasts, you run or hide. Don't stand around and take in the sight." He lets go of my arm and turns to his brother. "Erman, use your actare with me. Scare a few of them, and they should go around us."

Flashes of blue exit the Twins' weapons. The animals dart around us, moving farther into the city. Streaks of light move across the bottom of the clouds. Fearful screeches fill the air. I look up and see a winged figure swoop down into the mass of fleeing bodies. A cry of pain is cut short as the predator carries off its meal.

Pennas. The name encompasses all the flying animals that inhabit Solisternum. Few pennas fall into the family of caros, and only those would fly during a Sorbe. They don't fear the storm but are using it as a hunting opportunity. I only hope they don't see us as prey.

A small animal with a long, hairy snout stops next to us. Its small eyes are perfect for the constant sun that bombards the hillsides. But now in the storm's shadow, it struggles to adapt. I don't recognize the species, but I know most gradulas burrow into the ground during the darkness that follows the sunset. The storm's unnatural presence this far into the land disrupts everything.

"Zayne!"

Someone pulls me back as a four-legged caro pounces on the small gradula, ending its life in its jaws. The Twins don't fire as the animal snorts at us before disappearing into the shadows to enjoy its meal.

"They're using the city to trap their prey," I say.

Safon lowers his actare as only a few lingering creatures remain.

"I think that proves there are still beasts around," Erman says.

"That only complicates things," Safon says. "I was hoping Edwin and Cade were at least right about that."

I stand up and peer over the rubble. "We should find Cramen and—"

A streak of light erupts out of the clouds and strikes a pile of metal scrap. Safon yanks me down as a rush of air sweeps over top of us. Debris ricochets around us.

When I reach for my anro, I can't find it. By the time I return my gaze to the sky, the Sorbe comes alive with color. A bolt of light streaks across the clouds before slamming into a tall, slender building to our right. Metal creaks as the structure shifts, sending hunks of wreckage crashing into the ground. The bottom supports at corners snap with a metallic crack. What remains of the upper portion leans toward us.

"The building. Safon! The building!"

Erman's voice strikes fear into my body, paralyzing me. The Sorbe lashes out again. The building moans.

Safon grabs my arm with a painful grip. "We're leaving. Now move!"

He half drags me toward the other side of the transport path. I look back as the building topples over. It crashes into the ground, sending a cloud filled with debris toward us.

Erman screams yet is barely audible above the destruction. "Safon! The alley!"

His brother barely glances back before diving into an alleyway. He lets me go at the last moment. The edge of the cloud catches my shoulder and lifts me off my feet. I slam into the wall of the alley. I drop nearly five feet to the ground where the air exits my lungs all at once. I roll onto my back and let out a dry heave.

The air is heavy, and dust and debris surround us. I can hear the Twins coughing. They come up to me and help me into a seated position. My eyes sting, so I keep them closed. I feel hands on both my arms, lifting me up. My body resists, still sore from my first—no, sec-ond—near-death experience.

"Stop here," I manage to say. "The air feels better."

The Twins lean me against a wall, and I allow myself to slide down. I wipe what feels like dirt from my eyes before opening them to darkness. The storm is quiet, and the two buildings on either side darken the shadows.

"Zayne, are you injured?"

I run my hands around my body. I find sore spots but no open wounds. "Felt better, but I'll be fine. Remind me to find the designer of these clothes. They can take quite the beating. School uniforms ripped under far less stress."

"We have far bigger things to worry about," Safon says. "We need to get back to the others. Maybe Edwin and Cade will listen to reason when they learn everything they've believed is wrong."

"Why does that seem unlikely?"

Safon shakes his head. "They have to."

I force myself to stand up. "They gave you weapons. Doesn't that show some change?"

Erman sighs. "We stole them."

"So we're walking into an angry Edwin and Cade."

"Or they may be fearful." Cramen's voice exits the shadows. His body makes an appearance a few seconds later. "They must have heard the storm. A stray beast must have jumped the wall."

"Thanks for joining us," Safon says. "Find anything out there?"

He points to me. "I only sought to search for Zayne in other places. We were far more likely to find him if we split up."

I close the space between Cramen and me. "Did the storm strike anywhere else?"

Cramen slowly shakes his head. "I don't believe so. I heard the storm and saw activity in the clouds near this location. I noticed nothing in other directions."

"I don't know what you're getting at, Persolus, but we need to return now. There are caros lurking about."

Safon walks in the direction Cramen came from without another word. His silence forces us to follow him. I don't know if I should forgive the Twins so easily, but they are all I have out here. Despite his choice to side with Edwin and Cade, even if for a short time, I trust Safon's leadership. His willingness to lead allows me more space to focus on the Tech. The storm just showed me that my presence is necessary.

Erman walks up next to me and hands me my backpack. "Missing something? I put that anro-thing in there. It's scuffed up but seems to have survived."

My words stall in my mouth to thank him as he increases his pace to catch up to his brother. I can sense the shame in him about his actions.

Safon leads us to where their rotams are. The decision to leave the vehicles away from where they found me protected them. Mine lies in the rubble somewhere. With only three of the four, Erman rides on the back of his brother's rotam, giving me his.

The pace Safon leads us in is intense. Even understanding the relief the generator gives, my legs burn from pedaling. I don't say anything. Our velares do little to push back the shadow we move through. The blue hue from our rotams fades fast into the darkness. Seni mentioned the core of the storm not being here yet. I fear we haven't seen the worst of this Sorbe.

"Beasts lurk in the shadows," Cramen calls above the noise of the rotams.

"Keep going, we're almost there," Safon says.

Cramen knows that. The animals are close to the encampment.

We slow down as we near the wall. Safon hops off his rotam and slams his fist on the gate. To some surprise, the gate opens. Two boys appear, flashing velares in our faces.

Safon steps past them. "Where is Edwin?"

They point toward the center, where we now see a flurry of activity. The single stationary velare remains in the center, providing minimal light. We remain in dark shadow. Before we can approach the center, two silhouettes break away from a group and head toward us. Edwin and Cade.

Safon doesn't wait and walks to meet them. Our paths collide close to the main source of the activity. With a closer view, the boys are in a flurry of movement, shifting the containers once used as furniture. They appear to be making a secondary wall.

"What's the commotion about?" I ask.

Edwin ignores me and points a finger at Safon. "You stole actares. Everything that leaves this camp goes through us. There are no—"

"Shut it, Edwin," Safon says, causing the co-leader's eyes to widen. "I need your patrols out in the sector now."

Edwin shifts his weight back, glancing at Cade before stepping into Safon. Their chests nearly touch. "You're a Aemiin for the Tech Boy. That's all. You aren't anything special. Now return the weapons."

"Didn't you hear the storm? It destroyed part of the sector," I say, trying to pull them apart with words.

He looks past the twin to me. "Yes. And that's your problem. Not mine."

"And there are animals in the city. Hundreds."

"Not possible."

"Will you stop and think for yourself, just for a minute? We saw them. If you would only send out one patrol, you would see for yourself. Or are you afraid to be wrong?"

Cramen steps next to Safon. "The rumors were wrong. Beasts lurk in the shadows just outside this camp. The storm pushes them into the city. You have to act."

The three boys are far closer than I like. Anger permeates every word.

"This only proves the Council's inadequacies," Cade says. "They were the ones spreading the rumors that the beasts had been wiped out from the hillsides. They couldn't do anything—"

A fist from Cramen lands on Cade's face. Cramen kicks in the side of his knee, putting him on the ground in a wail of pain.

Within that violent moment, Edwin shoves Safon in the chest, knocking him off balance. Erman retaliates. His right hand swings around on Edwin's face. Edwin doesn't react in time; he stumbles, hand reaching for his face. Erman trips him, and Edwin cries in pain as he hits the ground with a thud.

All the while, my legs lock. Everything happens quickly. Whatever order the Council intended has broken apart. We're operating in chaos. I can only watch.

Safon gestures for Erman and Cramen to step back. "Enough. Persolus's word is the ruling authority here. At his word, you will do your duty to this city."

The tension remains. I don't imagine it lessening soon. But the threat of violence seems to have passed. If not only for the superiority of my Aemiins, which I now realize surprises me. I should feel safer, but a fear lurks in my thoughts.

Edwin and Cade rise to their feet, rubbing their injuries. Everyone looks at me. Safon is the far more capable leader here, but he's right to turn everyone's attention to me. He only has authority because I allow him to lead us. I can feel the blood in my neck throbbing, trying to escape. I keep my mouth shut to hide my abnormal breathing. Safon steps toward me, and as he does, the other two take it as a reason to do the same.

I take a deep breath. "The beasts are a present danger to our sector. Not only are they a threat to us, but they could threaten the stability of the lamis seals on the buildings. If a single beast breaches a building with a significant concentration of lamis, the storm will not hesitate to unleash its wrath."

Edwin shifts toward me, which causes Safon to step forward. "You are making that up. As long as we stay here, any *potential* beasts can't hurt us. And you have your Aemiins to protect you out there. The storm is out there. Why should I risk everyone else on pointless patrols to find beasts? Beasts you can't prove exist. We haven't seen or heard any. You're making things up to force us to do what you want. I'm not out here to listen to some lamis-sucking Council lover."

If the Council could see my memories now. See who they left in charge of their precious city. I only hope to survive to understand why.

Between the short-lived fight and Edwin's long-winded response, the other boys begin to gather. They aren't here to observe but to engage. A flurry of questions and other remarks bombard us.

"Was that the storm we heard?"

"Are there beasts in the city?"

"No, the Agmen killed them all."

"Are they caro or gradu?"

"The ground shook. That wasn't beasts."

"What do we do?"

"Enough!" Edwin says, his poise breaking. "Return to your duties. Cade and I will address your concerns later."

Many of the boys appear to want to continue with their questions, but they don't have the resolve to challenge their leader. But whatever feelings they have aren't enough to disperse them. They remain silent, probably because they have no duties to return to.

Edwin moves close to me. I push my arm out to stop Safon from intervening. He speaks so no one else can hear. "Undermine my leadership again, and I will make sure you don't come back through that gate. You can protect the city well enough out there without returning here."

The back of my head stings. I flinch. Edwin steps back with a smile. I look up as colors race across the clouds. No destruction. The Sorbe only chooses to remind us of its presence. I bring my gaze down and step toward Edwin, causing him to lose his balance.

"Send out your patrols. Or I will." I can sense some rebuttal, but without considering my words, I speak. "I don't need either of you. My Aemiins can direct the boys. Your presence here is a nuisance at best. If you don't want to do your duty, I will put you out into the city and you can remain there until the storm passes."

If I could exit my body and look into my eyes, I don't think I would recognize myself. Edwin doesn't. He steps away and looks at Cade, who is looking up at the storm. He is not the only one. Everyone is. The storm's constant presence has the sky lit up, but that isn't what's drawing everyone's attention.

Something else is in the clouds. Pennas soar beneath them. They pass over the square and go out farther into the city. A few larger ones draw my attention that I suspect are caros. They fly slower. They're hunting. A sweeping murmur fills the area as the boys watch the scene unfold.

Edwin and Cade yell at the boys, dispersing the crowd, trying to retain any authority they may have with the others.

Erman steps next to me. "They must cooperate now . . . right?"

"The others may force their hand," Safon says. "A sky full of penna beasts should be proof enough. They never fly over the city." He looks at me. "I didn't think you had that in you."

"Give credit to the storm. I don't think Edwin was going to listen."

"Those two will never listen," Cramen says. "The Council makes few mistakes, and those are two of them. The influence of traitorous parents. A failure of their education. They only know what their parents say. We have extensions of adults who don't trust their leaders out here with us."

Erman rubs his knuckles. "You sound almost as if you are working for the Council as those two accused Zayne of."

"We are all working for the Council," he says. "What form that takes varies."

I turn toward Cramen. He has some connection to the Council that is closer than mine. He isn't the son of a Representative. And the actual Members don't have families. Whatever connection he has, it doesn't exempt him from the danger of the storm. How different are we, then?

"Yes, we are," Safon says. "But not in the same way as you. You struck at Cade for his comment about the Council. Not an attack on Persolus or personal insult."

"Is this a conversation we should have with beasts overhead?" Cramen asks.

"You grew up in favor," Erman says. "I can tell that much. Never wondering if the Council would reject your parents' visas at the end of each cycle. Yet watching them stay when given the opportunity to leave. I guess that's the illusion of this city. Everyone thinks this is the best our Nation has to offer. But it's worse with you."

"My loyalty to my leaders is not a fault. You could learn from your parents' choice to remain here."

"Persolus's disconnect with us from lesser sectors is obvious, but what about you? He would know you if you were from Sector Two. Where did you grow up in the city? How close are you to the Council that they hold such loyalty from you at your age?"

I look at Safon, and his words sting. Does he hold where I live against me? My upbringing. Everything I have no control over. Yet I have chosen a path that has me remaining in the city. A city I feel he wants to flee, not because the law dictates, but because he wants to? Yet he seems eager and willing to be my Aemiin.

Soriina has something to do with this. Did she convince them to tolerate me? To act in my favor despite feelings that urge them otherwise? Is that why Edwin and Cade were able to turn them against me?

She's also from Sector Two. What makes me different? My father. They only see my father's connection to the Council. Or does she share more similarities with the Twins than I know? Why would she not tell me about the Twins' mistrust of the Council? Or was it my own ignorance of those not her? My singular focus, my desire to understand the man who engenders their distrust of me, blinded me to everything else.

My eyes shift from my Aemiins to the sky. This all seems important until I see the storm. This squabbling is a temporary escape from the real problems we face. Why Cramen trusts the Council, or why Edwin despises our leaders, or even why the Twins trust me—when facing the Sorbe, none of it matters. If I were ignorant, I might claim the storm was affecting our minds, drawing us into conflict.

It waits above us.

Waiting to strike.

"Stop prying, you two," Cramen says, drawing me back to their conversation. "Being Zayne's Aemiins doesn't grant you access to my life. My presence here doesn't mean I'm trying to make friends. We go our separate ways after—"

My anro beeps from inside my backpack, but before I can look at it, the flashes of the storm stop. Darkness falls over the area. A stillness sweeps across the encampment.

A voice cries out, breaking the silence.

"Beasts!"

Dream Theory

"Dreams are how we communicate with ourselves." —an excerpt from a joint-faction study on sleep

When I want the storm to provide us with its light, it refuses. In the illumination of the single stationary velare, boys run toward the center of the encampment, fleeing the shadows that may hold caros. The noise of the boys' fear is enough to mask any predators. What if the animals are gradulas and are only here out of fear?

"Beasts! Beasts near the gate!"

The words pierce the shadow. I've already turned myself around. I don't know which direction the gate is.

Safon's voice brings order into the chaos. "Erman, Cramen, stay with Persolus. Go to the center with the other boys. They may not have actares. Use yours to fight off any beasts."

"Where are you going?"

"To convince Edwin and Cade to arm the other boys. Then if I get that far, to organize them. I doubt this will be our last encounter with beasts."

Smaller lights move erratically around the single velare at the center of the camp. Edwin and Cade have left them in their fear. They aren't leaders in any form.

As we draw closer, I see movement to my left. Eyes flash in the darkness. A growl precedes something taking my legs out from beneath me. My arms brace my impact with the ground.

A flash of blue fills my vision. "Zayne, are you hurt? I didn't see it until it was too late."

"It's a caro," Cramen says. "But that species isn't common on the hillsides."

"We don't need a species lesson, Cramen. Help me get Zayne to his feet."

The two boys lift me up by the arms. We reach the light source to face anxious boys. Vels shining without reach, trying to fight back the shadows.

"This isn't good," Erman says. "We'd be better off on our own."

Screams turn us around to face an animal on the other side of the light. It—clearly a caro—stands overtop of the bodies of four boys. It's not trying to feed on them. It flashes its teeth at us, set in a long snout beneath tall ears, listening to us. Four legs carry its slender body with a tail swishing behind it, nearly longer than its entire six-foot body. Sharp claws protrude from its paws. The light gives it a menacing appearance, though I cannot imagine it looking friendly in a better light. It twists its paws as it looks at the boys frozen in fear around it.

Two streams of blue zip through the air. Both make contact with the caro's side. Sparkling blue light lingers as the creature stumbles. It shakes its head before retreating into the shadows. Erman swings his actare around, looking for additional threats. The boys shake off their paralysis and help those injured.

"This isn't right," Cramen says, holding his actare close to his body. "Caros don't act like this."

"The storm alters animal behaviors," Erman says. "We just need to focus on making them second-guess attacking us. They'll leave us alone when they realize we aren't easy prey."

Cramen has more to say, but he withholds it.

Erman grabs the nearest boy. "Don't you have actares?"

He looked confused. "Of course not. Until five minutes ago, there weren't any beasts in the city."

The twin pushes him away. "Where's Safon with those two incompetent leaders? We need weapons."

I look out into the darkness. The storm's silence makes it difficult, but as my eyes struggle to adjust, I see movement. "Erman, in front of me."

He turns and releases a long stream of energy from his actare. He doesn't hit anything, but on either side of the blue light, caros appear. Their eyes catch the blue light, and their teeth flash. I count nearly a dozen. Just as soon as they become visible, they disappear.

A scream comes from the other side of the group. We push our way through the bodies to see a boy drop to the ground. The next second, something drags his body into the shadows. Another scream, another boy gone.

"Everyone down!" Cramen's voice commands immediate obedience from everyone, including Erman and me.

His actare glows bright blue without releasing its energy. He builds up the weapon's stored Lamis for nearly twenty seconds. When it seems he can't hold it any longer, he whips the actare in a horizontal arc. The blue energy sweeps overhead, and even as I duck, I watch it make contact with at least half of the approaching caros. The beasts twitch backward, their coats singed, and howl in pain. The light lingers long enough to show the creatures in retreat.

His actare sparks blue. He tosses it out into the darkness.

"How'd you know that would work?" I ask.

He looks at me. "I once saw an Agmen do something similar. I just wasn't sure if the power source in this version was enough to mimic it. Almost wasn't."

Erman stands up and straightens his shirt. "We can't do that every time. Someone shut off that light. Beasts may find the light as a place of refuge. We want to look uninviting."

He gives a few quieter orders. Several boys use vels to search for the missing boys. Another two go to find Safon, Edwin, and Cade. The rest hold on to their fear and settle down. No intention of dispersing. Despite not knowing these boys, I have no plan of leaving to sleep in private. I put my back on the ground and let my exhaustion sweep over me.

This dream feels different, as if I can wake up at any moment, but I choose not to. A sparkling blue mist covers the area in front of me but not around me. Something is in the mist. As I stare, my father forms. He gestures for me to walk to him. Flashes of my memory of him fill my mind. His place on the Council. His constant absence. I want to step toward him, but as I consider, a sharp pain erupts in the back of my head.

My father extends a hand. It offers freedom from the pain.

I step back, and Diask replaces him in the mist. Generators flash in mind. Unfinished schematics. The Linam. Agony shoots through my body as I take another step back. The mist is painful.

Diask steps forward.

Understanding.

I jerk my head around. A voice? No. A metallic clang. It comes from the mist. The mist holds the secrets that Diask left. His death. The generators. I need this knowledge to protect the city. I just need to walk in. Embrace the mist. My hand moves just out of reach of the mist. I almost touch it, but the tips of my fingers start to burn. I pull my hand to my chest and step back.

A silhouetted figure surges out of the mist. I lose my footing and hit the ground. It's featureless in the face and body, but it smiles.

Resistance. How interesting.

It grabs me and pulls me into the mist.

I jolt upward, my hands racing across my body to get rid of the mist. It feels like nearly a minute passes before I realize there's nothing on me. I hold my knees close to my chest, trying to keep my heart from bursting out. Any second it could burst out. I don't care how unrealistic the sensation is. It feels true.

When my heart slows, and I can take in my surroundings, I realize how bright it is. I look up and realize it isn't the sun. Large sections of the storm flash in unison. When one fades, another takes its place, giving an almost constant light source. It's beautiful. Then the memories of the storm's destruction surge to the forefront of my mind.

I push the images down before looking across the encampment. The light makes it easy to see and realize there's almost no one here.

"Zayne sleeping Persolus." I turn to see my three Aemiins approaching. Judgment spews from Cramen's words. "You're awake."

I stretch out my arms. "What's that supposed to mean? I sleep in once and you get all worried?" I extend my legs out, rubbing my knees before standing up. "How long has the storm been like this?"

Cramen looks at the others. "The storm's been doing this for the past sol and a half."

My eyes widen as I try to comprehend what he says. "What? Why . . . why didn't you wake me? Has the storm struck again? What about the caros?"

"Slow down, Persolus. We tried waking you, but you wouldn't wake."

"Clearly you didn't try hard enough. Where is everyone?"

"You wouldn't wake," Safon says. "Look around you. We moved you halfway across the encampment. You didn't stir."

I glance quickly, and he's right. "It must have been some sort of Lamis somnus. It's rare—"

"But you weren't glowing blue," Erman says. "Safon and I have seen the condition. You weren't in some deep state of recovery."

"The dream was so short this time," I say, with no intention of anyone hearing.

Cramen leans toward me. "What was short this time?"

I shake my head. "Nothing. Did the storm—"

"No, Persolus," Safon says. "You just connected this to why you haven't been sleeping. No more secrets."

"It's complicated," I say, hoping I can push the conversation in another direction. "We have bigger things to worry about. I need to get out into the sector. The storm, these beasts—"

"None of which matters if when you go to sleep you don't wake up," Safon says.

I'm not escaping this time. Not unless I can convince them I don't need sleep. Their trust in me already wavers. How will they react to these dreams? To the reality that I'm allowing these dreams to affect me so much.

"I'm . . ." The three boys stare at me. "I'm having dreams."

Cramen's arms extend forward and freeze halfway to full extension. "Dreams? This all has to do with dreams."

"Yes," I say. "They wake me long before I want to wake up. And the intensity keeps me from returning to sleep. Why should we bother talking about something that is out of my control?"

"Dream theory."

I look at Erman, then at his brother, to see if he understands. Erman's words confuse Safon as much as me.

"Can you elaborate, brother?" Safon asks.

"Dream theory?" Erman repeats the phrase as if it'll make more sense a second time. "Were Soriina and I the only ones studying in school? Dreams are an extension of our mental state. Or a reflection, if that makes sense. This makes perfect sense for Zayne."

Safon crosses his arms. "No one else is going to contribute to this. Please, continue."

"Don't you see? He's stressed. Edwin and Cade refusing to do their duties. This Tatem title put on his shoulders. All this pressure is affecting his mind, and therefore his dreams. He's the son of a Council Representative with significant expectations laid upon him. His dreams are trying to make sense of it all."

Cramen scoffs. "That's perfect. We just need to remove all the stress from his life and he'll be better?"

"That doesn't explain him not waking up," Safon says.

Erman shakes his head. "I think it does. Zayne, at a mental level that he may not be conscious of, is refusing to deal with his stress. This choice is revealing itself in his dreams. He doesn't go back to sleep because he refuses to face his problems. He's pushed his body too far, and it refused to wake up to force him to face his stress. Maybe it was some type of somnus, but of the mind and not Lamis."

If this conversation were about anyone else, I may find it fascinating. But Erman's far too excited to pull apart my mental state. I just need the words to explain how he's wrong. I've always felt a weight from who my father is. My dreams have never reflected my mental state.

"You would think the Council would know about this," Cramen says in a low tone.

"What did they say during the preparation?" Erman asks, though we each know he's going to answer his own question. "We would each have Lamis tests after the storm passes over. The Sorbe may not strike us, but it can certainly affect our energy."

"Why wouldn't they tell us this?" Safon asks.

"This entire plan from the Council relies on us feeling secure out here. No, no, not us. Our parents. The citizens of the city. They feel safe knowing the storm can't affect us. Can you imagine if they thought the opposite?"

"So you mean that the storm's affecting my Lamis, which is, what?" I ask. "Amplifying these feelings and taking form in my dreams?"

"Children suffering from Lamis sickness don't sleep. If the storm's affecting your Lamis, there's no reason not to think that the storm can affect your sleep. These dreams are just your brain's way of reacting to it."

"What are these dreams about?" Cramen asks.

I thought this conversation would avoid this direction, but Cramen pivots us toward it.

"You aren't dreaming about pretty girls or peaceful skies," he continues. "What scares you so much that you can't go back to sleep? And what about this recent one? What held you in there?"

"I think that's enough," Safon says. "He will tell us when the time is appropriate. He was right earlier. We have other things to concern ourselves with. I appreciate your honesty with us, Persolus."

"You're still going to trust him?" Cramen asks. "He's a liability. He's in no condition to protect this city, let alone be at the forefront of its hope for survival."

Safon has an uneasy calm about him. "We should trust you? You find any reason to be alone, away from us. Let's not forget your initial absence. What was the reason for your prolonged stay at the Linam?"

Cramen shrinks back.

Safon has no intention of pressing the topic but only uses it to silence him. I want him to ask Cramen more. My curiosity about Cramen's secrets grows every sol. Safon's growing mistrust of him only strengthens my desire to know more.

"Nothing is ideal out here," Safon says. "We have to admit this isn't as the Council planned. Right now, we need to endure until the end. That means trusting each other, even when it seems wrong. We'll make up the difference when it becomes necessary."

Cramen says something under his breath and walks away.

Erman drops his head as he walks in front of me. "I'm sorry. I thought dream theory would help. I didn't think it would undermine your position."

I put a hand on his shoulder. "I won't say I enjoyed that, but Cramen looks for a reason not to trust someone. He would have found something else."

Erman lifts his head and smiles. "If you want to discuss it more, I did several research projects on Lamis and memories. There are theories that connect memories with dreams."

I laugh. "I said I didn't enjoy it."

Erman shrugs. "Sometimes the things we don't like are the best for us."

I shake my head and feel around my belt. There's nothing attached. "Where's my—"

"This?" Erman says, holding my anro. "I held onto it for safekeeping. Didn't want you to roll over and smash it. Noticed you always kept it in your backpack when you slept."

He hands me my anro, and I let out a breath. "Thank you."

"Didn't do much, so I think that's a good thing. But I didn't mess with anything."

"Zayne," calls a different voice. My finger pauses before it can activate the holographic screen on my anro. I look up to see Edwin walking across the encampment. "We need to talk."

I look at Safon, who shakes his head. I try to remember to ask the twin how they kept my absence a secret.

"What is it?"

"My patrols are finding beasts throughout the sector," Edwin says. "Have you been in contact with the other sectors? I need to know how widespread this problem is."

My grip tightens on my anro. "The other sectors have been silent."

"And does that worry you?"

"I trust the others to contact me if there are things out of their control."

"This whole storm is out of our control," Edwin says. "You should contact them. Find out the state of their sectors. You're our only connection to the others without traveling to their sectors. I can't risk that with so many beasts."

"Any updates I hear, I will share with you."

He holds a stare on me. "I know you haven't been out in the sector. I thank you for not giving my patrols something else to worry about. But I understand I can't keep you here. Let me know when you leave, and I'll have a patrol near you. I know you trust your Aemiins, but my boys will be present if you need help."

His offer surprises me. Words escape me, and I only acknowledge his words with a quick drop of my chin. Between the caros and my challenge of his authority, his perspective has shifted, if only slightly.

"Don't misinterpret my actions, Zayne," he says. "I still don't trust you. No Representative sends his son into this storm. You're out here for some other reason. Maybe you're not working with the traitor Diask." I bite down a response. "But your motives are beyond the Datum. I only hope there's enough of an overlap with your goals and ours."

He walks away, shouting at a boy.

Whatever positive change I'd perceived from him dies quickly. Any patrol sent out with us is not meant to protect me but to keep tabs on me. Fear creeps up in my thoughts. What if these boys suspect me of something dangerous? Is he going to order them to act?

The Sorbe rumbles seconds before casting us into darkness. A few flashes appear deep within the clouds, but the storm seems content in hiding its light. I only imagine it's because I'm awake. The others benefit from its light, but not me. I suffer in the dark.

I lift my anro to chest height and activate the holographic screen. Seni's name is highlighted. I press the icon, and a message appears.

Zayne, we need to talk. Meet at the sector border near the hillsides in one solpae from when you read this message, during the sixteenth hour of that sol.

There's no timestamp or datecode, but I don't doubt Seni's ability to know when I read a message. It's in the programming somewhere, but I don't have the time to find it. To be sure he knows when I received the message, I send a quick response.

The storm flashes brightly before returning to its darkened state.

A reminder I won't be alone out there.

Out of the Shadows

*"Twenty-nine hours make up a sol. Depending on the time
of the cycle, the moon may spend more than ten hours of
this time covering the sun, which most Vox spend resting."*
—an excerpt from Solisternum: The World We Live In,
page 24

The Sorbe flashes, illuminating its destruction. We look upon the
tenth building with its side blasted off. Metal shrapnel covers
the ground. We leave our rotams some distance away as I inspect the
damage. The smell of burnt metal stings my nose as I examine my anro's
scan results. The other nine locations were quick and simple to evaluate.
An upper portion of the outer wall is damaged here, so I can't see inside.

I press the bridge of my nose with my fingers. Exhaustion continues
to haunt me. Even after sleeping for over a sol, my body finds no rest.

Even though the Twins have more understanding of my tiredness, I still feel the need to hide it.

Erman steps next to me, kicking a piece of building away. He follows it with his velare. "Hurts the nose. You're better off holding your breath."

"I'll try to remember that for the next one."

"Is this one the same?"

I lower my anro. "Appears so."

With information from Edwin and Cade's patrols, we're tracing the storm's destruction. A short detour from our destination at the edge of the city. I want to collect as much information as I can for my meeting with Seni. I know he'll have information from his sector.

Safon tosses a fragment of a wall in between two buildings. A metallic thud echoes out from the alley. "What does this mean?"

Cramen approaches the damaged building in front of us, pulling my attention before I look back at Safon.

"This is the tenth building we've found that the storm struck," I say, tightening my grip on my anro. "And there's still no generator present. No excess Lamis concentration that my anro can detect."

"And this is bad?"

"Generators present give a clear and tangible reason for the storm strikes amidst the preparations that went into securing the city. Without this piece, I can only come to two conclusions. Either the city wasn't ready for the storm, and this is just the beginning of the destruction we'll see, or the storm is acting contrary to our understanding of Sorbes. These strikes are random in nature."

Only one of these conclusions pushes the blame off Diask. The other further accuses him. I try not to let either influence my conclusion.

"Is there any good news?" Erman asks.

I smirk. "The building's still standing."

"And more seriously?"

"The building's still standing," I say, trying to sound serious. "These random strikes from the storm aren't the full power of the Sorbe. We've seen what it can do."

Safon stares at the building, where Cramen stands at its base. We can see inside the upper levels from where the storm blasted off the outer wall. It's a small section in contrast to the entire structure. Shadows hide any details. Random doesn't mean illogical. A Sorbe still must adhere to a natural process. I simply don't know what it is.

"Why does that not comfort me?" Safon scratches his head, displacing his hair. "What have the others said? We've seen the storm strike across the city. Is it random or directed?"

My immediate thought is to say the others haven't responded yet. But I don't think they're going to respond. I don't want to theorize why. The thought scares me.

"You've sent them messages? You aren't waiting for them like you told Edwin?"

"No, no. Of course I've sent them messages."

"Then what have they said?"

"They haven't responded. They appear to be ignoring my messages."

"Anything else from Seni? You think he would have sent a follow-up message since yestersol. The sixteenth hour is nearing."

I shake my head.

"I don't like this," Safon says.

"We don't think . . . the storm has been quite active," Erman says, not completing his thought, but his meaning is clear.

Without any messages from the others, we don't know where the storm has struck in the other sectors. Have Seni and his group been as fortunate as ours?

Images of the storm fill my mind. The building crashing to the ground. Diask's death. Soriina's death. An acidic mist extending from the Sorbe. My death. No, no, none of that is real. I try to clear my mind. Separate dream from reality.

Safon snaps me back to what I think is reality before I can fully separate everything. "We're not thinking like that, Erman, not when there's no evidence to suggest it. We'll ask Seni when we meet him."

"Zayne!" We turn to see Cramen halfway up the damaged building. "You might want to see this."

Erman shines his velare across the damaged outer wall. "I'm not going up there."

We approach the base of the structure, and I call up to him. The building has shifted enough my neck doesn't strain to look up at Cramen. "What is it?"

Cramen looks down. "A generator."

My hand goes to my anro, and I press it against the wall. "How far?"

"No more than ten feet from the exterior wall."

I shake my head. "Not possible. I'm not picking anything up."

"Stop using that thing and use your eyes. Come up here."

I reattach my anro to my belt and start examining the wall. Climbing isn't a common activity in the city. I try to determine which path Cramen took up. "This might take me a moment."

"Pull your sleeves down over your hands," Cramen says. "The edges are sharp but climbable."

I feel the jagged edges of the wall try to pierce my sleeves, but the design withstands the attack. My feet struggle to find their place, so I second guess each placement. A few minutes pass before Cramen is shifting his position so I can sit where he is. A smooth metal beam is bent inward, so I rest there, breathing heavily.

Cramen points into the shadows with his velare. "See. That lump of metal there."

I follow the light to his crude description. Various wreckage covers a cylindrical device with a domed top. It appears similar to actare but much larger. Even with the velare, not enough is visible to determine the type of Tech. It doesn't appear to be a generator, or not one that Diask has listed in the anro. Not wanting to risk leaning too far, I can't see much around the device other than debris from the wall.

"I need to get closer."

"And how do you intend to do that? Quite the drop, let alone getting back up. You aren't the best climber."

His last comment is unnecessary, but I ignore it. I shift my body to start the descent back to the ground. "Every building has a door. I just need to open it."

"I thought we weren't supposed to be opening doors."

His words have to be a joke, but his tone doesn't give anything away. "I don't think we have to worry about an open door with his particular building."

Safon shines his light at us as we near the bottom. "Is it a generator?"

My knees jar as I hit the ground. "Could be. But I need to get inside."

"There is a door here," Erman says. "Locked up, though."

"Without power, all I need to do is to bypass the locking mechanism." I approach the door, and with the displacement of the building, the panel to the lock is partially open. I pry it away and let it hit the ground. "This will be easier with an actare." I stretch my hand out to Erman.

"Something tells me you've done this before," Erman says, handing me his weapon.

I smirk. "Certainly not. At least, not like this."

I step back and raise the weapon toward the locking mechanism. I release a sustained beam that I shut off within a second as my aim misses the target. I don't look at my Aemiins to see if they react to my poor handling of the weapon. I use my left hand to steady the actare and fire again. The beam stays on target until I hear the mechanism snap. The door lets out a hiss but doesn't open.

"The storm's attack shifted the building," I say. "We need to pry the door open."

Erman and Cramen push with open palms until the door shifts. A gap finally forms that Safon slides his fingers into and pulls as the others continue to push. The gap widens before stopping, despite Erman and Cramen gripping the inside of the door.

Safon lets go and shakes his arms. "Squeeze through, or we move on. That door isn't moving any further."

Erman flexes his fingers. "I don't think Cramen was doing anything. We should try again."

Safon glares at his brother.

I glance at the opening and hand Erman his actare back. "I should be able to get through. Thank you."

I slip through without much difficulty. My velare illuminates debris covering the floor. Stairs lay on the floor near the wall that the storm blasted through. Parts of the ceiling hang down, threatening to smash me. Beyond the destruction, boxes line the walls. It's some sort of storage building. Despite my curiosity, I ignore the rest of the room as I set my eyes on the mysterious device.

It takes all my strength to shift the wall fragment off the device. The crash brings several requests for the state of my wellbeing from my Aemiins. I quickly dismiss their concerns and run my hands over the outer casing of the device. Dents and scratches mar the surface, but the storm doesn't appear to have reached it.

I active my anro and scan the room. Even standing next to it, I receive no signal. Stepping around the cylindrical device, something catches the light of my velare. It's an arvos. I clear away debris to see it appears undamaged. The computer interface powers on with little effort. The tug on my Lamis is minimal. Various logs appear on the screen, tracking the movement of Tech in and out of the building. It's a manifest. The last entry matches the description of the device in front of me. The log doesn't specify its function.

I nearly drop the arvos as I read the last line in the entry. Diask's name. It is the only one with his name. The date places the domed cylinder arriving just before the storm. My curiosity propels me to examine the outer casing more closely. Within a few seconds, I find a panel that I remove. Inside the panel, I find a control pad and a small screen. The access code is on the manifest as required by law. The adherence to the law tells me the device is no secret. What purpose did Diask intend for it? I only hope he meant it for our good.

I start to enter the code when I stop at the last digit. I don't know how much energy flows through this device. The storm could very well be waiting to strike.

"Slow down, Zayne," I say to myself. "You don't know what turning this thing on does."

"You almost done in there?"

I turn back to the door. "Almost. Need a few more minutes."

"Hurry up. Cramen's starting to talk."

Withholding a chuckle, I return my attention to the device. The screen is on. I don't remember pressing the last digit. I look up at the hole in the wall. The storm's silent.

"There must be a separate power source for this control pad," I say, breathing slowly. "The main device is still off."

Then the outer casing shifts. It begins to turn, spiraling out to reveal a blue light. A Lamis core. The screen flashes the words: **Anro detected: Sequence initiated: 1 minute.**

The manifest hits the ground as I run across the room to the door. My feet slip several times. I slam into the door as I squeeze out. I fall out of the opening, which immediately draws the attention of the Twins and Cramen. They take a few steps toward me when I throw my hand up.

"Persolus, what's wrong?"

"Run! Just run!"

Thankfully, whatever mistrust they may have doesn't impede their legs. They join me in a sprint away from the building. I try to keep track of the minute in my head, but at some point, I lose count. The storm acts as a visual timer. The colors grow brighter until a flash of white races across the sky to the building.

I don't see the explosion. I feel it with every part of my body. I stay upright as heat and metal push me into the air. My feet hit the ground after what feels like minutes but can't hold my weight. I try to extend my hands out, but my face hits the ground. I stay down until the storm goes quiet.

My arms shake as I push myself up. I leave a small pool of blood where my face was. I can feel my life dripping from my nose and forehead. I stumble when a pair of hands catches me.

"Steady, Zayne."

With Erman's help, I return to the ground, my legs unable to sustain my weight.

I stare down into a small pool of blood. I touch my forehead and wet my hand in my blood. It's a dark red. No hint of blue displaying my Lamis healing me. Erman sees the Lamisless blood, but I shake my head.

"We can't be worrying about that right now," I say, wiping my hand on my pants. "We need to continue to meet Seni."

"Persolus, take a moment. Your body isn't healing as it should be. It seems the storm is affecting more than just your dreams."

"You don't understand. That wasn't just some generator. It was intentionally put there. Someone wanted the storm to strike." I look back. The building hadn't been tall enough to topple over but is now a smoking heap. Smoke shifts, showcasing the mark of the storm on the surrounding buildings. "Someone's using the storm to destroy the city."

Cramen raises his head, knowing I have more to stay. "Who?"

"Diask."

A False Exchange

"The simplistic nature of the anro communication network was seen as both a benefit and security risk."—Connecting Solisternum, an overview of Vox communication

Safon's face sparkles blue as his body heals its wounds. A deep gash marks his face. Without his Lamis, a scar would be a certainty, but the storm isn't affecting him. I check my wounds every few minutes. The bleeding has stopped, but with no sign that my Lamis is aiding my body's healing process.

The Sorbe stays silent above. We don't move for what feels like several hours. Safon insists.

"We have to leave," I say. "We have to meet Seni in less than an hour."

"Persolus, your body isn't healing. You need more time—"

"We don't have time. That's the last thing we have."

"Brother, Zayne's right. We need answers, and Seni may have them. He knew Diask. Who better to ask?"

"Fine," Safon says. He glances at his timepiece on his wrist. "You think we can make it to the hillside before Seni wants to meet?"

"Seni will wait," I say.

"Are you able to manage the rotam?" Safon asks.

If I had any option, I would say no. But I don't have a choice, so I tell him yes. Safon wants to call out my lie, but he doesn't. He knows we need to meet Seni.

No other words are necessary as we climb atop our rotams and continue to the edge of the sector. No more detours, even though we find more evidence of the storm's wrath. I can't focus on the buildings as my legs burn with pain. My whole body rebels against my effort to keep the rotam moving. But once I get to a reasonable speed, I ease off the pedals, and the rotam uses the lamis around us to maintain my speed.

We can't travel as fast relying on the rotam's limited power, but Safon recognizes the necessity. He keeps us down the center of the main transport path that cuts through Sector One toward the hillsides. We stop short of our destination and leave our rotams tucked away in an alley.

Safon stares into the shadows before turning to us. "Erman, take Persolus and meet Seni. Cramen, you and I are going to check the area, make sure there are no beasts or other surprises."

I want to ask what other surprises he thinks there could be. He can't detect generators or whatever other devices Diask has hidden throughout the city. My thoughts are slow, and he walks into an alleyway before I can pull the words out of my mind.

"Well, Zayne. Where are we supposed to meet Seni?"

"He didn't specify a certain spot. There's a walkway around the edge of the city, so I say we start there."

Walking's worse than the rotam, but I try not to verbalize my discomfort. Not that Erman can't tell. He walks ahead of me, keeping watch on the shadows. His left hand holds his actare just tightly enough not to trigger the pressure sensor. He has no limp or other sign of injury from the storm's latest attack. If not for the injury to Safon's face, I might think the Twins were invincible.

Erman shines his velare back at me. "Don't worry about keeping up with me. Just let me know if you see anything."

"How do you do it?"

He stops. "What do you mean?"

"You faced down that animal back at the encampment. And just now, we were almost obliterated by the storm. But you walk away without a scratch. No fear lingering from what could have been."

He tilts his head and smacks his lips. "I guess it's tough to be fearful with my goal in mind. And that's to protect you. No storm or beast is going to get in my way." He chuckles, and I hear pain in it. "With all honesty, we all handle pain differently. I'm just better at hiding mine."

We walk the rest of the way to the path in silence. Without the storm's light, Erman moves the velare in a sweeping motion, covering every inch of shadow. No beasts. Not yet.

Erman stops suddenly, putting his palm toward me to pause my movement. I look beyond, trying to see what he has found.

He whispers, barely audible. "There's movement ahead."

"Could be Seni."

"Or a beast."

"If the animals are coming into the city, I don't think they'd be out here. Has to be Seni." I step next to Erman. "Get ready to shoot. Seni! Is that you?"

A few seconds pass before a light floods the path. A silhouette steps out of the shadows.

"Zayne, is that you?" the shadow calls out. "I hope so, else beasts now have the ability to speak."

I outstretch my arms. "It's me, Zayne."

In a strange helpful moment, the Sorbe lights up, giving enough light to confirm who I look at. Seni looks uninjured. His time in the storm seems less eventful than mine. Or his Lamis heals him. He recognizes me in the storm's light and moves to meet me.

We stop short of each other. He has a limp. I see a sparkle of blue just below where his shirt ends at the wrist.

Seni glances over his shoulder. "When you didn't specify where to meet, I wasn't sure if I would find you."

"We thought you might be something else. Erman was about to shoot you."

"I thought you were a beast at first too." He touches his wrist. "Now that we're here, what did you want to discuss? I think you can understand we need to be spending as much time as we can closer to our encampments. I still don't think this was the best meeting spot."

I look back at Erman to make sure one of my other senses is working. I hear Seni's words, but they don't make sense.

"You wanted to meet."

Seni's eyes narrow. "You sent me a message wanting to meet. You were ignoring my other messages. I thought the worst when you didn't respond. I heard the storm. Saw the storm."

"Seni . . . I didn't send you a message to meet. You did."

He opens his mouth to respond, but nothing escapes.

The storm laughs before blanketing us in darkness.

The Novitae

"Redlanders refuse technology and thus are in self-exile from the Vox Nation. We show them mercy by allowing them to live in the voids of the land, where cities cannot be built." —early Council recording on the Redlander presence in Solisternum

"We're here on the account of someone else."

Seni breaks the silence. I'm not sure how long it lasts, but it lasts long enough to fill my head with a hundred different thoughts. The storm waits, either trying to hide its secrets or listening for us to uncover the mysteries its darkness shrouds.

"It appears so," I say. "We need to talk. About this and much more."

"I hope your injury is a part of that."

I raise my hand to my forehead but stop short of touching the wound. "This is just a small part."

Unsure how much of our communication was real, I start from the beginning. Edwin and Cade refusing to help. Cramen's absence. The generators. Caros. The new device. I gloss over my near deaths. And my dreams. The storm affecting my Lamis's ability to heal me is enough of a topic. I suppose near deaths are implied.

I talk quickly, hoping not to take too long. The shadows shift, causing me to look away several times. Seni never does. He listens to every word. I know he's analyzing each one in his head, preparing questions to clarify my story where I miss a detail or jumble the words. I do my best to answer his questions.

Then silence.

He breaks eye contact as his eyes search the shadows. They hold secrets. But not the answers to our questions. The storm is nothing but a tool. It's not here to help or destroy us. I can't be angry at nature.

"You're leaving something out," Seni says. "From what I can tell, the last *real* message I received from you was about the others not trusting Diask."

My eyes shoot up to meet Seni's judgment. I try to recall everything. Did I miss something? Some crucial observation or piece of information?

"You think Mr. Diask is responsible?" he asks.

I left my judgment out of my story. I wanted Seni to come to the same conclusion without my interference. My influence. My anger burns quietly against the Tatem. I'm still uncertain. The evidence condemns him, but it doesn't make sense. The reasoning behind his potential actions avoids rational thought.

I can't look him in the eyes. "I . . . wanted you to come to your own conclusion. I'm still not—"

"Your accusation dulls your analysis. And now I can't think about everything without your condemnation clouding my judgment. You can't accuse the city's Tatem of trying to destroy the very city he helped build."

My heart pounds. My throat throbs as my emotions dictate my words. "What if he had regrets? Is it not the creator's responsibility to tear down what he built up? Would you rather someone else do what you're afraid to do?"

"And when the creator hands over his creation, he relinquishes his rights and responsibility. This is the Council's city. Not Mr. Diask's. You believe he would seek to destroy what the Council possesses? His memory is already lost to the Historical Record. You now seek to defame him even further with yours?"

My hands are sweaty. I want to pull them off my body and toss them into the storm. "Give me another explanation. I refused to believe the rumors the others were spreading. But what do I do with the evidence that grows against him?"

"Did you even try? Or did you let their ideas fester in your head until they overwhelmed you? You didn't try to defend him. Their thoughts were yours but louder."

"That's a lie!" I jab my hand forward, forcing Seni to step back. "He put me out here. I wanted to be here, and if it weren't for Diask, I wouldn't be. He's given me a chance to prove myself before the Council . . . my father. He didn't know me, yet he put all the responsibility on me."

"Then why aren't you seeking another solution?" Seni's words cut deep. But my loyalty isn't to Diask but to the Council. "You owe him."

"The device went off when it detected my anro," I say. "It knew we would be scanning Tech in the city. Then someone hacked into the anro network and disabled our anros. Who else is capable or would have access?"

"He's dead. Do you think the dead can rise to finish what they couldn't finish when they were living?"

"No, but he had a plan. He certainly could have set this all into motion before his death. Anyone with any knowledge of Tech knows you can't always be there. You set automation. The way he died. Don't you see how it makes sense?"

"Wait!" We turn to Erman. The storm seems to light up at the sound of his voice. Vibrant colors flash across the sky. "For a moment, let's say Diask didn't do this or that he probably needed some help. No one's stupid enough to try something like this and hope everything works after they die. Even with your auto Tech or whatever."

"Speak your meaning," Seni says.

"You said it earlier, Seni. Haven't you two figured it out? If that fake message brought you both here, doesn't that mean someone wants you here? Now. If someone is using Tech to attack the city through the storm, who's going to stop him? Well, I'd say the two smartest boys capable of standing beneath a Sorbe."

"And we never would have come together with everything happening," I say.

The storm plunges the area into darkness.

The shape of Seni moves away but stops before completely disappearing into the surrounding shadow. "We need to leave. Erman's right. Whoever is responsible wants us here. We're the only ones capable of protecting the city. And this traitor knows that."

"We can't leave yet," I say.

"No, Zayne, we have to. Let the Council pass judgment when the storm ends. We can't go on arguing this."

"We need to be able to communicate," I say. "Whoever's responsible has disabled our anros. We need to fix that before we separate. Talking to each other is more important now than before."

"And Soma and the others need to know what we do," Seni says. "The anro network can't maintain a constant signal. It's the reason we can't do direct communication. It receives bursts of information. Whatever's disabling our anros has to be in the fake message. Delete it—no, full reset. That should remove the altered program or virus."

My hand comes to a rest on my anro. "What if I isolate the message? I can try to figure out who sent it. Diask's work will have his signature. I can clear his name."

And I can prove my worth to the Council. They will want to know who has attempted to undo their plans and destroy their city.

"We need to be able to communicate now. If Mr. Diask is responsible, which I don't believe he is, why would he use his known signature? You would have to look at the smallest intricacies to figure out who designed the invasive message. No, it'll take too long."

"This may be the only piece of evidence the storm doesn't—"

"Brother!" We turn to see a figure emerge from an alleyway. The shadows shift, revealing Seni's twin, Arsen. "Brother, we need to leave. Beasts on the hillside. And a man."

His words process slowly through my mind until the last word. A man?

Erman mutters before his words have meaning. "No. No. That isn't possible. No adult can survive out here. Not unless we admit even the storm is a lie."

"Give my brother a chance." Seni steps closer to Arsen. "What did you see? Speak with clarity."

He takes a deep breath in. "A man. It wasn't a boy. Beasts were alongside him. Caros. We have to leave."

Seni looks at me. "Arsen, you must have been seeing things in the shadows. The storm strikes any adult. Was it one of my other Aemiins?"

"We can argue this back at the base," Arsen says. "I don't want to stick around to prove myself right or wrong."

My body freezes as a shadow rises behind Arsen. Jaws latch onto his shoulder and pull him backward. He fires off his actare, but all it does is illuminate the terror on his face. Seni draws his weapon and fires into the shadows. Erman sends the light from his velare after the beast and Arsen but finds nothing.

"Curse the Prava," Seni says. "What was that?"

"A caro," Erman says. He looks at me. "It looked just like the ones from the encampment."

"We have to go after him."

I grab Seni by the arm. "Wait, we can't run off into the dark after a caro. We need a—"

A blur rushes past me and slams into Seni's shoulder. He falls into me, and I can't stop us both from hitting the ground. I look up in time to see a caro with its jaws around Erman's arm pulling him up the hillside. He fires his actare without success.

Seni crawls off me and grabs his actare, which had landed a few feet from him. His actare sends a sustained beam up the hillside. His attack falters. Blue sparks replace the beam, forcing him to drop the weapon. The caro disappears over the crest of a hill. The storm silhouettes its escape.

Seni retrieves his actare. After slamming his hand down on the dome, the sparks die out. "Where's your weapon?"

I force myself to stand up. My limbs shake. "I don't have one."

"After everything you told me about, you don't have one? Stupid."

"They aren't attacking us," I say. "They singled out Arsen and Erman."

"What are you saying?"

"I don't think they're wild caros," I say. "These are trained like Soferas."

"Soferas don't attack people, but I think you're right. Someone is commanding these beasts."

"Erman was right. They want us."

A heavy sound exits the shadows, causing us both to turn in the same direction. It sounds like a voice, but what should be words have no meaning. As the voice fades into silence, a flickering yellow light appears at the base of the hillsides. It moves toward us. It floats through the air, well above our heads, fighting the darkness reflecting off the metal of the nearest building. As it draws closer, a figure takes shape behind the light.

I fight my arm to raise my velare up. The light pushes through the darkness, revealing the face of a man, but not any man I have ever seen. He has short hair, almost bald. His face has some sort of tattoo or mask covering it. He raises his arm up, blocking my light, and lets out some sort of yell.

Seni grabs my arm and pulls me. "Now, while it's distracted."

A part of me wants to remain and learn more about the man the storm ignores. But Seni pulls me until we turn a corner, and I give up the desire and run without his encouragement, ignoring the painful protests from my body. The light from our velares swings with our arms and becomes more annoying than helpful. But we run straight with only the thought of gaining distance from our attacker in mind. We finally turn two consecutive corners before stopping. I drop my velare and put both hands on my knees.

Seni shines his light at me. "That . . . that was a man? But the storm."

"Did you hear it speak?" I ask. "Or I think it spoke. I couldn't hear well enough to understand."

"What does that matter?" He paces back and forth. "It commanded those beasts. Took my brother. We have to go back. Find them. Hope they aren't hurt."

I pick up my velare and shine the light around. "And if that thing is following us? We can't go back. Not the way we just came."

"Then we go the long way—Zayne! Behind you!"

Before I can react, something slams into my back. My body hits the ground hard. My velare spins on the ground before it stops, illuminating a four-legged beast. Claws extend out from its paws. Its head is wide with small eyes. Short ears twitch. It turns from me to Seni. He raises his actare. A flickering light appears behind him.

"Seni!" It is the only word I can force out of my mouth. My head throbs alongside the rest of my body. I struggle to comprehend what happens in front of me.

Seni turns away from the beast, raising his actare. Using his velare to find his new target, the caro leaps through the air, striking him in the shoulder. His light hits the ground before going out. His actare sputters blue sparks. He drops to one knee, slamming the weapon into the ground. Jabbing his hand forward, a blue stream of energy seeks its target. A blue sheen envelops the man as his yellow, swirling light drops to the ground. He doesn't fall.

The man steps forward and speaks. I can hear the words clearly, but I don't understand them. He isn't speaking the common language. The beast understands.

Seni aims his actare, but only sparks exit the half-dome front. Before the beast can attack, three streams of energy streak overhead. Two strike the man. Another the caro.

"Zayne!"

"Seni!"

The words reach my ears, but I cannot distinguish the voices. As the shadows draw in, a tingling sensation surges up my back. I collapse fully onto the ground. The darkness overwhelms me. I allow it.

"—that thing demands it. We have to discuss it."

"Not until Zayne wakes up. I don't want unnecessary repetition."

"That man could be back at any moment. We don't have the time to wait."

"Stop calling it a man. We don't know what we're dealing with."

My eyes open to the voices and the Sorbe above. It flashes. I let out a wordless grunt. I try to sit up, but a pain urges me not to.

"Persolus!" Safon comes into my field of vision. He helps me into a sitting position. "Having more of those dreams? Not the best time to take an extended rest. Take this." He hands me a green bar.

A smirk crosses my face. "I wouldn't call that rest." But the absence of the dreams gives my unconscious state the illusion of rest. After I take a bite of the sour bar and swallow, I speak. "What happened?"

"Now may we discuss it?" Cramen says. "That thing commanded the beasts."

Cramen, Erman, and Seni stand around me.

"It was only one beast," Erman says.

He's holding his arm close to his body. His clothes aren't ripped, but the caro still left its mark. How did he escape?

"One beast, two beasts, it doesn't matter. It commanded them to attack you and Arsen. Not kill. That's rare control over a caro beast. No, it's not rare. It's unheard of among the civilized."

"Keep your voice down," Safon says. "That man, or whatever it was, could still be near. Our actares didn't put him on the ground. I don't want a second encounter."

"Perhaps if our aim was better," Arsen says from a shadow to my left behind the others.

I can't tell if he's injured. His voice reveals no pain. This man, or whatever it is, didn't care to kill either twin. It only wanted Seni and me.

I look at Seni. He's quiet, waiting for the right moment to speak.

"We need to get back to the camp and warn the others," Safon says. "If that thing did indeed command the beast, it could have used them to attack our camp before. And could again."

"It was out in the storm," Cramen says in a low tone. "You realize it could be only one thing, right?"

"What are you talking about now, Cramen?" Erman asks.

"Are you all so oblivious? That was no child. Yet it stood out in the storm."

"Spit it out already. We don't have the time."

"It had to be a Redlander. They are the only ones able to survive out in a storm."

A silence clings to the darkness as the storm remains idle.

A Redlander? Was the Council telling the truth about the Techless society being near the city? Why wouldn't they warn us about them during our time in the Linam?

I rub my head. "We should discuss this with Edwin. My responsibility is Tech, not beasts and Redlanders."

Seni looks at me. "Despite everything, even you cannot believe those Lamisless *things* are capable of this?"

Safon helps me to my feet. My legs shake, but he plants his feet firmly, letting me lean on him until I find my balance. "I don't know what to believe. But we shouldn't be discussing it here. You were right before. We need to head back. Update everyone and figure out what to do."

Erman shifts his body. "Do we understand the implication of Redlanders? The Council wanted us to keep Tech from turning on and scare away a few beasts. Not deal with Redlanders. We have to tell Vitus. We need the Agmen."

They don't understand. Redlanders didn't hack the anro network. They didn't place a device to cause the storm's destruction. Someone else did. Not even the worst of us would work with the Lamisless beings of the Red Plains. That means we face two threats. No one's going to say it. I won't.

"And how do you suppose we do that?" Arsen asks. "Knock on a door and expect them to open it? Send out soldiers to be obliterated by the storm?"

"Of course not," Erman says. "But we have to find some way. They need to know about this. Seni, perhaps you can get some message to those in Sector Two."

Soriina comes to mind. She is sheltering from the storm in her home. In Sector Two.

"No," I say louder than I want. I lower my voice and continue. "Risking the lives of those in the sector—any sector—is too great. We can't forget about the storm."

"Zayne is right," Seni says. "The storm's activity is unsettling. You felt the ground shake when Zayne was unconscious. The foremost danger is the storm and its threat to the generators. Give this new information to the Edwin and the others. Let them come up with some plan. We still have to monitor the Tech."

Safon stops his brother from saying something else. "Enough of this talk. We need to return to our sectors. Persolus can communicate with the other Tech leaders and coordinate with the other leaders. No matter the threat, our responsibility remains the same: protect the city until the storm passes."

Seni looks at me and speaks across the others, intending for them to hear. He wants everyone to know so they can enforce his will. Why doesn't he just say so? His trust in me wavers as mine does in Diask. "Zayne, reset your anro. I expect a message upon your return. Staying in contact is more important now than before. You must contact the others. They have to know the potential danger."

The Redlander sends fear coursing through him. He regrets not having my position. I don't blame him. The Lamisless things that reject our technology seek the Council's city. They risk war. We're on the frontline. No one's ready to admit we have to risk more to serve the Council.

Those Remaining

"The origin of Redlanders is unknown, though the unnatural language they speak points to somewhere other than Solisternum." —*an excerpt from* A History of Solisternum

The Sorbe stays silent, letting my thoughts eat away at my sanity. Safon refuses to allow us to use our velares, so all I have to stare at is the shadows. My thoughts all the more powerful in dark.

We travel slowly, which makes things worse. Any shadow may contain a Redlander. An occasional flash from the storm reveals the shorter constructions that surround the square. No damage to the buildings or signs of the invaders. The Sorbe's wrath remains away from the place we shelter. Is this a part of the Council's plan? Do they have extra protections in place here to keep us safe? I didn't have time to ask Seni where in Sector Two the storm struck.

Is Soriina still alive?

I dread the interaction with Edwin that has to come. I have to tell him everything. When he learns of the new evidence against Diask, he'll lose all trust in me. I can't prove Diask's actions are separate from his decision to bring me into the storm, let alone his appointment of me as the Tatem within the Datum.

We turn the last corner before the gate. Before we reach the entrance, a smell reaches my nose. It stings. I stop my rotam and illuminate the area with my velare.

Safon speaks just above a whisper. "Persolus, what are you doing?"

I lift my nose higher. "Do you smell that?"

"It stings. I am trying not to."

"The storm struck nearby."

Erman shines his velare over the buildings, his light visibly shaking. "There's no damage here. We haven't seen any new signs of the storm on the way here." He licks his finger. "A breeze. It could be carrying the smell."

"From inside the square," Cramen says. "After the Redlander, I only imagine the worst."

His comment discourages any further discussion as we approach the gate. Safon steps up to it and slams his hand on the metal. "Open up, Tech patrol returning."

Erman looks at him. "Tech patrol?"

"Would you rather me list off each of our names?"

It doesn't matter what he says; the gate remains closed.

Safon reaches up to the top and pulls himself up. "No one's here." With a quick maneuver, he is over the wall. The gate opens a moment later. Safon stands in the opening. "This doesn't look good."

He moves so we can enter. I expect to hear the boys, but silence has a hold of the area. "Where is everyone?"

Erman shines his light as far as it goes. "I . . . I don't think that Redlander is alone."

Safon shakes his head and mutters before his words are clear. "How can they all be gone? The gate was locked. Did they lock it and then climb over?" His velare barely reaches into the encampment. He points to the right. "Erman, take Persolus and walk the edge. Cramen and I will go this way. Meet at the other side. Something must be present to explain what happened."

Erman drags his hand across the metal wall. "How much of this do you think the Council anticipated?"

I know the correct answer, but I don't burden him with it. "It's the reactions of the Council that prove their strength and wisdom. It's their responses to disaster that comfort us. We don't have any of that out here."

Erman lets out a laugh. "Sometimes I forget you're the son of a Representative."

We continue walking in silence. When we nearly reach the halfway mark, the wall shifts. The top is bent. Surface cracks span the entire wall. At the edge of our velares' light, a hole appears. Debris fills the area, causing us to think extra about each step. The buildings beyond the square showcase the fury of the storm and mock any previous thoughts that we have extra protection here.

We see the lights of Safon and Cramen approach from the other side.

"Well, we know where the storm struck," Cramen says. "But where are the boys?"

The Sorbe ignites, flooding the encampment with its color. The showcase of its beauty solidifies that the boys are not here.

Despite our protests, Safon has us stay in the square until we figure out what to do next. And I cannot convince him that our next step should involve Tech. I can't blame him. Without the support of the other boys, traveling the sector is a far too high of a risk to take. We try to sleep when a lack of ideas arise. I try. The storm stays silent above, which should make falling asleep easy. But with the shadows shifting around us and invaders in the city, any rest evades me. I am not alone. The others don't seem to sleep much.

Erman mutters to himself.

Safon keeps his eyes on us.

Cramen watches the shadows.

"A test," Erman says out loud. "What if this is all a test? It has to be. Perhaps the storm is such a non-threat that they are testing us before we leave for our Eteros."

Cramen lets out a laugh. "That makes sense. Which must be why they blew up half the city. Maybe they wanted to replace those build-ings." He scoffs. "They don't care enough to put that much effort into a test."

"No one else is coming up with any ideas."

Safon turns toward us as the storm flashes. "I appreciate the thoughts, brother. But that is far from our priority now. We need to find the others before . . . whatever that thing was finds us."

Cramen's hands move uncertainly in front of him. "And it knows where we are, yet you still have us here."

Erman stands up and walks in a circle. "All we know is that the storm struck. We don't know if that thing was here. The boys may be finding some other place to use as a base."

I continue to listen with a half-mind. My attention is on my anro. Without sleep, I try to disable whatever hinders my device. The intrica-cies of the anro are far more complicated than I expect. I can't find any differences between the fake message and the ones I know are real. Either

I am missing something or the problem could be more widespread than I think.

This message holds the information I can use to earn my place among the Council Representatives as my father did. Or do I do this to clear Diask's name? Will the Council be as grateful to know their Tatem isn't responsible for the destruction that sweeps across their city?

Safon looks at me. I avoid his glare. I know what he means to ask. He has given me until the moon sets. We can't see the moon, but the temperature warms slightly. And Safon wants me to send a message.

"Persolus."

"I know—"

He stands up and speaks with enough force that I look at him. "No. You have had more than enough time to mess with that thing. Reset it. Send a message to the others."

"Fine."

I stare at the false message. The secrets it holds. Secrets that will solidify my place under the Council's teaching. But time is not on my side. I twist the anro in my hand. The only way to interfere with the anro is through the network. A continuous signal is impossible. They only had seconds of connection to render our communications inert. The complexity of this virus has to be minimal. If I move the message and reset everything around it, that should reset everything to before the virus. The message will be intact for me to continue to analyze.

The message itself isn't dangerous anymore. It was only the method of infiltration. I create a folder in the anro's back end and place the message there.

Safon watches closely, but he doesn't know what I am doing. He has to trust I am resetting my anro—which I am. I won't tell him the risks. It takes longer than I realize to isolate the folder and purge my anro. The system glitches, acting as if the purge is unsuccessful, but the process completes after a few seconds. The folder remains, but everything else defaults to when I first received the device.

I compile messages to each of the other leaders and send them. "Persolus?"

I raise my anro up. "Done. Now I await responses from them."

"And what do we do before then?" Cramen says. "We've been waiting here. We need to be doing something."

"We don't know how many Redlanders, or whatever they are, are out there," Safon says. "The more we move, the more likely we could run into them again. It's time we break down these sector barriers and face this storm as a whole. When Persolus hears from another sector, we will make a plan."

"And in the meantime, we sit here and do nothing?"

"You are welcome to suggest something."

"We are just sitting here, acting scared—"

Erman points his injured arm at Cramen. "Scared? What gave you that idea? Was it the man that controlled a beast to attack us? Or the storm overhead that strikes as it wills?"

Cramen shifts his weight and stands as he talks. "Did they not think this would be terrifying? We have to rise above—"

"Enough, Cramen," Safon says. "Not all of us are able to hide our fear behind blind loyalty."

"You wait until we have to explain our actions to the Council. We won't be judged on our survival, but on what we did amid the fear."

He turns his back to us and walks off. The storm doesn't tell us where he goes.

Erman smirks. "Should have done that earlier."

"We need to be working together, Erman," Safon says. "No matter his insanity, we need to stop creating more division. Especially after all this."

He crosses his arms with a flinch. "But we can ignore any cries for help he may make, right?"

Annoyance flashes across Safon's face. "No more. Do you understand?"

Blue light moves across the darkness. Cramen's voice cries out from somewhere up ahead. His words aren't discernible, but his need for help is without question.

The skies remain dark. The Redlander has found us.

We don't need any instructions to move. We half walk, half run toward Cramen's voice, wary of the shadows. The storm ignites overhead, revealing a piece of debris by the fallen wall and Cramen crouched behind it.

He sees us. "Get down! He is out of his mind."

As he speaks, a blue streak shoots over us. We drop to the ground and crawl the rest of the way.

Safon tries to look over the debris. "Tell me the Redlanders don't have actares?"

"No," Cramen cries out, as another blast goes overhead. "Edwin. He either cannot hear me or thinks I am a Redlander."

Erman smiles. "Or he saw Cramen and wanted to take out some frustration."

"I said enough of that," Safon says. "Move to the side and see if you can get around him. Make sure he can see you. I will—Persolus, where are you going?"

I stand in sight of the broken wall. Safon's plan would be good, but there's no reason to prolong this. I shine my velare into the opening. "Edwin! Stop, it's me, Zayne."

A figure emerges from the shadows. "Careful, there . . . there is a Redlander somewhere in the square."

I look at the others. "There is no Redlander. You were firing at Cramen."

He steps into the light of my velare. Blood, sparkling blue, seeps from several wounds on his face. "You are certain?"

I point to Cramen and the others who stand up. "Yes. Now what happened here?"

As if he doesn't recognize me until now, his tone shifts. "Can you not guess? They attacked us. And I had so many patrols out making sure you were safe. We were left vulnerable. Beasts . . . beast-men. They . . . they took everyone." His anger shifts to fear as he recalls the terror.

Safon steps forward. "Do you know where they are? Or what happened to the others on patrol?"

His response is informative but doesn't answer the question. "We could fight the beasts. Even those Techless abominations. But together . . . we couldn't fight both. They must have followed a patrol back here."

"How did you evade them?" Erman asks.

Edwin shifts his actare in his hand. "Not . . . not sure. Drained four actares escaping. Found a few other boys. The Redlanders took us by surprise, but their number was only a dozen, maybe a few more or less, not enough to take us all. Beasts . . . beasts struggled to see when we turned off the velares, but not the Redlanders."

The only thing that makes sense. Beasts are used to the constant sun. The darkness is unusual for them.

"Why are you here?" Cramen says. "Why out here where the Redlanders could capture you?"

The Sorbe flashes. "We agreed that if anyone escaped or avoided them, they might return here. But I didn't expect to find anyone. Thought you would be taken first, so close to the city-edge."

"Which is why you shot at me."

"The Redlanders . . . their voices sound like ours, but with no meaning. Your words were unclear . . . I didn't know."

Safon extends an open palm to Cramen to quell any more questions. "That doesn't matter. You said there were others. Where are they?"

Edwin steps toward the wall. "Not far. We should move. The Red-landers will have seen my blasts. They aren't as dumb as our leaders describe them."

Safon places a hand on my shoulder. "Have the others responded to your message?"

I place my hand on my anro but don't look at it. "No. Nothing."

His shoulders drop. "We can assume they attacked the others in a similar method. Edwin, take us to what remains of our boys. We will figure something out there."

Cramen shifts as if he wants to speak but stays silent.

Edwin guides us through alleyways, moving at a slow pace. No lights. Only the storm reveals our surroundings, and even then, it awakens for sparse moments. I want to move faster, but Edwin checks every shadow for danger. We never know when he is going to stop. After nearly an hour of what feels like wandering, he stops at the edge of a tall, narrow building and hesitates. The immediate area appears empty, but that seems to worry him. He expected to find something here.

Safon moves up alongside him. "What's wrong?"

Edwin points across the shadows to a compact structure that pales in comparison to the towering structures around it. "The smaller building there. We found it unlocked. The others are inside, but . . ."

"How many were outside?"

"Supposed to be at least two unless Redlanders were near."

Cramen brushes my shoulder. "With your leadership, they are probably neglecting their duties."

Edwin turns, and I see some spark of his prior defiance in his posture. "That may be intended to demean me, but that is the best-case scenario now." He points to the building where the Datum hides. "Otherwise, we are all that is left."

No Redlanders in sight," Safon says, moving forward to cut off the argument. "We should check now before we lose our chance."

We walk through the shadows to the building. Edwin taps on the metal. Minutes pass before the door slides open and light floods out. As it blinds us, an actare emerges inches from my face.

"Don't fire," Edwin says in a harsh whisper. "Why is there no one out here?"

The actare retreats. A boy half steps out of the light. "Redlanders were everywhere. Inside, now."

We move out of the darkness. The boy closes the door with a soft click. As he lets the door go, Edwin grabs him by the shirt and slams him into the wall. I take the moment and look around the small room. A blank message board sits on the wall but is void of anything else except a door that leads deeper into the building. It remains closed, locked for obvious reasons. I suspect the Council meant this place as some sort of shelter from the storm. Whether for us or people before the Sorbe's full wrath descended, I don't know.

Less than a dozen boys are present; the rest captives are of the Redlanders. Cade is among the missing.

"You left the light on with the door open!" Edwin tosses the boy into the others, who gather around their leader. He stares at them. "What are you doing? Who knows how many saw the light? Turn off your vels."

The room plunges into darkness. Not even the storm can illuminate us in here. Soft murmurs spread across the boys. Fear rises quickly, and Edwin's leadership does nothing to stop its surge.

"Everyone shut up! They may hear us."

He only adds to the noise.

I make out someone moving through the room. Whispers fade before reaching my ears as the boys' fears diminish.

Safon speaks, not that I can be certain, but the calm belongs only to him. "We can't be certain that anything saw the light. We saw nothing when we approached. The door closed quickly. Redlanders are stupid, and with the storm's light, they may confuse the two."

The fear in Edwin's voice stands out. "Listen to me when I say these Redlanders aren't dumb. Every moment you think they are gives them the advantage. Why do you think they are in the city? The Council thinks they're so dumb that they didn't even imagine their presence. They're here to take the city. To prove to our leaders they deserve more than the Red Plains."

The Redlanders embody the lack of control he believes the Council has. Now that his belief is reality, he's struggling. I understand. None of this makes sense. Is it possible the Council overlooked the threat of the Redlanders? Or worse, they knew and held this truth from us. The storm rips away all illusions. That's the only certainty we have.

"Persolus, what do you think?"

I turn on my velare. "To start—"

A metallic crack fills the room as the floor shakes. A rush of air slams me into the wall. I drop to my knees, gasping for air. My throat stings as I inhale. I look up. Pieces of metal drop from the ceiling. The side of the building is missing. The storm comes alive, giving us its light, displaying its destruction.

My vision blurs before refocusing.

The others lie on the ground. No movement. A dancing orange light fights the shadows. Redlanders. I try to force myself to my feet, but a pain shoots up my back. My legs collapse under my weight.

The swirling light fades to black.

21

Loyalty

"Lamis is a natural part of the Vox body, healing it of its wounds and giving strength in times of need. Research suggests healing begins within minutes of an injury, which can always be seen in the glimmer of blue." —an excerpt from A Study on Lamis: The Energy that Protects Us

Brilliant colors roll across the sky. They feel dangerous, but I cannot find a reason why. It must be a sunset. The vibrance rarely reaches the city, though. Time escapes me. Is it even the right mansii for the sun to set?

A figure sits in front of me. It speaks. Words pass by me, but I cannot determine their meaning. A voice, no, a breeze. The voice surrounds me but drifts off in a cool wind. The colors envelop the area, casting everything in beauty.

The figure stands and approaches me. Its appearance stings with familiarity, but it disappears into a blue mist with each step. Diask emerges out of the mist. Hours must pass as the Tatem appears to ask me questions. I can never give him answers, yet he seems content with my silence.

The mist expands as my father steps out. He makes demands I cannot understand. Demands answers to questions I don't know. With each step, his size increases until he blots out all the color, and all there is is the mist. His questions, his words weigh me down. He separates from the mist. The blue color calls to me.

I step into the mist, and my father's words disappear. A chill sweeps over my body.

Let us speak.

The mist shifts around me, filling my vision until everything turns black.

Pain spreads out from the back of my head to my eyes.

A cough overcomes me and reveals more pain in my chest. It is enough for me to want to return to whatever dreamless state I was just in. No dream. A peaceful silence. My head ignites in agony again.

As the misery subsides, I find myself on my back. I sit up and try to examine my surroundings. My vision is blurry, and my eyes sting when I try to focus on anything around me. It takes almost a minute before my vision returns to something resembling normal. No Redlanders.

In the darkness of the storm, I am alone.

My hands are free, and I feel no type of restraints anywhere else. Perhaps the Redlanders did not expect me to wake so soon. No lights are visible. I rub my eyes, trying to make sense of my situation. The buildings around me have wide bases and narrow as they climb into the sky. I'm nowhere near where Edwin had taken us. Am I a prisoner? Or did they discard my body thinking I was dead?

That seems most likely. Perhaps I am the only one who didn't wake.

A sharp pain surfaces at the back of my head, less intense than before. The discomfort fades after a moment. A wave of exhaustion sweeps over my body. I cannot be certain, but each sol brings more weakness, as if the storm is slowly draining my Lamis. But that isn't possible. The storm can't touch me. Erman is wrong.

The Council is right. The storm isn't affecting anyone else. There's something else wrong with me.

I muffle a scream.

I press my hand into my forehead and flinch.

If only my father would have explained how he enters the Council's reality and can see clearly. I can't see anything. Or does the Sorbe dilute everything beneath it? The only truth is the storm's. Here, Redlanders rule the city and command beasts. Are they even capable of understanding our Tech?

My legs shake as I use whatever my back's against to stand. Smooth and cold. That describes every building in the city. It's not a residential building as it towers nearly ten stories in the air, so I may still be in Sector One. Or Sector Five. Or even a small section of Two. The storm flashes, illuminating my surroundings for just long enough to confirm I don't know where I am. In the light, I might have some chance to orient myself, but not in the dark.

I take a step and hit my foot on something soft. My backpack. Did the Redlanders think it was a part of my body? No, they aren't that stupid. Edwin is right about that. I reach down and open it. A few green bars, my map, a velare, even my anro, and—the device Vitus gave me from Diask.

I activate the device and scroll through the files. Why Diask wanted me to have this escapes my comprehension. It's been useless so far. Nothing about generators or mysterious devices that draw the storm's wrath. Not even information about the anro, which I could use to figure out who hacked the network. The last two entries still hold no place in my memory. They aren't from any version of the Tatem handbook.

When I'm about to turn the device off, I realize the letters in the last two entries are a faint red. I was so busy trying to find meaning in the order of the symbols that I didn't look closer. I press the sequence of letters varying in color, and another file opens—my anro beeps at the same time. I reach down into my backpack and pick it up. The holographic screen pops up, but rather than the control interface, an image of Diask extends out. I feel the tug on my Lamis grow as the device requires extra power.

He stands in front of me, untouched by the storm. A few seconds pass before I realize what's happening is real and not a dream. He speaks to me.

"Seni—" I let out a gasp. I try to contain my confusion and shock as he continues talking. "I trusted Vitus to give this device to you. You should be familiar with the information from the endless hours of my instruction. I couldn't risk someone not giving you the device and discerning the information. The anro is an unfamiliar tool, but I trust you will realize its usefulness to understanding this device. Your excellence and resourcefulness is why I've selected you to serve in this Tatem role. My absence has been necessary, so I hope you still hold the same trust in me.

"This device's capacity is limited, so forgive my short remarks. By this time, you should know you face a Sorbe, a devastating force of nature that reveals the foolishness in even the smartest Vox. Many have tried to tame them, and all have had their stories stricken from the Historical Record. You are young, immune but not invulnerable. Caution is your best ally. And that is the reason for this message. I cannot speak of this to you in person.

"I fear someone works to undermine my preparation for the city. They hope to have the storm destroy or cripple the city. They must be targeting the Council. Or the unique research that happens away from the public's gaze. I don't know what methods they will use. The storm is the obvious weapon, with the city being vulnerable. So I urge you caution when you monitor the city's generators and other Tech I assign you. Take nothing for a mere circumstance of the storm. Your diligence will stop them. No matter their goals or strategies, only you can stand beneath the storm."

Diask's holographic image retracts into my anro.

I take Diask's device and smash it into the wall. It shatters. I let out a yell. I don't care who hears. Nothing makes sense. Diask knew someone threatened the city. He didn't tell the Council. He left it on some device that the wrong boy received.

I look at the pieces on the ground. Why didn't I mention the device to Seni? He would have recognized the Tech. Maybe some of it was useful. I gasp. This proves Diask's innocence. He wasn't trying to destroy the city. He was trying to help it. I destroyed the only evidence not condemning him.

I drop to my knees and plunge my hand into my backpack. With my velare, I search the wreckage. The memory core has to be somewhere. It's small. The outer casing would protect it. I can salvage the file Diask embedded. Prove his innocence.

I catch a breath when I find the small green disk. It's shattered in a dozen pieces. Any chance of salvaging the information on it is impossible. I imagine Seni's reaction. First, I accuse Diask of heinous crimes. Now I destroy the only evidence supporting the truth.

"I never imagined you being one to destroy a piece of Tech."

I turn toward the voice, blasting my velare in the person's face. A hand covers their face until I lower my light. Cramen. He limps forward. Blue glistens from his shoulder. His shirt is ripped, showcasing the bloody skin underneath.

"I would turn that thing off. Redlanders still rule the city. You haven't been out that long."

Extinguishing the velare, I sit back with my back to the wall. "How long?"

"Not quite a sol. I couldn't stop them from taking you, but I followed."

He grabs his arm near his wound.

"My backpack?"

"You thought the Redlanders brought it? I saved it. Thought you may still need that stuff. Well, I guess not all of it." His eyes look at the broken pieces.

"Where are the others?"

"Not sure. I think the blast killed a few. They kept the bodies separate. Probably some Redlander ritual to ensure they stayed dead."

He doesn't mention the Twins. Certainly that means they are alive.

"And your wound?"

He grimaces as he moves his shoulder. "A gift from a Redlander. Nasty blades they have. Cut clean through."

Not that I don't care about Cramen, but my questions are only to avoid asking about the Twins. They were closer to the explosion. But they're tough. Strong. And the storm isn't affecting their Lamis. Any injuries they sustained would heal. Despite being able to rationalize their survival, I don't ask Cramen, and he doesn't offer up the information.

The storm comes alive, casting its light into the alley. Cramen stares at the ground.

"Why'd you destroy that?"

I look at the pieces. "Doesn't work."

"Couldn't fix it?"

I glance at him quickly before returning my gaze to the broken Tech. "It was beyond my abilities."

"So you smash it?"

I turn fast enough that pain erupts across my chest. "Do you have an issue with something, Cramen?"

The space between us shrinks. "I want to know why the boy in charge of the city's Tech is smashing valuable assets on the ground. I saw you use that thing. It helped you combine two pieces of Tech. Or did your modification to the anro cause its malfunction?"

I underestimated Cramen's competency with Tech, though he doesn't realize Diask's device didn't help. "If you're questioning my abilities—"

"I'm questioning whatever thought caused you to destroy something Vitus gave you."

I pause for a second as I process his words. "How do you know that? You weren't with the boys in the Linam when Vitus addressed us for the last time."

He speaks without recognition of my response. "You're trying to prove something, earn your way into something you already have. Tell me, what do you have to prove to the Council? You're already the son of a Representative. You have the Alfaron name and a path to anything you want. What more do you need?" His voice cracks.

I now doubt how close Cramen is to the Council. He only sees them from a distance. He desires to know them more. Is that why he's out here? He's trying to gain their attention.

"I'm out here to serve the Council by protecting the city."

"No, *I'm* out here serving the Council. You're serving your own purposes. That's what you all are doing. Surviving for your own self-interest. After all this, you don't have to face *him*."

"Who are you talking about? *What* are you talking about?"

"You can't understand," he says. "I thought . . . I thought maybe you could, but I was wrong."

I lock eyes with Cramen. "Give me a chance, and I might. I know more about the Council than most."

A half-smile flickers across his face. "No. No, you don't."

A quick flash catches my attention. A blade arcs down toward Cramen. A Redlander is on the other side of the weapon. I dive forward, shoving Cramen away. Metal clashes with the ground. Sparks shoot into the air. I stumble backward, trying to create distance from the attacker. The Redlander drags the blade across the ground in the direction Cramen rolls. It swipes the blade up with a flick of its wrist, catching the boy in the back. His clothes offer no resistance.

Cramen screeches. The storm laughs.

It twirls the blade effortlessly in its hand. Glimmering blue blood falls off the tip. The Redlander looks at me but turns to Cramen. He's crawling backward, pain flashing across his face with each movement. The blade barely misses his head as the Techless creature moves closer.

It doesn't see me as a threat. I can use that.

Lowering my shoulder, I run through the pain that erupts in my body. I collide with the Redlander's backside. It stumbles forward and slashes with its blade over my head. When it looks at me, rather than strike with its weapon, it grabs me by the neck. My feet leave the ground as it stares at me. Its skin is pale, untouched by the sun. Scars cover most of its face. Red eyes look into my blue ones before it tosses me back. My heels hit first before my back slams into the ground.

Cramen must have taken advantage of my distraction. When I look up, he's jabbing the Redlander with something in his hands. Shrieks of pain fill the alleyway. It stumbles back, red blood dripping from multiple spots on its body.

No blue. No hint of Lamis in the Redlander's blood. They reject Tech, yes. But it's only because we've made it impossible to use without the energy that runs through our blood. No wonder they hate us. No wonder they want to destroy us. I still don't understand their presence here. The city and its technology are useless to them. Perhaps if we used solar-powered Tech it wouldn't be, but we don't.

Cramen points a small blade at the Redlander. He breathes heavily, grimacing with each breath. "He'll . . . destroy you . . . all. You aren't . . . you aren't supposed to be here. Not yet."

The Redlander responds. Its words are angry but empty of meaning. Cramen's face betrays recognition. He understands it. The Redlander stands straight, blood still dripping from its wounds. It points its blade at Cramen before sliding it into a long pocket. It limps away as the storm goes quiet, concealing its retreat.

Persolus

"When danger arises, seek a friend." —a Vecco saying

We remain silent as the Sorbe flashes with color but doesn't share its light. The shadows press in around us. The mysteries around Cramen grow denser. Before I didn't care, but now they suffocate me. He's providing no relief.

Cramen restricts his movement, allowing his Lamis to heal his wounds. Silence is not required, but he remains quiet regardless. I can still see the blood where the Redlander's blade struck him. The blue glimmer persists as the stains dry. It's the only thing that makes sense. The only thing that's acting within my understanding. Nothing else is.

Learning the language of the Redlanders is forbidden. No one tries. I have heard stories of others teaching them our language. The regulations around the practice dissuade most. The brutality of the Red Plain dwellers is a far more effective deterrent. I now only need to reference my own experience to confirm such reports.

"What's next?" I ask, refraining from the questions I want to ask. "That Redlander will come back with more. I don't think you can fight them all off."

"What's next? Nothing for us."

I shine my velare on him. "What do you mean by that? You followed the Redlanders to find me. We need each other."

He stands up faster than I think he is physically able. "You need me. The Datum needs me. I don't need any of you. I heard the recording. You were never even supposed to be in this position."

I gasp at the change in direction of the conversation. "We still have the same goals. Even you'll fare better with help."

He laughs and lets the confusing act linger. "Haven't you figured it out yet? You may claim we both serve the Council, but our goals are distinct. I've used the Datum for as long as it was manageable."

He then raises what appears to be a smaller version of an actare. It sits on the palm of his hand. The small dome glows blue. He grimaces as a flash of blue sends me into the darkness.

The city's dark when I wake. I keep wanting this all to be a dream. That I never woke from the first dream, and when I finally do, I will find out the storm never reached the city. Diask never died. I simply accepted my place with the Council. I now study under with the Representatives, learning their ways, their secrets.

The Sorbe casts its color over me.

Rejecting the truth of my reality does me no good. The storm remains. The Redlanders have the Datum, and Cramen has an agenda that surpasses my awareness. He's working for the Council. I do not understand how.

I rub my head. He has a good aim.

Words pierce the darkness. Flickering orange lights have me grasping my backpack and running in the opposite direction. I glance back to see a dozen dancing lights floating through the dark. I force myself to go faster, but my body fights back. Pain rips across my body. My legs sting with agony. I slam into a wall when my weight becomes too much to bear.

My breaths come out heavy. I've heard stories of people forcing their bodies to do the unthinkable in situations like this. Fantastical stories are all they are. Dragging my body against the wall, I move forward. I have no idea where I am. I could be walking into more Redlanders. I am faced with no other choice.

Words echo off the walls. They have not seen me or are taking their time in overtaking me. I turn a corner and stumble over my feet. I slam into the ground. Blood drips from my hand. Broken metal lies on the ground. I pick the pieces out of my hand, trying to withhold the screams of pain I want to unleash. Dropping the last bloody piece, I look up. Soft colors move across the clouds. They silhouette a corner missing from a building.

I search the side of the building for an entryway or a way to climb up to the hole. Halfway down, I find a door. I rip into the panel next to it and manually release the lock. I feel my wounds spike in agony as I put all my strength to release the pressure lock. An actare or anything else would make this faster. I lose my balance as the mechanism finally comes free. I hear the air release and the door slides open.

My first thought is to bounce to my feet, but I drag myself up and limp into the building. Leaving my blood behind on the door, I slide it shut.

I collapse on the floor.

My hands burn.

Just red drips onto my shirt as I look at my hands. Not even a speck of blue. Why is my body failing me? A stupid thought. I know why. The storm affects me. The Council refused to challenge their own truth, so they let me out here. All they had to do was admit the truth, and they could have refused my entry. But they didn't.

Voices draw my attention to the door. I let my head touch the floor and lie in silence. If they find me, perhaps they will think I am dead. Without my Lamis, death is inevitable. I only hope enough energy remains to power my implant. When the storm passes, they can find my body and enter what little I have to contribute into the Historical Record.

After a few minutes, any noise fades except for my labored breathing. I force myself up to a sitting position. My body aches. I look up and can see up into the storm. A variety of colors cast shadows into the room. Empty walls and debris surround me. I turn around to face a short, cylindrical device with a domed top. I don't need to approach it to realize it was set by Diask.

I start laughing and try to stop, but it is the only thing that numbs the pain.

Time passes with uncertainty. The pain rises and falls without warning. I feel my skin grow cold. The Sorbe steals my Lamis. It refuses to kill me quickly. It has to kill me differently. I wonder if my father had something to do with that. The Historical Record will ensure everyone knows I died different. A normal death is unfit for someone like me.

The device chirps behind me. Ignoring the pain, I turn around, crawling on all fours. I sit back on my heels and press my hand against the outer casing. The metal is cold, sending relief through my fingertips into the rest of my hand. I press my palm onto it and flinch before the coolness pushes back some of the pain. I stand up. My knees shake, but I ignore it.

"Why should I have to die alone?" The words slip quietly off my lips. The storm wants to kill me quietly, but I can control it with Tech. It will act on my terms. The Redlanders will fear me with their final breaths.

I retrieve my anro from my backpack and open the door. I step out into the darkness and scream as loudly as I can. The storm responds. Colors crack across the sky. As the colors quiet, voices grow louder.

Yellowish-orange light fills the small transport path that runs between the buildings. I try to count the individual lights, but I stop at twenty-one. The number grows. My heart beat increases, then my breathing. But I stand still and let out another scream. No more hiding.

The Redlanders move faster, closing in on my position. I turn my velare on and drop it in the doorway. I step inside and approach the domed device that waits to draw the storm. Removing the access panel, I use my anro to activate its systems. **Anro detected: Sequence initiated: 1 minute.** The automated voice does not bring fear but relief. It ends now.

The outer casing shifts, expanding to bring about my end.

I turn to face the door. Orange light creeps through the shadows. I drop my anro into my backpack.

Diask was wrong. You cannot tame a storm. But you can direct it.

Silhouettes enter the doorway. Blades reflect the orange light. I smile. I almost do not notice the pain across my body diminishing. My legs stop shaking. My heart beats more slowly. I glance down at my hand. Speckles of blue form and disappear.

I sense fear in the Sorbe.

The irrational thought is all I can think of as a Redlander stabs me with its blade. Straight through my chest. It is too low to hit my heart. I gasp for air. I look down and grin. My blood coats its blade with a shimmering blue.

Then the storm strikes.

Renewal

"Lamis is the great mystery of Solisternum. Those who claim to know its secrets know very little. The true researchers of our energy know our knowledge will never be complete."—unknown source

The Council is wrong about death.

Death is not quiet or painless. I am not lost to oblivion. My body burns with agony. Death is everything suffered in life twice over. I want to return to the living and warn others of this torture. No place in the Historical Record is worth this suffering. But no one returns from death. No chance to teach others the Council's lie.

But this cannot be death. I cannot accept the Council is wrong about something else.

I am on the edge of life. My body is refusing to let go.

My eyes are stuck shut. My limbs refuse to obey my commands. I only want to cry out. Death will come as a pleasure when it comes for me finally. But now, it only watches me suffer.

A breeze moves across my body. It coincides with the pain subsiding. It lingers, but lessens. My eyes open to a blue haze. My head refuses to turn, leaving me to look up at the storm. It mocks me. The storm refuses to submit to me in my moment of triumph. It was never going to let me die a quick death.

Or the Council is right. I am immune to the storm. It can hurt me but cannot kill me. My death is at the hands of the Redlander. I can feel the wound in the middle of my chest. It burns.

A hooded figure moves within my limited eyesight. Their face is dark with shadow. Baggy clothing hides any other discernable features. They grab my arms, and my skin burns. The sky moves as they drag me. They struggle. It cannot be a Redlander. They are tall and strong.

My neck gives way to my control. Remnants of the storm's wrath surround me. I feel the occasional piece of debris hit my back. This is my doing. How did I survive?

The pain from the figure's hands flares. It spreads out to my hands and neck before traveling down my back. I gain control of my limbs and writhe in agony. The figure lets me go. The pain does not linger but moves until it stops at the back of my head.

My eyes burn before I slip back into oblivion.

When I wake again, everything feels to be a distant memory—the pain, the figure—and in its place is a resurgence of energy I thought impossible to feel again. I have control over my body. I expect pain or at least soreness as I sit up, but nothing comes. I feel amazing. I touch my forehead, and my wound is gone. My hands search my chest, and my skin is whole.

My Lamis is whole.

I pull at the hole in my shirt where the Redlander's blade pierced me. The smile I feel on my face fades slowly. A scar remains, smooth, but a discoloration of my skin betrays its presence. My Lamis is not entirely normal. It fails to remove the mark that I now have to live with. Does my head still hold on to its wound?

Or this all is another dream? My Lamis's adverse state reflects this false reality. I am dying, and this dream is the only thing I have left before passing into the Historical Record. The scar is my failure.

I stand up, still expecting some pain, but find none.

A crack of color reminds me of the storm's presence.

Buildings surround me, tall, but general in appearance. Their image does not bear any markings from the storm.

"If this is a dream, just end this! Strike me! Show me your power and wipe me from existence." My words drop to a whisper. "What are you waiting for?"

I close my eyes and stretch my arms out.

Then another voice answers mine. "I've heard stories of people surviving Sorbes and going crazy."

Familiarity rushes over me. I know the voice, but refuse to turn around.

"Never met a crazy person before," the voice continues. "You'll have to let me know what it's like when you survive this storm."

I press my hands into my temples. "No, no. Why do you torture me? End this already. Let me wake to whatever truth I have to face. Not this. Not again."

A hand touches my shoulder. A slight pain grows in my chest. "Zayne, turn around and face me."

"And witness the storm destroying . . . I can't. I won't."

She pulls on my shoulder, but with my returned strength, I resist. "Face me, Zayne. I don't know what's happened out here. But I'm here now. I can help."

"But you aren't here," I say. I look up. "What are you waiting for? Strike already. End this dream and bring me back to reality, whether that means death or life for me."

Her hand slips off my shoulder. "Zayne, this isn't a dream."

"Prove it."

"That burden lies on your shoulders," she says. "But this isn't the first dream you've been trapped in. Ask yourself, what's different about this one?"

A clear voice. Her voice.

I turn to face Soriina.

Along the Network

"Complementary parts are key to greater innovation."
—Tech Development Guide, *version 20.131217*

The storm does not strike. It stays silent as Soriina and I reunite. Her embrace breaks any doubt I have of whether this is real. I push back every question and thought as we hug. My senses dull as my arms squeeze. My eyes water underneath my eyelids. All I want to do is collapse and have everything but this moment be a dream. I want to wake up to clear skies and to the time where Soriina was my only friend. And death was a story, not a reality.

My dreams strike in my memory. Soriina dies from the storm, over and over again. I open my eyes and release her, stepping away. The Sorbe makes its presence known, causing me to step away further.

I can feel Soriina's stare. She does not have to ask. I tell her everything. Diask and his preparation. His death at the hands of the storm. The device. Edwin and Cade. The Redlanders and the beasts they command. My choosing of the Twins—she is not surprised; she knew I would make such a decision.

I know I miss a few details, even mess up the order of things. I tell her enough. Enough that she forms questions and seeks clarification on many of my points. Her questions help bring clarity even to points I was uncertain about. A few still are murky. That's because I omit the details.

"This Cramen appears to be the least of your concerns," she says after a few minutes of silence. "I don't care if he shot you. He didn't kill you." She points to my chest. "The Redlanders are the greater concern. They tried to kill you."

Soriina faces most difficulty without flinching, a quality that always surprises me. But here, it speaks to something she is not telling me. She knows my story, but I do not know hers. She doesn't appear willing to share it. She shouldn't be here. She knows that but doesn't share her story as willingly as I have.

"How did you come to be out in the storm?" I ask.

She avoids my gaze. Her thoughts searching for ways to avoid my question. She's focused on my words and descriptions to avoid thinking about her own.

"Soriina, you cannot expect me to see you and not question your presence. Only one of us is supposed to be here."

"What matters is that I *am* here," she says, raising her eyes to me. "Let me help."

I raise and lower my hands as I force out my words. "You are asking the impossible. How can I focus when your presence brings uncertainty?"

"You are focusing too much on this."

"No, Soriina, I'm not. The last person whose secrets I ignored shot me. I need to know what happened in Sector Two."

"I'm not going to shoot you, and nothing I know means anything now." She steps closer. "You trust me. You're out here to protect the city. Let me help you do that."

I can't stop a laugh from coating my first words. "Did you listen to what I said? I haven't been protecting anything. Our only option is to outlast the storm and hope nothing else goes wrong." My voice trembles. "How many died when the storm forced you from your home?"

"Don't say it like that," she says, her lips quivering. "I am here of my own accord. Nothing you did or didn't do is the reason."

I let a silence sit between us, but she doesn't let it last long.

"The Council put you in an impossible situation," she says. "They lacked the foresight to see the People's Representative taking advantage of the storm even after his speech."

She still believes my lie. Or she allows me to continue in my lie.

"How do you know it's him?"

Vitus thought Carius played some part. How have I not seen this?

"You haven't put it together? He had advanced research to predict the storm's first strike. Certainly he can influence the storm to some extent. His downfall was his inability to predict the Redlanders taking advantage of the Sorbe. We now pay that price for both his and the Council's mistakes."

My focus was entirely on Diask until recently. I never thought to consider the People's Representative as the man behind what we face during the storm. He can no longer be a threat, for he is under the Council's judgment, unless his power supersedes the Prava and he acts even while under their watch. Soriina points out such obvious points. How can I think with any clarity when her presence demands answers?

"The Council placed Carius under their judgment," I say. "He's no threat."

"Use that brain of yours. This is one elaborate plan to force us to use solar energy. He knew he would either be captured or killed during his speech. He set everything into motion to move ahead without him."

"Wouldn't his plan fall short if everyone knows he's involved?"

She laughs. "The Sorbe's presence is all his plan needed. The Council now faces a new reality—one they don't control—about how Sorbes can reach the city. It doesn't matter if Carius predicted the storm reaching us or forced it upon the city. The Council will spew some lie that protects the truth they want the people to see."

With all that has happened, it still feels wrong to doubt our leaders. But I can't ignore their recent failings. "Certainly the Council will find some way to counter this."

Her head tilts to the side. "Perhaps, but I think the damage will be too much to control. The people will see some weakness in the Council, regardless. But will they be strong enough to do something about it?"

I watch her carefully. Whatever she refuses to tell me has changed her.

"You want them to."

Soriina shakes her head. "Don't tell me you think the Council has handled this all well? If the people don't respond, the Council won't change." She stretches her arms out. "And this all happens again."

She regrets the division she is causing, so she changes the conversation. She shifts closer and points to my head and chest. "Our wounds don't scar anymore. What caused these? You didn't specify."

I also left out the recording on the device meant for Seni. And how I didn't fully reset my anro. I guess I missed the detail about the Sorbe affecting my Lamis, too. She has her secrets, and I have mine. A part of me wants to tell her and help me understand these things. Another part doesn't sense the same trust in Soriina that I always seemed to have before.

"I guess we both have our secrets," I say.

I regret the words, no matter how insignificant they seem. The girl with nothing to hide now seems to hold more secrets than the Council. As a sign of peace, I shift the topic.

"What's with the weird clothes?" I think the question is less divisive, but she averts her eyes. The sleeves hide her arms as she crosses them, while a hood hangs behind her head.

She avoids the question, which only pulls at my curiosity more. "You mentioned the Redlanders had taken the others. Do you know where to start looking?"

I let silence hang in the air, so she knows I recognize her avoidance. "Cramen never told me where they took me. I don't even know where to begin."

Soriina pulls her oversized coat tighter. The temperatures are cooler but nothing requiring additional layers. The clothing pulls at some thread of familiarity, but even with my renewed strength, I can't grasp the connection. She pulls a backpack off, which I do not notice until she is extending it out to me. "This was with you when I found you. Not much in it, but I thought it would be important."

I open the bag and pull out my anro. A single green bar is all that remains. My map is missing.

"Does that help us?" she asks.

I squeeze my anro. No messages. I should have listened to Seni.

"No, no one's responding to any messages," I lie. "We think the Redlanders attacked everyone. No one's been responding since."

Soriina stares at the useless device in my hand. "How many of those are there?"

"Each Tech leader had one," I say.

"You still have yours, so the Redlanders don't understand Tech enough to have taken it. The others should still have theirs."

"What are you getting at?"

"Certainly you can track them, right?"

"I haven't tried that," I say. "No one mentioned that."

"And when has that stopped you before?" She points at the anro then up. "The network connects each device. Even if they don't respond, you should be able to trace their location. You can access the network from the anro, so with a little tweaking, you could follow a message through the network to where it stops. Presumably, another anro."

She's right. Soriina has never understood Tech with such precision. Anros and the network are not common Tech. Asking her how she knows will only frustrate me and delay any useful course of action. The curiosity stings still.

I connect my anro to the magnetic clip on my belt. She's almost right. "In theory, yes, but the anro doesn't have a map function. It tells me the general direction of a signal. Being short-range, that's enough. We don't know where the others are. We could be walking for hours before we know we're headed in the right direction."

She tosses something at me. "What about this?"

I nearly drop it before securing it with both hands. I turn the item over and realize it's a map. The same design the Datum had. "Where'd you get this?" She would tell me if this was mine.

Her answer comes a few seconds later than I think necessary. She's coming up with a lie.

"Stumbled across a pile of rubble and junk," she says. "My goal was to find you, so I thought you might find some use for it."

It's not even a good lie. "And how did you even find me?"

"No one told me where to go, if that's what you're getting at," she says. "I know this Cramen seems to be here with some ulterior motives, but that doesn't mean everyone is."

"Forget I asked anything." The storm is cooperative, maintaining enough light for me to work. Soriina probably has a velare, not that I'm going to ask her. She shouldn't have one, and if she does, she'll lie about how she received it.

I drop to my knees and place the two devices on the ground. I flip the map over and remove the back panel. My anro gives a general direction for the Tech it detects, but with a few tweaks . . . I can send the scan details to the separate map. The two devices are easier to link than I first expect. As long as my anro can detect a signal, the map will show its location.

Soriina squats next to me. "Are you done yet? I don't like standing around the same place."

A genuine fear laces her words.

"I think so," I say. "I just need to send a message and hope it shows up on the map."

"It will."

I don't know if she trusts my abilities or whoever told her about tracing the signal. Not that she'll confirm that. She met someone beneath the storm. But she's not with them now, so either they left her or something worse happened. Perhaps her avoidance of my questions is her way of protecting herself. Memories flash in my mind of the storm's victims.

I write out a short message and send it. The map's screen flashes before settling on a building near the border of Sectors Five and One.

"Where are we going?"

I reset the map to our position. We're near the border of Sectors Two and One.

"I picked up a signal on the far-center edge of Sector One," I say. "Not far, but if the Redlanders are holding them at this location, we should stick to the alleys. It'll take longer but will be safer."

"Just in Sector One?"

Does she realize her questions are betraying her dishonesty? I have to bite back a response. I know it'll only delay us further.

"Only one signal pinged on the map," I say. "Could mean they are all in one spot, or only one device received my message."

"We should be moving."

I should be happy to be with Soriina. She's the one piece I was missing being out here. But her secrets push me away. She doesn't trust me, but I don't know why. Cramen comes to mind. The Council sent him. Our leaders never intended to put their trust in the Datum. Not even me.

Why then would they trust me with their secrets? If not them, why should Soriina?

The thoughts eat away at my mind as we walk. Soriina checks every shadow while I keep my eyes on the map. The dim light of the screen is enough to affect my ability to see within the darkness. I'm not sure if the storm is trying to help us or hurt us.

The shadows keep Soriina quiet, and the last thing I want to do is talk. I silently thank the storm.

Eyes

"Three out of four sets of twins die at birth. Less than ten percent reach the age of ten."—A Study of Children: What Makes Them Different, *chapter 4, page 14*

The Sorbe stays quiet. It makes our path more difficult, but the darkness maintains a silence between us. I need to focus on what's ahead and not what Soriina's hiding. We walk nearly an hour in between the buildings of Sector One. Most alleys are wide enough to walk comfortably, while others require us to squeeze through, which slows our progress.

We have to cross the Sector at a diagonal to reach where the map leads us to. We have to exit the alleyways and cross smaller transport paths five times. I have us walking parallel with the Sector Five border now.

The next transport path will lead straight to where the Redlanders are keeping the Datum. Or that's what I hope.

"Zayne, I know Redlanders roam the city, but must we walk in silence?"

I try to keep my voice low and flat. "What would you have us talk about?"

Soriina senses my true tone. "Please, understand I don't keep secrets to hurt you. You will understand and even thank me, but not this sol."

She's delusional.

"What's the difference between this sol and next? You used to be careful with your words to ensure clarity. Now you bring nothing but confusion."

Soriina turns away from me. "I cannot force an understanding upon you." She looks at me. "But do you trust me enough to leave this alone for another sol?"

The Sorbe blankets us in color.

I see fear in her eyes.

I offer her a smile—a genuine one. "Let's find the others and deal with these abominations."

An uneasiness fills me as we encounter nothing the closer we get. Will the Redlanders keep the boys near their main encampment, or are we headed to a remote area where they keep their prisoners?

The storm occasionally flashes, pushing back my anxiety. We take advantage of the colors, moving faster.

We stop at the edge of the alley we're in. The transport path lies ahead of us. There's no connecting alley behind us as I had hoped. We're two subsections away from the building. I lean my back against the wall facing the direction we need to go.

"We have to go that way, down the main transport path," I say.

Soriina pulls on her hood. "What are we waiting for? Let's go."

"Stay on the sidewalk close to the building and try to keep to the shadows," I say. "We're going to be out in the open. If there are Redlanders around, we won't have many places to hide."

Soriina nods, and we step out. A slight ledge separates the sidewalk from the section containing the hover tracks. The smooth metallic track glistens with the storm's colors. A blue hue extends from the tracks when transports glide overtop. The air is stagnant now.

Soriina tugs on my arm. "I don't think the Redlanders are flying transports. If they are, we might as well abandon the city."

A grin forms on my face. "Maybe they'll give us a ride out."

Soriina shakes her head. Her smile tells me she's holding onto this fleeting moment of normalcy. If it wasn't for her smile, I may have cursed myself for my humor. The city is in danger, and I make a joke.

I make note of several alleys across the metallic tracks.

The storm sends blasts of light, ensuring if there are Redlanders, they would see us. But as my heart beats faster, the Sorbe also shows us we are alone. My uneasiness only grows at the realization.

We reach the edge of the sidewalk before it turns to the left around the corner of the building. A smaller transport path crosses in front of us. A small building with windows across the top section and a single door below marks where the boys should be. A taller structure stands behind it, which I believe connects.

"Is that it?" Soriina asks.

"My message pinged off another anro from that building. Probably is a small entryway, where they're being kept. The main part of the building is probably closed off."

"That's a lot of probablys," Soriina says. "And is there a *probably* about why there aren't any Redlanders around?"

I force a half-smile. "Let's hope the Redlanders are *probably* keeping the boys separate from where they're gathering." I place my backpack on the ground and put the map and my anro inside. "It could be a trap."

"This wouldn't be the first one you've walked into."

I stand up, securing my pack. "Thanks for the reminder."

"We're here, so we should check. We can hide in those alleys by the transport path if we have to. A few looked pretty cramped. I don't think a Redlander would fit."

She's right. The Redlanders I've seen won't fit. A beast may squeeze through, though. I push the thought down.

We cross the stagnant transport path to the door. It's unlocked. I place my hand on the door and stop. I close my eyes and push the door back into its compartment in the adjacent wall. The storm doesn't strike, so I open my eyes. The immediate space inside is dark and silent. No sign of the boys or Redlanders. But the unlocked door told me that from the start.

I turn back to Soriina. I keep my words soft. "You didn't find a velare along with that map, did you?"

She walks up to me and looks inside. The storm provides enough light to produce a few details. A few chairs and a table, but no evidence the boys were ever here. "No, but this just looks like a waiting area. There should be another . . ." She walks in a few feet, and I hear another door slide open. Flickering lights outline a larger room. Before I can object, Soriina walks inside.

I look back, expecting the storm to rush in, but it doesn't.

I follow her into a room with a ceiling nearly fifteen feet high. The farthest wall is nearly thirty feet away, but the shadows make determining the actual size impossible. I expect to see another device waiting for me to activate it and unleash the storm's wrath, but the room is empty. Not even a storage box. The layout is void of any specifics, so I cannot even determine a purpose or why the building is unlocked. A few dim lights line the nearest walls. They don't appear to be natural to the room. It feels like another trap by whomever hacked the anro network. Soriina lets her arms drop to her sides, allowing her sleeves to extend beyond her hands.

"Will you wait?" I speak softly.

Soriina's voice rises, echoing off the walls as she walks further in. "There's no one here, Zayne."

With my eyes on Soriina, I hear something to my right in a deep shadow. Before I can look, a voice reaches my ears. "Zayne." The intensity of the lights increases twofold.

When my eyes adjust, I face the dome of an actare. Cramen holds the weapon out. His arm is steady, but his eyes waver. He looks over at Soriina, then back to me.

"What are you doing here?"

The actare doesn't scare me. It should, but my hatred for Cramen numbs the appropriate emotions. "You think you can ask questions after you shot me? You left me there for Redlanders to find me. They nearly killed me."

He jerks the actare at me. "Don't blame me for the results of your actions. Now what are you doing here? Answer me before I shoot you again." He twists the weapon so I can see its full size. "This isn't like the one I shot you with before."

He wants me to think he's going to hurt me, but his actions betray his words. He isn't pushing any energy through the weapon. The dome remains idle. He was expecting someone else.

"I followed a signal here. Was that you?"

His words are uncertain, half directed at me and half directed to himself. "The signal. I didn't expect it to be you."

I soften my tone. "Why did you bring me here?"

His eyes harden in the flickering light. "You're here to face the Council's judgment." He sees the change in my eyes. "You thought the Datum served the Council. I serve the Council. Your presence has only been a nuisance."

"I don't believe you."

He laughs. "I would say ask your father, but your presence here means you're not leaving the storm. The son of a Representative with all the potential in Solisternum. What a waste."

"Then tell me before I breathe my last breath. Why is the Datum out here if not to serve the Council?"

"The Council's plan never needed them," Cramen says. "They needed me. You are simply the means that they hide their will from the people. Not everyone understands why the Council acts as they do, so they aren't allowed to know."

"What does the Council have you doing?"

"I'm maintaining their control," he says. "You would understand that if you were even a fraction of the Alfaron your father is."

Soriina moves, and he jerks the actare toward her. "Stay there! Who are you?" She pushes back her hood. "You're not supposed to be out here."

"What, because I'm a girl?"

I need to act. Disarm him.

He turns his weapon back to me. Too late.

"You're entering buildings? Bringing people into the storm? You're compromising everything. I understand why they want you here."

"He had nothing to do with my presence here."

Cramen takes an exaggerated step toward Soriina. "I don't know who you are, but shut your mouth."

I don't hesitate this time. I lunge forward, grabbing him by the wrist. I push his arm up before sending my fist into his stomach. He grins as he rips free from my grip. He smashes his actare into my face. I feel my skin break. I stumble back. My vision blurs.

Blue flashes fill the room.

My vision clears. Cramen isn't the one firing. Soriina is. My former Aemiin lies in the corner. His actare lies on the ground next to him.

Soriina has her own weapon. Blue sparks spit out, forcing her to drop it.

She runs over to me, pulling me to my feet. "Let's go before he gets up. My actare didn't have much power. Only enough to stun him."

"Where . . ." When I come up with one question, another forces itself forward, leaving me mute. I plant my feet and force Soriina to stop. "What's going on?"

"Not here, Zayne."

Cramen struggles to his feet, using the wall to balance himself. He looks at us with heavy breaths, then reaches into his pocket and pulls out a small rectangular piece of Tech. "Sorry, Zayne. I have no choice."

I take a step forward. "What do you mean? What does the Council have you doing?"

He laughs. "I thought of anyone out in this storm, you would understand. But I was wrong." He raises his hand up and squeezes the device with his thumb.

The lights on the wall turn a bright blue. He's drawing the storm here. Any previous understanding shatters. My thoughts freeze my body, trying to reconnect the lines that lay broken in my mind.

Soriina barrels into me, breaking the hold my thoughts have on me. We crash to the ground. Light from the storm floods in through the doorway. No shadows remain as vibrant colors bounce across the sky. Soriina is on her feet quickly, pulling me. I scramble, barely making it out of the second doorway before the storm crashes into the building. Metal cracks as an explosion propels me to the ground. I feel hot air rush overtop of me. I crawl forward without looking back. I can hear the metal crashing in on itself.

"Zayne!"

Soriina pulls me to my feet. My Lamis flows freely to my limbs, energizing my movement. The storm's too busy striking the building to hinder me.

We reach the nearest alley and dart inside. We run without worry of Redlanders or beasts. The sound of destruction is only a distant rumbling after a few minutes. But when the shadows return, our steps slow and my anxiety returns.

Swirling lights sharpen my focus about a hundred feet in front of us.

"Soriina." My words are low but sharp. She sees what I do and immediately darts into another alley with me close behind.

The Redlanders don't come close, but we can hear them. Their heavy steps persist for nearly ten minutes. I even hear the scuffling feet of beasts. I stifle my breaths until the sounds fade. Soriina glances around the corner and looks back at me.

"They're gone." She steps out before I grab her arm.

"Soriina, stop. We don't know where we're going. We could walk into another group of Redlanders."

Her hands drop to her knees. "That boy . . . he tried to kill us."

My first thought is to turn the conversation on her. She had an actare. But I push down the impulse. A thousand other thoughts replace it. I can't concentrate on a single one.

"And he used the storm."

She tries to pull my thoughts away from her.

"I think you know who's behind some of the things you've experienced."

Cramen is the last person I want to settle on. He's dead now, and he took every secret with him.

"Soriina, did you not hear him? He directly connected himself with the Council."

"You believed him? It's more likely he was helping the People's Representative."

She's wrong. He would boast in defiance of the Council. Why pretend? No, he sought their approval. Only the Council is worth dying for. But I don't understand what our leaders hope to accomplish by his actions.

"We can't believe anything he said," Soriina says. "The storm affected his mind."

I jerk my head at Soriina faster than I intend. "What did you say?"

"Sorbes affect Lamis, which affects the mind. The Council broadcasts covered this after you left. They said you were immune to bring ease to the people, but anyone with common sense could figure out they were lying. Certainly you figured that out. Cramen wasn't thinking well." She pauses, if only now realizing he didn't escape the building. "You aren't. No one out here is."

"And you are?"

She knows I misspeak. I take a couple of breaths.

"Sorry. You're right. I feel the storm messing with my thoughts." I let out a chuckle. "You may be the only one thinking straight, at least for now."

She tugs on her hood. "On that thought, we need to find the others."

"Any ideas?" I ask, placing my backpack on the ground and pulling out my anro and map. "We can't risk relying on this again." The temptation creeps up to try again, but I don't know how many others like Cramen lurk in the shadows. The Council wouldn't rely on one person. But do I even understand how the Council would choose to act?

"Which direction is Sector Five?"

I glance at the map and point in the direction the Redlanders went. "That was a large group. If they intend to take the city, occupying Sector Five is their best strategy."

"We go in the opposite direction, then. If the Datum are alive, they're back there. The Redlanders have no need for prisoners. The storm is their leverage."

"If they're alive."

Soriina squeezes her eyes shut. "Keep your mind straight. They're alive. I know it."

Confidence lines her words.

I don't know where she finds it. I felt mine bleed out as my Lamis returned.

But I trust Soriina.

We risk walking along the metallic tracks of the smaller transport paths. Ash tells us the Redlanders traveled the same way. We hope we are headed in the opposite direction. We determine the boys may be kept in a storm-damaged building. We don't think the Redlanders can access sealed buildings. Not ones big enough to hold all the boys.

It feels wrong to discuss the Redlanders having some reasonable intelligence, but I relent.

I keep my mind focused on finding them. Being so close to Sector Two, I hope Seni is with them, even if he's a prisoner. I can apologize for not fixing my anro. I know it's still broken. That's why Cramen was able to lead us into his trap.

I wonder how the Twins will react to Cramen's betrayal. I don't think Erman will be surprised.

"Zayne, look there."

Soriina points to a series of buildings with varying levels of damage.

"If the Redlanders took this path, they may have used these buildings. Keep the boys from interfering."

"Why not just kill them?"

I regret the question. It diverts my thoughts.

Soriina doesn't answer.

The storm does.

Beneath the color, I can see metal panels on the ground near the doors of two of the buildings. The Redlanders must have accessed the manual controls. I ignore the ramifications of the idea as I run up to the closest one. A metal fragment jams the locking mechanism.

I slam my hands on the door.

"Is anybody in there?" I look at Soriina. "Check the other building. Someone's accessed the manual controls there as well."

I press my ear up against the metal. I slam my hand against the door again. This time, there's a response. I can hear voices growing, echoing off the walls and escaping through the damaged walls. Unable to contain myself, I slam my hands into the door, jumping up and down.

"Who's in there? Are you alright?"

Overlapping voices make it impossible to discern who's behind the door. I grab hold of the fragment trapping the boys. My hands burn as I wiggle the piece until it comes free. Ignoring the pain, I grab the lever and push it to the unlocked position. A hiss of metal precedes the door moving slightly.

Before I can try to push it the rest of the way open, someone on the inside does. I see hands reach around the edge as the opening grows. After a few seconds, I come face-to-face with a bloodied boy.

His eyes beam. "Persolus. You're alive." Safon moves forward and embraces me. His hug is strong, despite his appearance.

I fear it isn't his blood.

We take a step away. I try to look past Safon.

"Who's here?"

"Not everyone," he says. "We don't know where they took the others. There are boys from Sectors One and Two here."

"Zayne." I turn to Soriina sprinting up. "There are boys in the other—Safon." Soriina jumps forward, gripping the twin tight. Their embrace warms my heart, and I tuck the memory away in my mind.

"Don't forget to ask about the other twin." Erman steps out around his brother. I can't stop a chuckle as I hug him. He squeezes me hard, but with my renewed strength, I do the same.

"Never thought I would see you hugging one of the Coffer boys," Soriina says.

Erman shoves me away. "Yeah, it was his idea. He forced me to hug him."

"Come here." Soriina hugs him, but not as tight as his brother.

The other boys slowly exit the building. They keep their eyes to the shadows rather than the storm. It greets the boys with vibrant colors.

I watch each one as they exit, waiting for Seni. The boys finally stop appearing in the doorway. He has to be in the other building.

Several of us make quick work of unlocking the door and freeing the remaining boys. Fearful faces turn to joyful reunions as boys greet each other. I stand there, accepting friendly smiles and formal and informal gestures of thanks, even the occasional hug.

The last two boys to exit support another boy on their shoulders. Makeshift bandages made from shirts wrap his right leg from his knee down to his ankle. Soriina pushes past me and grabs him by the face. I hear tears in her voice. "I thought they killed you. Oh, Seni—"

I don't hear anything else. He's here, and he's alive.

I step closer, and when he sees me, he looks into my eyes. My knees buckle. I stumble back.

His eyes aren't Seni's.

To Bear the Weight

"The anro network was a primitive tool for cities with insufficient energy stores to maintain a more efficient communication network . . . Anro networks deteriorate over time as messages are never lost but are stored along the network pathways until they find their destination at a proper device."—Ancient Tech and Their Replacements, *chapter 59, page 2*

Every color imaginable streaks across the sky. That's when Arsen collapses. The boys struggle to keep him up. I now realize his wounds show no sign of his Lamis healing him. Whatever energy flows through his body barely keeps him alive. We carry him back inside the building. Safon and Erman watch over him as I pull Soriina to the side. I've had enough of her secrets.

"You met Seni," I say. It's not a question, and Soriina doesn't add or subtract from the statement, so I continue. "The actare and the map were his. He gave them to you. Why? What happened to him?" I know the answer, but I want to hear it from her.

Arsen's painful breaths fill the somber silence. Seni's brother deserves to know the truth. I pull Soriina with no resistance over to him, and he coughs before rolling on his side.

"You shouldn't be moving," Safon says.

Arsen's bicolor glare rises to Soriina as he ignores the advice. "I need to know."

"Know what?" Erman asks.

Arsen only talks to my dearest friend. "What happened to my brother?"

Soriina steps forward. "You don't—"

"I do."

I take hold of Soriina's hands. "He deserves the truth." I whisper my next words, so only she hears. "I deserve the truth."

A part of me doesn't want her to tell me. I know the answer, but in her silence, I can reject what I know to be true. But that won't help Arsen. He needs to know, though I'm not certain he's come to the same conclusion I have yet. His hope tears at me with no mercy.

Soriina kneels next to Arsen as another coughing fit ends. "Your brother saved me."

She pauses, remembering something she is choosing not to tell us.

"I think the Redlanders liked seeing the storm strike the homes. They had their beasts rip into walls and windows of homes we knew were empty. We heard the storm strike, but the preparations were enough. The damage was minimal. We were one of the few families sheltering in Sector Two. You don't live there without some important job, so most were given invitations to shelter in Five. We weren't certain the Redlanders knew which homes had people or not.

"We couldn't risk the Redlanders breaching our walls. When the periis left our home, they told us they couldn't complete the purge of our systems. The seals would be enough to keep the storm from detecting the Lamis. Any breach would cause at least enough of an explosion to level our home. That's when my parents sent me out into the storm. Gave me this jacket to reduce any spikes in my Lamis. I had a better chance out here than in my own home."

She pauses at the absurdity of her comment.

"We waited for the storm to strike another part of the city, and out I came. Turns out the storm doesn't strike multiple places at once. Or that's what my father said. I know there's more to it, but I didn't have time to ask questions. When I came around to the main path, I saw the Redlanders descending upon my home. I should have run as my father commanded. But I couldn't. I tried to stop them, but that abomination didn't hesitate. He drove a blade through the door . . . such simplicity compared to our Tech. The hands of the cruel don't need much. And the storm needed less."

My chest tightens, and I feel all the breath in my body escape all at once.

Arsen coughs as he manages a few words. "What of my brother?"

"That's when I met him. The explosion was enough to scare the Redlander off. Seni and a few other boys were nearby when they found me. He said the Redlanders had attacked his sector camp. Everything they had worked toward was gone. Storm strikes increased. We kept to the shadows for the next two sols. He wouldn't allow even the simplest of conversations.

"The third sol, we remembered to share our names. How improper of us as Alfarons. No time for proper introductions in the face of the storm. I don't know how the conversation formed, but we realized we both knew you, Zayne. He even sent you several messages that I was in the storm. But . . . but clearly you never received those."

My hand instinctively goes to my waist even though my anro isn't there. How many other messages did I miss?

"My brother?" Arsen repeats.

Does he not know how this story ends? I try not to think about it.

"I convinced him to return to Sector Two to see my home. He didn't want to, but he relented. They were waiting for us, it seemed. I know that wasn't possible, but it felt that way. With the use of beasts, they singled the boys out, capturing them one by one. They singled Seni out differently. All I could do was watch as the Redlander drew its blade on him. It didn't hurt any of the others. It didn't make sense. What sense does it make to rationalize the actions of the senseless?"

"What happened to my brother?"

He lets out a horrid cough.

Emotion overwhelms Soriina's face.

I spare her the final detail. "The Redlanders killed him."

The storm screams with Arsen.

That's the last time we hear Arsen. His physical pain and now emotional trauma cause him to pass out.

I separate myself from the others. A sol passes. Or perhaps only a few hours. Time escapes me as guilt washes over me. I blame myself.

My arrogance led me to ignore Seni's command. He knew how to restore our communication, but I disregarded him. Not because I knew better, but because I wanted to prove myself to the Council. Would he still be dead if we were able to communicate? Could I have helped him?

I squeeze my anro in my hand, trying to break it. My hand burns with pain before I come close, so I stop.

A chuckle escapes my lips. Now none of it matters. It never did. The Datum never had any purpose out here. I was never going to prove myself to the Council. They knew that. Even if such a thing was possible, doubt creeps into the belief. Did my father know such things when he earned his place with our leaders? Does he know now how the Council uses us for no purpose other than to deceive the public?

Does he know they want me dead?

"Persolus."

I don't look at him. "Safon."

"Soriina caught us up on some of the most recent activities. We're meeting now to discuss what we do next." I don't answer him, prompting him to continue. "We thought you might want to join us."

"You thought wrong."

"Zayne." His use of my real name causes me to look at him. "I don't know why you're putting so much blame on yourself. And I don't really care. We're still Alfarons. We still have a duty to uphold."

"Soriina must have left out the part about Cramen."

"She didn't."

I stand up. "And you're still trying to be of some value out here?"

"No matter what the Council intended for us," Safon says, "this is our city. We're the only ones who can help it. The Redlanders were never a part of anyone's plans."

He walks away, leaving me to sulk.

I can't manage that. I have to make things worse. With my anro in hand, I fully reset it. If the Council truly cares, any messages sent will be lost along the network. If they hate me—my anro beeps six times in succession—if they hate me, my anro will beep. Six messages appear on the screen as the device finishes the reset cycle. Each one from Seni.

Each message feels like a piece of shrapnel ripping through my body. I don't get out of the way. I let each one hit me. Each one does a little more damage than the last.

Dishonesty Among Friends

"While Lamis prevents sickness and heals wounds, when the body experiences a loss of Lamis, the body suffers repercussions that often last for cycles even after the Lamis has been fully restored." —an excerpt from A Study on Lamis: The Energy that Protects Us

I write responses to Seni only to remember he'll never receive them, and not for the reason of my own arrogance.

When I can't take looking at the messages anymore, I rejoin the others. The Sorbe darkens my steps, but I find them easily enough. They must think the Redlanders aren't in the Sector anymore. Their voices carry out of the place that once held the Datum captive. There's almost a joyful tone to their words.

They're formulating their own plan. I have my own now, but it doesn't involve them. Soriina will object. The Twins also.

"Zayne!" Soriina runs up to me and takes my hand, leading me into their little group. Hiding her true feelings must come easily. I expect to see three, but a fourth stands amidst my friends. "Join us. We were about to go over the details of our plan."

I try not to show any surprise, but I am unsuccessful. Edwin turns to greet me, raising two fingers to his chin. "Zayne, good to see you well."

I return the gesture and turn to Safon. "You haven't discussed a plan yet."

Safon pats me on the shoulder. "We weren't going to start without you."

"You should have."

"You may find this interesting."

"You can't beat the Redlanders."

"We aren't trying to," Safon says.

He knows he has my curiosity. My greatest weakness.

"Go on."

"Arsen's sick, real sick. He needs help we can't provide. Soriina said there's a medical building in Sector Two. We're going there."

I want to laugh at the absurdity, but I can't. He's serious.

"Yes, we know the storm still remains."

"Good, because I thought I was imagining the swirling colors above."

"Soriina actually gave me the idea," Safon says. "The storm doesn't strike in more than one place. If we can time it right, we can access a sealed building without the storm striking any potential Lamis or the people sheltering inside."

"And have you discovered some way to predict when the storm will strike?" I know the answer, so I don't allow him time to answer. "No, you haven't. You're going to get yourselves killed. And risk destroying a building in the process. Who knows how many people may be sheltering there."

"I hope at least one doctor is sheltering there," Soriina says.

"Did your father give you some way to track the storm?"

I want to take back the words.

"No, he didn't. The plan isn't perfect, but it's all we have. Arsen won't live much longer. Look at him. Don't you recognize what's happening?"

He isn't here, but I don't need him to be to see his wounds flash in my mind. The storm affects his Lamis as it did mine, but something is different. It's worse.

"Lamis sickness," I say.

Soriina slowly nods. "He must have been near a storm strike. It absorbed his Lamis, and his continual presence underneath the storm has made it impossible for his body to restore his energy. His wounds have made it worse. If he doesn't get treatment, he'll die."

I owe it to Seni. I couldn't help him, but I can help Arsen.

I squeeze my eyes shut and speak. "What you need is a big enough storm strike that you can get him into a building safely. You can't wait for one." I open my eyes. "We'll have to cause one."

Safon glances at his brother. "Something tells me you've already thought about this."

"I have an idea," I say.

"Why aren't we going to like this?" Soriina asks.

"It involves me going to Sector Five, alone," I say. "Now knowing what you plan, this can work for both of us. You will take Arsen and the others to Sector Two. I will go to Sector Five and draw the storm there."

"Zayne, you can't stop the Redlanders," Soriina says. "You said it yourself."

"No, but they don't fear the storm. And they should."

"Will it work?" Safon asks.

Soriina steps in front of him. "You can't be considering this."

He looks past her to me. "Will it work?"

I skip any long explanation. "Yes."

Safon shakes his head. "No, it won't work."

Soriina's shoulders noticeably drop. "Thank you. Now may we talk about—"

"You're wrong," I say. "It will work. All I need to do is cause a big enough storm strike to—"

Safon holds a silencing stare on me. "It won't work with you going alone."

I hold his stare, refusing to blink as I speak. "I have to go alone."

"Maybe you didn't notice every Redlander in the city headed to Sector Five. That's what you told us. Were you lying?" Safon takes a step away. "No, I'll go with you. I can give you the time necessary. Too many unknowns. We can't risk the storm striking the building we take Arsen to, not only for his sake, but the city's."

"I don't think you understand the risk involved with what I'm planning."

"I do," he says. "But you're overlooking what needs to happen even to give you the chance."

"All I need to do is find a generator—"

"Which you could do right here, but you're not just looking for any generator. You need one close to where the Redlanders are in Sector Five, but in an area that won't risk the Council."

No, I don't want to put the Council at risk. But I want them to feel the storm. And I want them to know it was me that brought it down upon them.

Soriina moves toward me. "You're angry at them. We all are. But this isn't the way."

Does she mean the Council or the Redlanders? It doesn't matter. She's right either way.

"This is how we get Arsen the help he needs," I say. "I'm not asking anyone to come. This is my risk."

Safon waves his hands. "It's decided. Persolus and I will go to Sector Five. Draw the storm there and show the Redlanders why they fear Alfarons. Soriina—"

"If this is the plan, I'm going with you. Someone needs to make sure you're planning on coming back."

Her words give me pause. She wasn't there before. She found me after. Or was that another one of her lies? I made that decision thinking death was inevitable. I can't be certain this one act will be enough to drive the Redlanders out. I may have to do it again. And again until the invaders realize whose home this is. The Council's. They didn't want me out here, but they will see that they needed me.

"The four of us—"

"No, brother." Safon grips Erman's shoulder. "I need you to go with Arsen and the others. You know better than most the pain of Lamis sickness. We suffered alone. Arsen doesn't deserve to suffer this alone."

"We haven't been apart since we suffered the same sickness. You sure you remember how to act without me?"

Safon shoves him. "Get him to a medical building. Wait for the sky to light up." The twin turns to Edwin, who to my surprise, hasn't spoken a word or caused us to turn in his direction. "The Datum isn't complete, so I need you to find where the Redlanders are keeping the others. They're probably going to be in similar buildings. Take whoever you choose and find them. After that, move into the other sectors and gather the others."

The storm has—no, the Redlanders have diminished the boy. I barely recognize him. Even with Safon addressing him, he responds with a nod, not asking for any clarification. He doesn't leave yet either.

A painful cry from Arsen reaches our ears as the ambient light from the storm surges. Safon watches the clouds. "We can't wait any longer.

We have a few things the Redlanders left with us. Let's split it up and get going."

We take a few green bars to replenish our strength and a velare. Safon takes the only actare, but its power source is nearly depleted. He hopes the mere appearance will cause the Redlanders fear.

The goodbyes are dishonest. Safon expects to see his brother again. Soriina intends to return to see Erman and some of the other boys she spent a short amount of time with. The farewells are a formality, testament of our Alfaron blood.

I feel uncertain when I reciprocate the others' gestures. I have no intention of dying, but even with Safon and Soriina, the risk transcends my abilities. Now their lives are my responsibility. I risk making their goodbyes honest.

Safon shares a silent word with his brother before we head toward the towering buildings. The Council hides there. Will they feel the walls shake when I bring the storm so close? I will make sure they know it was me.

"How do you plan on finding a generator?" Soriina asks. "You can't trust your anro."

"A generator is the last thing I need to find," I say. "Too big of a risk of causing a reaction into the deposit beneath us."

Safon shines a light into the shadows in front of us. "Then what's your plan?"

"The Linam."

Safon stops.

Soriina walks past us both before turning around. "What's this Linam? I haven't heard of it."

Safon laughs. "You want to blow up the Linam?"

I look at Soriina. "Until the storm arrived, we stayed there. Most of our preparation was there. It has independent generators with no connection to the Lamis deposit. They could overload without causing a chain reaction. Diask designed the building to survive strikes from the storm. I can use the Linam to distract the Sorbe without endangering the rest of the sector."

Safon smirks as he processes my words. "You want to blow up the Linam."

I look at him, matching his smile. "I want to blow up the Linam."

The Linam

"It is proper Alfaron custom to greet a person with whom you are familiar, with both names, unless you know that person's preferred name."—an excerpt from A Closer Look at Alfarons, *a Vecco text*

The walk is long. And the Sorbe tries to slow us down by darkening our steps. Safon and Soriina don't mind. They trust my plan will work. But all my mind settles on is the potential scenarios that may unfold. The outside of the Linam can withstand storm strikes, but what about the inside? Will the building contain the explosions from the generators? What if the Lamis has been purged and the storm doesn't strike? Why is the best-worst-case scenario the storm striking before I can escape? Can I survive a third time?

The worst-case isn't the city's destruction. What if Safon and Soriina don't survive this, but I do? I have to keep them out of danger. I have to be only one risking my life. I cannot—

"Zayne." Soriina's voice pierces the dense shadows around us. "Zayne, stop overthinking this. You have a plan. A good one."

"Stop reading my mind."

"Stop making it so easy," she says. I can't see her smile, but I know she does, and it tries to push back my worries. "Your face twitches when you worry. And it has been twitching a lot lately."

"You can't see that. It's too dark."

"Both of you need to be quiet."

We look at Safon, then ahead. We are at the City Center. Our alleyway ends, and just beyond, I see flickering lights. Hundreds of them.

"Did your plan account for this many Redlanders?" Safon asks.

The lights move throughout the square, revealing silhouettes of both beast and abomination. Do they realize how close they are to the Council? How long before they breach the buildings and bring down the storm's wrath? Soriina said they did such in Sector Two. Does the Council know the danger they are in? Or do their agents remain silent, waiting to intervene?

I point to the tallest silhouette on the cityscape. "That's the Linam."

"I never knew they named that building," Soriina says.

Safon moves his head around. "We could go around through the alleys. It'll take longer."

"The Redlanders are congregating near the Linam," I say. "They may be in the alleyways as well. Beasts too."

"We can't stop now. My brother is waiting for a sign. If he mistakes an errant storm strike for our signal, it could be disastrous."

"Zayne has to go alone," Soriina says.

I look at Soriina, unsure if I heard her correctly. I agree with her, but thought it would take more convincing. But she is the one suggesting it.

Safon shakes his head. "Sure, one person will slip by more easily. But what if they catch him? The three of us have a better chance of escaping if that happens."

Soriina points away from the Linam. "We are going to help him, but in order to create his distraction, he needs a distraction. We can use the actare, get them to follow us away."

My head shakes slowly. "No. I can't let you both do that. If they catch you . . ."

Soriina takes my hand. "Even if they capture us, they won't hurt us. After they follow us, we won't attack them again. They won't see us as a threat."

I imagine Seni. His body. Soriina squeezes my hand, bringing me back to the present.

"We don't know why that happened," she says. "What we do know is that they came here for a purpose. They have some grand scheme that doesn't involve killing all the children the Council left in the storm. Why leave the others alive? Even if they catch us, we'll be fine."

Safon steps next to Soriina. "You think they are going to catch us? Where is your confidence in us?"

My lack of confidence isn't in their ability but mine. "The risk—"

"The risk is ours to take, Zayne. We know nothing of the generators. That is why you are here. No one else can do this but you. You do your part, and we will do ours."

"And if you get hurt?"

Safon grabs my shoulder and squeezes. "We aren't doing this for you, Persolus. Take the burden off your shoulders. This is for Arsen. This is for our city. Those things are here because they think this storm makes us powerless. Show them they're wrong. Show them we control the storm. Make them afraid of Alfarons again."

He means his words to give me courage, but nothing of the sort arises within me. Doubt creeps in. My clothes feel tight around my neck. My hand clenches my anro. "And if your distraction is not enough?"

Soriina squeezes my hand. "If they don't follow us, certainly their attention will be in our direction, away from the Linam. We have to hope that will be enough to get you safely across the square."

"We should leave now, while the storm is dark," Safon says as his hand leaves my shoulder.

Soriina still has my hand. She releases her grip to hug me, speaking softly as we embrace. "Stay safe. And make those Redlanders regret ever stepping foot in our city."

I squeeze her tight before letting go. "Protect him. His brother would never forgive me if you let him get hurt."

Soriina fights a laugh. "No goodbyes. We will see you after that building comes down. Wait for the signal. Should be almost as obvious as the one you're about to create."

We exchange no more words as my two friends disappear into the shadows. The storm stays silent, helping them stay hidden. They keep to the edge of the square in the opposite direction I will be going. I move back away from the opening of the alley. The Redlanders are not close, but I don't want to risk being seen.

The silence allows the doubt to grow louder.

The distraction has to work. No matter how smart the Redlanders are, they can't predict I would want to cause the storm to strike. They won't have any reason to look anywhere else other than at Safon and Soriina. I just have to wait.

A sharp pain stings the front of my head. An exhaustion sweeps over my body. I step into a deep shadow and put my back against whatever holds me. Time is short. But I need to rest my eyes for a moment.

An angry wind jolts me awake. Voices fill the air. Words I don't understand, but a tone I do. Fear and worry. The Redlanders are moving. I reposition myself to see more of the area. The flickering lights are moving across the open space and away from the Linam. Not just a few, but every single one. My path is clear. My eyes linger in the direction the Redlanders are moving.

"Be safe. Now it's my turn."

I exit the alley and stay near the buildings, sticking to where the shadows are the darkest. The storm flashes, and rather than slow down, I move faster. No shadows for any beasts to hide in. As the colors surround me, my path becomes clearer.

I look around at the buildings so often housing the most powerful people of our city. One open door from complete destruction. Where does the Council hide? How much are they aware of? Do they realize the boys they sent into the storm are powerless? I'm the one they're relying on, whether they realize it or not.

My feet freeze. Dancing flames exits an alley in front of me. The Redlander doesn't look toward me. It walks toward where the others are running. It stops. A dozen others exit the alley behind it. Each one has its full attention on the far side of the square. I cannot be more than ten feet from them. A stench fills the air. The storm goes silent, keeping me hidden from their wandering eyes.

I peer up at the storm and speak nothing more than a whisper. "How long do I have your cooperation?"

The thought lingers in my mind as the towering building draws closer. The area feels familiar, but the darkness keeps it at a distance in my memory. The glass buildings seem to sway in the darkness as they reflect the storm's terrifying, yet beautiful, presence. I feel the storm close in around me. The clouds shift, causing me to flinch as my peripheral senses the movement.

The storm silhouettes the Linam as it towers over the other buildings. I feel small as I approach one of its doors. No metal columns or sections of the wall reveal where a manual release hides. I may need to search the entire outside for a way in. My anro beeps on my waist. I remove it and hold it up. A small section of glass lights up, revealing an input pad.

Diask intended for us to return here. But why? The Linam holds secrets that he intended for his Tatem to find. I now regret not having the time to discover them. I hope he would forgive me for destroying it all. He would understand I have no choice.

I enter a command sequence, and the door hisses. I squeeze my eyes shut, waiting for the storm to strike. It doesn't. The walls must mask the power that still flows in the Linam.

I take a breath. "Thank you."

I return my anro to my waist and lay my hands flat on the glass. The door slides easier than I expect. I walk inside and look down the dark hallway. A few lights line the wall, but they barely make a dent in the shadows. I press my hand into the wall. I can feel a vibration. It's slight, but Vitus was serious. They left the power on as a test. Diask's design works.

It hurts to think I have to destroy Diask's creation. Sorbes may never have to be a threat again. No more blackouts or Lamis purges. His legacy beyond the Historical Record. But I can't think about that.

Now I need to find the generators.

I walk down the hallway with my hand on the wall. I hope to sense some variation that will lead me to a generator. When I reach a doorway, my anro chirps. It's not the same sound it usually makes. Detaching it from my waist, the holographic screen pops up. The words flash: **Primary Generator Detected**.

"Why did you want us to come back here?" I ask aloud, then push the question to the back of my mind. The secrets are tempting, but I don't have time. This primary generator is what I need for my goal at hand. My anro tells me it's on the top floor.

Every step I take, I fear is an extra step I don't have time for. Did Soriina and Safon evade the Redlanders? Does the storm remain quiet so as to not confuse Erman? Every minute I spend in here risks the lives outside. The darkness of the hallways fills my mind with dangerous thoughts.

The vert lift works. The control interface flashes a soft blue. Even with power, this surprises me. I push my curiosity away and set the lift to bring me to the top of the Linam. The door closes slowly before it moves upward at a fraction of its normal speed. Minimal power moves the lift. It's less disorienting than when it runs at full power.

I should turn on my velare and bring some real light into the lift, but I don't. I allow the soft light from the controls to wash over me. I close my eyes, and the thoughts come in waves. They don't feel natural. My father, the Council, my decisions that hurt my standing with both. The first sols in the Linam spring in my mind. Diask's actions confuse me with how he met his end. The storm was going to trap him with his enemy. Did he fear the Council? He prepared the message for Seni to thwart an attack on the Prava leaders.

The secrets are here, but I have to sacrifice them.

The lift stops. The doors require me to open them manually. It strains my muscles enough to annoy me. I step out into yet another hallway, dark save for a blue glow emanating from a door. The color seeps out of the edges onto the floor and ceiling. I approach slowly. I know there's no danger, but I still can't bring myself to rush in. I push on the door. It oddly swings open to reveal a single generator. Transparent coils fill the room, exiting and entering through ports on the walls. The ceiling is nearly ten feet high with coils extending down almost two feet. Lamis flows through them, pulsating the color that brings life to the Linam.

I approach the generator and press my hand to it. I breathe softly as the vibrations move through my arm. The access panel removes easily to uncover a control interface. My anro beeps. Bringing the small device up, I discover it's already interfacing with the generator. Within a minute, primary control is mine. Twelve other generators are powering the Linam, and I can control each one from here. The power levels are enough to run basic systems, but I can change that. But that's not what I want. I set each one to overload.

My anro beeps again. **Download Complete**. The words appear on the holographic screen. My curiosity pushes me to check, but I resist. I don't have time. Soriina and Safon don't have time. Arsen doesn't.

I set the main generator to send an overload signal to the others in ten minutes, but I won't activate the command until I'm on the bottom floor. Multiple warnings appear, which take several minutes to disengage, allowing the overload to occur. The timer connects to my anro, so I can activate the signal when I'm at a safer distance.

I step back into the hallway and look up. "Why did you put this generator here?" I look into the darkest part. "This is familiar. I didn't take a lift here before. We took the stairs." I jerk my head to the ceiling. It's the same hallway that Diask took us to gain access to the roof.

This is how I ensure the storm can reach the generators. Diask's design may prevent explosions from breaching the wall. But I don't need such a thing to let the Sorbe in. Without even thinking if it will work, I walk down the hallway with my anro raised above my head. It nearly touches the ceiling. After a few feet, an outline appears above me. The roof access hisses before the ladder extends down. The opening in the ceiling looks to be a portal to another world. From darkness to light. But I want to let the light in. Destroy the darkness.

It feels cycles ago that I was hanging onto this ledge, watching Diask sacrifice himself. A sacrifice I still don't fully understand. I squeeze my anro. Maybe he knew that.

I look up. "Okay, you dreadful thing. I know you're hungry. Don't disappoint me."

I stand idle for nearly a minute, waiting to see if there's enough energy escaping the generator to cause the storm to strike. But Diask's design isn't that shortsighted. The coils are transparent, but no detectable Lamis escapes. The storm will strike when I say.

Pulling my eyes away from the storm, I return to the vert lift. It moves quicker. Accessing the generator has pushed more power into the systems. The doors open partially on the ground floor; not entirely, but enough that I can squeeze through.

I stop just before the doors to the outside and turn around. I use my anro to activate the overload command. "I would apologize, Mr. Diask, but I think this is what you wanted."

When I turn around, a hand lashes forward and grabs me by the neck. A Redlander. My feet come off the ground. It's nearly two heads taller than me. Its grip tells me not to resist, but I can still breathe. It wears some type of uniform. No insignias or markings, but I don't think Redlanders have those. Its face is pale, which is odd for living on the Red Plains.

The abomination carries me outside. Nine minutes.

Its long strides take us nearly to the center of the square, where it tosses me forward. My legs buckle when they hit the ground, but I'm able to use my hands to brace my fall. Eight minutes.

I look up to see Safon and Soriina. They're on their knees. Fear washes over them, and it's not because we are too close to the Linam. A man stands next to them. Yes, a man, not a Redlander. He's shorter than they are, but still taller than me. He lacks the pale skin of the Redlanders.

A hundred flickering lights surround us, but he doesn't carry a weapon or flame. He's different. A leader, maybe. Seven minutes.

He walks with the confidence only an Alfaron can have. He kneels in front of me, and his lips curl as the storm flashes.

"Hello, Zayne Persolus."

29

Dreams No More

*"Epis City was built in the early sols of the Prava Council.
But the Council did not preside in the city until many cycles
later."—an excerpt from* A History of Our City

The buildings magnify the colors. They almost react to the man's words. They suffocate me with familiarity. There's nothing significant about him, but a terror grips me. I know something, but my mind refuses to grab hold.

Six minutes.

The man stands up and walks halfway to Safon and Soriina. He wears dark, loose-fitting pants that flap as he moves. A cloak covers his upper body and makes him appear shorter than he actually is. I can't see any symbols or insignias on his clothing. He doesn't flinch at the storm as the colors crack around us. He stands with calm confidence, unlike the Redlanders, who can't seem to stop moving, swaying back and forth with their flames. But he stands beneath the storm. He cannot be Alfaron or even Vox. Yet he stands distinct from the inhabitants of the Red Plains.

Are Sorbes not dangerous? Is the threat to adults a lie so the Council can work without interference? No, this would be a lie too big, even for the Council. This man hides in my ignorance of the Redlanders. He's one of them. He has to be.

He walks back to me, remaining silent as to allow my thoughts to clash. He knows he confuses me. He speaks our language, and he knows my name. But not my real name. He knows the name I hold beneath the storm.

He doesn't kneel this time but towers over me. "Now, child, I need answers. My understanding is that you have them."

I look at Soriina, but she doesn't meet my gaze. She fears him. What has he done?

The man holds a stare on me as I force out a response. "Answers? Wh-what answers?"

"Ahh, so you do speak. I had hoped the Novitae hadn't damaged your vocal cords. I gave strict orders, but you understand they aren't like us." His eyes narrow. "This whole ordeal is far more pleasant when you can speak." He points behind me. "You were found in that building, which I know will survive the storm. What did you do there? Did you leave a message, something for your leaders to find?"

I let his question drift with the wind. My curiosity propels my next words. "How do you know my name?"

He squats down with a smirk. "Now is that an answer to my question? No, no, that sounds like a question, Zayne Persolus."

He speaks with confidence that he knows me, the city, of Alfaron ways, but his knowledge has limits. He fears something I did in the Linam. The secrets Diask hid there. He wants them.

Soriina moves behind him, shifting my attention. Safon tries to grab her as she stands. "What place does a Redlander have to ask us questions? We are Alfarons, and you—"

The storm goes dark as the man turns. The flickering lights reveal a frightening expression across his face. He outstretches his hand toward Soriina. She's too far for him to reach, but he twists his hand as if he can touch her—and Soriina gasps. She grabs at her neck, trying to pull at something taking her breath away. She collapses onto her knees before slumping to the side. Safon stops her head from hitting the ground.

"Stop!" The word tears out of my mouth.

But the man's next action seems to have nothing to do with me. He relaxes his hand as the storm fills the sky with its color again. Soriina gasps for air as Safon cradles her in his lap.

The man jabs his finger at Soriina. "Offend me again with the notion that I am as small as the Novitae, and you will be the only victim the storm doesn't take." He turns back to me. "Give me the answers I want."

My curiosity wins again. "If you aren't a Redlander, then to who do you belong?"

The man waves his hand at me. "You are a different abomination than the Red Dwellers, but you have manners they don't. Don't you know respect? You ask questions yet answer none of mine."

An anger swells in me, but I hold it in. I need only delay this man for three minutes more. I try to keep my words calm so as to not trigger the anger that boils within this man. "You know my name. You command Redlanders but call them by a different name. You even respect my name but withhold yours. How can you demand respect from me when you lack the very thing you ask for?"

Soriina lets out a dry cough, which draws my attention for a moment. Within that brief glance away, the man descends upon me and places three fingers on my neck.

"I don't answer to *his* abomination. I owe you nothing." His fingers tense. He keeps calling me that, but I don't understand. We call Redlanders abominations. "But I have tried to receive answers in a pleasant manner. Now comes the unpleasant. You'll have to tell me what the pain's like."

"Pain?"

I regret the question as the answer comes immediately. A sharp tingling sensation surges through my body from my neck. It seems to pulse along the edge of my skin before sending a stabbing pain into the back of my head.

My vision goes black. One minute.

When the pain becomes unbearable, my mind clears as the agony fades. A voice replaces it, washing over me with familiarity.

Hello there, Zayne.

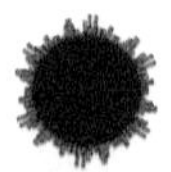

"Shall we try again?"

The voice is clear, but everything else is a blur. We appear to be standing in the same place. The storm remains overhead, but a blue mist surrounds me, shifting slowly. I turn to face the man. His words come from his mouth and also from the mist. It's disorienting.

"Do you recognize this place?"

I look around again. "The City Center. We didn't leave."

"From a certain perspective. Do you not recognize the place we first met?"

He speaks with a calmness that makes his previous state seem chaotic. He's confident here. The place feels familiar, but I can't see beyond the physical appearance.

I finally comprehend his words. "We just met. Obviously, this is the first place we met. Your words lack clarity. You aren't Alfaron. Who are you?"

"It is not I who lacks clarity, but you who lack understanding. Look closer. Understanding is close by, even for you."

The mist shifts. I look past the man. The Redlanders. Safon. Soriina. They're all gone. "What did you do to everyone? Where are they?"

"Only the two of us can enter this place." He moves through the mist, but it never touches him. "How you would perceive it with your lack of understanding? A dream. Fleeting, hard to hold onto, as this mist is."

A dream? He knows about my dreams.

"I don't just know about those. I created them."

My eyes widen. My thoughts are as audible as my voice here.

"Your surprise tells me how little you know. But you are young, and based on your thoughts, you haven't studied under the Council. You don't know who you truly are."

"I know who I am," I say. "I am Alfaron."

The man laughs. "A pawn, yes. When I first encountered you, I thought you brought me into your dream. But now I know it was an accident. My careful prodding after that was pointless. My fear held me back." He stretches out his arms and laughs again. "But that means I reached the city in time."

My head stings. "Who are you?"

"Manners!" His voice surges through the square. The mist expands, then it settles as he speaks again. "Answer my questions first. Then, perhaps I will give you some understanding before this city's destruction."

The storm's havoc across the city flashes in my mind. "You're responsible for the storm strikes. Why would Redlanders want to destroy the city? You inhabit our abandoned—"

"Silence! Do not consider me an equal with the Novitae. They follow my command." He moves his hand through the mist. "Now, what did you do in that building?"

The Linam comes to the forefront of my mind. He doesn't need me to speak, only think. I refocus my thoughts on the storm's destruction. The Redlanders' presence. "Which faction are you? You aren't Alfaron, for you have no respect for the Council's city."

He turns his back to me with his hands clenched at his sides. "I care nothing for *your* Council. No power lies there. I am here with one purpose, and I must know what your intentions were in the Linam. Your mind is easier to access while you sleep, while you find comfort in your dreams, but don't think I won't find what I need. This waking dream is where my power is strongest."

"The dreams weren't real?" I say. "My dreams are my own. You can't control them, let alone share them. This is something else."

"Your perspective is so naïve," he says. "You think every word means the same thing in every context. I don't have time to teach you what you cannot use. Now, the Linam."

The Linam fights to the surface of my mind again. He can influence what I think about. I allow the thoughts to rise, but turn them at the last moment. To Diask. The Twins. The endless lectures that I now realize were pointless to our survival in the storm. I wonder if Vitus knew the entire time. Did he know how the Council planned to use Cramen?

The man walks past me, speaking just above a whisper. His voice no longer surrounds me. "You resist for no reason. This city will fall."

I turn to him. "And the rest of the Alfarons will seek you out."

He laughs. "How do you seek out a storm? How do you hold a grudge against something that vanishes into the air?"

"What?"

"I need no credit. Only the truth that this city lies in waste. And to know that will be enough to stop him."

Images of the Council shift in my mind before changing to the Sorbe. He speaks of the Prava as a single entity. "I don't understand. Why would they seek the storm? They will seek the man."

"Your confusion clouds your thoughts and blocks what I need. So let me clear something up for you." He raises his hand up to the sky, and the storm shifts in color. "I am the storm. I am the Sorbe. And with it, I will wipe this city off the face of the land."

He tries to mislead me, confuse me. He cannot be the storm. Sorbes aren't living. "Why the city and not the Council? You could destroy them without leveling the city. Would that not show your power more convincingly?"

"Ah, you mistake my goals. You mistake where the power lies here. The city is what I want destroyed. And the fate of those who stayed is their own, whether that be the Council or a simple child."

What Tech does he possess that allow him control over a Sorbe? To access my mind is simple, really. My implant allows such a possibility in theory, but to control a storm? "Why not force them out? With your Redlanders and their beasts, you could sweep the city and leave it abandoned before you level it. You have unfathomable power. Let the people leave if you seek only the city's destruction."

The man stares intently. "And risk the retribution of his wrath? If a storm strikes down the city, no one will look for me. Another natural tragedy. The people had their choice, and they chose to stay."

He intends to kill everyone. He has no quarrel with them. Pointless killing. Meaningless death. All to attack one person? Who is so important that isn't a part of the Council? "But how could they know?" The words come out with more intensity than I intend. He intends to kill everyone. All because he hates the city? Buildings? Metal?

"Yes, Zayne!" His voice roars through the area. "I want the buildings crushed and ripped apart! I want this monstrosity to lie in rubble! But how can I expect a child to understand my intentions? You are nothing but a pawn of your people. You don't know the power this city holds for him. You don't know its purpose."

A part of me wants to step back and be quiet. But something urges me forward. This is my mind. He came here to find information. I may not understand this all, but this place is mine. He only created this environment for him to enter, to interact with me. This place is still mine.

"You think you can stop me? You are a child. Killing you would be simple."

An anger fills me. A truth that escaped me earlier becomes clear.

"You killed Seni!" The words send the mist flying. It doesn't rest but continues in an agitated motion. "You say your actions here rely on secrecy. The deaths have to come by the storm because of the one you fear. That's why you didn't allow the Redlanders to kill anyone. But why Seni? Why make an exception for him? Why is his death unique? Why send them after me?" I pull at the hole in my shirt to reveal the scar on my chest.

He swipes his hands through the mist. "I had no part in that boy's death."

"Liar!"

The man covers his face as the mist explodes from between us.

"Your Redlanders killed him. You may not be a Redlander, but you brought them. You command them. Are you so weak that they act outside your will?"

"My presence here relies on my anonymity. Why would I risk everything on a boy I know nothing about? You are mistaken and waste your final moments emotional over the loss of a friend."

Images of Seni and my anro flood my mind. I take a step back, my anger changing to grief.

An ugly smile crosses the man's face. "Guilt. In your final moments, you choose to push the blame onto me. You think my admission will absolve your guilt. Poor child. You've never experienced death before now. How does it feel to be powerless?"

Weakness floods my body, and I drop to my knees. "No. You lack the power you say you have. Your Redlanders killed him. If you didn't command them, you are just their pawn."

He screams, forcing the mist out of the Center. "The Linam! What were your intentions there?"

The Linam forces itself into my mind. But I shift my focus to the storm. How much control does he actually have? How much is he simply guiding the Sorbe's wrath to where he wants? He has no control over it. He has no control over the Redlanders.

He knows my thoughts, so I disconnect my next words. "Does time move differently here?"

His anger falters. My words confuse him, so he lets out a breath and allows the shift in conversation. "As long as a dream takes. Moments. Seconds. I could keep you here for cycles, and only minutes would pass outside. No matter how long you delay, I'll still have time to accomplish my task."

I keep my thoughts simple, not betraying my words. "Then let me help you with your task. Let me bring down the first building for you."

He looks as if to say something, but no words emerge. I smile. My thoughts move to the Linam and the generators.

"You aren't the only one who can control the Sorbe."

He pulls back. "You seek the wrath of the storm for what? A boy? Your guilt will remain."

I stand up. "You control nothing."

"Alfaron abomination."

He swipes his hand, and all the pain returns.

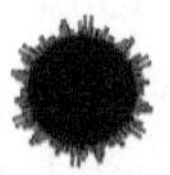

I gasp for breath. This time, waking up doesn't feel like I had been asleep but something else entirely. The man stands behind me, gazing up at the Linam. Smoke rises from the roof into the vibrant colors of the storm. The generators have overloaded.

"You fool. With that much energy, I cannot hope to control the storm."

Though weak, I stand up and move toward Safon and Soriina. "You stand in front of my *intentions*. But does it not help you? You want the city in rubble. Let's start with this building."

The man lets out a roar as the storm strikes the Linam.

An Ignorance of Truth

"No man can hope to control a Sorbe. The storms from be-yond the mountains transcend both nature and Tech. This study concludes that further research on the taming of these storms is a misuse of time and resources."—an excerpt from an Alfaron study on the Triones storm patterns

The sky erupts in colors beyond my comprehension. Below the beauty, the storm unleashes its devastating power on the Linam. Fragments of the building strike the ground, sending shrapnel flying. The glass of the surrounding buildings shatters. I hold my breath, waiting for the Sorbe to spread its attack. It doesn't.

Does the Council feel the destruction? Do they feel their control lessening? They will know this was me. But will they thank me or fear me?

The shrapnel increases as the storm strikes the Linam from every angle. Whatever masks the energy within fails, and the Sorbe takes advantage. An explosion rocks the ground each time the storm strikes a generator. The building's metal creaks, giving way to the possibility it could come crashing to the ground. I found the limits of Diask's design.

I look down from the building to the man. He stands in front of us with his hands extended toward the Linam. He projects some sort of transparent shield. A blue shimmer pulses from his hands, showing where the shield is. The debris deflects around us. A ten-foot-long beam slams into his shield, but his defense holds as the debris breaks in two, passing us on either side. He inadvertently protects us.

This man's Tech is powerful. He not only could control the storm but also withstand its devastation. Shields require tremendous power, and he seems to have no shortage. But he can't protect the Redlanders. They try to run, but the shrapnel shows no mercy. They don't even look to their leader. I see fear in them for the first time.

"Zayne." I look at Soriina, who points up. The storm's color remains above us while the sky extending over the rest of the city is dark. "The storm strikes only here. Your plan worked."

I smile before dropping to my knees. My eyes water, blurring my vision. I close my eyes and press my hands into the ground. I feel the vibrations from the destruction, every piece of the Linam crashing down. "Your brother is safe, Seni. Forgive me for only saving him."

"Persolus. The man."

I wipe my eyes and see the man dropping to one knee. His shield flickers, turning a brighter blue, now completely visible. His power supply falters. Shrapnel pierces his defense and strikes the ground in front of us. A piece of metal slams into the ground in front of me. Before I can blink, my right eye stings in pain.

I press my hand into my eye as five separate white bolts erupt from the clouds. They streak across the sky and strike the Linam. Something different happens this time. There is no immediate explosion. A silence overtakes the area. I feel blood wetting my hand.

Without warning, the rest of the Linam explodes, sending a shockwave through the square.

Our unwilling protector lets out a scream of agony as his shield shatters. I extend my hand out as a rush of air knocks me to the ground. The man lands nearly twenty feet behind me. He took the brunt of the storm's final attack. Blood drips from my face as I drop my hand to my side. Exhaustion sweeps over me.

The Sorbe goes silent. Shadow falls over the area. Despite an occasional flash, the attack is over. All lamis is gone from the Linam. As I force myself up against the wishes of my body, I see nothing remaining of the building. The entire City Center will bear scars from the attack. I try to wipe my vision clear, but it's no use.

Safon helps Soriina to her feet, then me. My legs falter, so Safon lends me his strength. "Your eye, Persolus."

We watch the man struggle to his feet. He collapses twice before his legs hold his weight.

"This isn't over," I say. I pat Safon's arm, and with a soft grip of my shoulder, he lets me go. I limp forward.

The Sorbe casts a soft light over the City Center.

The man slams his hands into the ground. His eyes narrow on me. "You are nothing but a foolish child. I saw your thoughts. You want this city's secrets, yet you are too close to claim them." He coughs, spitting out crimson red without a hint of blue. "I came here with a purpose beyond myself! But you wouldn't stay in your place. You lack perspective."

He drops to his knees. His arms hang limp at his sides.

"I cannot maintain the storm. It will dissipate soon. And your people will emerge from their hiding. And he will seek the others as my punishment. You bear this guilt as well."

I look back at Soriina, wiping my eye again. Fresh blood limits my view while I fight a constant headache. "Who is this *he* you keep referring to? It's Carius, isn't it? You were at his speech."

The man forces out a laugh, coughing afterward. "You think I fear Carius? I don't. I attacked Mauris for him. He told me the secret of this city, so I came here. He then promised me *he* would be at the speech, but Carius lied. I tried to kill Carius there, but those generators drew in the storm's attack."

Diask designed those generators. He was working with Carius. Soriina was right. This all was the People's Representative's plan, but Diask sought to undo whatever he helped the traitor with.

I put my arms out to the side. Blood drips from my hand. "Diask stopped you. Not Carius. He placed Tech throughout the city, not to help the storm destroy it, but to hinder your control. I only wish he could see that his plan worked."

He spits blood out of his mouth. "Oh, I know Diask. I had ever the pleasure of killing him on that roof." With a painful groan, he rises to his feet. "I have yet the strength to destroy you also. Do you feel the remnants of the storm?" He reaches forward with his hands. His next words are just louder than a whisper. "Aria give me strength."

A blue mist appears in front of him and swirls around him. His hands twist back and forth, then thrust forth. Two streams of energy, similar to actare fire, burst out of the mist. I raise my hands up to my face. I feel only one blast strike me. The impact threatens to knock the air out of my lungs as I struggle to maintain my balance.

"Zayne, get down," Soriina says. "He is using the storm's energy to charge his weapon."

I look at her. A weapon? "The actare? Where is it?"

She extends her hand out. "Here. It's useless. It's out of power."

No Tech is useless in my hands. I look at the man. He continues to twirl his hands around the pulsating blue mist. Whatever weapon he is charging, it gives me enough time to prepare. He's been in my mind, yet he still thinks I'm helpless.

I wipe my bloody hand on my clothes and remove the actare's dome casing. Even with half my vision, it is simple work. I try to keep my blood from dripping into the inner workings. No one would waste time to redesign the weapon just for us. The added power source disables its haur function to pull energy from the user. As soon as I remove it, the actare reverts to its default setting.

"Zayne? What are you doing? We need to leave."

"Persolus, Soriina is right. We've accomplished what we set out to do. And if the storm is dissipating, we can let the adults deal with this man."

My eye stings as I replace the dome's casing. "No. He killed Seni and Diask. He has to face the consequences."

Without use of both my eyes, I aim toward the man with no certainty of my accuracy. I squeeze the handle. My hand goes numb as my Lamis fuels the actare. A final twist of the handle sends a bolt of bluish-white energy racing toward the man. His eyes widen. He puts his hands out in front of him. As the light fades, the man remains standing. He shakes his arms and smirks.

He pushes his hands forward, and a flash of blue sends me backward. My legs cannot keep me up as my back hits the ground. My eye stings as fresh blood floods my vision.

"Zayne!"

My body feels numb. A weakness sweeps over me. But he will not win. I roll over and force myself to my knees.

Soriina rushes to my side. "We need to leave. He is stronger than you, let alone you trying to power an actare yourself. You're trying to kill yourself."

I struggle to my feet. And as if to help her argument, Soriina doesn't help me. My breathing increases as my legs struggle to keep me upright.

A sinister grin fills the man's face as he stands idle, letting his weapon remain depleted.

"No. He didn't just kill Seni and Diask. He destroyed Mauris. All those people. Everything that's happened falls on his shoulders. He doesn't get to walk away."

I squeeze and twist the actare in one motion. A stream of energy exits the weapon and darts toward the man. He grins before raising one hand. My attack stops just short of his body. But something is different. The stream of energy remains suspended in the air. My hand burns as the pain moves up my arm.

Soriina stands next to me, barely visible in my bloody peripheral vision. "Zayne. Stop. You are going to drain yourself of all your Lamis. He isn't worth it."

I can't turn my head. "I . . . can't . . . let . . . go."

Even as I try to release the flow of energy, I feel the drain on my body increase. The pain encompasses my entire right arm. My arm feels as it should be limp by my side, yet it remains up. The pain travels through my chest before a sharp pain explodes near my heart, then down my other arm before the agony sweeps across the rest of my body. It pulses out from my heart. My vision blurs. It snaps back into focus every few seconds.

"Persolus. Just let go. You can't break through his defenses."

The pain hits my legs. They lose strength as I drop to my knees. "He is . . . preventing me."

He is doing this. I have to overload whatever Tech he is using. As the pain increases, I urge more energy into the actare. The surge in my attack takes the man by surprise, but a shift in his footing is all he needs to maintain his hold on me.

His Tech is astonishing. He enters minds and controls storms. Now he drains the Lamis from my body. Perhaps he is part Sorbe. A part of me wants to talk to him, learn about his Tech. But he killed Seni and Diask and consorted with abominations.

He cries out over my pain. "Do you feel the life leaving your body? I don't know what you are, but you are weak, like all Alfarons. All Vox. You will be the last of your kind."

Soriina goes down to her knees and looks me in the eye. I can't see her as my entire vision blurs. Her voice calms me. "Zayne, let go."

She gently places her hand on mine. As our skin touches, what vision I have snaps into focus. The pain fades into a cool, tingling sensation. I feel my energy renew.

The man's voice carries through the air. "Your Council can't save you. They stand idle and watch as I pull the life out of your body."

I wish the man could hear my words to see his reaction when he fails, but they escape as just a whisper. "I don't need the Council. My strength alone is enough."

I send a surge of energy through the actare. Every ounce of my concentration propels every drop of energy I have through the weapon. The man twists his hands, but whatever defense he has, he doesn't have enough power to stop it. The area ignites in a bright flash of blue. Shadows retake the City Center as the man collapses.

Soriina stands up, removing her hand from mine. As she gasps at what transpires, a wave of exhaustion overtakes me. My hand goes numb. The actare strikes the ground seconds before I do.

I gasp for air as my eyes shoot open. My body rejects the air, forcing it back out in a dry cough. My entire body throbs, but the pain is not enough to keep me from getting up. I force myself to stand. My surroundings swirl. I squeeze my eyes shut and press my hands into my head.

I open my eyes. The area falls into focus. My vision is back.

A group of boys stand in front of me. No one is looking at me. Their eyes are on the sky. The actual sky. The Sorbe is dissipating. Patches of the yellow are breaking through what remains of the storm's clouds.

I allow myself to drop back to the ground. I wrap my arms around my knees. It's over. My eyes water before forming tears. I allow the tears to roll down my cheeks.

"Beautiful."

With some pain, I turn to see Soriina. She moves to sit next to me. She pushes her shoulder against mine.

"I would hug you," she says, "but you still appear to be in pain."

I shift my gaze to the sky. "How long?"

"Two sols."

"And the man?"

"We left quickly. We are back in Sector Two."

"They will never believe any of it."

"The bodies of the Redlanders should be proof enough. The Sorbe's last attack killed many of them. I doubt that man had time to take them if he survived."

I turn to her. "Proof of a small portion. Not all of it. That man had powerful Tech. That means he was Alfaron. A traitor—"

"Whatever he was, wherever he came from, he isn't our problem anymore. We survived. We—you protected the city. Let the adults worry about him. You have done enough."

"I was never supposed to do anything." I turn to look her in the eyes. "I did what was necessary, and that's the problem. The Datum was a mask, and I was never supposed to be here."

"Zayne." Her words are soft. "Look upon the sky and the beauty that returns. Maybe you weren't meant to be out here, but you did this. They have to recognize that."

"They will be angry," I say. "I went beyond the limits they set."

"Their plans didn't account for the Redlanders or that man. You did what that Cramen couldn't. You saved their precious city."

"They will want explanations for everything. I'm not sure I can give them what they want."

"Yes," she says. "They will. But not now. They remain in hiding for just a little longer. The city is still ours."

A pain shoots up my back, causing me to spasm. Soriina jumps back from me.

"What is it?"

Words are impossible as the pain envelops my entire body. I slump to the side. My right eye stings. The pain stands out from the rest of my body. My head slams into the ground. I lay paralyzed before everything goes black.

The Age of Choice

"The extent of what an implant captures is different with each person and not known until it is uploaded into the Historical Record."—an excerpt from Our Implants: The Defining Tech of the Alfarons

Something is pressing into my eyes, making me blind. My arms are stuck at my sides but not paralyzed. Something restrains me. Before I can identify anything else, a pain spreads out from the back of my head. It is unlike anything I can imagine. Each flash of pain brings a memory.

The Linam. Grief. Seni. Sorrow. The Sorbe. Torment. Soriina. Misery. The Twins. Agony. Cramen. Despair.

The memories shatter as the pain subsides. I gasp for breath. Whatever is covering my eyes comes off. Bright lights above me sear my vision as voices reach my ears.

"Is he alive?"

"How long was he conscious?"

"He is going to kill us when he finds out. You should have checked the dosage before we started."

My eyes adjust to see two men standing a few feet from me. They wear light blue shirts and loose pants with green belts. The Alfaron symbol stands out on their shoulders and backs. One is gripping his hair, nearly pulling it out.

"If you release me, I may forgive you," I whisper as the pain fades back into memory.

They whip their heads toward me. "He's alive. Thank the Council."

I am alive despite the Council, but I fight the urge to say that to them.

The one man releases his hair and moves toward me. He reaches down near my side. Something clicks, and I can move my arms.

"We apologize. We needed a few more tests of your implant—"

"Where am I? Who are you?"

I don't care about whatever they did. They glance at each other, seemingly happy I'm not asking other questions.

"You are in a Sector Two medical facility. We are the dothyris assigned to your recovery."

"This was the closest facility to where they found you. And you needed immediate attention. Your—"

"And the Datum?"

They glance at each other again.

"We should allow someone else to answer those questions. There are many questions to be asked of you. The Council's procedures haven't been satisfied yet."

I shift myself so I am sitting upright. I am wearing only a grey medical garment that fits loosely against my skin. I put my knees together and pull the clothing closer to my body. "After what I went through, I deserve answers. What's happened since the storm—"

"Gentlemen!" The voice freezes the men and cuts off my question. They turn, revealing a doorway where the Curator stands. "You were supposed to inform me the moment he regained consciousness. Not start a conversation. Observation only after your tests were complete."

"Our apologies, Curator," one says. "The tests were incomplete—"

"Because he regained consciousness. I will address that with you both later. Now, leave."

The men dip their heads and exit.

The Curator steps closer. "Zayne, may I call you that? Yes, I apologize for their error. Accessing an active implant in a conscious person . . . the pain is great but does not linger."

"I don't care about that," I say. The pain was nominal compared to everything else. "Where are the others?"

He takes another step forward and places an arvos down next to me. "You are no longer out in the storm. You have to act like an Alfaron again. You have questions, as you should. But we have questions for you also."

"Then ask them."

"It is not my place to do so."

I hop to the ground and walk until a wall stops me before turning around to face the Curator. "Then at least tell me where my friends are?"

He shakes his head slowly. "It is not my place—"

"Then whose is it? Is the risk that I took to protect the city not worth answers?"

"The Council acts in their own time."

I feel as if I blink a dozen times before managing a word. "T-the Council . . . of course . . ."

"Your memory is intact, so you should recall the bodies of Redlanders that we would have found in Sector Five. Or were you not there? The bodies of our enemies are of great concern. And the buildings shattered by the storm, especially within the Council's sector. You were one of this *Datum's* leaders. They will have questions. And they will ask them when they are ready."

The Curator doesn't understand the Datum's false nature. He thinks I was important. I wasn't.

"They blame me?"

He picks up his arvos. "Not you entirely. But we all lack perspective on what happened. When the moment comes, the Council will ask questions to help us understand what happened. It is clear to the people that something went wrong. They must find where the fault lies."

"And what if the fault is their own?"

He points his arvos at me. "That insinuation cannot leave this room. When you go before the Council, you are going to act as an Alfaron. Your tone and language are important when before your leaders."

I can't manage anything else as my mind imagines various scenarios. What if they blame me? Will I receive the benefit of the doubt as my father's son? Their city still stands, but what if that isn't enough to absolve me?

"Zayne," he says, pausing for me to make eye contact. "I'm not here to talk about such things. I have been your Curator for many cycles. I care about you. Now, I need to ask you other questions. Please, stay focused."

I breathe in through my nose and let the breath out slowly.

"We found you in a terrible state," he says. "We found numerous signs of severe Lamis deprivation in your body at one point. Are you able to recall what may have caused this?"

"At one point?" I ask.

"Stay focused. One question at a time."

"Not to deviate, but that may have been from using an actare."

The Curator lets out a loud breath. "An actare? How—no, I will not digress. That was incredibly dangerous. Actares are dangerous even for trained Agmen soldiers, let alone a child. Did you kill those Redlanders—no. That is not for me to ask."

His curiosity pounds at the door, but he won't open it. If I can talk to him first, maybe my thoughts will be clear for the Council.

"I used the weapon when no other choice was presented," I say.

He stares at me, unblinking. "That is a childish answer for a graduate. If the only choice leads to your death, then you choose another. You were simply too narrow-minded to see another way."

"I had no expectation to die."

He forces his lips together. His face contorts before he can manage more words. "That comment only shows your childish perspective. Something you need to limit when you address the Council."

"What else is wrong with me?"

He pauses, as if collecting his thoughts. "You certainly suffered from a lack of Lamis at one point. But you also suffered from a Lamis surplus, most often seen from feedback from Tech modifications. In your case, it occurred in some other way, as actares can't cause a surplus."

Did the storm restore the Lamis it took? "W-what?"

He lowers his head and inputs something into his arvos. "Highly unusual. I was optimistic you could provide some insight. No matter how it was caused, you have to live with the consequences now."

"The consequences? I feel fine."

A single finger extends from his fist. "You should, for now. But the dothyris were scanning your implant to create a timeline. Zayne, your implant is failing."

My mouth hangs open for a moment. My place in the Historical Record is at risk. How much is already lost? What happens if my memories are lost?

"I can sense your fear," the Curator says. "This is our connection to our people."

"Put a new one in."

He gives a half-smile. "I could, yes. But it's not that simple. We have to develop an implant just for you. Your Lamis levels are steady now, but higher than average. Implants are already intricate devices. We cannot guarantee the implant will work if you have another spike in Lamis production. Without knowing what happened, I cannot guarantee the implant will work for the rest of your life."

My hands slowly move to my face as I contemplate his words.

"The choice is yours," the Curator continues. "You are a graduate, but with your initial intent to remain in the city, where your life separates from your parents is an . . . unsettled debate. And as the law considers an implant a modification, you must assent to have a new one put in. No law requires an Alfaron to have one. Each parent chooses for their child before graduation. You are in a void that has never happened before."

"And if I choose not to have one? What happens with the old one?"

"The old one still has to come out," he says. "I can't risk a failure that may cause brain damage. But think carefully about this."

Will my memories enter the Historical Record now, or will they wait until I die? No, they won't wait. My memories will hold answers to their questions. But I won't be able to fight this intrusion.

"What happens to the old implant?"

"The Council will have experts examine the implant and determine what information is still viable. These devices are intricate, and the process takes a long time."

"So they still need me to tell them everything."

"My guess would be yes."

"When do I have to decide?"

"Before your old one comes out," he says. "The procedure is extensive, so I would like to put the new one in as the old one comes out. It will be less traumatic on your body. There's good reason we implant them when we do."

I feel the back of my head. "And when does the old one come out?"

"Not before your inquiry with the Council. As I said, the procedure is extensive."

"The Council's answers come before my health."

He closes the gap between us. "Zayne. The Council expects answers, but as Curator, your health comes first. I wouldn't allow their agenda to jeopardize that."

I see the sincerity in his stare. "When is my inquiry?"

Leaning back, he glances quickly at his arvos. "The Council is expecting you before the moon rises. I cannot keep you here any longer. Your Lamis is stable, and your ability to converse with me tells me more than enough. I will have someone bring clothes in. And a transport will be here to take you to Sector Five within the hour."

He enters something into his arvos.

"I almost forgot. How is your eye?"

I hover my hand in front of my face, focusing on my fingerprints. "My eye?"

"A piece of metal damaged your right eye. We had to remove it. I was able to replace it. Eyes are simpler than implants, so it should adapt to any changes in your Lamis."

I fight the urge to touch the eye. "Why did I not have a choice in that?"

Hypocrites.

"Your city profile showed we needed no permission when the modification is a full replacement for continuous sol-to-sol regularity. The Council further approved the procedure. You should thank them. LiorTech best holds when installed as soon as possible."

"And if they do not like my answers. Will they take it back?"

He drops his arvos to his side. "I wish my scans could tell me where your anger comes from. You have the rare choice to remain in the city after graduation. You should be grateful for everything you have. Grateful to be an Alfaron. Ensure the Council sees as much."

He turns from me and exits the room.

I press my hands into my head, fighting the urge to rip the eye out. The anger feels distant. I know I should be thankful for the Council, but I can't rectify their actions in the storm. Or is it my arrogance to think I can understand them before joining their ranks?

I miss the simplicity before the storm. Or was I just ignorant? How much more has the Sorbe shattered beyond buildings?

I tug on my shirt as I exit the medical building. The fabric is itchy, and the Alfaron symbol on the back protrudes. It feels heavy and makes me want to rip it off with each step.

The sun hits me in the face as I leave the cover of the building. I close my eyes and let the warmth wash over me. When I open my eyes, the city is smaller without the shadows, still silent. A few Esidio guards walk by. Their calm contradicts the terror that had controlled the city.

A rush of air breaks the tranquility. A volant's hover pads vibrate straight ahead. The operator half opens his door and leans out. "I would rather not keep the Council waiting."

I consider some remark but hold the words. The operator doesn't say anything else as I enter the volant. The vibrations are inconsistent. He is not Mr. Auctor, so I make no comment as I find a seat. I know the Council doesn't send him on purpose. They don't want me talking about anything before I meet them.

The windows are small, and the volant is dark. The inactive lights above mock me. The operator runs on minimal power. I find the largest window in the back and sit down. The operator directs us into the air, then turns toward Sector Five.

We soar above the buildings. The Sorbe is gone, but it left evidence of its presence across the city. Black scorches mar the rooftops of the tallest buildings that somehow remain standing. Windows are missing from most places. A whole section of residences in Sector Two are now piles of rubble. How many flashes of the storm were strikes? How many people were harmed? Killed?

I don't have any evidence to give the Council for what I think happened, but the storm left enough evidence to condemn me for my failures. For if I claim the success, I have to accept I could have done more. That man will destroy me in another way, whether he meant it or not.

I sit back in my seat.

How do I tell the Council their failures resulted in the destruction so evident across the city? They won't accept that. Or will Cramen take the brunt of the blame? No, they won't acknowledge his presence. That much seems obvious.

The transport tilts, descending into Sector Five. A glance out the window shows the rubble that remains of the Linam. The surrounding buildings are intact but still bear the damage from the Sorbe's last attack, except the building the operator lands the volant in front of. The Council building's undamaged nature makes me question my leaders more. I should be happy they are unharmed, but that feeling is as distant as Mauris and in the same condition.

The doors open, and two Agmen soldiers board the volant and exchange a few words with the operator. They then look at me.

"Zayne Radi. Come with us."

I hesitate. I haven't heard my full name since before the storm. I have no intention of disobeying, but I force them to ask again.

"Zayne Radi. Exit the transport. The Council awaits you."

They don't move as I walk in between them. I pause in the entryway as another Agmen soldier stands on the ground. He looks up at me.

"Please, follow me."

I step down. The volant is several hundred feet from the building. Agmen soldiers are spread throughout the area in sets of three. The storm may be gone, but the Council still sees some threat in the city. No Esidio guards are present.

Six soldiers stand on either side of the entrance. They make no move toward me or the Agmen who guides me. The doors automatically open as we draw closer.

"Excuse me, soldier." The voice comes from behind us. Its familiarity pains me. I turn, hoping it is anyone but who it actually is. "May I have a moment with my son?"

32

Before the Council

"A Council Members never speaks publicly. Only their respective Representatives may hear their voice."—an excerpt from How the Council Unites Us

My father's appearance challenges the notion that the Sorbe ever touched the city. His white coat is pristine, and the silver plates on his shoulders glisten. No concern rises from his voice. Is that a requirement of his position, or was he so well hidden that the fear of the storm never reached him? He certainly never feared for my life.

The Agmen soldier places two fingertips on the center of his forehead. "Of course, Representative."

He walks away, and my father gestures for us to enter the building. We walk into a lobby with a ceiling nearly two levels in height. On the right side, a broadcast monitor sits on the wall with three chairs surrounding it. A broken light allows the shadow to fill the left side of the room that sits void of anything. A door splits the two sides.

My father stops on the left side of the door, and I step to the right. "Zayne—"

"I'm changing my name." I don't know why I tell him now. I have so many other things to say, but he needs to know. "I don't want to carry your name beyond this city."

His mouth opens before closing. He doesn't expect my words because he isn't here as my father. He's a Representative now. I question if I have ever talked with him as my father. He acts in secret, not letting me know anything. A father talks to his son. Doesn't make him guess his intentions.

"I look forward to hearing the name you will soon carry with you. But now—"

"Should you not already be in there? About to question me?"

He purses his lips and speaks through a forced smile. "Your anger is not helpful now."

I point at the Alfaron symbol on his coat. "Are you here as a Representative or my father?" I know the answer.

I want to let him speak, allow him to provide me answers, but I can't. He's given me no reason to think he acts apart from the Council. That's why I wanted to study under them. To understand the Council was to understand my father. But now, after the storm, I don't know if I want to learn more. Our Prava leaders act without reason, preparing hundreds of boys only to send others out in secret and undermine their own Tatem.

My father is only here to prevent further embarrassment. He was my advocate. Even with my rejection, my choices in the storm reflect his decision. It speaks more to him than me. He knows that.

"Watch your tone." He takes a deep breath and exhales. "I am still a Council Representative."

"And that's all you've ever been," I say. "Never my father. My father would know I strive to be like him. I see the way people look at you. I wanted that. I thought you would set me on the path that would give me that. But you didn't." My heart beats faster with each word. "But I don't understand. Why did you give Mr. Diask my test scores if not to send me into the storm? Was that not your way of ensuring my path was like yours?"

"Zayne, I tried to keep you out of the storm. I wanted to protect you. I begged the other Representatives to admit you early so you could go into hiding with them. They almost refused me."

I withhold a gasp and turn from the Council Representative. He never was my father. What I previously thought was only my hopes lying to me.

"I never wanted you to be like me, Zayne. You are meant for better things. My path was long and difficult. Do you not trust me to make good decisions for you?"

"Why are you here?" I ask, squeezing my eyes to keep the tears inside.

He lets out a sigh. "The Council needs answers, and you were one of the Datum's leaders."

"You want me to trust you, but you don't trust me."

"I never said that—"

"Then why are you here?" I face him again. "What type of precedent does this set? A Representative's son being questioned before the Council? What are you afraid of?"

Anger flashes across his face, but he controls it. "You act as if this is bad. This is not a punishment. This is protocol."

"And what if they don't like what I say?"

"They seek truth. Give them that."

"Don't lie to me." I spit the words out. "We both know the Council isn't seeking truth. They only want to know enough to control the people. You know why the Datum was out there. Anything the Council can't explain, we will take the fall." I stop short of mentioning Cramen. I want to see the faces of the other Representatives when I say his name. "The people will turn against us. Your own son."

He puts his shoulders back and straightens the silver plates with careful precision. He now speaks as a Representative; any attempt to masquerade as my father is gone. "The others have all had their inquiries. The Council was divided on having official inquiries so soon after the storm. The people demanded answers. The questions were not thorough. Rushed. But the law restricts us from having such a formal inquiry more than once. You are the last. And the questions may not be easy. We ask you to bring clarity."

We. He has always stood before me as a Representative.

"And if I do not?"

He raises his head. "Less formal inquiries may take place. But if the Council wishes to take part, they will charge the Datum with a crime. Then they will have their answers."

"You didn't want to protect me from the storm," I say. "You wanted to keep your secrets. You didn't want me to learn how the Council operates. You failed. I know how they and you think. Everything is manipulation. I should have let that man destroy this city."

A mix of emotions flash across his face, but he controls them well. He steps toward the door and places his hand in the center. "We have talked too long. The Council is waiting. Please, put your feelings aside and answer with respect. You owe us that much."

"And what do I owe my father?"

His face lowers slightly as he pushes the door open. A red glow spills out. The Council Representative enters first. Inside, two men stand on either side of the door. They are neither Agmen nor Esidio guards. They each wear a red vest with a helmet that shows only their eyes and noses. My stare lingers before a voice directs my attention forward.

"If you would approach."

Lights along the ceiling exaggerate the red color that lines the wall, only the occasional strip of yellow breaking the consistency. White lights above the oval table the Council sits around push the red hue away. The seat opposite of the head of the table sits empty. I presume I stand there. I don't dare to sit down else I claim equality with the Council members.

The seat at the head is empty. The Speaker is absent.

My father steps behind the Members seated first—Council Members Isa. Presuming they sit in order, Tosa is next. My eyes stop on Kaz. Vitus stands behind him at the back end of the left side. He lifts his head at me. Arba, Pak, and Anam sit on the right side. I recognize their Representatives well. I wonder what they're thinking after I rejected my father's advocacy in their presence.

I try to look at the Members, but their faceless masks make it hard. My stare returns to their Representatives. Vitus exchanges a glance with the others.

"Zayne. May we call you Zayne?"

My eye snaps to Vitus. "You may not. Call me Persolus."

Murmurs spread across the Representatives.

"You haven't made an official declaration to change your name," Vitus says, directing the others to silence with his hands. "As this is an official inquiry, we will call you by your name given. When your city profile marks a change, the recording will reflect your choice."

I look at the faceless leader before looking at Vitus. "Is that what *he* is concerned with? My name? Does what happened during the storm not take precedence over what to call me?"

My father shifts but stays silent.

"Zayne Radi," Vitus says. "The Council wishes to treat its people with respect. And you are Alfaron. If we are to use your name, we wish to respect the choice you have made. This is a formal gathering of the Prava Council. Recorded for the Historical Record. We want to make sure everything is correct."

Simply nodding and continuing the proceedings crosses my mind, but my mouth opens first. "That sounds wasteful. You want answers. I am here to provide those. Anything else is just a ploy. Or is this all a formality? What happened out in the storm really doesn't matter. You are going to tell the people what you want them to know, no matter what I say."

Vitus glances at my father. "You don't trust the Council. You think we will twist the truth to accommodate ourselves. A misdirected thought. A wasteful thought. Shall we continue?"

I close my mouth before I can say anything. He dismisses me so easily. I expect more pushback, but he shows no concern at my defiance.

"Now, since you are so keen to start, we have reviewed the anro network and found that you ignored numerous messages from the other Tech leaders."

My eye darts from Members to Member. No one else says anything. I look at Vitus. "Is that a question or a statement of what you already know?" Cramen used the network to trap me. They know this. But this is an official inquiry, so they have to keep their lie going.

He smiles. "We simply lack an understanding we hope you have."

"The network was compromised," I say without a question in my tone. "False messages were sent, and I received genuine messages sols after the others sent them. I ignored nothing."

"Impossible," Anam's Representative says. "The network was closed. Only active anros had access. This boy clearly didn't understand how to use it properly."

Vitus raises his hand. "We must not come to any conclusions yet. I doubt he lacked the knowledge to use a simple network interface. Zayne Radi, were you able to fix the problem?"

"Not before everything went to chaos."

Kaz's Representative whips his arms to either side. "This was your pseudo Tatem? If the network was compromised, it was his inadequacy that led to it. We should have put Tatem Diask's prodigy in command."

They did go against Diask's wishes. He wanted Seni. They wanted me. I see the regret overflowing.

I slam my hands on the table. "He was deceived as well. You all were."

"Zayne!" My father tries to control his tone, but he falters.

"Silence, Stephan," Vitus says. "You are well respected, but as this is your son, you may not speak during this inquiry."

I look at my father. His eyes widen as he knows I am about to speak. "And why do you speak, Vitus? If my relation to my father forbids him, you should not—"

"Silence!" Vitus steps out from behind his member. Kaz remains motionless, not even a twitch. "Not only do you speak out of term, but you accuse me of breaking Council law?"

I know I shouldn't speak, but he asks a question. "You were in charge of the preparations for the storm. This failure is yours as much as it is the Datum's. Does that not create a conflict?"

I challenge their lies. The Datum had no purpose, but they can't admit that without revealing their failure.

Vitus returns to his position behind Kaz. "It is my connection to the storm and the Datum that qualifies me to lead this inquiry in your father's absence. I have given you much freedom here; do not make me restrict it."

The room falls silent as I hold back more words. My freedom was restricted the moment the storm left. This city restricts my freedom.

"Now, if there are no further interruptions, let us continue. You say the anro network was compromised and communication disrupted. What was your solution to this?"

"My solution?"

Vitus gives no response.

"I had no time for a solution. When I discovered the network was unreliable, we were attacked. Redlanders invaded your city and decimated the Datum. A traitor commanded not only the Redlanders but also the storm. He stood beneath the storm unscathed, without fear."

The Representatives exchange glances with each other. The man behind Anam to my right speaks. "You aren't the first to use words suggesting the storm was unnatural. But the first to suggest a traitor."

The other Representatives' voices collide.

"A traitor? A traitor to who?"

"The Alfarons?"

"Perhaps the Vox?"

"To the Datum. Was this traitor one of the boys serving alongside you?"

Silence takes the room when I realize a Representative directs the last question to me.

"This man who controlled the storm was no boy. Did you not listen to me? He commanded Redlanders. His use of Tech insists he was Alfaron. He controlled the Sorbe. Am I to believe you know nothing of this type of Tech?"

They hear my words but talk over me again.

"Could we have a traitor in the city?"

"We should consult the new Tatem about who would have such advanced knowledge of Tech."

"But to produce Tech to protect one self from a Sorbe? To withhold that knowledge is worthy of death."

"We should focus on the Alfarons for this traitor. No other faction is that capable with Tech."

Vitus raises his hands, silencing everyone. "We should not worry about a single faction. This is the act of an individual. Any Vox citizen could hold this expertise."

"He commanded the Redlanders. Are you not listening?"

Every eye in the room stares at me. I want to say more, but I can't manage it as my heart beats faster. My neck throbs with apprehension.

"The boy is mistaken. Not even a traitorous Vox would work with those abominations. We should strike those words from the Record."

"He is either lying to us or lacked perspective to view the full truth of what happened."

I slam my hands on the table again. "Why would I lie? Unlike the Council, I want the people of this city to know the truth."

Vitus raises his arm quickly. "Watch your words. We act for the benefit of the people. Do not accuse us of otherwise."

"Do they not deserve to know their own people are cooperating with the Techless monsters? Do they not deserve to know that this city was in real danger and that its Council was helpless to protect them? Or that you never trusted the Datum. Or you had others in the storm doing your will. How does trying to kill me benefit the people? Do I know enough of your secrets now that you see me as a threat? Or do you simply have no control?"

I expect Vitus to interrupt me, so I stop, but he doesn't say anything. Silence envelops the room. My heart beats as if it is going to rip through my skin, but I continue. "What purpose did Cramen have that the Datum could not fulfill?" A stronger silence floods the room.

They are not silent out of secrecy, but confusion.

"This inquiry is a waste of our time," someone finally says. My heart stills beats so hard that I don't realize who. "The boy does nothing but argue and throw out accusations. We should end this and find answers elsewhere."

"This boy has a name." It's irrelevant, but this is an official inquiry. The next part is completely unnecessary. "Or are you afraid to think I may have been one of you? You were mere words from accepting me into your own."

"That is enough, Zayne Radi." Vitus speaks my name as a warning. "You would be well to recognize you are in the presence of the Members, not just their Representatives. Their words are silent, but their judgment is not."

Isa's Representative doesn't look at me. I wonder if my father would look me in the eye if he were here. I prepare to say something else when the door behind me opens with a hiss.

I turn, sparing the Council from another bombardment of my thoughts. My opportunity at a mentorship is over. I know that. My actions in the storm only have the Council questioning me, not praising me. The boy at the beginning of the Sorbe is not the one standing here.

A man in plain black clothing enters, keeping his eyes on the floor. His apparel is absent of any markings. His breathing is irregular. The two red-vested men bar his way.

"My apologies, Prava Council and its Representatives." He pauses, taking a deep breath. "I have news that impacts this inquiry."

Vitus waves his hand, and the guards step aside. "Approach and deliver your news."

The man keeps his eyes on the floor as he approaches each Representative separately. He speaks quickly and leaves as soon as he finishes. The Representatives look at each other.

Vitus steps out from behind Kaz. "Zayne Radi, your cooperation has been appreciated. You can see the Speaker is absent. We must consult with him about all we have heard."

The Council Members stand up. The red-vested guards at the door move to safeguard the Prava leaders' exit through another door across the room. My father lingers with Vitus before exiting. Vitus looks at me once we're alone.

"You're smart, so I know you connected these dots. But the Council is not considering you for a mentorship among the Representatives apart from advocacy." His next words have a shift in tone. "You either beg your father to give his again or leave this city."

His words surprise me. They haven't completely rejected me, only my effort to gain their approval apart from my father. I don't need the approval of either. The answers I seek aren't here. Does he still think I want to remain in the city?

"Mr. Diask acted against Carius," I say as Vitus turns. "He saved the city more than once. But you didn't trust him, so you put me in charge and made him announce it as if it were his decision. You thought he would use Seni against you in the storm. You gave that device to me, knowing he wanted Seni to have it. You unknowingly compromised everything. And all for what?"

"The Council's power holds this Nation together," Vitus says, his back still to me. "You should be thankful we take the measures we do to ensure the Vox remains strong."

He exits without another word.

A new voice enters the void that is now the room. "Zayne."

I turn around to face Soriina.

Her timing is always perfect.

33

Betrayal Without Choice

"Upon the deaths of a child's parents, the family name enters the Historical Record and those left behind may retain the name, but only if they have come out from under the law of the parent. By law, this moment is marked when a child declares and leaves for their Etero. Otherwise, the now-orphan gives up their family name and the Prava leaders will provide a new name."—from An Interpretation of the Council's Law, *subsection, Orphans of the Council*

Soriina holds me tight. She's afraid if she doesn't, I may not come back. After she lost her parents and watched Seni die, I refuse to be the first one to let go. I need this as much as she does. My world crashes around me. The storm is gone, yet nothing is the same. This city was never my home, but now I feel it's pushing me away. I'm happy to oblige.

Soriina pulls away. "This is the second time you haven't listened to me. Might I note you had nearly the same consequence."

"I won't make that mistake again."

She grins and shakes her head. "Yes, you will."

I chuckle. "But how do I ever learn if it isn't through mistakes?"

"You need a bit more practice in that area."

"Why are you here?" I hate to redirect the conversation, but I don't think anyone just enters Sector Five anymore.

She rubs her hands together. "I had to give an official testimony about what I witnessed. I wasn't a part of the Datum, so it wasn't before the Council. The Twins had theirs." She scratches the top of her hand.

"And?"

Disappointment stresses her words. "I have been declared an orphan."

She knew this when her parents died. No child is ever left to earn their own way, even this close to leaving for Eteros. The Council's mercy protects those in the Nation. The words taste sour in my mouth.

"We can't discuss it here," she says.

"You refuse to—"

She moves forward and grabs my face. Her words are low, as if trying to keep someone from listening. "This time, I will tell you everything. But not here. Power still isn't flowing fully through the city, but they still listen with what they've restored."

"Where?"

"You there." We turn to face an Agmen soldier. "You aren't scheduled to be here anymore. You both must leave. If you would follow me."

Soriina and I barely exchange a look as we cooperate with his order. He guides us out of the room and building. A transport hums outside. The doors are open with the operator in his seat. Without waiting for the soldier, I redirect my steps toward the vessel. He places an arm out. "The transport is for her. Not you."

Soriina walks past me. She stops at the base of the transport door and turns. "I hear the hillsides were untouched by the storm. You should visit them next sol."

She enters the volant and flies off toward Sector Four.

After the rush of air passes, I look at the soldier. "Where is she going?"

He doesn't have to tell me, but the look in my eye must convince him. "The Pillus. The storm made many orphans. The Council's normal accommodations are unfit at the present."

"And where do they intend to send me?"

"Your father has a residency here in the Sector. The Lostra." He points in the direction. "May I trust you to find your own way?"

"You can."

The Lostra is still empty the next sol. The ten-story building isn't my father's, only the top floor with its spacious accommodations. It has enough room for five people, more if people share the private spaces. There's no evidence anyone has ever lived here. The metal shines, and the chairs don't have a single crease. Everything is in order.

My father never comes, nor does my mother, not that I expect either to. I am alone, which makes leaving for the hillsides easy. The uncomfortable bed makes waking up early the easiest thing I have to do. The sheets are itchy, and old cleaning gel leaves my skin dry. I change back into the previous sol's clothes.

A note flashes across a screen: a message from the Curator. My implant comes out in three sols.

A transport operator responds to my travel request within the hour. He alters my request and asks that I board on the ground and not the landing pad outside the top level. It's early. The moon barely leaves its place over the sun as the volant lands. I hope for Mr. Auctor, but it's not him. I had to use the public transport system. I doubt he checks that system for travel requests. I no longer have access to the system my father uses.

The operator is quiet and significantly younger than Mr. Auctor. He reluctantly leaves me in Sector Two. The ruins of my house and Soriina's are here. She didn't tell me the storm had destroyed them, but she didn't have to tell me other details for me to know those things. It gives a reason to be here, or reason enough for the operator. I consider asking him to leave me near the hillsides but refrain. I can use the walk to waste some of the extra time I have.

The man from the storm creeps into my thoughts. His words repeat in my mind, drawing my curiosity out. He controlled the Sorbe. He initially came to the city after destroying Mauris for Carius. Carius left the Etero Grex Ludus untouched. Why wouldn't he have the man destroy both?

But one thing is now clear. I have to leave the city. I could forgo an Etero and seek an apprenticeship, but that requires Council approval. Grex Ludus doesn't make sense for me to attend from a skills standpoint, but that's not the reason for me to go. The rubble its host city lies in holds secrets. Whose, I don't know. I can't discover anything here with the Council watching, not that they will allow me to remain after rejecting their guidance.

Soriina will never agree. Not that I need her to, but her support would make the decision easier.

I reach the hillside. I'm thankful for the distraction my thoughts give. I barely notice the houses lying in ruin and sections of the transport path cracked from storm strikes. I try not to imagine the place where Seni lost his life.

The grass shifts colors as I climb. When I reach the top, Soriina sits cross-legged among some yellow flowers sprouting from the red grass. I glance back toward the city. Remnants of the storm create an assortment of color in the sky. Despite its beauty, Soriina's gaze is away from the city and the color. She gently runs her fingers across the flowers.

Her head barely moves. "You are early."

I smirk. "Says the girl who is here before me."

"I have things to think about. They rarely let anyone up here. But I suppose with everything else, they can overlook some minor things." She grips the grass in her hand. The colors shift. "The grass makes thinking easier. Never liked the hard surface of the city."

"Good place to think," I say. "I used to think this was the biggest strife I would have against my father. Stepping on grass."

Soriina shifts her positioning. "And what did you come to think about?"

I take a seat next to her with my legs bent enough that my arms wrap around my knees. "I can't stay in the city now. I have to think about my future, just as any normal graduate would."

"You're far from a normal graduate."

"Well, yes, and that's probably why you won't like this next part." I take her silence as a sign to continue. "I'm going to continue my studies at an Etero or else find myself working in the lamis deposits."

"The path of a normal graduate is a terrible thing."

My eyes narrow on a single blade of grass. It shifts to a bluish green as I run my finger across it. "I still have some details to figure out, so no decision is official, but I'm choosing Grex Ludus."

I feel Soriina's head snap toward me.

"Mauris's Etero? Zayne, you must be kidding. Your head isn't recovered from the storm. Grex Ludus's host city can't support the school.

It has the finest medical facility, so unless you intend to get your head checked, there's nothing there for you."

"The city is in rubble," I say, plucking the grass blade from the ground. It turns a dull brown. "They have to rebuild. If I'm not to follow in my father's footsteps, Tech is my obvious venture forward. What better place than a new city?"

Soriina moves to in front of me, forcing me to look at her. "You're chasing the storm. That man."

"And what if I am?" I ask. "You sit there without a single care about him. He killed your parents, Soriina. Yet you don't seem to care. Don't you want to know why?"

"Zayne, you don't understand."

I stand up and throw my arms to the side. "What is there to understand? He controlled the Redlanders and the storm." I pause, closing my mouth to control my breathing. "He tried to kill you. He killed your parents. Why don't you care? Didn't you love them?"

Soriina's up on her feet and throws a finger in my face with tears in her eyes. "Don't accuse me of not loving my parents."

My eye widens. "They're alive."

Her parents have abandoned her to be an orphan of the Council. No reasonable solution seems possible.

Soriina gasps. "You can't say that." Her eyes dart around. "You can't repeat that. Never. Zayne, promise me."

"Did you know? When you left your home, did you know they were alive? Or did they find you after? Are they still in the city?"

Fear shrouds her words. "Zayne, please, we can't talk about this."

"Isn't this what you wanted to come here to talk about?"

"Yes, but now I realize how dangerous it is. Promise me you won't bring this up again."

"How can I make such a promise? Your parents have abandoned you."

Anger flashes across her eyes. "Don't accuse them of such things. Your parents betrayed them." Her accusation stops any response I may have. "They promised to house me, to keep me from falling into the Council's care. Now I can't leave the city. Can't get away from this place."

"Soriina—" I cut myself off. I have no words.

Soriina wipes her eyes. "I'm sorry. This isn't your fault." Her words soften, but the pain remains. "Your father won't respond to my messages. They promised to look after me in an event the storm hurt my parents. I don't know if he knows my parents' true intentions. But we can't talk about this. You have to trust me."

"I can talk to my father," I say. He won't listen to me. "He may listen. I can beg him if necessary. After my implant comes out, I'll plead with him to bring you in under his family name. You'll have access to any Etero you want."

Her lip quivers. "What did you say?"

I step forward and rest my hands on the sides of her shoulders. "I'll beg my father—"

She shakes her shoulders and steps back. "Not that. Your implant."

"That doesn't matter."

She screams. The grass swallows the sound.

"Soriina, what's wrong?"

Tears fill her words. "Your implant. When does it come out?"

"Why does that matter?"

"Just tell me."

"In three sols."

"Is it still functional?"

I can't find a connection with her questions. "I believe so. But it's failing. The Curator wants to remove it before it fails. He thinks it could hurt my brain if that happens with it still connected. Why does any of this matter?"

"Zayne, how can you not understand?" She pulls at her hair before letting go. Strands float to the ground. "An implant records everything you experience. Your sights, sounds. Even dreams. Thoughts. All for the Historical Record."

The Council ended my inquiry because that man told them my implant was being removed. They didn't know at the start. No, why wouldn't they know? Unless those two dothryis determined my implant contained information they could use. They didn't need my cooperation anymore. "Zayne, the Council will know everything. The Council can't know about my parents."

"Soriina—"

She starts to pace, crushing the flowers around her. "You should have told me sooner."

"What does it matter? Why would your parents fake—"

"No, Zayne." She moves toward the slope of the hill, heading back into the city. "I have to go before they remove your implant. There may still be time. I'm sorry."

"Soriina." I try to follow her, but my legs freeze. "Soriina!" Only my voice chases her, but it's not enough. She disappears over the crest of the hill.

My knees buckle before they strike the ground. I try to scream, but nothing escapes.

Into the Historical Record

"Alfarons have the promise of inclusion in the Historical Record through their implants. Only the destruction of an implant forbids an Alfaron's place in history. No Alfaron person has refused such an honor, which brings surprise that the small piece of Tech is a choice and not embedded in Alfaron law."—an excerpt from Our Implants: The Defining Tech of the Alfarons

Three sols pass. Soriina avoids me, and I avoid her. There are no such things as secrets until my implant leaves my head. To protect Soriina, I cannot risk learning anything more. No matter how insignificant it seems.

Her parents *are* dead. Killed by the storm.

Eteros don't accept students without families. With the storm's delay of Etero procedures, she has to remain here. I doubt the Council is going to pass a law that works in Soriina's favor. Death separated her from her parents, not the law. My parents betrayed hers, leaving her as a child of the Council. The people meant to protect her are responsible for her parent's deaths.

I hit the side of my head. "Stop thinking about this. Every word is the Council's."

My implant comes out in a couple of hours. The medical facility has sent numerous requests for information. I avoid the last question: do I wish for a new implant? The decision should be easy, but I hesitate. I know what I want, but anxious thoughts freeze me each time I begin to record my answer.

I press my hand into the back of my head. My hand doesn't find the wound I gave myself the first night alone in the Lostra. My Lamis made quick work of the injury. Something in my mind thought I could damage the implant and destroy everything it collected. It hurt. A patchwork of blood still lines the floor.

The thought returns several times late at night, but I push it away. I don't get any sleep.

Maybe my Lamis deprivation caused a failure in the intricate systems of the device. I know the thought is hopeless. They tested the implant. The Curator would have told me if it wasn't working.

A travel request flashes across the screen in the Lostra's main room. A volant's scheduled to take me to a medical facility in Sector Two. The operator isn't Mr. Auctor. His profile—that I'm not entirely certain I should be able to access—says he's out of the city. I know the Council sent him away so I couldn't talk to him. They thought I would seek him out. And they were right.

A flashing light illuminates the space above the door. The transport is close. I stand outside on the deck connecting to the transport platform overlooking Sector Five. Volants and veheres fill the sky. The busyness of the area represents almost that of before the storm. Not quite. A stillness still envelopes the City Center. Soldiers walk the paths.

I consider jumping. The impact with the ground may damage the implant's information beyond repair. But Soriina would never forgive such a drastic attempt to protect her secret. Or would she?

The volant's blast of air snaps me out of the thought. It hovers several feet away before resting on landing supports. I enter the volant without a word, and I take a seat next to a window as the operator directs the vessel away from the building. The Lostra's outside appearance matches the inside, untouched by the storm.

I quiet my thoughts by staring at the buildings we pass. Repair crews are working on the storm damage, but they have made little progress yet. The clouds are colorless, resuming their position over the sun, comforting us rather than covering us in darkness.

We are in the air for just a few minutes. The operator leaves me in front of the medical building without a word. The outside area appears empty until I notice a familiar figure near the edge of the facility, away from the entrance. I consider ignoring him, but something urges me forward.

I stop a few feet from him. His back is to me. "Forgive me, but I can't tell who is who without seeing your eyes."

Safon turns around with a wide grin. "After all this time, you still cannot tell us apart?"

I smile at his comment. "It was dark . . . and I don't know if you're Safon this sol, or Erman. You like to switch it up . . ." I pause to trick him. I don't think I will ever forget who the Twins are. They seem like distinct people now. "Safon."

His smile widens. "Correct, but you only had, like, two options." Safon grabs my shoulder with one hand and shakes it. "Good to see you.

You had us worried for a moment." He removes his hand and puts his palm out toward me. "Don't worry. Soriina has given us all the details."

I want him to ask questions. Soon, the Council will tell everyone what they want them to know. Will anyone believe me if I speak contrary to their truth? I want him to ask me so he knows how to discern what our leaders publicly announce.

I only nod and speak to avoid the topic. "Why are you here?"

He pats the side of the building. "They had everyone from the Datum come here for treatment. Limit the stories we can tell, I suppose."

My eye traces his body. "Are you hurt?"

"No. My wounds have healed, as have Erman's. I was actually visiting Arsen. The storm struck the building his family lived in, and with what happened to—well, he has no one. Erman and I visit him when we can. You know, twins stick together."

He lost everyone. I can only think about how much more I could have done. Was it even my responsibility? Does this guilt rightfully rest on my shoulders?

"My parents have taken him in, so if you see him, by law, he's Arsen Coffer now. Triplets, if you look past the part where we don't look anything alike." He laughs.

I sour the mood. "Did Erman get him here in time?"

"Thankfully a few doctors sheltered in the medical building, so they were able to stabilize him. Your plan worked perfectly. They had a generator operating in the building, but the storm didn't strike. Erman said they scared everyone quite a bit when they opened the doors." Safon drops his voice. "But his Lamis levels are out of whack. I overhear the doctors. They don't have any idea what's wrong. They're forcing Lamis into his body, but his body's rejecting it. But the Curator is tending to him, so it's only a matter of time before they figure it out. Just look at you."

Did the Council not anticipate anything? They knew the storm struck me yet refused to acknowledge the truth to better prepare us. But we had no purpose, so I can only imagine they wanted us to die. See how the storm affected us. Will they tell the public what I truly think about them when they release my memories?

"I suppose all that destruction was worth it," I say. The words don't seem enough, almost a cop out to avoid the conversation. A boy is dying, and I can't find the words to speak. "At least now he has a chance. If the doctors are struggling, we didn't have a chance to help him."

"Not according to the Council. They spent most of Erman's inquiry condemning him for his actions. The risk was not worth the *desired outcome*, or some nonsense like that."

I can't help but smile at his mockery. "And what of your inquiry?" I'm glad the conversation has shifted. The mention of Arsen only helps to bring Seni's face fresh into my mind.

"Not as exciting as yours, I hear. My inquiry lasted three extra hours because I told them a Redlander possessed Tech that controlled the storm. Tried to explain as clearly as I could, but I still questioned it all myself. Then their questions just made me question everything I think I saw."

I turn my back to him. "Don't worry, they will have clarity soon."

He lightly grabs my shoulder, and I turn back. "And what does that mean?"

I point to my head. "My implant is coming out. That is why I'm here. The Council will know everything I know."

He steps back in a slow, exaggerated motion. "So I should stop talking to you, right? Run away before I say anything illegal?" A snicker betrays how seriously he takes the revelation.

Soriina didn't tell him her secret. Would he joke if he knew the dangerous knowledge my implant contains? She didn't burden him with it, so neither will I. "That or know whatever you say is between us and the Council."

He smiles and closes the gap between us. "I can deal with that, but I need to be going. Lingered for a bit . . . still not used being home again. Many are displaced from the storm, so most residential houses are overfilled more than they already were. Still getting used to so many extra neighbors."

I want to ask him about his home, learn more, but my hesitation moves the conversation to an end.

"We have Eteros to look forward to," he says. "Soriina said you are leaving the city. We should meet up later and discuss where we are all going. I need to know where the next Tatem is going to spend his Etero cycles, but not now. I'm late, and if I fear anything more than a Sorbe, it's my mother."

He presses two fingers into his head and wiggles them, then laughs as he walks away. I turn away but stop and call back. "Safon, what does Persolus mean?"

He turns around and walks backward, shouting with a smile. "I have no idea! I liked how it sounded."

He turns on his heels and keeps going. I laugh and approach the entrance with a smile I cannot remove. I envy his ability to shed the horrors of the storm, the fear and uncertainty it brought.

My teeth disappear behind my lips as the doors slide open. The whiteness inside the facility is off-putting. I linger until someone walks in behind me, forcing me to enter completely. A woman with long hair tucked behind her shoulders stands behind a desk. The Alfaron symbol stands out against her grey shirt. She stings with familiarity. Varet. The woman from when I first awakened with my implant. Her attention is on an arvos. She looks up when I stop in front of her.

She smiles. "Welcome, your name?"

She doesn't recognize me. "Zayne."

"Ah, Zayne Persolus, welcome."

I spent the last three sols navigating the Prava's systems, changing my name. My last effort to see if I can make the Council angrier with me. Not quite.

"We have been waiting for you. In fact, you are a bit late. Was your transport delayed?"

"Um—"

"I will request a report from the operator. We must get you to your room. The Curator's dothyris are waiting."

Varet walks out from behind the desk and gestures for me to follow. She inputs information into her arvos as she walks. I lag behind, but not enough to lose her through the series of hallways. She stops in front of an open door and waits with a smile for me to catch up.

I enter the room and take a seat without instruction.

She taps on her arvos, and her eyes narrow. "There is only one question that needs to be asked before preparation for the procedure begins. Certainly more of a formality than a real question, but one we have to ask." She pauses. "Do you grant permission for the implantation of a new implant to replace the failing one? As I said, it's a formality. Sometimes we forget to send all the questions, or it gets lost along the network. Who would choose to forgo the pinnacle of what it means to be an Alfaron? Especially at such a young age as yourself. I certainly do not want to die, but to know my memories will become one with our—"

Varet laughs.

"I apologize. I just started rambling. I will have them prep the new implant."

Her fingers move across the screen of the arvos. Before they stop, I interrupt her. "Wait—" I pause to ensure she stops. The next words should be easy, but I hesitate. If my life ends here, my impact on the Historical Record will only be my time in the storm. My failures. But what does that matter? I am not important enough for anyone to want to remember. No one will have reason to access my memories. Or will the Council make me into some hero? My name will be synonymous with the storm. My memories will be the only visual information.

Varet gives an awkward grin, waiting for me to break the silence.

I may become more well known than my father. The thought scares me.

I meet her gaze and take a deep breath in. "You should tell the Curator that . . . that I don't want the new implant."

She lowers the arvos and certainly wants to speak, but cannot find the words. She forces a smirk as she taps her arvos. "Yes, of course. Please forgive my rashness. I will inform the Curator."

She exits the room.

I sit back and exhale.

Closing my eye, I try to imagine the Council's reaction to my decision. An Alfaron refusing his place in history. Refusing his perspective embedded into the narrative of our people. But that isn't true. They control truth. Everyone would see me as they want. Not as I am or will be.

This is what it means to be an Alfaron. But if that is true, then I refuse. If an implant makes me an Alfaron, then I choose another path.

Let my last thoughts show that to those who may see my memories. I am not an Alfaron.

The Mendax

The realization shames me. The Alfarons' implant steals their narratives from me. I condemn them so easily I never try to learn about them. I refused to look inside their cities to see those whose stories were open to me. I now know why this story of the city and the storm was given to me. It was to humble me, teach me. The boy was no mere instrument to tell me this story; this was his story as well.

This boy sacrifices the only way he knows to exist beyond himself. Now, without his implant, his story ends when he dies, at least from his perspective. But I see it all now. How blind I was not to realize how their lives were kept from me. But Ario grants me vision with this boy's life.

I see the connections previously hidden. I see his decisions and the direction they take him. I see his death and life.

Persolus. A fitting name for where his story leads. Yes, because what I thought must be his death is simply the end of this part of his life. His story continues. I now can see.

His story is not alone. I see others that refuse to allow the historical record to tell their tales. And others who yearn for inclusion but are forbidden.

They all are a part of Solisternum's story. Bless the Great Ario for His sight. May He bless my steps, and if not, end my compilation here.

Messages

The words hurt. They speak to his failure. Despite the pain, he forces himself to read them. He has to remind himself of what he did. He knows the Council wants to hurt him with it; for what other reason would they give him back his anro? Even with that thought in mind, he cannot stop himself from rereading the messages.

Each word breaks apart the friendship he thought he had. The friendship he now doubts ever existed.

15.1.518 Anro Designation: Seni Daw

I have lost track of how many messages I have sent you. Perhaps one will reach you. Everything is chaotic here. Redlanders attacked our main camp. We are scattered across the sector hoping to remain in small enough numbers to avoid the abominations. I fear the same is for you. I hope that is the reason you are ignoring my messages.

Please give some indication that you are receiving my messages. We need to meet. This time at a place of our choosing. Our sectors need to join if we are to fight back against the Redlanders.

16.1.518 Anro Designation: Seni Daw

We are fewer now. The Redlanders are using beasts. There is no doubt now. They somehow command them. I fear they have overrun your sector as well. That has to be the reason you have yet to respond to my messages. Or you foolishly choose not to reset your anro. I hope you have more sense than that.

We found a girl after the Redlanders forced her from her home. What a coincidence that she knows you. Soriina assures me you are hardheaded but not stupid. Though we have only met I have to agree with her. So I can only assume you are hurt and unable to respond.
        Perhaps one of your Aemiins finds this and is able to respond.

17.1.518 Anro Designation: Corrupted

This is my last message. If these words could reflect the pain I am in, they may not be legible. But at least then you would know what you have caused. I sent her away to find you. She does not deserve to witness what is coming for me. But I hope she finds you dead. Else I know you refused to reset your anro or worse, tried your own method to fix the problem. We needed you. You failed us all. I fear the city may share my fate.
        May this message act as evidence of your guilt.

Zayne Persolus can't bear to read the rest.

Glossary

Actare: a weapon that fires energy projectiles, often fueled by the user's Lamis, but can also be utilized with a self-contained power source with reduced functionality

Agmen: the Vox military, those belonging to this specific designation reside outside of cities and respond to the aid of the Esidio (see **Esidio Guards**) when called

Alfarons: The faction with the largest population and the most proud. This faction uses the most Tech and leads advancements every cycle in Tech research

Anam: The last mansii (see **Mansii**) in a Vox cycle (see **Sun Cycle**) and the title of the sixth member of the Council

Anro: A multi-functional device designed specifically for the Datum (see **Datum**)

Arba: The fourth mansii in the Vox cycle and the title of the fourth member of the Council

Arvos: small portable, computer-like devices that are able to connect to a mainframe in a house or the main information network of a city

Balons: the second most populous faction in the Vox Nation, holds strongly to Tech usage but are less dependent on technology

Beasts: a general term for animals that the Vox people believe to be pests, often untamed animals from natural areas, usually meant as a derogatory term

Caro: carnivorous animal, feeds off the Lamis from the flesh of others

Center or City-Center: similar to a square, a place for people to meet, often a place where the entrance to buildings are

City School: A school held within every city to instruct children in the history and culture of the nation and the basics of each specific skill they will pursue at an Etero

City Visa: A document indicating a person has permission to reside within a city for a temporary stay as a visitor or worker

Council Representative: a citizen appointed to a Council member and speaks on their behalf to the people, appointed every five cycles

Curator: a city's expert on Lamis development of children, manages and oversees city dothyris (see **Dothyris**)

Cycle or Sun Cycle: a length of time equal to six mansiis (see **Mansii)**, six mansiis complete a Sun Cycle or Cycle

Datum: a term given to the boys who served during the storm in the five hundredth and eighteenth cycle of the Council

Dothyri: An expert on Lamis, subject to the Curator, **see Curator,** often presides over the Lamis health of adults

Epis City: The capital of the Vox Nation, home of the Faction's leadership, the Council

Esidio Guards: men belonging to the Agmen military who are positioned within cities, acting as peacekeepers and protectors, often wear no uniforms or hide their uniforms to remain discreet. They are the only Vox allowed to carry weapons on city ground

Etero: A school that operates for six cycles, training children in specific skills, so they may return to cities and serve the Council. Eteros are often near cities that support them and provide non-school opportunities for students

Exan Tech: Tech that is no longer used, put out of service

Generator: a device that processes raw Lamis energy in order to be distributed to the appropriate places that require power to operate, receives raw Lamis from natural, underground caverns

Gradu: herbivore animal, feeds off the Lamis in plants and other ground sources of food

Haur: a part of Tech that allows the use of a person's energy to power systems

Isa: the first mansii in a Vox cycle and the title of the first member of the

Council

Kaz: the third mansii in a Vox cycle and the title of the third Council member

Lamis-5: the designation for Lamis energy in its raw form, most often found in underground deposits, volatile in its raw form

Lamis: a unique energy that can power all forms of Tech, but also is found within every member of the Vox Nation, animals, and plants

The Linam: The building used as the central area for the preparation of the Datum (see **Datum**) for their time out during the storm

LiorTech: Tech that is used to enhance a person's natural abilities or replace missing limbs or other body parts, this Tech is powered by the person's Lamis

Mansii: the six separating marks during the cycle (see **Cycle**) and are defined by 90 solpaes (see **Solpae**) or 50 in the case of Kaz.

Novitae: name stricken from Vox records

Operator: a person who runs a Volant or Vehere (see **Volant** and **Vehere**) and is often designated to a certain person of high status to move them around the city

Ora: the separating mark within a mansii comprising 10 solpaes (see **Solpae**)

Pak: the fifth mansii in a Vox cycle, and the title of the fifth member of the Council

People's Representative: a citizen appointed to address the Council on behalf of the people with no connection to the Council and can bring the people's needs and desires to the leadership of the Faction, travels to other cities to meet with City Representatives (see **City Representatives**)

Perii: an expert in Tech, working in the field under the orders of the Tatem (see **Tatem**) and will sometimes assist Tech Specialists (**see Tech Specialist**) in teaching assignments in city schools

The Prava Council: also known as The Council, a group of six men, led by Giovanni, who are replaced every five cycles. Members wear masks in public and have no identity outside of their titles

Redlander: inhabitants of the Red Plains. These people have no Lamis, reject all Tech, and are considered abominations by most Nation citizens

Rotam: a manual-powered vehicle that utilizes small amounts of Lamis to ease the movement

Sofera: animals tamed by Vox members, these animals feed off the residual energy of their owner providing physical relief from an excess of energy

Solpae: the full cycle of the moon shifting through the sky, covering the sun, then uncovering it and is the separating mark within an Ora (see **Ora**). Also referred to as a 'sol' or 'pae' for short, a twenty-nine hour period

Sorbe: a powerful, natural storm that drains Lamis from people or machinery to sustain itself

Tatem: The title for the overseer of Periis (see **Perii**) and Tech specialists (see **Tech Specialist**) in a given city

Tech: a general term used for machinery that uses Lamis to be powered, can be on a person and enhance certain attributes (see **LiorTech**) or can be a transport, ex. A Volant is a piece of Tech

Tech Specialist: those designated with the responsibility of teaching school age children about Tech in cities

Teg Bed: a cocoon-like bed for sleeping outdoors without any cover. Fits tightly to the sleep to trap warmth.

Tosa: The second mansii in a Vox cycle and the title of the second member of the Council

Veccos: the least populous of the factions within the Vox Nation and the most liberal in holding to the normal uses of Tech, are more curious to the uses of Lamis without Tech, often hated by the Alfarons for their lack of appreciation for technology

Vehere: large transports (see **Volants)** that are specifically designed to carry large cargo, not people

Velare: a small, portable light with a self-contained power source

Volant: transports that travel via hover pads, vessels that carry people or supplies, capable of traveling along predetermined paths or along hillsides for short periods

Vox Nation: a nation which uses focuses on Tech as a part of their culture. The Nation is split into three factions, Alfarons, Balons, and Veccos (see **Alfarons; Balons; Veccos)**

To my readers

I may have written *The City and the Storm*, but you, my readers, bring life to the pages. When you read the words, you bring meaning and add depth to my story that I could never imagine. Your experiences help shape my world in ways that transcend the words on the page. But with all this, I must ask something of you. Would you help me spread this story to others, so they may experience what you have? Please consider leaving a review on Amazon and Goodreads and even social media if you feel compelled.

Would you reach out to your local library and request them to purchase a copy for their shelves, so others may enjoy the story without the financial burden?

Thank you for your support!

Acknowledgements

This book has been over ten years in the making. Many, many people have taken a part in this story, some small, some big. These are just a few, and I don't know if I could fully include everyone, but I'll try.

First and foremost, I want to thank God for blessing me with this gift. When I revisited this story in 2020, I did so with the intent that this story would be His. Without Him, this story wouldn't be where it is today. I thank you, God, for this story and ask that You use it for Your will.

God blessed me with parents who would occasionally make starving artist jokes, but were supportive of my writing endeavors from an early age. My mom, who helped cultivate my love for reading and was one of my first Beta readers for *The City and the Storm*. My dad, who was willing to help with the tech side of things as I moved from handwriting novels to working on the computer. The perseverance I've had through this entire publishing process is a testament to the work ethic my dad instilled in me. This story stands where it is today because of the early support I had growing up from my parents.

Though she never saw the fruition of her efforts, to my grandmother, who helped me transcribe my handwritten novels to the computer on a floppy disk. I hope God gives you updates on my progress and what you helped cultivate.

To my brother, Joseph, who made me my first cover (with stolen images, but we don't talk about that) and was always willing to provide feedback on my design choices. And reminded me my cover needed to be in CMYK.

To my friends, who have stayed supportive despite the end seemingly never coming close and always asked for updates even if I could barely put into words what I was presently working on. To the friends who asked about my stories and kept listening as I struggled to encapsulate my story early on. And to Dale, who accompanied me on a whirlwind trip to experience a total solar eclipse, which was really just a research trip for my book, but the pictures turned out pretty cool too. There's probably a Dollar General in Solisternum, I just haven't found it yet.

I have to thank the various designers and readers who gave input on my cover. I received invaluable insight and no one ever judged me for choosing to design the cover myself.

And to my Betas and editors, this story is stronger because of you. I never would have been able to do it without your help. You were the first people outside of family to read this story. You taught me the importance of letting a story go that you've held so close to you for so long.

And I can't write this section without mentioning the community I found on Instagram. I showed up and disappeared, but my fellow Indie authors were always willing to answer questions. I thank you all for sharing your journeys, whether you realize it or not, you're willingness to be transparent has been a tremendous help on my journey.

I want to thank the printers, the binders, the laminators, case makers, cover makers, the trimmers and the people in-between that make indie publishing a reality through POD. I have had the unique experience of not only seeing this process happen, but learning it and being a part of it. It would be unfitting not to recognize the people that work almost completely unknown. Thank you.

And to anyone who has ever asked about or listened to me talk about my book, I thank you.

My name may be on the cover, but publishing a book is not a solo act. I would be arrogant to say I made it here on my own. Thank you to everyone.

Beyond the Book

Don't want to leave the land of Solisternum yet? Scan the QR code or visit **jeremiahsaterauthor.com** and discover 2 additional bonus chapters from the Mendax as well as learn more details about this fantastic land and its inhabitants. A world beyond ours is just moments away. What are you waiting for?

Bonus chapters contain spoilers: use the password **themendax** to access.

Clarifying the Mendax's Story

Thank you so much for reading this story and visiting Solisternum. The Mendax is not perfect, and his compilation will occasionally have an error. If you found an error, please report it using the QR code or visit **jeremiahsaterauthor.com**. Thank you for helping the story of Solisternum be as accurate as possible.

About the author

Jeremiah Daniel Sater has always loved stories, whether he was reading a hundred books a year or handwriting novels as a young boy. He grew up in fantastical lands, reaching them through wormholes and on spaceships.

Now, he creates these worlds for others to explore. When Jeremiah is not forming worlds with words, he captures the natural beauty of God's creation with his photography. He hopes his art reflects the truth told first by the original Creator.